M000213235

Swan Song

Elin Hilderbrand

Little, Brown and Company

New York Boston London

The characters and events in this book are fictitious. Any similarity to real persons, living or dead, is coincidental and not intended by the author.

Copyright © 2024 by Elin Hilderbrand

Hachette Book Group supports the right to free expression and the value of copyright. The purpose of copyright is to encourage writers and artists to produce the creative works that enrich our culture.

The scanning, uploading, and distribution of this book without permission is a theft of the author's intellectual property. If you would like permission to use material from the book (other than for review purposes), please contact permissions@hbgusa.com. Thank you for your support of the author's rights.

Little, Brown and Company
Hachette Book Group
1290 Avenue of the Americas, New York, NY 10104
littlebrown.com

First Edition: June 2024

Little, Brown and Company is a division of Hachette Book Group, Inc. The Little, Brown name and logo are trademarks of Hachette Book Group, Inc.

The publisher is not responsible for websites (or their content) that are not owned by the publisher.

The Hachette Speakers Bureau provides a wide range of authors for speaking events. To find out more, go to hachettespeakersbureau.com or email hachettespeakers@hbgusa.com.

Little, Brown and Company books may be purchased in bulk for business, educational, or promotional use. For information, please contact your local bookseller or the Hachette Book Group Special Markets Department at special.markets@hbgusa.com.

ISBN 9780316258876 (hardcover) / 9780316577854 (large print) / 9780316579964 (signed edition) / 9780316579940 (B&N signed edition) / 9780316579148 (Nantucket Book Partners edition) / 9780316581677 (Walmart edition)
LCCN 2024932745

Printing 1, 2024

LSC-H

Printed in the United States of America

I will end where I began: This book is for Chip Cunningham—with friendship and profound gratitude.

Swan Song

Prologue

Thursday, August 22, 6:00 p.m.

Rumors about Nantucket Police chief Ed Kapenash's retirement have been swirling around for the past two years, though when asked directly, the Chief said, "I'm far too busy to contemplate retirement." However, three days after the Big Scare in February, Ed told his wife, Andrea (from his hospital bed at Mass General), "That's it, I'm finished, I'll just stay on through the summer while we find someone to replace me."

"Another *summer*, Ed?" Andrea cried out. She was shaken—and for good reason.

Ed had been giving a safety talk in the gymnasium of Nantucket Elementary when his left arm started to tingle. He felt short of breath, his vision splotched—and the next thing he knew, he was being loaded onto a medevac chopper and flown to MGH for emergency bypass surgery.

"You had the kind of heart attack we call the widow-maker," Dr. Very Important said. "A full blockage of your LAD artery. You were lucky the paramedics were right there. Otherwise this could have ended differently."

Yes, the fire chief—Stu Vick—and EMTs from his department had been in the school gym as well, waiting for their turn to speak, when Ed hit the floor.

As Dr. Big Shot gave Ed a lecture about exercise, diet, and, above all, *stress,* Ed gauged Andrea's reaction to the term *widow-maker.*

Not good.

"You should retire *now,*" Andrea said. "You might not survive another summer." She looked at Dr. Master of the Universe because she needed him to hear the backstory. "Ed has been admitted to the Nantucket hospital three times in the past two years for chest pain. They wanted to send him up here for testing but he *refused.*"

Ed sighed. He'd married a tattletale. But also, Ed felt guilty. Had he played fast and loose with his health? Yes. Could he just give two weeks' notice and leave the public safety of the island up for grabs? He could not.

He would retire in the fall.

Now here it is, August 22, and the Chief is celebrating: His last official day of duty is Monday, August 26. His replacement, Zara Washington, was the deputy chief in Oak Bluffs on Martha's Vineyard, so she understands island life as well as Ed does. Zara has moved into her housing, and after two weeks of shadowing Ed, she is eager to take over. Andrea has planned a big retirement party for Ed at the Oystercatcher in a couple of weeks and there will be some official hoopla arranged by Governor Healey.

But for now, the Chief is enjoying a night out with his people: Andrea; his son, Eric, and Eric's girlfriend, Avalon; his best friends, Addison and Phoebe Wheeler and Jeffrey and Delilah Drake; and his daughter, Kacy, a NICU nurse who moved back from California this summer.

Kacy had intended to bring her friend Coco as her plus-one but . . . Coco works as the "personal concierge" for the Richardsons, a couple whom Ed and Andrea (and the Wheelers and the Drakes) became acquainted with this summer, and when Ed opted not to include the Richardsons in tonight's dinner, the Richardsons turned around and threw a sunset sail on their yacht, *Hedonism*—and so Coco has to work.

"I guess everyone has abandoned the Richardsons," Kacy said. "Coco didn't recognize the names on the guest list—they're mostly strangers."

Strangers who evidently hadn't been warned about the Richardsons, Ed thought. Some weird things had happened this summer.

Back in June, the Richardsons were a hot commodity; they'd nearly become part of "the Castaways," which is what the Kapenashes and the Wheelers and the Drakes call their friend group (because they all "washed ashore" on Nantucket decades earlier). Part of the appeal of the Richardsons was that they were younger, still in their forties. The Castaways, Ed in particular, had been feeling their middle age.

For tonight's dinner, Ed chose Ventuno, a restaurant housed in one of the historic residences downtown, and Andrea reserved the entire upstairs for them.

They ascend a narrow wooden staircase and find their table draped with white linen and lit by candles near the windows that overlook the charming brick sidewalks of Federal Street. All their guests have already arrived.

Ed takes his seat at the oval table and reminds himself to appreciate the things that Andrea accuses him of missing: the crystal wineglasses, the low centerpiece of dahlias and roses, the fact that Eric has worn a tie without being asked. The air smells of garlic and herbs; Tony Bennett croons in the background. This is exactly the evening Ed wanted—and yet he can't help but feel melancholy. The summer is ending, and so is his career.

After Addison assesses the wine list—it's long been his job to serve as their sommelier—he catches Ed's eye over the top of the menu.

"There's no time to get in your feelings, Ed," he says. "A bold yet subtle Barolo awaits."

The wine, Ed has to admit, tastes divine even to his unsophisticated palate (left to his own devices, he's a beer drinker), though he holds himself to half a glass. What he's really interested in tonight is food. Andrea is seated next to him but she's whispering with Phoebe and Delilah about the Richardsons. *They couldn't leave it alone; they had to one-up us!*

The Chief is going to use his wife's obsession with the Richardsons to his advantage. He does some ordering for the table—two fritto mistos, the farfalle with crab and local corn (sourced from Jeffrey and Delilah's farm), the strozzapreti with sausage and broccoli rabe, the ricotta crostini, the stuffed clams.

"Ed," Andrea says in a warning tone. Andrea is the police chief now, at least where Ed's diet is concerned.

Ed throws in an order of the giardiniera and a Caesar salad. He waits until Andrea turns away, then says to the server, "For the main course, the Fiorentina." This is the finest steak on the island; Ed dreams about it the way some men dream about Margot Robbie. It's a thirty-three-ounce porterhouse served with roasted rosemary potatoes. Ed pushes away thoughts of the salt, the fat, his heart. At home, it's been chicken, fish, and vegetables for the past six months.

When the steak arrives sizzling on the platter—the scent is enough to bring Ed to his knees—he helps himself to two rosy-pink pieces. This might be what kills him, but what a way to go.

Andrea notices the fried shrimp and squid, the helpings of pasta, and the rare steak, but she zips her lip. She's proud of Ed—he's lost thirty-five pounds, started jogging three mornings a week, switched to decaf coffee, stopped going to the Nickel four times a week for lunch (the shrimp po'boy is his kryptonite), and he's at least pretending to meditate ten minutes each day. Andrea is also relieved that

they made it to the end of the summer without any major inci-
dents. That's not to say the summer was boring—au contraire! The
moment Phoebe introduced them to Addison's new clients the Richardsons, their summer became a blur of lunches at the Field and
Oar Club, pickleball, sailing excursions, and parties, parties, parties. Andrea hasn't had a summer like this since before her kids were
born. For most of the summer, the Richardsons seemed like a gift
sent from the heavens to remind them that they weren't too old to
have fun.

But when Andrea thinks about the Richardsons now, she…no,
she won't let them live rent-free in her head. She'll just feel happy
that Ed is enjoying his steak.

Addison makes a toast. "To our fearless leader!" Everyone raises
a glass; Ed is honored but also a little embarrassed. He drinks his
red wine—he thinks Addison might have refilled his glass without
his noticing—and suddenly he grows reflective.

He moved to Nantucket from Swampscott thirty-five years earlier
when the chief of police position opened. People had warned him
that policing on an island would be different than on the mainland.
It was like a small town except that it was thirty miles out to sea, so
there was no getting away. This has been tricky enough to navigate
even in the off-season, and during Ed's tenure, the year-round population has doubled. But come June, the island explodes with summer residents, short-term renters, and day-trippers, some of whom
feel inclined to rent mopeds despite not having a clue how to oper-
ate them. There's traffic to deal with, scores of parking tickets on the
daily, kids from the cities and fancy suburbs with their designer
drugs and entitled attitudes giving his officers lip.

Beyond that, there's real trouble—domestics, vandalism, drunk
driving, overdoses, accidental deaths. Ed worked a case out in
Monomoy half a dozen years earlier that he still believes was murder, though they never quite figured it out.

Their server shows up with a dessert sampler for the table—an apple crostata with cinnamon gelato, baba au rhum, and cannoli.

Phoebe takes a bite of the crostata and says, "This tastes like fall."

"Blasphemy," Delilah says. "There's still an entire month of summer left."

Ed is considering a cannoli, but he's afraid he's pushed the limits of his diet far enough. Andrea is the one who places a cannoli on his plate, her cheeks flushed from the wine. She leans over and kisses him on the lips, a good kiss, one that promises more later. "It's your special night."

Ed gazes around the table, and his eyes land on Kacy. She looks wistful, maybe even lonesome; she keeps checking her phone. *It's funny,* the Chief thinks. *No matter how old your kids get, you still worry about them.* Kacy and Coco were close all summer, a Millennial Laverne and Shirley, but things between them seem to have cooled. When the Chief asked Andrea if Kacy and Coco had a falling-out, Andrea said, "They're grown women, Ed." Whatever *that* meant.

After coffee is served, there's another surprise. Their server turns up the music—Harry Connick Jr. singing "It Had to Be You"—and moves the other tables so they have room to dance. Andrea takes Ed's hand. "Come on, Chief, let's show them how it's done."

Phoebe and Addison join them on the improvised dance floor, then Jeffrey and Delilah. In that moment, the word *retirement,* a term that previously evoked only dread for the Chief, seems filled with promise. The weight of the island's problems will be lifted from his shoulders. He and Andrea can travel; he'll be able to go out fishing on Eric's charter boat whenever he wants—maybe he'll even take a job as Eric's first mate. They'll enjoy other nights like this when the Chief can have more than half a glass of wine.

He'll be free.

"Are you sure you won't get sick of me hanging around all the time?" he asks Andrea. Before she can answer, Ed's phone buzzes in his pocket.

Andrea groans. "Please just let it go."

He checks the screen. It's the station, line four, which means it's an emergency.

"I'm sorry," Ed says. "I have to—"

He steps off the dance floor, lifts the phone to one ear, and plugs his other ear with two fingers. It's his dispatcher, the aptly named Jennifer Speed, whom they just call Speed. The woman defines *efficiency.* "Do you want the bad news or the bad news?" she asks.

The Chief doesn't want any news and Speed knows it. He has one hundred hours left as Nantucket's police chief. "What is it?"

"There's a fire out in Pocomo," Speed says. "The NFD is on the scene. I talked to Stu, who says it's a total loss. Burned to the ground."

"Pocomo?" the Chief says. "It's not..."

"The Richardsons' house, yes, it is," Speed says. She pauses. "Was."

The Chief closes his eyes. He feels Andrea's hand on his back.

"What else?" he says.

"Their assistant, woman by the name of Colleen Coyle?"

"Coco, yes," the Chief says. "I know her. She's a friend of Kacy's."

"Apparently the Richardsons were having a party on their yacht when someone called them about the smoke at their house, and they hightailed it back. The girl, Coco, was on the boat, but when they got back to the mooring, she was gone. As in, no longer on the boat."

"No longer on the boat?" the Chief says. "Where did she go?"

"Nobody knows," Speed says. "She's missing."

"Is she the only one?"

"As far as I know, everyone else on the boat is accounted for, and Captain..."

"Lamont?" the Chief says.

"Yes, Lamont Oakley called the harbormaster. The harbormaster called us."

The Chief turns back to the table. Kacy's face is bathed in blue light from her phone; she gasps and looks up at him. The *Nantucket Current* must have just broken the story.

"Thank you, Speed," he says. The Richardsons' house burned down, and Coco is missing? The Chief wants to believe this is a prank, a gotcha for his final days. But he knows it's real. If he's honest, he would admit he feared something awful like this would happen with the Richardsons. "Tell them I'm on my way."

1. The Cobblestone Telegraph I

Most towns have a rumor mill. We here on Nantucket have what's known as the cobblestone telegraph—and Blond Sharon has long been the switchboard operator. *Everything* goes through her.

But this summer, a twist: Blond Sharon is now the topic of gossip. Everyone on the island is talking about how Blond Sharon's husband, Walker, left her for his physical therapist, a woman who is less than half Walker's age. Walker tore his ACL skiing over the holidays, and in March, he announced that he'd fallen in love with "Bailey from PT." He was leaving Sharon; he wanted a divorce.

Ouch, we thought. It's hardly a new story, a middle-aged man leaving his wife for a younger woman, but we thought Blond Sharon's family was bulletproof. Sharon is an exemplary mother. She secured her sixteen-year-old twin girls, Sterling and Colby, coveted internships at the Nantucket Historical Association (unpaid, but so good for their college applications). Sharon's thirteen-year-old son,

Robert, has type 1 diabetes, and Sharon monitors his blood sugar using an app on her phone. We feel bad that Sharon has been dropped like a hot potato at the age of fifty-four, but none of us feel guilty talking about it. When we think of how many hours Blond Sharon has spent blabbing about other people's business, we can't help but see this moment as a kind of poetic justice.

The good news, we all think, is that Sharon has her sister, Heather, to lean on. Sharon and Heather are polar opposites: Sharon is blond and Heather is brunette; Sharon is a stay-at-home mom, Heather is an attorney with the corporate finance division of the SEC in Washington. Blond Sharon is like the flight attendant who overshares about the pilot's hemorrhoids and the famous talk-show host seated in 3C; Heather is the black box. The only thing Heather has ever done with a secret is keep it.

Heather is also the voice of reason. When Sharon admits that what bothers her most about Walker leaving her is being a cliché, Heather says, "Just promise not to wear statement necklaces and fake eyelashes and take cruises in the Mediterranean looking for a rich replacement husband."

Sharon blinks. That had been her plan exactly.

"This is your chance to reinvent yourself," Heather says. "Do you remember the quote you taped to your bedroom mirror when we were young?"

It wasn't a quote, Sharon thinks. It was the last two lines of the Mary Oliver poem "The Summer Day": *Tell me, what is it you plan to do / with your one wild and precious life?* Sharon discovered the poem one summer when she worked shelving books at the New Canaan Public Library. The lines, which Sharon typed out on her father's electric Smith Corona and taped to her bedroom mirror, had always seemed like a challenge—but when she thinks about it now, it feels like one she has failed to meet. She has spent her one wild and precious life selecting wallpaper and scheduling the pool cleaners; she has spent it reading *People* magazine in line at the market and fruitlessly trying to improve her backhand. She has spent it scrolling through her phone.

But there is something that Sharon has dreamed of doing, something we never would have guessed.

It has been Blond Sharon's secret lifelong desire to become an author.

Well, we think, she's certainly demonstrated her keen interest in other people's stories, the seedier and more salacious, the better. Since beloved local novelist Vivian Howe died a few years ago, there has been no one to write about the dramas that occur every summer on Nantucket. Could Blond Sharon take her place? Does she know the first thing about writing fiction?

Summer is a prime time to embark on a self-improvement project, Sharon thinks—and she signs up for a virtual creative-writing workshop. The instructor's name is Lucky Zambrano, which makes it sound like he's a Mob boss, but in fact, he's a recently retired Florida Atlantic University English professor. He tells his students that he's teaching this online class to keep busy because his wife passed away last year.

Lucky is a widower, Sharon thinks. She sits up straighter and yanks at the bottom of her blouse to show a bit more cleavage. There are two other students in the Zoom class, both of them women and both about Sharon's age, though neither quite as well preserved as she is. One is named Willow, the other Nancy.

"Oh," Lucky says. "Nancy was my wife's name."

Does this give Nancy an advantage with Lucky? Sharon wonders. Nancy has one of those short, no-nonsense haircuts that means she's probably already married. Willow is wearing long feather earrings and has never seen a Botox needle.

"Let's get to your first assignment," Lucky says. "Character. What I'd like you to do is venture out into the world somewhere, could be your local farmers' market, your office building—Nancy, I see you work at the RMV, that's a fertile environment—and choose two individuals to observe. Then I'd like you to dramatize a scene between the two with an eye toward developing this scene into a story. The late great novelist John Gardner famously said that there are only two plots: One, a person goes on a journey, and two, a stranger comes to town." Lucky pauses and Sharon furiously scribbles on her legal pad. Sharon is hopelessly old-school; both Nancy and Willow type on their laptops. "Go forth and observe, then, my friends. We'll meet again next week and you can share what you've written with the group."

When Sharon clicks Leave Meeting, she's energized and, dare she say, inspired. She won't be one of those orange divorcées on a cruise ship; she's going to create a dazzling second act for herself as a published author. She snatches up her legal pad, ready to venture out into the world to observe. In a way, this has always been Sharon's mission—to find out what's really going on. But now she has a more noble mission. Now she's going to write about it.

Sharon plops herself down on a bench at the Steamship Authority ferry terminal. Where better to observe a person going on a journey or a stranger coming to town? Sharon wears her enormous Céline sunglasses and a white tennis visor, though those of us who are waiting for the ferry to arrive—notably Bob from Old Salt Taxi and Romeo, who works for the Steamship Authority—notice Sharon right away.

Why, Romeo wonders, *does Blond Sharon have a notebook and pen at the ready?* He can't think of a single reason, but Romeo loves a mystery...especially one that involves a beautiful woman.

* * *

As soon as Sharon gets settled, the boat pulls in. She scans the people coming down the ramp. Does anyone look promising? No, no, no; it's all day-trippers, the women in roomy sundresses, the men in cargo shorts, everyone in ugly sensible shoes. Fanny packs, backpacks. Why is the casual traveler in America so decidedly unstylish?

Her eyes latch onto a young woman over by the luggage cart. She has a look not seen often on Nantucket—she's like a human piece of art. Her black hair is short and cut in angles and spikes. She's wearing a tight black tank that leaves an inch of her midriff bare. She has a tattoo of a flamingo on her left shoulder and another that looks like a gecko just above her ankle. Sharon sees a gemstone sparkling in the girl's nose as she lifts a lumpy army-green duffel off the luggage cart. This person is more than a casual tourist; this is someone arriving for the summer.

A stranger comes to town! Sharon thinks. She abandons her spot on the bench and creeps over to get a closer look. Should she offer this girl a ride to wherever she's going? Sharon is about to tap the girl on the shoulder when a second young woman appears. This young woman has honey-colored hair cut in a neat, sassy bob and she's wearing slim white jeans and a fitted navy blazer. She hoists a brightly patterned Vera Bradley bag off the cart. Sharon has the exact same bag at home.

"Here, take my number, Coco," the second woman says. "Keep in touch, okay? Let me know where you end up staying."

"I'll figure it out," Coco says. "I always do. And hey, Kacy, thanks for the chowder—it meant a lot."

The second woman, Kacy, waves a hand as if to say *It was nothing.* She walks into the snarl of traffic in the parking lot. Coco's shoulders sag as she pulls out her phone. The poor girl has come to Nantucket with a giant duffel bag and doesn't have a place to stay? Sharon is about to offer to walk her over to Visitor Services to see about available hotel rooms — but then a couple of things happen in rapid succession. One is that a black Suburban pulls up, and Romeo from the Steamship opens the tailgate door and slides Kacy's suitcases into the back. It isn't Romeo's job to help with luggage, so Kacy must be some kind of VIP. A second later, Sharon realizes the person driving the Suburban is the chief of police, Ed Kapenash. The young woman must be his daughter. Yes! Kacy Kapenash! Last Sharon heard, she was working as a nurse out in San Francisco. She must be back for a visit.

The second thing that happens is that Sharon's phone rings. Inwardly, she groans. Before Walker left, Sharon's phone was attached to her ear; this had been one of Walker's major complaints (but how was Sharon supposed to get any news if she didn't chat?). In a few short months, Sharon has turned into a full-blown Millennial when it comes to talking on the phone — she'll do anything to avoid it.

The display says Fast Eddie. Eddie Pancik is Nantucket real estate royalty and Sharon's male counterpart in the gossip department. He's one of six people she'll answer her phone for.

"Eddie," Sharon says.

"Hey there, beautiful," Eddie says. Eddie has, of course, heard the news about Walker trading Blond Sharon in for a younger model but he won't mention it. "I just closed on Triple Eight Pocomo Road. A couple appeared out of nowhere and offered the full asking price. Twenty-two mil."

What? Sharon thinks. The house at 888 Pocomo Road has been something of an albatross for Eddie. It's famous for its octagonal deck, and Jennifer Quinn recently gave the interior a complete cosmetic refresh (it was the last project she took on before *Real-Life Rehab,* her HGTV show, took off). But... Triple Eight sits right on the water, and, thanks to climate change, harbor levels have been rising each year, eating away at the property's small private beach. The forensic geologist reported that the first floor of the house would be underwater in eighty to a hundred years. Unfortunately, there's not enough land behind the house to move it back, and neighborhood bylaws prohibit lifting it up.

Who pays twenty-two million for a doomed house? Sharon wonders. Someone either stupid or crazy.

"I want to introduce you to the wife," Eddie says. "She's a self-described 'party animal.' "

Sharon cringes. *Party animal* brings to mind someone like Keith Richards in the 1970s, Rob Lowe in the 1980s. But Sharon could use a new friend, even a shortsighted one. *A stranger comes to town, part deux!* she thinks. "Great, feel free to give her my number."

"Already did," Eddie says. "She wants to join the Field and Oar Club."

There's no chance of that happening, as Eddie well knows, but instead of reminding him about the lengthy wait list and the nominating and seconding letters, Sharon says, "Proud of you, honey."

"Thanks, bae," Eddie says and he hangs up because he needs to get to the bank with his commission check. He's glad he called Sharon with this news before going. If Blond Sharon doesn't know about it, has it even happened?

During the short time that Sharon was on the phone, Kacy Kapenash has reappeared at the luggage cart; it seems she isn't finished with Coco. "I just talked to my dad, and he says it's fine if you stay in our guest room for a few days."

"You're kidding!" Coco says. "That's amazing — thank you, you're *such* a lifesaver." Coco follows Kacy to the waiting Suburban.

Sharon returns to her spot on the bench and scribbles down all the details she can remember, including the flamingo tattoo, the army-green duffel, the "I Love Rock 'n' Roll" haircut.

As she's describing the heartwarming scene between the two women, Romeo approaches; his large form casts a shadow on her page. "Hey, Sharon, what's up?"

Sharon glances at him. *Is Romeo single?* she wonders. "I'm writing a short story."

Romeo grins. How has Sharon never noticed how attractive he is? "Cool, can I be in it?"

"I'll have to think about that," Sharon says. "It's going to be pretty scandalous."

"*Scandalous* is my middle name," Romeo says.

Sharon writes in her notebook: *Romantic hero — Romeo Scandalous Steamship Guy?* It feels a little unlikely, but then she reminds herself that it's fiction — anything can happen.

2. "Sherry's Living in Paradise"

One month earlier

The song is playing when the couple sit down at the bar. Each track on the Banana Deck's Spotify playlist has *paradise* in the title; Coco is weary of all of them but especially this one. What that really means is that Coco is tired of St. John. It's nearly Memorial Day weekend, which marks the end of high season here in the Virgin Islands.

"I have a question for you," the gentleman says in a broad Australian accent. The guy is overdressed for the Banana Deck — he's in a linen blazer the color of wheat bread and a crisp white shirt. His wife has long chestnut-brown hair styled in sumptuous barrel curls; her silk bias-cut dress is giving Academy Awards–presenter vibes.

Coco sighs and sets down her book. She's reading *The Secret History* by Donna Tartt. She can't believe it's never been made into a movie.

"No, this song isn't about me," Coco says, though most of the lyrics apply. She *is* living in paradise, she *is* slinging drinks at a bar down by the beach. She's both chasing something and running from something; she's had a lot of lovers who were good for nothing. As for thinking about leaving—well, these days Coco does nothing but.

"That wasn't my question," the gentleman says. "I want to know if—"

"Yes, Kenny Chesney does sometimes come in here," Coco says. "Though not usually this late in the season."

"Shoot. We were hoping we could buy him a drink," the wife says. She sounds American.

You and everyone else, Coco thinks. Wow, she's in a foul mood. She slaps down a couple of Cruzan Rum coasters. "What can I get you?"

"A bottle of very cold Veuve Clicquot, please," the gentleman says.

Coco nearly laughs. "We don't have Veuve Clicquot."

"Moët?" he says. "Taittinger?"

Coco holds a finger up. "I'll be right back."

She heads over to the hostess station. "I think the couple at the bar is in the wrong place," she tells Clover. "They ordered champagne, and they're all gussied up." Coco can't believe she just used the word *gussied;* from time to time, she opens her mouth and Arkansas slips out.

"They didn't make a reservation and I won't have an open table for at least forty-five minutes," Clover says. She lowers her voice and says, "The guy called me *mate* and tried to slide me a hundred-dollar bill. I was like, *Whoa, are you trying to bribe me?* Then he tells me he's a movie producer and I'm like, *Good for you, mate. I'm a restaurant hostess without any available tables.*"

Coco perks up. She just finished her screenplay last week and has been contemplating her next steps. *This,* she thinks, *is what's known as* manifestation.

When Coco returns to the bar, a dude who works for WAPA, the Virgin Islands power company, has taken a seat next to the couple, and they've struck up a friendly conversation — so friendly that the movie producer introduces himself. "I'm Bull Richardson and this is my wife, Leslee." To Coco, he says, "How'd we do with the bubbly? I'll need a third glass for my mate Harlan here."

"We don't carry *any* champagne, unfortunately." Coco wonders if this couple thought the Banana Deck was more like Nikki Beach in St. Bart's, where, if Instagram is to be believed, your server parades through the dining room holding your ten-thousand-dollar bottle of Dom Pérignon with Pitbull playing and sparklers shooting so everyone knows just how much money you spent on your buzz.

"No worries!" Bull Richardson says. He looks at Harlan. "What are you drinking, mate?"

"Bud Light, please," Harlan says.

"I'll have a double-shot rum punch with a Myers's floater," Bull says.

Coco raises her eyebrows. That's a serious drink.

"I'll have the same," Leslee Richardson says. "And we'd like to eat."

Coco slides menus in front of everyone and mixes up the double-shot rum punches with generous Myers's floaters. She presents the drinks to the Richardsons and cracks open a Bud Light for Harlan from WAPA. The song changes to "Two Tickets to Paradise," and Coco washes glassware while casually eavesdropping.

She learns that the Richardsons are renting in Peter Bay, aka Billionaire Hill. When he's asked where they're from, Mr. Richardson says, "We bounce around a lot. We did the holidays in Palm Beach, then we skied most of our winter away in Aspen. The snow was so good that we stuck around longer than we planned, which is why we're here so late in the season. We're going to spend the summer on Nantucket. I should say we're moving there, finally putting down some roots. We've been looking at houses."

When asked what business he's in, Mr. Richardson says, "I own a beverage-distribution company. We supply water, soda, and sports drinks throughout Indonesia."

Coco's spirits deflate. Did this guy lie to Clover just to get a table?

"*And* Bull is a movie producer!" Leslee says.

"On the finance side," Bull says. "I have people who tell me what's going to be big, and I invest. For example, did you see *The Main Vein?*"

Harlan admits he hasn't seen it, and neither has Coco. She can't help but think of her mother's boyfriend, Kemp, who announced he was going to "drain the main vein" every time he took a leak. Eww.

"What about *Snark?*" Bull asks.

Nope.

"They were big overseas," Leslee says. "All the cinemas in Kuala Lumpur were showing *Snark.* There were lines down the street."

Coco is glad to hear that Bull Richardson's producer credits don't include movies like *Top Gun* and *Avatar.* That means he might be open to taking a chance on a first-time screenwriter.

She asks if they're ready to order. Bull slaps down the menu and says, "Give us all the appetizers."

"You'd like—"

"All of them," Bull says. "Please."

Coco punches in the conch fritters, spring rolls, mozz sticks, wings, and quesadillas; she skips the peel-'n'-eat shrimp as a favor to the wife in her silk dress. The song changes to "Paradise City," and Coco checks her garnishes. Harlan is sitting next to Leslee; he's a white dude with a hard-hat sunburn that cuts neatly across his forehead. He's explaining his job as a lineman, and Coco would like to ask how he can, in good conscience, work for a company that charges forty-one cents per kilowatt hour. (It's ten cents per kilowatt hour in Arkansas; Coco looked it up.) But she doesn't want to be rude. She needs to seize this opportunity.

She considers saying, *I've written a screenplay*. And when Bull Richardson quips, *Hasn't everyone?* Coco will tell him that *her* screenplay is *based on a true story*. Is there a more seductive phrase in the English language?

But what if he asks her to pitch him right then and there in front of his wife and the WAPA dude? Coco learned everything she knows about pitching a movie from watching *The Player* a dozen times, and although she practices her pitch in front of the bathroom mirror every morning as she waits for the shower to heat up, she can't quite convey the magic of her screenplay, which is in the writing, the details, the emotional depth of her main character. She wants this guy Bull Richardson to *read* it — but why would he? He doesn't know her; she's just tonight's bartender, and therefore she'll be easy to dismiss.

There has to be another way to finesse this. There *is* another way, Coco realizes, one that nicely dovetails with her burning desire to leave the Virgin Islands for the summer.

She sets down the order of conch fritters, and Bull Richardson growls. *He's more Mad Max than Crocodile Dundee,* Coco thinks. She can easily picture him cruising across the outback in a Ford Falcon seeking vengeance and justice.

"I heard you mention Nantucket," Coco says. "I'm heading there myself this summer."

Bull dips a conch fritter into the roasted red pepper aioli and seems to take an interest in Coco for the first time. Bull holds her gaze (Coco has been told her entire life that her eyes are something special; the irises are icy blue with a dark blue ring around them). She expects his attention will drift down to her chest, but happily, Bull isn't as coarse as her typical bar customer.

Leslee, meanwhile, has taken the moment to squeeze Harlan's grapefruit-size biceps. She turns to Coco. "That's quite a coincidence. Do you know people on Nantucket?"

"Yes," Coco lies. Then she scrambles. Who? *Who?* "I grew up in Rosebush, Arkansas, and our town librarian, Susan Geraghty, introduced me to Nantucket." *Technically,* Coco thinks, *this is true.*

"Rosebush, Arkansas?" Leslee says.

"Yes, ma'am," Coco says. Coco's screenplay is titled *Rosebush*. Her opening shot is of the town sign, which announces a population of 423, then the camera pans to Rosebush's seen-better-days Main Street, which boasts two businesses: Grumpy Garth's Diner and the Pansy and Petunia Vintage Market, where you can buy anything from a donkey saddle to Aunt Sally's amethyst brooch missing all but one of the amethysts.

The screenplay follows a high-school girl named (for the time being) Coco, who wants to get the hell out of Rosebush. Most people in Rosebush care about nothing but college football and NASCAR, but Coco is obsessed with grander things: film, literature, art, music—culture.

The screenplay starts during Coco's senior year, when she attends a program for exceptional students in Little Rock. She takes a screenwriting seminar with a professor from NYU who tells her she has a "good ear for dialogue" and a "keen sense of story arc." These two compliments set Coco on her path; she returns to Rosebush energized, inspired, *aroused.* She wants to hitchhike to LA but before she goes, she needs at least a little money. She steals from the register at Grumpy Garth's and then the safe, but she's caught by Garth himself, which is awkward and horrible because Garth is a wonderful man (Coco imagines Morgan Freeman playing this part). September arrives and there's no money even for community college in nearby Searcy, so Coco moves up to Missouri and gets a job bartending near the Lake of the Ozarks.

A montage of Coco at her new job follows: She pulls draft beers and pours shots of bourbon; she counts her tips, then looks across the dull mirror of the lake in which the Hollywood sign appears as a mirage. She's gotten away—but not far enough.

Coco is named employee of the year and wins a weeklong cruise to the Virgin Islands. There's a scene where Coco leans against the railing of a cruise ship marveling at the green peaks of the islands, the clear turquoise of the water. She has reached a land of palm trees and steel-drum music, hibiscus and white sandy bays. She wanders through Cruz Bay and sees a Help Wanted sign at a bar not unlike the Banana Deck, and the viewer realizes she's going to stay.

The script ends there, but in real life, Coco wants a more meaningful dream to come true. She wants to enter the world of producers and first ADs, of craft services and second units. She will do whatever it takes to see *Rosebush* on the big screen. Only then will she have fulfilled her purpose.

When Coco turns her attention back to the Richardsons, she notices Leslee's hand resting on the WAPA dude's thigh. Coco's eyes flick over to Bull. Is he seeing this?

"Anyway," Coco says. "I'm really looking forward to this summer on Nantucket." And suddenly she is. She will leave behind three o'clock happy hours and wild donkeys in the road for...what do they have on Nantucket? Lighthouses, clam chowder, cocktail parties on the croquet lawn?

Bull takes a long swig of his rum punch. "Do you already have a job nailed down?" he asks. "Because we're going to need a household assistant. A...girl Friday." He turns to Leslee, who lazily lifts her hand from the WAPA dude's leg. "Right? We talked about finding someone."

Leslee says, "We talked about hiring someone who's familiar with the island since we'll be brand-new there. We don't know a soul."

Coco says, "I'm deciding between two offers for the exact position you're talking about. Personal concierge."

"Yes!" Bull says. "Personal concierge! Well, don't take those other offers. Come work for us instead. We'll pay thirty-five an hour and provide housing."

Wait, Coco thinks. *Is it going to be this easy?*

"Thirty-five an hour!" Harlan says. "Hell, I'll go to Nantucket."

"Bull," Leslee says. *Here it comes,* Coco thinks, *the velvet hammer.* "We haven't even bought a place yet."

"But we're close. You liked the one with the party room."

"Party room!" Harlan says, hoisting his Bud.

Bull shoves the final conch fritter into his piehole. He has sun-scorched cheeks and a nose that looks like it's been broken half a dozen times, so you couldn't call him handsome, but his confidence and his accent are appealing.

"The party room is an orgy waiting to happen," Leslee says like this is a good thing. "But isn't that the house with issues? The ero-sion problem? Climate change…"

"By the time we need to worry about climate change," Bull says, "we'll be long dead." He smiles at Coco. "We don't have kids. Who cares if the house falls into the sea fifty years from now?" He slides his business card across the bar and Coco picks it up. BULFINCH RICH-ARDSON, it says. SWEETWATER DISTRIBUTION AND PRODUCTIONS. There's a cell number and two email addresses, one for the distribution, one for the productions. "Send me your information tomorrow," he says. "I'll let you know when we close on the house, and we can reconnect on Nantucket. How does that sound?"

"Maybe we should ask her name first," Leslee says fake sweetly. "Before you invite her to live with us."

Bull says, "She already told us — it's Sherry."

"That was the *song,*" Leslee says.

"My name is Colleen Coyle, but everyone calls me Coco."

"As in…Coco Chanel?" Leslee says dubiously, giving Coco the up-and-down.

Only if Coco Chanel wore Chuck Taylors and had a pierced nose, Coco thinks. "I'll probably take one of the offers I already have," she says. "But thanks anyway. Maybe I'll bump into you up there."

"No, wait!" Leslee says, practically jumping off her barstool. Coco has read her correctly: She's a woman who wants only what she can't have. "Bull is right, you should come work for us. Besides, I could use another woman around."

"In that case," Coco says, cheesing up the moment for all it's worth, "you have yourself a new personal concierge." She reaches across the bar and shakes hands with Leslee and then Bull. "Now, let me check on the other apps."

As Coco heads for the kitchen, she hears Bull say, "How about that? I can't believe our luck."

"Me either," Harlan from WAPA says. "She's hot."

3. Level 4

The patient who finally breaks Kacy is named Gideon, though Kacy calls him Little G. Gideon arrives in the level 4 NICU at UCSF Benioff Children's Hospital as a twenty-four-weeker (technically, twenty-three weeks and six days), and, as with all babies this premature, he has only a 25 percent chance of survival. Little G weighs in at one pound, four ounces; he fits in the palm of Kacy's hand. His lungs are the size of lima beans; he has no hair; his eyes don't open; and, like most extreme preemies, he looks like a tiny, translucent doll.

What Kacy has learned during her seven years as a NICU nurse is that her itty-bitty patients are stronger and more resilient than most people realize. The human body wants to survive. Through the thimble-size bell of her stethoscope, Kacy can hear Gideon's heart beating as rapidly as the wings of a hummingbird.

Kacy learns that Little G's parents went through nine rounds of IVF and his mother suffered three miscarriages before she became pregnant with Gideon. Kacy has known some nurses over the years who grow impatient with the parents—their crying, their worrying, their questions that don't have answers, their interfering, their praying, their self-blame, their pessimism, their optimism. However, Kacy excels with parents. She embraces Mama and Papa G, tells them, "We're going to give Gideon the best care." She wants to add, *I will personally see to it that your child survives,* but the head neonatologist on the unit, Dr. Isla Quintanilla, has gently reminded Kacy that the cruelest thing she can do is offer parents false hope and make promises she can't deliver on.

Gideon has an umbilical venous catheter and is given trophic feeds to prepare his gastrointestinal system. He's on a vent, but still, his O_2 levels drop so low that Kacy fears they're going to lose him right away. His lungs are too stiff to accept oxygen. But somehow, he hangs on.

On the second night of Gideon's life, Dr. Quintanilla sneaks over to Kacy's apartment on Filbert Street. Isla's fiancé, Dr. Rondo, is the chief of pediatrics at the hospital. Rondo volunteers at clinics in Oakland's underserved neighborhoods on Tuesday and Thursday nights, so for the past eighteen months, those are the nights Kacy and Isla make slow, torturous love, then order takeout, which they eat naked in Kacy's bedroom. But on this night, when Kacy is halfway through her fusilli lunghi from Seven Hills, Isla says, "I don't think Gideon is going to make it, Bun."

Kacy sets the takeout container on her nightstand and goes into the bathroom; she takes a few deep breaths and starts her skin-care routine.

Isla stands in the bathroom doorway and touches Kacy's shoulder. "Hey, this isn't like you."

"It's exactly like me," Kacy says. The smaller and weaker a patient is, the harder Kacy falls for him.

"I think you're just upset about your dad," Isla says.

Kacy douses a cotton pad with micellar water and tries to keep her expression steady. Kacy's father, Ed Kapenash, had a heart attack a few weeks earlier; he was medevaced off Nantucket to Mass General, where he underwent bypass surgery. Kacy had been at work when it happened, so by the time she spoke to her mother, Ed was "out of the woods" and expected to make a full recovery.

Kacy *is* worried about her father, especially since he went right back to work and is refusing to retire until the end of August. But Kacy is bothered by something else as well.

She starts to remove her makeup. "When are you going to tell him? When are you going to *leave* him?"

Isla hisses like a balloon losing air. "It has to be soon. We're looking at wedding venues in Napa this weekend, which means picking a date, which means it's getting real, which means...yeah, I have to tell him."

"Or don't tell him," Kacy says. "Marry Rondo. Give birth to four or five little Rondos. Hire a nanny to raise your kids or quit your job, because you can't work sixty-hour weeks and be on call every other weekend while at the same time getting the kids to their fencing matches and oboe lessons. And we both know Rondo won't be stepping down so he can 'be more present at home.'"

"Bun, stop," Isla says.

Kacy sighs. She doesn't like herself when she dumps on Rondo; the dude is Mister Rogers with a medical degree. "Marry Rondo and live the dream." She meets Isla's gaze in the bathroom mirror. "Only you and I will know that the dream is a lie."

"Bun," Isla says. When Kacy bends over the sink to splash water on her face, Isla runs her finger down Kacy's spine. "I'm going to tell him."

That night, Kacy wakes up from a dream certain that Little G is dead. She calls the unit, and Sunny, her night-shift counterpart, says, "Little G is a tiny warrior. He's doing great."

Kacy wipes away a few tears, then goes back to sleep.

Like most extreme preemies, Little G is in the hospital for weeks and weeks. Kacy wishes she could put together a time-lapse film showing Gideon gaining weight, Gideon's eyes opening, Gideon's hair growing in, Mama and Papa G changing his diaper, Mama G reading him *The Runaway Bunny,* Papa G singing him "If I Had a Million Dollars" by the Barenaked Ladies.

Isla and Rondo look at wedding venues in Napa; they like Auberge du Soleil for the rehearsal dinner, the Charles Krug Winery for the reception. They go to a cake tasting; they register at Sur La Table. Isla assures Kacy that the wedding date is still more than a year away—she has plenty of time to back out, and she will, she *will*! It's not as though the invitations have gone out; it's not like she's bought a dress.

Gideon comes off the ventilator and starts taking feedings by mouth. Kacy finally allows herself to imagine his future: Little G on a pitcher's mound, Little G picking up his date for prom, Little G graduating from Stanford, Little G developing a new source of sustainable energy or becoming a civil rights attorney. He will do something that brings people joy, hope, peace of mind—and Kacy will have been a small part of it.

Then, only eleven days before Gideon is scheduled to go home with Mama and Papa G, something happens in the middle of the night. It's not his lungs; it's his heart. It just...stops beating. He crashes, the peds cardiac team are called in, they can't save him. When Kacy gets to work in the morning, she learns that Little G is gone.

Kacy has dealt with hundreds of losses, but this one is cataclysmic. She goes into the break room and cries. Traditionally, the nurses create a memory box for each baby they lose—a lock of hair, a swaddling blanket and cap, the baby's ID bracelet. Kacy can't bring herself to do it, so Sunny handles all of it. *It's not fair!* Kacy thinks. He was doing so well; he was so close to being discharged.

Isla tells Kacy she'll come over that evening, even though it's a Wednesday. Kacy is grateful; she's always been good at keeping work and home life separate, but she can't bear to face her empty apartment. And childishly, she likes the idea of stealing Isla from Rondo for a night.

Isla arrives and orders fried chicken, shrimp and grits, and a big bag of beignets from Brenda's, but when the food gets there, Kacy can't make herself eat. She cries in Isla's arms, and Isla shushes her, smooths her hair, and reminds her that she was one of the most important people in Gideon's brief life, every bit as important as his parents. He survived so long, Isla says, because of you.

In a way he was lucky, Isla adds. He knew nothing but unconditional love.

The following week, Kacy is functioning but still tender. She takes one morning off to attend Little G's service. Mama G tries to read *The Runaway Bunny* but gets through only the first page before breaking down. A young woman with a guitar sings "If I Had a Million Dollars." The coffin is the size of a shoebox.

When Kacy returns to the hospital that afternoon, she spies Dr. Rondo in the lobby. *No,* she thinks and she casts her eyes to the floor, but a second later, he calls her name. They've met on numerous occasions; Rondo often comes to pick up Isla after work.

"Kacy at the Bat!" he says. Rondo is famous around the hospital for using nicknames. He calls his young patients Champ, Trouble, T-Swift. "I just wanted to say thank you for agreeing to be Isla's maid of honor."

Kacy blinks. Rondo's black hair is damp and freshly combed, as though he's just taken a shower. In the middle of the day? Kacy would like to tell Isla that Rondo might also be having an affair, but then she remembers Rondo often plays squash in the afternoons with Dr. Dunne.

"Oh…" Kacy says. Maid of honor? Kacy would most definitely be Isla's maid of honor if Isla were getting married, which she claims she isn't.

"She doesn't have a lot of women friends and she was really nervous on Wednesday when you two were having dinner because she thought you'd think it was weird. Since you guys have a strictly professional relationship."

Kacy stares at the cleft in Rondo's strong chin. She longs to tell him that her "strictly professional relationship" with Isla includes kissing her eyelids, braiding her hair, making her orgasm so loudly that her next-door neighbor has learned to play Puccini arias at top volume on Tuesday and Thursday nights. *I love her more than you do,* Kacy would like to say—but Rondo's adoration of Isla is much talked about in the NICU. He sends flowers to the unit weekly, urns of coffee from Blue Bottle, boxes of Topogato truffles that look like they belong in a museum. Not only that, but he has created his own Pinterest board for their wedding. (The other nurses swooned at this news.)

Kacy privately feels Rondo might be too soft for Isla—he has no edges; he doesn't swear; he doesn't lose his temper. What Kacy resents most about him is that she can't point to any obvious flaws. The other male docs at Children's tend to be mansplainers or total bros who think nothing of talking over women. But not Rondo. He's a gem.

"But she said you happily agreed," he says. "Which is so great. We finally picked out invitations last night, and her mother is flying in from Mexico City at the end of the month to go dress shopping."

Invitations, Kacy thinks. *Dress shopping.*

Rondo's phone buzzes. He looks genuinely apologetic as he checks it. "Shoot, I have to go. But thank you, Kace. Truly." He squeezes her shoulder and rushes for the elevator bank, then seems to think better of it and goes dashing up the stairs, taking them two at a time, like a superhero off to save the world.

On Tuesday, when Isla sneaks over to Kacy's apartment, Kacy tells her she's made a decision.

"What do you mean, you're *leaving*?" Isla says. "Leave of absence? A week, two weeks, you're burned out, you want to drive down to Big Sur? You want to go to Ojai or LA and sit by the pool at the Beverly Hills Hotel?"

All of those options sound lovely and Kacy wishes that a short break was all she needed. But her father's health, Isla's impending nuptials, and tragically losing Little G (why had she let herself grow so attached when she knew better?) have brought her to a crossroads.

"I'm leaving for the summer," Kacy says. "I'll reassess in September."

"Reassess?" Isla says. Her cheeks flare pink; her normally unflappable composure cracks. "Are you breaking *up* with me?"

"I'm going to Nantucket," Kacy says. "My dad...I want to spend some time with my family."

"You promised the next time you went home, you'd bring me," Isla says.

"Isla, you're engaged," Kacy says. "I saw Rondo the other day. He told me you've chosen invitations. He said you're going dress shopping." She laughs unhappily. "He thanked me for agreeing to be your maid of honor. You're getting married, Isla. How can I break up with you when you aren't mine to begin with?"

Kacy realizes she's issuing an ultimatum. Isla can save their relationship now. She can choose Kacy now.

But instead, Isla drops her head into her hands. "When are you leaving?"

"Two weeks," Kacy says.

On their final night together, as Kacy packs, Isla lies across Kacy's bed, as lush and naked as an odalisque in an Ingres painting. "Leaving on a Jet Plane"—Kacy's choice—is playing over the speaker.

"You're taking all your cute clothes," Isla says.

"That I am."

"I love your style," Isla says. "Have I ever told you that?"

"Yes."

"Even in scrubs, you look like Grace Kelly."

"You're being dramatic."

"I want you to stay, Bun. I'm afraid you're going to meet someone on Nantucket and I will have lost the only person I've ever really loved."

"So kiss me," Kacy sings along, *"and smile for me."* She folds her silky camisole tops, her white jeans, her floral sundresses. There's only one thing Isla can do to get Kacy to stay, and she knows it. *"Hold me like you'll never let me go,"* Kacy sings.

Isla is crying, and Kacy won't lie, the moment is gratifying, but an hour later, after Isla has dressed and gone, Kacy wonders if she's made the right decision or a rash one.

She crawls into bed and checks Instagram. Isla doesn't have an account but Rondo does; if the man has a fault, it's that he overshares on social media. Only three minutes earlier, Rondo posted a picture of two glasses of wine side by side on their coffee table with the flames of their gas fireplace flickering in the background. The caption reads *Unwinding with my love.*

Yes, Kacy thinks, *I made the right decision.* She's going home.

4. Meet-Cute I

As soon as Coco's plane touches down in Boston, she texts Bull Richardson: I've landed.

There's no response and Coco wonders if now is the time to panic. Her previous three texts — one sent yesterday afternoon from the St. Thomas airport, one sent last night from the Orlando airport (where she shoplifted the new Kristin Hannah book from Hudson News because she'd finished her Jesmyn Ward novel on the plane), and one this morning before takeoff — have gone unanswered. She checks her email. There's nothing new from Bull Richardson but she's at least able to reread his previous correspondence: We'd love to offer you the job of personal concierge... Errands, light housekeeping, party prep (Leslee throws a lot of parties)... Thirty-five an hour plus room and board... We're scheduled to close on the house June 11... From Boston, take the Plymouth-Brockton bus line to Hyannis, then the fast ferry to Nantucket... Let us know your travel plans.

Coco had written back that she would be arriving on Nantucket on June 11, and she included her flight itinerary. There had been no response to this, which Coco assumed meant it was fine. Now, however, it feels like she missed a crucial step, which was getting Bull's confirmation. Was something wrong? Did Leslee change her mind about having another woman around? Did Bull suspect that Coco's intent was to worm her way into his good graces, make herself indispensable, then use him to get her screenplay produced?

Or is she just paranoid because she's tired? When she's off the plane and in the terminal at Logan, she calls Bull; she is jettisoned to his voice mail.

"Hey, Mr. Richardson, it's Coco. I'm taking the nine o'clock bus, then the eleven o'clock ferry, arriving on the island at noon. I can get a taxi to your house. I just need the address? Looking forward to hearing from you and excited about the summer. Thanks!"

It's not until Coco has boarded the bus that her phone buzzes with a text from Bull: We closed on the house this morning. Leslee says we need some time to move in and get the place ready, etc. If you could just hang tight, that would be great. We'll let you know about a start date. Thx!

What? Coco thinks. He does realize she's in Massachusetts, right? On the bus, headed to the ferry. By noon, she'll be on Nantucket, where she knows no one but them.

She texts back: Where should I stay in the meantime?

Bull says, We thought you had someone on the island? The librarian?

I said my librarian introduced me to Nantucket, Coco thinks. *I never said she* lived *there.*

Bull texts again: We're at the Hotel Nantucket, which is fully booked, but I think the White Elephant has rooms? Or you could try a B and B?

Coco types, Will you be paying for my room?—but then deletes it, because it's clear that the answer will be no. She's on her own until they get the house ready. How long will that take? A few days? A week? Longer? Are they having it painted? Has their furniture arrived?

Coco has to figure on a week. Unfortunately, she couldn't find anyone to sublet her room in her St. John house-share, so she has to eat three grand in rent and utilities, leaving her with a little over eleven hundred in savings. She owes sixteen hundred bucks on her Visa, which she wants to pay off; she will *not* be like her mother and Kemp, perpetually living in debt.

Deep breath.

Thirty-five dollars an hour means a gross of fourteen hundred for a forty-hour week, and she won't have to worry about rent or meals. Then, once she sells her screenplay...

She runs a hand through her hair. She's getting ahead of herself.

She checks out the White Elephant's website on her phone. The cheapest room is $1,095 a night. Seriously? The bed-and-breakfasts start at $310 per night. There are no motels, there's no Holiday Inn Express; there used to be a hostel, but not any longer. *Looks like I'm camping,* Coco thinks, which is fine; she grew up camping with her mother and Kemp, and she can rough it without a tent or even a sleeping bag. But it turns out Nantucket doesn't have a campground.

Where do poor people stay? she wonders.

At the ferry terminal, Coco begins to understand what *going to Nantucket* means. Everyone is preppy and wealthy-looking; the clothes are tasteful; there's a lot of navy blue and white. One woman carries a woven basket purse on her forearm and holds the leash of a yellow Lab in her opposite hand. Her silver-haired husband wears pinkish pants and loafers with no socks. He bellows, "Larry!" and another gentleman turns around and exclaims in delight. "Ha-ha-ha, Talbot, old pal! How was your winter—Vero, was it? Let's get a drink at the Field and Oar next week—my first order of business is getting my boat in the water."

Coco has a recurring nightmare where she's onstage at the Rosebush Middle School spelling bee and all the words are in a nonsense language. She feels that way now. *Can I have the definition for* Field and Oar, *please?*

Coco had had a steep learning curve when she moved to St. John—driving on the left, respecting West Indian culture, realizing that *painkiller* was a drink, not a pill. But St. John was so low-key it was almost no-key; it was populated by outlaws and renegades, pirates and mermaids. You could go to the grocery store in bare feet.

Nantucket is something completely different. There isn't a tattoo in sight.

Coco waits in line carrying everything she owns in the enormo canvas duffel Kemp used in the Gulf War. She feels a sharp jab at her back and turns to see the gentleman named Talbot in his pinkish pants scowling at her. "You can't carry something that big and... *unwieldy* onto the boat, young lady. It belongs on the luggage rack."

Coco's duffel was the last piece of baggage to slide down the chute of the carousel at Logan (Coco had spent anxious minutes certain it was lost and that she was royally screwed). She held the bag on her lap for the entirety of the bus ride and she isn't exactly eager to let it out of her sight again.

"It's fine," she says. "I'll just hold—"

"I'm telling you, it's not allowed," Talbot says so loudly he must be either extremely important here or going deaf.

The chick in front of Coco whirls around. She's wearing white jeans with a blazer and has really good hair—glossy, the color of honey, cut into a bob, tucked behind one ear. She leans toward Coco and says, "He thinks he's the chief of police. Just put your bag over there on the blue luggage rack."

"Thanks," Coco says. She doesn't know the rules here; she messed up, and everyone is now looking at her. She trudges over to the luggage rack. Her bag *is* unwieldy and a part of her is grateful to relinquish it. When she returns, the chick with the good hair is gone. Thankfully, so is Talbot. Coco joins the end of the line, and once she's on the boat, she takes a window seat in the first empty row. Her mortification lessens somewhat. *Talbot is a scrote,* she thinks as she pulls out her book. Almost immediately, she closes her eyes.

A few minutes pass. The boat gets under way; there are some announcements over the loudspeaker: life jackets, restrooms, the trip will take about an hour. Coco dozes on and off. She didn't get much sleep last night on the floor of the Orlando airport. She can't believe the Richardsons' house isn't ready, although, now that she thinks about it, what did she expect? Closing on a house doesn't mean moving in the same day. She should have waited for Bull Richardson to give her a firm date before she fell prey to a sale alert from Expedia. She can't afford even $310 a night, so what is she going to do? She could've just pitched Bull Richardson her screenplay at the bar. What made her think the long game would work any better?

But it *will* work. Somehow, Coco knows this.

She hears a rustling near her; someone has taken a seat in her row. Coco likes to be aware of her surroundings and knows she should open her eyes and make sure it's not some dude creeping on her—maybe old Talbot is a perv—but she's tired, and her eyelids are heavy...

Suddenly she smells something delicious—briny, oniony, herby. She's dreaming; she's just hungry, starving. She wants lunch or a snack but she needs to save her money.

Coco opens her eyes and there, on the tray table in front of her, is a bowl of clam chowder with two packets of oyster crackers. Coco turns her head to see the chick with the good hair. She's taken the aisle seat, leaving the seat between them open. She too has a bowl of chowder in front of her.

Coco straightens up. "You got this for me?"

"One little-known fact about Nantucket is that ferry chowder is the best chowder." The chick blows on a spoonful and smiles at Coco. "I take it this is your first time to the island?"

Not at all, Coco thinks. *I'm a regular at the Field and Oar.* "Is it that obvious?" She opens a package of crackers, dumps them into her soup, and watches the fragrant steam rise. "Thank you for this. You're very kind."

"I hope Talbot Sweeney didn't freak you out. He's the old guard, the kind of person who gives Nantucketers a reputation for being snooty. I'm Kacy, by the way."

Coco offers her hand, a gesture that feels hokey and old-fashioned but also like what's maybe expected? "I'm Coco. Do you live on the island?"

"Born and raised," Kacy says. "But I've been living in California for years. I'm just going back for the summer. My family is there." She pauses. "How about you? Are you...visiting? Going for work?"

"Work," Coco says. "A couple who just bought a house on Nantucket hired me to be their 'personal concierge.'" She uses air quotes so Kacy won't think she's a total douchebag.

"Nice," Kacy says. "Where's the house?"

"On Nantucket," Coco says. Did she forget to mention that part?

Kacy laughs. "Right, but where on Nantucket? Squam? Monomoy?"

Squam? Coco thinks. *Monomoy? Can you use that in a sentence, please?* "I'm not really sure." She takes a spoonful of soup; it's so delicious, her eyelids flutter closed. "I feel like such a charity case."

Kacy laughs. "It's just soup."

The best and worst thing about Nantucket, Kacy thinks when she gets to the ferry, is that it never changes. She spies the summer people with their battered boat shoes, needlepoint belts, and natural ease and the day-trippers in CAPE COD T-shirts and Keen sandals.

Kacy is surprised to find an outlier behind her in line, a young woman with retro-punk-rock hair, piercings, and tattoos. Kacy immediately thinks of that old jingle from *Sesame Street: One of these things is not like the others, one of these things just doesn't belong.* Talbot Sweeney gives the girl a hard time about her bag; she seems uncomfortable, disoriented, or, at the very least, uninitiated. Kacy decides to do the welcoming thing and buys the girl a chowder.

Coco is shy at first, or maybe just hungry. She devours her soup and both packets of crackers, down to the dust. But then she loosens up and tells Kacy that the personal-assistant job she's accepted comes with housing, but just that morning, her employers told her the housing wasn't available yet.

"What?" Kacy says. "So where are you going to stay?"

"I'm not sure," Coco says. "A hotel, I guess. Unless you have any friends with a flophouse? I'm kind of on a budget and I didn't anticipate this..."

"Of course you didn't," Kacy says. "What's the couple's name?"

"The Richardsons."

Kacy doesn't know them, though they might know her; she has one of the most recognizable last names on the island. "I've never heard of them," she says. "But they're new and I've been gone for a while."

Coco waves a hand. "You were so cool to buy me this chowder, I don't expect you to solve my housing issue. I was an idiot for not confirming with this couple. I'll figure something out. I'm just happy that someone on this boat is being friendly instead of looking at me like I have fleas." She tucks the cracker wrappers and her napkin into her empty bowl. "So what were you doing in California?"

Over the course of the boat ride, Kacy spills her guts about her job in the NICU, her clandestine affair with Isla, Isla's engagement to Dr. Rondo, losing Little G—and Coco says all the right things. *Wow, you're such a hero, talk about making a difference every single day when you go to work; I can totally see how you and Isla fell in love,*

I can't believe the fiancé created a Pinterest board, that's so funny; I'm so sorry, your heart must be broken, I understand why you came home.

Kacy laughs. "I can't believe I unloaded all that when I literally just met you."

"Sometimes that's easiest, right?" Coco says. "Believe me, I'm the last person who's going to judge you."

The ferry slows down, and the captain announces that they're entering Nantucket Harbor.

"Let's go up top," Kacy says. "We want your first time seeing the island to be memorable."

Coco follows Kacy to the top deck. Kacy points out the Nantucket Beach Club, where green, blue, and yellow umbrellas are lined up in rows. Next to that is a beach bar called the Oystercatcher. Coco sees kids building sandcastles, a gentleman flying a kite; she catches the scent of fried seafood on the breeze.

"That's Brant Point Lighthouse," Kacy says. Her voice is thick. "The white steeple is the Congregational church, and the clock tower is the Unitarian church." She wipes a finger under each eye. "I'm not sure why I'm getting so emotional. I guess it's just being... *home.* I haven't been home since the Christmas before last, and it's been forever since I was here in the summer. I forgot how pretty it is."

It's more than pretty, Coco thinks. Sailboats in the harbor bob on colorful buoys. The row of summer cottages fronting the water all have gray shingles and crisp white trim, window boxes bursting with spring flowers, snapping flags. Coco didn't have a clear picture of what Nantucket would look like, but it's everything she wanted it to be: classic, charming, a freaking postcard.

She doesn't belong here. Like, at all.

She thought it was a good thing that the Richardsons were new to the island—they could all be new together!—but now she sees the downside. The Richardsons don't know a soul, and neither does Coco.

Except now, she knows Kacy.

They disembark side by side, and when Kacy's feet hit the wharf, she thinks, *I'm home.* The NICU; her apartment on Filbert Street; the cable cars; the Golden Gate emerging from the fog in the morning; Coit Tower; casual carpool; Crissy Field, where she used to run on the weekends; Hog Island Oyster Company in the Ferry Building... and Isla's liquid brown eyes, her beauty mark, her nimble hands— all of it seems very, very far away.

Kacy receives a text from her father: Here. She spies the black Suburban pulling into the parking lot; it's impossible to miss. But Kacy can't just abandon Coco, can she? "Take my number, Coco," she says. "Keep in touch, okay? Let me know where you end up staying."

"I'll figure it out," Coco says. "I always do. And hey, Kacy, thanks for the chowder—it meant a lot."

Kacy walks toward her dad's car, but she's hesitant to leave. Coco was such a good listener, exactly what Kacy needed. She can't imagine explaining about Isla to either of her parents, and after being gone seven years, Kacy doesn't have many friends left here.

Romeo from the Steamship, whom Kacy has known for eons, helps her roll her suitcases over to her father's car. *Romeo must have a speeding-ticket fine he wants reduced,* she thinks, *because he never helps anyone.*

Kacy opens the passenger-side door and sees her dad, the Chief. He looks older, grayer, and way more exhausted than she remembers. But then he smiles. "Hey, you," he says. "Hop in before someone writes a letter to the editor about how I blocked traffic."

Kacy climbs up into her seat and gives him a fierce hug; she doesn't care who has to wait. She could have been coming back to

Nantucket under very different circumstances, ones that are almost impossible to imagine. Ed Kapenash is a strong, solid, unimpeachable human, the kind of man who deserves a statue at the top of Main Street. Kacy feels ashamed of her recent transgressions — conducting an affair with Isla when she was engaged to someone else, running away from a job she was good at in a place where she was needed. She could go further down this rabbit hole, but as they're navigating their way out of the parking lot, Kacy spies Coco standing by the luggage carts looking…well, the word that comes to mind is *forlorn*.

Ed Kapenash glances at his daughter. He can't get over how elegant and mature she seems — and yet he can still see the little girl in pink ballerina pajamas. He recalls the year she made her own slime, when the house was filled with glue and borax; he remembers the glasses and the braces, the bloody nose from catching a basketball with her face at the Boys and Girls Club. He pictures her on the lifeguard stand at Nobadeer in her red tank suit, a stripe of zinc down her nose. He thinks about the day he and Andrea took her to Logan Airport. Kacy had finished her master's in nursing at Boston College and accepted a job in San Francisco, and he and Andrea had been equal parts proud and heartbroken. *So far away,* they thought. *They'd never see her.* For the most part, this has been true. They fly to San Francisco for a week every fall; Kacy comes home for holidays when her schedule allows. But it isn't the same. Eric and his girlfriend, Avalon, are always around, meeting the Chief and Andrea at the Anglers' Club for Friday appetizers, coming for dinner every week. Chloe and Finn, the twins Ed and Andrea adopted after Andrea's cousin Tess and her husband, Greg, died, are both in college. Chloe insisted that the Chief join Snapchat, and thanks to this, he can follow the twins' every move; he probably knows more about their lives than he wants to. Only Kacy remains a mystery.

She's home now, Ed thinks. She's in his car; her luggage is in the back, and boxes have arrived at the house. She's moving home for the summer, taking a leave of absence from UCSF.

"Why?" Ed asked Andrea. "Did something happen?"

"All she told me was that she wanted to come home for a while. She didn't offer anything else. You know Kacy."

You don't give up your life and move across the country for no reason. *Was it because of work?* Ed wondered. *Or a relationship?*

Ed knows Kacy is gay, though she never officially came out to him—she'd told her mother and asked Andrea to tell Ed. In some ways, this was a relief. Ed isn't much for dramatic emotional moments in his personal life; he gets enough of that on the job. But he does wonder why Kacy wasn't comfortable telling him. Did she think he'd disapprove? Andrea handled the whole thing with great equanimity. There might have been a single beat where Andrea had to let go of whatever vision she'd held for Kacy's future—a traditional husband and family. But hey, she said, there could still be a wedding, still be babies. Andrea told Ed that she'd always suspected Kacy was gay, and Ed thought, *Really?* In high school, Kacy had boyfriends—admittedly nobody serious, but she'd gone to both the junior prom and senior banquet with a terrific kid named Lamont Oakley.

Now Kacy says, "I have a strange request. Feel free to say no."

She's smart, Ed thinks. He's so happy to see her, he would say yes to nearly anything. "What's up?"

"I met this girl on the boat," Kacy says. "She has a job as a personal concierge with some wealthy couple who just bought a house here, but wires got crossed and the house isn't ready and this girl has nowhere to stay. Would it be all right if she crashed with us for a few days?"

"Oh." Ed isn't sure what to say. He just got his daughter back after seven years, and Andrea is planning a family dinner for tonight with

Eric and Avalon. Selfishly, Ed wants Kacy to himself, and wouldn't it be weird, celebrating her return with a complete stranger? He's about to pass the buck—*You'll have to ask your mother*—but he can see Kacy practically vibrating with anticipation.

"We have room, right? Chloe and Finn…"

Right. Chloe and Finn are both abroad this summer—Chloe in Florence, Finn in Dublin—so their rooms are vacant. Ed reminds himself that it's Kacy's nature to help people. He clears his throat. "A few days?"

"Four days," Kacy says. "Max."

"I'm agreeing to this without consulting your mother—"

Kacy hops out of the car before he can finish his sentence. "Thanks, Dad!"

The Chief swings his car back into the melee of the Steamship parking lot, blocking the cars that are trying to exit. The Chief hears a horn and looks over to see a kid with blond floppy bangs sitting behind the wheel of a silver Range Rover (license plate: BEAST) flipping him off. The Chief sighs. *Summer,* he thinks, *has officially begun.*

Kacy and her new friend approach. The friend is smaller than Kacy, with short dark hair, a pierced nose, and a fair number of tattoos. The Chief's first thought is that she looks like she works at a carnival or plays acoustic guitar at a coffeehouse. But he won't stereotype; he'll just smile and hope for the best.

The friend climbs into the back seat and moves her sunglasses up into the bird's nest of her hair—her eyes are a startling glacier blue. The Chief wonders if this is a love interest. Would Kacy pick up a girl she just met on the ferry and bring home? Ed chastises himself. Kacy is allowed to have friends who are women.

"I'm Coco," the girl says.

"Ed Kapenash, nice to meet you."

Coco eyes all the bells and whistles inside Ed's SUV—the scanner, the screen, the lights. "Are you..."

"Chief of police," Ed says, and Coco gets that *Uh-oh* look that Ed has seen thousands of times. Mentioning his job title tends to be a conversation killer. "Sorry to hear about your housing. Who is it you're working for?"

"The Richardsons?" Coco says. "Bull and Leslee."

"Don't know them," Ed says, then laughs. "Though in my line of work, that's probably a good thing."

5. The Castaways

"The Richardsons?" Addison says that night at dinner. "They're my clients."

Ha! Andrea thinks. What does Ed say each and every day? *It's a small island.* She catches his eye and can tell he's thinking what she's thinking: *Thank god Addison knows the couple Kacy's new friend is working for. Thank god they actually* exist *and that Coco isn't some con artist preying on our daughter's kindness.*

Andrea wasn't exactly overjoyed when Ed showed up from the ferry with an extra person, one who was evidently staying with them for a "few days." She tried not to let either her dismay or her irritation show on her face. It wasn't a big deal, Andrea told herself. They had plenty of space. *Roll with it.*

"So nice to meet you, Coco," Andrea said. "Let's get you settled in Chloe's room."

Because dinner was no longer just family, Andrea invited Addison and Phoebe and Jeffrey and Delilah too. The more the merrier; why not make it a party? They could eat out on the back deck. She doubled the ingredients for her lobster mac and cheese, Kacy's favorite dinner; she made an extra batch of garlic knots. Phoebe showed up with half a case of champagne, and Delilah picked up a Triple Chocolate Mountain ice cream cake from the Juice Bar.

They all gather on the back deck, and Andrea is impressed when Coco is able to remember everyone's name. And what a coincidence that Coco will be working for Addison's clients.

"He's been talking about this couple nonstop," Phoebe says. "Bull and Leslee Richardson."

"Bull?" Andrea says.

"Short for Bulfinch," Addison says.

Andrea rolls her eyes. She tends to be judgmental where names are concerned; Nantucket has a lot of offenders when it comes to using last names as pretentious first names. "Who names a child Bulfinch?"

"He's Australian," Addison says as though that explains it. "He's a charismatic guy, one of those larger-than-life types. Personable, engaging—"

"And loaded, obviously," Phoebe says. "These are the people who came in with a full-price offer on Triple Eight Pocomo Road."

"I thought Fast Eddie was going to kiss me," Addison says. "He's had that house on the market since before the pandemic."

Jeffrey clears his throat. "They know that property is compromised, I hope? The water levels in the harbor—"

Delilah turns to Coco. "You'll have to excuse my husband. We own a farm and he's the consummate environmentalist."

Coco remembers Leslee saying that the house had "issues,"

something about climate change and erosion. Bull dismissed that, not because he was a climate denier (Coco hopes) but because, he said, they'd be dead before it mattered.

"I told them the land is vulnerable," Addison says. "They didn't seem fazed."

"But surely there are homes in the twenty-million-dollar range that are better investments?" Andrea says.

"None that were featured on the cover of *Town and Country*," Addison says. "Triple Eight has provenance. It's an icon."

"Like a society matron on her deathbed," Delilah says.

"Don't be morbid—that house has another hundred years, at least," Phoebe says. "And it has the best views on the island."

Yes, Andrea thinks. Rumor has it that the deck of 888 Pocomo is one of the few places where you can see the beacons of all three lighthouses at once. Do the Richardsons care about the lighthouses? Do the Richardsons *know* about the lighthouses?

"So they're from Australia?" Delilah says.

"He's Australian, not the wife. She's from…well, I'm not sure," Addison says. "Their paperwork had a Perth address. But I didn't get the sense they were living in Australia. He mentioned Palm Beach, Aspen, and the Caribbean."

"Where he met Coco!" Andrea says.

"They had dinner at the bar where I was working," Coco says. "They told me they bounce around a lot."

"I'll get the scoop," Phoebe says. "Addison asked me to take the wife to lunch next week. I guess they want to join the Field and Oar Club."

"You can't let her jump ahead on the list, Phoebe," Delilah says. "Jeffrey and I have been waiting nine long years."

There's an uncomfortable silence. Andrea knows how badly Delilah wants to join the Field and Oar. In private conversations,

Delilah tells Andrea that she suspects the club's membership committee is prejudiced against locals. A very awkward situation, as Phoebe sits on that membership committee.

"I won't, Dee," Phoebe says. "But you know it helps if you play tennis or sail."

"Do the Richardsons play tennis or sail?" Delilah asks.

"I'm not sure about tennis," Addison says. "But Bull told me he's buying a yacht."

"So these people are plunking down twenty million on a house—"

"Twenty-two million," Addison says.

"And who knows how many million on a yacht," Delilah says. "And they want to join the Field and Oar Club with all the old Nantucket summer families?"

"Well, they have good taste in assistants," Andrea says, smiling at Coco. They should probably change the subject. Andrea isn't a stickler for etiquette, but discussing Coco's employers in front of her seems tacky.

They're buying a yacht? Coco thinks. *Snark* must have done *very* well in Kuala Lumpur. She finishes her champagne. She's so exhausted, it feels like the space where her brain should be has been filled with bubbles. And yet she's handling herself okay, she thinks. She's figured out who's who: The Chief is Kacy's father; Kacy's mother, Andrea, seems like the beleaguered mom in a laundry-detergent commercial. The bald one who wears horn-rimmed glasses and a tailored shirt is Addison; he's the real estate agent who represented the Richardsons. The glamorous blonde in the flowing white dress with the diamond studs the size of dimes in her ears is his wife, Phoebe. Jeffrey is the farmer; he showed up with a basket of hothouse tomatoes and a bag of hydroponic lettuces, and he's wearing a T-shirt that says WHO'S YOUR FARMER? (Coco assumes this is meant to be funny/ironic, since it's him.) His wife is Delilah; she has curly hair and freckles and is wearing a long prairie skirt and a tight white T-shirt. She gives off sexy-earth-mother vibes.

Coco isn't used to attending dinner parties, especially not with people her mother's age. Georgi, Coco's mother, is what the internet would call "broken"—so broken that if you shook her, it would sound like dry beans in a jar. Coco never knew her father. Georgi had a string of boyfriends when Coco was growing up—Sam, Jimmy Pyle, Rodney Fever—until, finally, Kemp, who moved in when Coco was thirteen and who brought his daughter, Bree, and Bree's four kids with him. Georgi and Kemp didn't entertain at home; if they had, it would've been a reality show. Bree subsisted on cigarettes and Little Debbie Oatmeal Creme Pies. Her kids whined about Georgi's cooking (it was pretty bad—brown stew, hot-dog casserole), there was always a two-liter bottle of soda on the table, and at some point during the meal, Bree's baby daddy, Larch, would walk in, grimy from doing oil changes at Valvoline and also sometimes drunk, which was when he and Bree would start fighting.

No, Coco's family did not entertain at home. Coco used to make herself a bowl of Cap'n Crunch or a grilled cheese and eat in her room, where she either read the classics or watched DVDs from the 1980s and 1990s that she borrowed from her high-school library. Books had raised her (Jane Austen had taught her how to comport herself at a dinner party like this one), and movies allowed her to escape the chaos going on outside her bedroom door.

"Would anyone like more cake?" Andrea asks. "Another glass of champagne?"

"I'd love more champagne, Mrs. Kapenash," Coco says. "But I can get it—"

"Stay where you are, I'm going in anyway," Andrea says. "And please, call me Andrea!" She takes Coco's glass and enters the kitchen to find Kacy leaning up against the counter, engrossed in her phone, texting. Andrea blinks; she didn't realize Kacy had left the deck.

"Everything okay, honey?" The downside of having all these people here is that Andrea hasn't had a chance to properly welcome her daughter home. She forgets the champagne for a second and opens her arms for a hug.

Kacy doesn't even seem to notice her; she's furiously typing, eyes fixed on her screen. Everything is clearly *not* okay. Andrea isn't sure what happened out in California. All Kacy would tell her is that "stuff fell apart." Andrea assumes that included a relationship. But with whom? Kacy hasn't mentioned anyone special.

"I'll leave you alone," Andrea says, touching Kacy's shoulder. She grabs the last bottle of champagne from the fridge and gets back to the deck in time to hear Delilah say, "If the Richie Richardsons want to get involved in the community, they should donate to the food pantry."

Yes! Andrea thinks. Delilah's on the board of Nantucket Food, Fuel, and Rental Assistance. Everyone thinks of Nantucket as a wealthy enclave, but there's an underserved community—service workers, day laborers, many of them foreign nationals—who struggle with the insane rents and high cost of absolutely everything, especially in the desolate off-season.

"That's a great idea," Phoebe says. "Why don't you come to lunch with us and you can talk to Leslee about it?"

"Maybe I will," Delilah says, making it sound like a threat.

"Maybe I'll come to lunch too," Andrea says.

"You can ask Leslee if she plays pickleball," Addison says. "You ladies are always complaining about not having a regular fourth."

Andrea, Phoebe, and Delilah *are* always looking for someone to play pickleball. Andrea has tried to recruit Avalon, but Avalon says competitive sports aren't her thing—and Andrea, Phoebe, and Delilah are *very* competitive when it comes to pickleball.

"Maybe we should hold off before inviting the Richardsons into every aspect of our lives," Andrea says. "Let's meet them first."

Coco is so buzzed—not only from the champagne but from the lobster mac and cheese, the best ice cream cake she's ever tasted, and the energy on the deck—that *she* nearly volunteers to be the fourth in pickleball. Coco strikes up a conversation with Eric's girlfriend, Avalon, who, Coco is relieved to see, has a tattoo of a mandala on her shoulder. When Coco asks what she does for a living, Avalon says she's a masseuse and a yoga instructor. "I have a private clientele for both massage and yoga," she says. "Eric and I are saving to buy a house. I'm on the lookout for a duplex so we can live in one half and rent the other half. I watch an obscene amount of HGTV."

Coco laughs. Avalon is such a queen!

The party breaks up a little while later. Eric has a charter at six the next morning; Phoebe has to drive her thirteen-year-old son, Reed, "all the way out to Sconset" at seven because he's working with the groundskeeping crew at the Nantucket Golf Club; the farmer, Jeffrey, wakes up with the chickens. Everyone says goodbye to Coco before they drift down the deck stairs. *So nice to meet you.* Jeffrey shakes her hand; Phoebe and Delilah give her a hug. Delilah says, "In a few weeks, you'll be able to answer all our questions about the Richardsons."

"Yes!" Phoebe says. "We'll have someone on the inside."

Coco feels like a spy but also weirdly relevant.

As the cars pull out of the driveway, Coco stacks the dirty plates, then carries the melting remains of the ice cream cake into the kitchen. Andrea and the Chief are there, but Kacy is nowhere to be seen.

"I've got all this, Coco—thank you, though," Andrea says.

"Are you sure?"

"Ed likes to help me," Andrea says. "This is when we catch up on our days."

That's Coco's cue to make herself scarce. "Good night, thank you for dinner, it was delicious, your friends are wonderful people." Has Coco forgotten anything? "It's nice of you to let me stay. It should only be a few days."

"Happy to have you," the Chief says. "Good night."

Coco climbs the stairs and finds Kacy waiting for her in the hallway. "I'm sorry I cut out," she says. "I'm not ready for all the questions."

Coco opens her arms and says, "Thank you for letting me stay here. It was a real act of kindness and trust, and I'm grateful."

Kacy gives her a quick squeeze. "Meeting you was so random," she says. "And yet I feel like this was meant to be."

Random, yes, Coco thinks. *Meant to be?* She supposes they'll find out.

6. The Cobblestone Telegraph II

The Richardsons close on 888 Pocomo Road at noon on June 11 and by 12:05, Leslee Richardson is on the phone with contractors.

"We aren't doing much to the house," Leslee confides to Avalon Boone, whom Leslee has summoned to the Hotel Nantucket to give her an in-suite massage. "After all, it was decorated by Jennifer Quinn, the host of *Real-Life Rehab.*"

Avalon *loves* Jennifer Quinn. *Real-Life Rehab* is the best show on HGTV, in Avalon's opinion. If Avalon were moving into a house that JQ designed, she wouldn't change a thing, but to each her own.

As Avalon sets up the massage table, she says, "Which house is this?"

"Triple Eight Pocomo Road."

Avalon takes a beat. *This* is the woman Eric's parents and their friends were talking about at dinner the night before. What does the Chief always say? *It's a small island.* She wonders if she should correct Leslee Richardson's pronunciation or let it go. "You know what's so funny?" Avalon says. "It's pronounced '*Pock*-ah-moh.' It took me a long time to get it right too, but yeah, that's how you say it."

" '*Pock*-ah-moh'?" Leslee says. "You're sure?"

Avalon smooths a sheet over the table. "I am very sure."

"I've been saying it wrong this whole time. In front of the real estate agents and the lawyers and everyone. Why didn't anyone *tell* me? I thought it rhymed with *Kokomo*. I feel like I've had spinach stuck in my teeth for the past week."

Avalon laughs. "I'm going to step out of the room while you get comfortable on the table."

"You won't tell anyone else, will you?" Leslee says. "That I don't even know how to pronounce the name of my own street?"

Avalon presses Play on her iPhone and the room fills with the sound of crashing ocean waves. "I won't tell a soul."

The next day, vans start pulling into the driveway at 888 Pocomo Road. Leslee has hired painters from off-island and a power washer from off-island, but, thankfully, we see a familiar face: Benton Coe, the foremost landscape architect on the island, who also happens to be *very* easy on the eyes.

Benton Coe has seen 888 Pocomo Road only from the water. It's a destination for every boater cruising around Nantucket Harbor; everyone takes pictures of its distinctive facade. It evokes old-school, gracious summer living—but with originality. Triple Eight is composed of two wings, each with a gambrel roof, joined in the middle by a spacious octagonal deck on the second floor and an octagonal screened-in porch on the ground floor.

Leslee Richardson meets Benton in the white-shell driveway. He agreed to take on this job—even though he stopped accepting new clients years ago—after Leslee called his office every day for a week. Benton has had people do that before, but he relented this time because 888 Pocomo is such a legendary property.

They walk around to the front of the house. The large sloping lawn leads to a slice of golden beach that's curved like a smile.

"The elephant in the room," Leslee says.

Benton sighs. Yes, big elephant, small room. He read the forensic geologist's report that Leslee sent him. The property is slowly being consumed by the harbor. The beach is eight feet wide, six feet at high tide; ten years ago, it was double that.

"There's nothing I can do about the beach, unfortunately," Benton says.

"I didn't hire you to perform a miracle," Leslee says. "Well, I did, but a manageable one. Follow me, I'll show you."

Leslee takes Benton to an area tangled with brush and Spanish olives on the far side of the garage. "I'd like you to clear this and create a hedged-in circular garden," she says. "I want it to feel like you're entering a secret room."

"Okay!" Benton's spirits lift a bit. He likes this idea.

"I want you to leave a space open in the middle. Guess why?"

For a fountain, maybe? Benton is known for his water features.

"I've ordered a custom octagonal hot tub," Leslee says.

"An octagonal hot tub?" Benton says. Did he hear that correctly?

"It's the third eight," Leslee says. "The deck is an octagon, the screened-in porch is an octagon, but we need a third to make it Triple Eight."

It's either a clever idea or a silly one—but Benton isn't there to judge.

Leslee leans into him and says, "When the hot tub arrives, you and I can test it out."

Whoa, whoa, *whoa*! There's no denying that Leslee Richardson is an attractive woman. She has long, flowing dark hair and a yoga body underneath her white jeans and tight white tank. But she's also *married,* and she's giving *I'm a handful* vibes. Was Benton a fool to break his no-new-clients rule?

He checks his phone. "I should go, I have a meeting out in Sconset in ten minutes. I'll get some sketches to you in a day or two."

He can't get back to his truck fast enough.

Not long after the Richardsons purchase the house, their yacht, *Hedonism,* arrives.

We see her come into Nantucket Harbor under full sail, captained by a man named Patch who works for the yacht broker. Patch later hits the Gazebo and tells anyone who will listen that Bull Richardson bought the boat sight unseen. "The guy doesn't know a jib from a spinnaker," Patch says. "Hell, he doesn't know port from starboard. He'd better hire himself a decent captain. I'm tempted to stay here and do it myself."

But Patch doesn't become the Richardsons' new captain because, in a development that makes us all want to tip our hats to the Richardsons, they hire Lamont Oakley for the job.

Lamont Oakley is a member of one of our oldest Cape Verdean families. Like so many of Nantucket's youth, he learned to sail on an Opti in Polpis Harbor at the age of seven through Nantucket Community Sailing classes. Lamont started joining crews for regattas at the Field and Oar Club when he was only twelve. He was courted by

St. George's School for their prestigious sailing program, but he stayed on island and skippered for the Nantucket High School team. When it was time to go to college, Lamont turned down both Howard University and Princeton and instead attended the College of Charleston on a full sailing scholarship. He was a four-time all-American and as a senior was named College Sailor of the Year. Lamont then became the captain of a boat called *Knock-Knock* and traveled to glamorous places like St. Bart's, the Canary Islands, Sicily.

Meanwhile, back on Nantucket, Lamont's mother, Glynnie Oakley, has been suffering from macular degeneration in both eyes, and just this spring her ophthalmologist, Dr. Ruby, declared it would be best if Glynnie had someone living with her.

The opportunity for Lamont to captain the Richardsons' boat couldn't have come at a better time. The boat the Richardsons bought is state of the art and can basically sail itself, but Lamont hires two brothers from the Nantucket High School sailing team, Javier and Esteban Valladares, to help out when he needs them. What a hometown hero.

While their house is being touched up, Bull and Leslee stay at the Hotel Nantucket and make the rounds of the island's best restaurants. Fast Eddie, who met the Richardsons at the closing (he represented the seller), sees them at the back bar at Cru enjoying lobster rolls and chatting with the people on either side of them. The next night, Eddie pops into the Pearl and again sees the Richardsons. Bull is quite animated and calls out to the bartender, "Let's get a round of drinks for my new mates!" The "new mates" Bull is referring to are the island's most-sought-after dentist, Dr. Andy McMann, and his wife, Rachel. Eddie could warn the Richardsons that Dr. Andy and Rachel are both as annoying as wet socks, but they'll find that out soon enough on their own. Eddie leaves the Pearl without ordering.

The following night Eddie sees the Richardsons at Proprietors, and the night after that at Lola 41. *What is going* on *here?* Eddie wonders. These people are out as much as he is—but it's Eddie's job to be out. That's how he finds new clients.

Saturday is Eddie and Grace's thirtieth wedding anniversary, and Eddie has scored a coveted table on the deck at Straight Wharf. It's a clear, balmy June night; their table overlooks the harbor.

"This is incredible, Eddie, well done," Grace says, and Eddie reaches for her hand. They've survived a lot—Grace's affair with their landscape architect, Benton Coe; Eddie's time in prison for running a prostitution ring; finally launching their girls—and this anniversary reminds Eddie how lucky he is to be in a good place. He's about to order champagne when a couple step out onto the deck like it's a stage and they're the stars of the show. And damn if it isn't Bull and Leslee Richardson. The hostess seats them at the table next to Eddie and Grace's.

"I love that woman's duster," Grace says. "It's so elegant."

"Mmm-hmm," Eddie says. He hasn't the foggiest idea what a duster is. He's trying to figure out how the Richardsons, who have been on island less than a week, managed to get a reservation on the deck at Straight Wharf. He wants to whisper to Grace, *Those are the people who bought Triple Eight Pocomo* (Grace would understand this meant that the Richardsons were to thank for the sizable commission that recently hit their bank account), *and this is the fifth time I've seen them this week.* Eddie wonders if now is the time to reintroduce himself—but Grace might complain that Eddie is conducting business on date night.

"And she smells delicious," Grace says. "I wonder what scent she's wearing."

Eddie says, "It's probably Eau de Cash."

A server appears with a bottle of Dom Pérignon swathed in a white cloth like it's a baby, and Eddie blinks. Is this a gift from their girls, maybe? They're growing up, but this gesture feels a little beyond them. Perhaps it's from Eddie's sister, Barbie? Or a grandiose send-out from the restaurant staff? Eddie did mention it was their anniversary when he called.

It's none of these. The server passes Eddie and Grace's table and presents the champagne to the Richardsons. Eddie feels deflated; the Richardsons have outclassed him.

"What are you thinking to drink?" Eddie asks Grace. "A cocktail? Wine?"

Grace is distracted by the exuberant *pop* of the champagne at the next table. She pivots in her chair and says to Leslee Richardson, "Is it your anniversary too?"

"No," Leslee says with a wink. "We just like to have fun."

The Richardsons *do* like to have fun. Later that night, Avalon Boone and her boyfriend, Eric Kapenash, are at the Chicken Box. Eric tends to be a little staid, like his dad—Avalon jokes that he's a police chief without a badge—but on Saturday nights, he lets loose. He and Avalon are out on the dance floor when she feels a tap on her shoulder. It takes her a moment to recognize the woman who wants her attention.

"You were my masseuse!" the woman screams over the band. "I'm Leslee Richardson! From the hotel!"

Avalon shrieks—she's on her fifth High Noon—and gives Leslee a one-armed hug. Avalon and Eric dance next to the Richardsons, and it gets pretty friendly. At one point, Leslee grinds up against Avalon's backside, and Avalon thinks, *Okay?* She gave this woman a massage a few days before and sometimes clients mistake that kind of touch for intimacy. Avalon takes Eric's hand and leads him to the pool tables in the back to get a little breathing room.

"*That* was the couple everyone was talking about at dinner the other night," she tells him. "That's the couple Coco is working for."

"Huh?" Eric says.

"They're the ones who bought the big house out in Pocomo? Coco is their personal concierge, but they're doing work on the house, so Coco has no place to go, which is why she's living at your parents' house."

"I guess I missed that part," Eric says. "I thought Coco was my sister's girlfriend."

Avalon sighs and goes to the bar for another round. She loves Eric, but he's completely clueless.

It's the end of the night, and Avalon is in the ladies' room when Leslee pops out of a stall.

"Oh, good, I found you," Leslee says. She steps in very close, as though she and Avalon are the best of friends, and whispers, "Why don't you and your boyfriend come back to the hotel with us?"

Avalon puts a hand to her abdomen. "I'm actually not feeling well, but thanks for the invite."

"Aww, come on," Leslee says. She fingers a strand of Avalon's hair. "It'll be fun, I promise."

"So nice to see you again," Avalon says, darting into a stall. "Have a good night!" Then she locks the door, her heart pounding. No wonder everyone is talking about the Richardsons.

7. Work It, Sell It, Own It

There's a knock on the bedroom door and Coco jolts awake, unsure of where she is. Fluffy white duvet, the scent of lavender, stripes of light through a slatted shade, birdsong.

Nantucket.

She climbs out of bed and opens the door to find Kacy holding a hot cappuccino and a mason jar filled with flowers.

"Good morning," Kacy says. "I wanted to let you sleep, but it's ten o'clock!"

Only ten? Coco thinks. On a normal day in St. John, she wouldn't wake up before noon. She usually bartended at the Banana Deck until close, then hit the Quiet Mon for last call, then went home and worked on her screenplay until three or four in the morning. She can tell, however, that sleeping into the double digits probably breaks some kind of house rule here. Kacy looks like she woke at dawn, ran five miles, whipped up an acai bowl or an egg-white omelet, and now is ready to conquer the day. Her hair is pulled back in a banana clip but it's still somehow shiny and sleek, with strands framing her face. She's wearing a white linen blouse, a patchwork madras mini, a collection of thin gold necklaces—real gold, Coco can tell—and gold hoop earrings. Kacy has a way about her, that's for damn sure.

"Go get ready," Kacy says. "Today is your proper introduction to Nantucket."

"You don't have to worry about me," Coco says. "You've done too much already just by letting me stay here."

Kacy blinks. "Don't be silly. I'll see you downstairs in ten. Put on something cute."

Coco closes the door, then rummages through her duffel bag. Put on something *cute*? She chooses a pair of faded jeans with rips at the knees and a navy tank top from Shambles in St. John. The back of the tank says DAY-DRINKING DONE RIGHT. Will the Nantucket fashion police write Coco a ticket? Her wardrobe staples include a lot of black, a lot of denim, and T-shirts emblazoned with the logos of her favorite bands: Tame Impala, Grouplove, the Killers.

Coco gazes into the bathroom mirror. When she was fifteen, she pierced each ear eight times using a needle, a tray of ice cubes, and a bottle of Wild Turkey. Her mother hadn't blinked an eye except to ask how she was going to afford sixteen earrings. Good question. Coco keeps silver studs in a couple of holes and a silver hoop at the top of her cartilage; she could do better. She has a diamond (by which she means "cubic zirconia") stud in her nose.

Once Coco got to St. John, she'd added tattoos. The first was the flamingo on her left shoulder; she had seen flamingos at Salt Pond, and it had blown her mind. Then she got a gecko just above her ankle, small and cute, head down like it was going to disappear into Coco's Chuck Taylor. She'd added a manta ray to the upper part of her left buttock and a tattoo of one of the wild white donkeys that roamed St. John on her right hip bone. When she swam at Maho Bay or Hawksnest, tourists would sometimes ask to take her picture.

She washes her face with the bathroom soap and applies her drugstore moisturizer, then rubs some moisturizer through her hair in an attempt to make it do something. (She cuts her hair herself with kitchen scissors; the style is best described as pixie-cut-meets-electric-socket.) She pulls a bandanna from her bag, fashions it into a headband, and pushes her hair off her face. She looks like Rosie the Riveter. All set.

"Coco?" Kacy calls from downstairs.

"Coming!" Coco says.

They climb into Kacy's Jeep, which has sat idle in the years since Kacy left but which her parents kept in perfect working condition. It's white with a sunset painted across the bottom parts of the doors. Kacy lowers the tan soft-top because today is nothing but blue skies. Coco puts on the hot-pink plastic sunglasses that some chick who'd drunk too many Bushwackers left on the bar at the Banana Deck. Kacy wears Ray-Ban aviators. Of course she does.

Kacy turns the key in the ignition. "Girls Just Want to Have Fun" is playing on the radio. It's too much, Coco thinks—but not for Kacy. She turns it up and peels out of the driveway. They're off.

Kacy goes into tour-guide mode, telling Coco how the streets were paved with cobblestones sourced from Gloucester, Massachusetts, in the 1830s. ("People like to say the cobblestones were brought over as ballast on ships, but that's a myth.") She points out the Civil War monument, then the Three Bricks—three homes built by the whaling captain Joseph Starbuck for his three sons. Coco hopes there won't be a quiz later; she's just trying to process how damn quaint the place is. The homes are stately, the fences and gates and gardens impeccable. They pass an inn called 76 Main that's basically a mansion—no wonder rooms on this island cost so much—then a place called Murray's Toggery. *Toggery?* Coco thinks. *Can you use that in a sentence, please?* From the looks of things, it's a store that sells cardigans and men's trousers with whales embroidered on them.

They get to the main part of town, where the shops all have tasteful wooden signs—LEMON PRESS, MITCHELL'S BOOK CORNER,

NANTUCKET LOOMS—and people are strolling around with their ten-dollar coffees, swinging shopping bags, taking selfies, living their best lives.

"There is so much unique shopping," Kacy says as though she works for the local chamber of commerce. "You'll probably want some new clothes for the summer?"

Want, yes, Coco thinks. But she can't afford even a new pair of underwear. "We can look," she says. She's pretty sure this is Kacy's way of saying that Coco's wardrobe needs an upgrade.

"I'll take you to my go-to." Kacy pulls up in front of a boutique called the Lovely. As soon as they're inside among all the dainty, fluttery, summery things, Coco feels like a cat in a wineglass. What is she doing here?

The salesgirl flashes a brilliant smile. "Welcome, ladies! My name is Olivia. Let me know if you have any questions."

This chick is straight out of central casting, Coco thinks. She has long dark hair, big brown eyes, and the kind of golden glow that can only be achieved by strolling through your family's vineyard in Tuscany.

"Thanks, Olivia," Kacy says. She slides dresses and tops along the rack, pulling out pieces she likes to get a better look. Meanwhile, Coco checks the price tags—a dress for $380, a simple cotton tank for $85.

Time to go, she thinks.

"This would be so cute on you," Kacy says, holding up a white eyelet sundress. Well, yes, Coco loves it; it's pretty enough to get married in. "And it's on sale."

Sale? Coco holds the dress up against herself in the mirror. The price tag shows it has been marked down from $385 to $168. "A hundred and sixty-eight dollars isn't *bad*," Coco says. (She is kidding. Coco has never spent that much on a dress, ever. She used to buy vintage dresses for six or eight bucks apiece at the Pansy and Petunia.)

"You *have* to try it on!" Kacy says.

Olivia floats over. "Would you like me to start you a room?"

"I'm not sure I'm ready for that kind of commitment," Coco says, and both Kacy and Olivia laugh.

Kacy takes the dress, hands it to Olivia, and says, "Please start her a room."

Coco steps into the curtained alcove and zips herself into the dress. Her panic escalates. The dress fits her perfectly; her boobs look a-*maze*-ing. When she steps out, Kacy and Olivia shriek.

Kacy says, "OMG, I have to take your picture." She whips out her phone and Coco gives her a fake pout that is actually a real pout as she envisions her eleven hundred dollars becoming nine hundred thirty-two if she uses debit, which she should so that her credit card debt doesn't get any heavier.

"Girl," Olivia says as though they're now the best of friends. "*Made* for you. As in, I wouldn't even sell it to anyone else."

It's a good line (although Olivia probably uses it on everyone), but Coco is too anxious to be flattered. Back in the changing room, she removes the dress and spends one second low-key *hating* Kacy for bringing her here and Olivia for working here. But the next second, like a paper airplane aimed straight at her by the hand of Fate, she gets an alert on her phone. An email from Bull Richardson.

Coco hesitates before opening it. She has a sick feeling that Bull is going to pull the rug out from under her: He's changed his mind; he's hired someone else, or Leslee has. They want a personal concierge who knows the island (and can she blame them?). Coco will have no choice but to spend the summer back in sweltering St. John. This might not have been such a bad option yesterday, but now that Coco has seen Nantucket, she desperately wants to stay.

She clicks on the alert. The email says: We'll be ready for you to start work on Monday. Our address is 888 Pocomo Road. Looking forward to seeing you again. —B.

Coco gets dressed and bursts from the changing room with Clark Kent–emerging–from–the–phone–booth–as–Superman energy.

She hands Olivia the dress. "I'll take it," she says.

Coco tells Kacy that she's starting her job on Monday, and Kacy says, "Let's celebrate! Lunch is on me."

At the Nantucket Pharmacy, they perch on leather-and-chrome stools at the lunch counter. Kacy orders a grilled cheese with bacon and tomato, and Coco is thrilled to see they have ham and pickle salad, which was her favorite thing at Grumpy Garth's Diner back in Rosebush. Coco asks what a frappe is and Kacy laughs and says it's a milkshake and it's pronounced "frap," not "frappy."

"Okay, sorry, at home we just call them milkshakes." To the eager-beaver teenage boy behind the counter, Coco says, "And one choco-late frappe, please!" When it arrives, in a frosty glass and topped with whipped cream, Kacy says, "Let me take a picture of you happy with your frappy." Coco purses her lips around the straw and bats her eyes while Kacy snaps a million photos. Then Kacy asks the eager beaver to take one of the two of them, a job he takes *very* seri-ously: "Get together. Closer. Okay, now work it, sell it, own it!" And they crack up, falling against each other like they've been friends forever.

That night, as Kacy is trying to sleep, her phone dings with a text from Isla.

I miss you, Bun.

Kacy runs her fingers over the words. Bun is short for *honeybun* — *honey* refers to the color of Kacy's hair. She wonders how things are going in the NICU, who the new babies are, how people like the nurse they hired to replace Kacy, if Isla has been acting sad and distant and, if yes, has Rondo noticed?

Another text comes in: I don't understand why you had to LEAVE. I was going to tell him, I just wanted to do it on my own timeline, not because you were pressuring me.

Kacy considers this. Did she pressure Isla to break the engagement? Maybe, but they were in love. Isla's relationship with Rondo, as Isla herself said, was a sham. Isla came from a fancy Mexico City family—five-story town house in Condesa, beach home in Tecolutla—and Isla's mother wanted all the California things for her daughter: UC Berkeley, Stanford School of Medicine, a Napa wedding to a man who was also a doctor, a home in Presidio Heights, three or four children, season tickets to the 49ers, a standing reservation at Gary Danko. Kacy and Isla had countless conversations about how Isla should be living an authentic life—she needed to break things off with Rondo, come out to her parents. "You don't understand how hard that conversation is going to be," Isla said. "My parents are traditional Catholics. My mother will faint; my father will schedule an exorcism."

"They'll get over it," Kacy told her.

"You're right, I know you're right. I just need more time."

"You don't have to tell them about me right away," Kacy said. "But please, for the love of god, break up with Rondo."

"I definitely will," Isla said—but what Kacy has learned is that she definitely won't.

Another text comes in: Leaving was manipulative. You did it to force my hand.

Isla and Rondo must have had a glass of wine or three in front of their gas-log fire, Kacy thinks.

Then, in a move so cruel Kacy can't quite fathom it, Isla sends a picture of Kacy holding Little G. The next text says: The unit needs you, Kace. It was selfish of you to leave.

Don't take the bait, Kacy thinks.

Another text: So that's it? You're not going to talk to me? Aren't you more mature than that?

What could be more mature, Kacy wonders, *than choosing not to engage?* Besides, it's ten forty-five, and Kacy wants to go for a run in the morning, then drive Coco out to Great Point.

Another text: I love you, Bun.

I love you too, Kacy thinks. She clicks out of her texts and hops on Instagram, where she sees Rondo's newest photo, posted that morning. Rondo and Isla are seated at a leather banquette with Dr. Dunne and his wife, Tami, who has enormous breast implants and microbladed brows. Behind them is pink-and-green tropical wallpaper that's so recognizable, Kacy doesn't even need to read the caption to know where they are, but she does anyway. *Champagne and seafood tower @leosoysterbar with my best man and the always-chic @totally_tami_.*

Unfollow Rondo, she thinks. *Then go to sleep.*

But Rondo's account is Coco's only window into Isla's world. Isla and Rondo went to Leo's with the Dunnes the night before; afterward, they probably hit the bar at Wayfare for a cocktail. Isla's texts sound lonely but she's been double-dating with Dr. and "Totally Tami" Dunne. Kacy wants to hurl her phone across the room. She types, Sorry, I've been busy. Then she attaches two pictures: Coco trying on the white sundress and Coco and Kacy at the pharmacy lunch counter, their faces squished together, cheesing. She presses Send.

There's no immediate response and Kacy chides herself for sending the photos. She's using the pictures of Coco as a weapon without Coco knowing it, and she's using them out of context. Her friendship with Coco is brand-new and already she's compromised it.

A minute or two later, a text comes in: Wow, you work fast.

Just friends, Kacy says, but her spirit is buoyed. Isla is jealous.

As if reading Kacy's mind, Isla texts, I'm sick with jealousy. Now I won't sleep. Thanks.

Mission accomplished, Kacy thinks. She turns off her phone and closes her eyes.

8. Thursday, August 22, 8:45 P.M.

On the way from Ventuno to the ashes of the house on 888 Pocomo Road, Ed throws on the lights and sirens; his heart is beating twice as fast as it should, and his thoughts spin out. He needs to calm down—what did Dr. Head Honcho say about stress? He doesn't want to alarm Kacy with the news that Coco is missing, but Kacy, in the passenger seat, keeps calling Coco over and over again.

"It just goes straight to voice mail," she says. "What do you think that means?"

Ed thinks, but does not say: *If Coco went overboard, her phone probably did too.*

Andrea wanted to come to the scene, but Ed asked her to go home with Eric and Avalon. Andrea had been drinking, and unlike him, she'd had a lot more than half a glass of red wine. He needs to breathe— what are his meditation cues? He can't recall a single one. Why did he succumb to temptation and order the Fiorentina, then eat a cannoli? He has only one hundred hours left on the job...and now this.

His phone rings. It's Lucy Shields, the Nantucket harbormaster. Thank god. He puts on his headset; he would prefer that Kacy not overhear any of this.

"Lucy."

"Ed," she says. "What a mess. A doubleheader like this in your final week."

"Who have you talked to?"

"Only the captain, Lamont Oakley. He called it in about twenty minutes ago: Guest on *Hedonism* no longer on the boat. Twenty-seven-year-old female named Colleen Coyle; five foot four inches tall; approximately one hundred and five pounds; dark, chin-length hair; worked for the owners of the boat."

The Chief clears his throat. "Yes, we know her. She's friends with our daughter, Kacy."

"Oh god, Ed, I'm sorry," Lucy says. "Was Kacy on the boat as well?"

"No, no, she's here in the car with me."

"Can she hear us?" Lucy asks.

"Negative," Ed says, and he hopes this is true.

"That's probably best," Lucy says. Lucy Shields has been the harbormaster for a long time. She was Kacy's boss back when Kacy worked as a town lifeguard in high school. *It's a small island,* the Chief thinks.

Lucy says, "It's unclear if Ms. Coyle had been drinking or what her mental state was during the party. Lamont told me the last time he saw her was as they were passing Eel Point heading east-northeast, so we'll go with that unless you and your officers find out anything different. Lamont was sailing solo—the Valladares brothers were at their abuela's birthday—so Lamont would have had his hands full with that boat and all those guests. He seems confident that Ms. Coyle can swim, which is good. The Coast Guard boarded the boat to do a search and they're bringing everyone ashore for questioning, but they'll keep them away from the house fire."

"Are you thinking what I'm thinking?" Ed asks.

"That she was disgruntled? Somehow arranged for the house to catch fire while they were out sailing, then ditched?"

Ed considers what he knows about Coco, which admittedly isn't much, though he's seen her a fair amount this summer, both at his own home and whenever the Chief and Andrea went to the Richardsons'. His first impression of Coco when she climbed into the back of his car was that she was a loner, a wayward soul. But she would have made Charles Darwin proud, the way she adapted to Nantucket life. She befriended Kacy; she seemed at home at Triple Eight Pocomo Road. She became as confident and as at ease as any other young woman ordering a mudslide at the Gazebo. Nantucket has a way of getting in your blood; Ed knows this firsthand. He and Andrea and all their friends arrived from elsewhere and now they're as embedded on the island as the bollards of Old South Wharf.

What do they know for sure? The Richardsons' house has burned to the ground, and on the same evening, an employee of theirs has gone missing. This feels like more than a coincidence, but if all these years of policing have taught Ed anything, it's that one should never jump to conclusions.

"Let's just worry about finding her for now," Ed says. "You've launched a search?"

"I sent one boat from Nantucket Harbor and one from Madaket Harbor," Lucy says. "I'm waiting on word from the Coast Guard in Woods Hole. If we don't find her in the next thirty minutes, they'll send a helicopter from the air station. We've authorized a track-line search from Dionis to Smith's Point, winds are fifteen to seventeen, seas two to four feet, which is good for sailing, bad if you're trying to swim—and the tide is going out, unfortunately. It would help if you could identify the last person who saw her."

"I'm almost to the scene," the Chief says. "I'll let you know what I find out."

The instant they turn onto Pocomo Road, Ed smells smoke. Once they reach the Richardsons' white-shell driveway, he can see a cloud hovering by the water and the smell changes from mildly pleasant campfire to bitter and acrid, then suddenly it's like he's driving through fog. Civilian cars line the right side of the Richardsons' driveway—guests attending the Richardsons' sail—but there's enough room for emergency vehicles to get through. The NFD sent Engine 4, Engine 1, and Tanker 1, since there's only one dry hydrant out here, at the start of Pocomo Road. There's an ambulance and an NPD squad car as well, probably Dixon's.

Ed parks and turns to Kacy. "How are you doing?"

She's as still as a statue in the near dark, but Ed can make out the expression on her face: a stoicism that she must have cultivated during her years in the NICU. "This isn't real," she says. "Coco missing is not a thing. She would never have fallen off the boat—that's ridiculous—and she didn't set a fire and then run. That's like something that happens in the movies."

Ed hopes Kacy is right, that Coco isn't missing—she was using the head in one of the suites or decided to take a swim in the harbor rather than go ashore, and by the time they find Dixon and the others, Coco will be among them, embarrassed to have caused such a fuss.

"Do you want to stay here or go with me?" he asks.

"Go," Kacy says. "Obviously."

Ed takes off his blazer and throws it in the back seat. One of the loveliest evenings in recent memory has been flipped on its head, but Ed can feel rotten about that later. Right now they have to find Coco.

A crowd of people are gathered in the Richardsons' circular garden, which is protected from the worst of the smoke by tall, thick boxwood hedges, though the Chief sees everyone has been given a mask. He hears one woman's cries above all the talking and catches a glimpse of Leslee Richardson in a long white dress that's soaking wet. Dixon whistles and asks for quiet; he announces that, to start, he'll need everyone's name and contact information.

71

Is Lamont here? He must be, but before the Chief can look for him, Stu Vick, the Nantucket fire chief, finds him.

"Fire's out," Stu says. Beyond Stu is a charred, smoldering pile of debris. The Chief has been to this house enough times over the summer to know he'll find the mangled, melted carcass of that exquisite jukebox and maybe a couple of intact pool balls among the ashes.

"Can you confirm no one was in the house?" the Chief says. It occurs to him only now that maybe everyone *thought* Coco was on the boat but she'd accidentally, or intentionally, missed the sail. He can't quite bear to take this idea any further.

"No one was in the house," Stu says.

The Chief exhales. He turns around and nearly bumps into Zara Washington, who on Monday will become Nantucket's new chief of police. She's in full uniform, and the Chief shakes his head. "Zara?"

"I was at the station when the call came in," she says. "Jennifer Speed gave me the heads-up that you were out tonight, celebrating with friends, so I thought I'd better make an appearance. You can go on home; I'll help Dixon with the questioning."

The Chief isn't sure how to respond. While shadowing him on the job for the past two weeks, Zara has proven to be intelligent, calm, steady, and thoughtful, and she has twelve years of experience as a chief over on the Vineyard, but that was one town, not an entire island. Fifty percent of the job—maybe more—is knowing the people you're serving, and that can be learned only with time. Lots of time. The Chief also finds himself bristling at Zara Washington telling *him* that *he* can go home. Unless something has changed that he doesn't know about, he's the chief of police here until Monday.

"My daughter"—the Chief turns around to find Kacy standing among the party guests looking like a lost child—"is friends with the girl who's missing. And I know the couple who own this house. They're…acquaintances."

"All the more reason for you to step away from this one," Zara says. "It's possible this investigation will take more than a few days, Ed. Just let me—"

"I'm going to lead this investigation, Zara," Ed says, leaving no room for misinterpretation. "I don't care how long it takes."

Zara studies him for a second, and Ed feels exposed. Does he feel like he can assert himself because he's a man, a white man? Is he (predictably) refusing to hand over power because he fears becoming irrelevant? He's been training and prepping Zara so that, in a situation like this, he can get in his car and go home, maybe check in tomorrow morning, put Zara in touch with the Massachusetts State Police if a body is found.

A body, he thinks. He has to stay on this for Kacy's sake. There's no way she'll want him to go home and let someone brand-new to the job figure out what happened to Coco.

"I'm sorry, Zara," he says. "I'm not looking for a power struggle here, but I am the chief until the end of the day on Monday."

Ed waits for her to ask him if he's had anything to drink tonight. But instead, she says, "I'll partner with you on this one, how about that?"

"Thank you," Ed says. "You and Kevin should ask the guests the last time they recall seeing Coco and anything they remember about how she was acting." He pauses. "Please."

The Chief has been to a number of parties at the Richardsons' house this summer, but from the looks of things, the usual guest list has drastically changed. (What did Kacy say? *Everyone has abandoned the Richardsons.*) Ed doesn't recognize a soul except Busy Ambrose, a bigwig at the Field and Oar Club. Ed weaves his way through the crowd. Kacy has found Lamont Oakley, and the two of them are sitting on the stone wall at the back of the garden. Lamont has his head in his hands and Kacy has her hand on his shoulder as she talks in his ear.

The Chief approaches. "Lamont?"

He jumps to his feet, shakes the Chief's hand. "She was on the boat, but when we got back here, she was gone."

Gone, the Chief thinks. There are three options: She fell off the boat. She jumped off. Or she was pushed off.

"Let's start at the beginning," he says.

9. Meet-Cute II

Nothing makes Kacy happier about being back on Nantucket than going for a run out to the ocean, then grabbing doughnuts from the Downyflake, still warm in the box. When Kacy gets home, she finds her parents sitting at the kitchen island.

"Is Coco awake yet?" Kacy asks.

"Haven't heard her," Andrea says. She waggles her fingers at the bakery box. "Bring those over here, please, darling."

Kacy sets the box down, Andrea eagerly breaks the tape and helps herself to a sugar doughnut while saying to Ed, "I'd suggest having half of one, Ed, and not the chocolate."

"Oops, sorry, Dad," Kacy says. "I didn't mean to bring temptation into the house." She selects a chocolate doughnut so there's one less for her father to stare at. "By the way, Coco moves into Triple Eight on Monday."

"I'm glad the Richardsons were true to their word," Andrea says.

"Why wouldn't they be?"

"Well," Andrea says, "nobody knows them."

"Phoebe and Addison know them."

"As clients, sweetheart, not as people."

"Do you hear yourself?" Kacy asks. "God forbid this island should have some new blood. Would it kill you to welcome them?"

"As a matter of fact," Andrea says, "Phoebe, Delilah, and I are having lunch with Leslee Richardson next week."

Kacy isn't sure why she's picking a fight with her mother; it's as though the house is turning her back into a teenager.

Ed breaks a plain doughnut in half and stands up. "I'm going to work," he says.

When Coco finally comes downstairs at ten thirty, Kacy makes her coffee and offers her a doughnut. She feels bad about sending those pictures of Coco to Isla. It was pathetic.

"I thought we'd go to Great Point today," she says. "I've packed a picnic."

Coco dunks her sugar doughnut into her coffee and takes a bite. "My god," she says.

"Downyflake," Kacy says. "Best in the world. So anyway, I made chicken salad and BLTs—I hope those are okay? And I packed two bottles of rosé, but do you drink rosé? It's kind of a Nantucket summer thing. I also have beer if you'd rather—"

Coco waves a hand. "I eat and drink it all, but, Kacy, please stop catering to me."

"It's no trouble," Kacy says. "I just want to make sure this weekend is fun for you. Before you start working."

Coco wipes the sugar from her fingers and reaches for Kacy's hand. "You're amazing, Kacy Kapenash. What would I have done if I hadn't met you?"

"Thankfully," Kacy says, "we don't have to worry about that."

* * *

They drive out a winding road, rolling past a farm on the left with fields of flowers and knee-high corn. *It's country,* Coco thinks, like Rosebush (but minus the hot rod up on blocks in her next-door neighbor's yard; the screen door falling off its hinges at her friend Tash's grandmother's house; the Rawleys' Doberman chained up in their yard). Here, they pass weathered split-rail fences, round ponds that glimmer like green glass, a girl riding a bike with a basket on the front and, in the basket, a chocolate Lab puppy. They're headed out to a lighthouse, Great Point, which is at the end of a long curved arm of sand. It's a nature preserve, a big deal, apparently, Nantucket's only true destination. The top of the Jeep is down; the wind is rushing through their hair. The music on Kacy's playlist—"Love on the Brain," "Anti-Hero," "Waking Up in Vegas"—isn't quite Coco's taste, but she sings along like a teenage pop queen.

Kacy points to the left. "There's Pocomo Road." Coco snaps out of her reverie. There's no street sign, just a white rock at the corner with POCOMO painted on it. Coco almost asks Kacy to turn down the road. Wouldn't it be fun to get a peek at the house where Coco will be spending the summer? But Kacy is driving full speed ahead.

At the Wauwinet gatehouse, Kacy pays a hundred and sixty dollars for a beach sticker for her Jeep. The woman working for the Trustees of Reservations—her name tag says PAMELA—has steel-gray hair clipped short and a weathered face and seems utterly humorless. "Kapenash?" she says.

"Yes, ma'am."

"You related to Chief Kapenash?"

"I'm his daughter." Kacy wonders if this entitles her to a discount or if maybe Pamela will waive the fee altogether, but the woman only frowns more deeply. She must have some kind of grievance against Ed. "Do *not* go over ten miles an hour, *respect* all signage, and take your tires down to fifteen pounds, *minimum.*"

Kacy smiles. "I grew up driving on this beach. I won't get stuck." She takes her sticker. "Thanks. I'll tell my dad I met you."

"Ask him to do something about the traffic on Old South Road," Pamela says. "It's appalling!"

Kacy beats a hasty retreat. She searches for her tire gauge but can't find it. That's okay; she can let the air out with her car key, and she'll just eyeball the tires. She moves around the Jeep, enjoying the satisfying hiss of air being released, the scent of rubber, the tires softening like butter left out in the sun. As she pulls out of the parking lot, Kacy waves to Pamela in the gatehouse, though what she wants to do is flip her off.

Coco drinks in the view. They pass an extremely fancy and beautifully appointed inn. "The Wauwinet," Kacy says. "Super-bougie." They hit a sandy road that cuts through the dunes and Kacy shifts the Jeep into four-wheel drive. They bounce around like they're riding a rodeo horse and Coco grabs the roll bar while Kacy whoops. In another minute, they're over the dunes and on the most pristine coastline Coco has ever seen. The golden sand stretches uninterrupted in front of them as far as she can see. The ocean is on their right, the dunes topped with swaying eelgrass on their left. Seagulls seem to hover overhead; smaller shorebirds scurry along the waterline, and a few yards off the coast, Coco sees a dark, sleek head.

"What is that?" she says.

Kacy follows Coco's finger. "Seal."

"There are seals here?" Coco says.

"Lots of them," Kacy says.

Ahead in the distance, Coco spies the lighthouse. It's white with a black top. This is exactly what she dreamed Nantucket would be like.

Kacy hits the gas and they go flying down the beach, sand spraying from the tires. Coco raises her arms over her head and tries to imagine what they look like from above—two women cruising down the beach in a Jeep, leaving tire tracks in their wake, not another soul in sight.

Free.

Later, Kacy will count her mistakes: forgetting the tire gauge, being smug with Pamela, blatantly breaking the speed limit—and drinking so much rosé.

In the moment, however, everything is coming up Kacy. They park just beyond the lighthouse on the very tip of the island. Kacy points out the visible line in the water that marks the cross-rip.

"It feels like we're standing at the edge of the earth," Coco says.

Kacy finds a flat spot for a picnic, spreads a blanket, opens the wine. Meanwhile Coco shucks off her shorts and her T-shirt and says, "I'm going in."

"The riptide is notoriously bad up here," Kacy says. She served as a town lifeguard as a teenager, but even she wouldn't swim today. "Plus the seals mean there could be sharks. And the water is freezing this time of year."

Coco skips toward the water, undeterred. "I'm a good swimmer," she says. "I grew up in Arkansas with a pond in my backyard where I had to outswim the snapping turtles. Then I moved to the Lake of the Ozarks, where I had to avoid the water moccasins. I'll take a shark over a swimming snake any day." With that, Coco splashes into the water and freestyles out. She has a nice stroke and her kick is strong, but all Kacy can think of is the woman who went swimming out here at night—she and her friends called themselves the night swimmers—and disappeared. Kacy keeps her eyes trained on Coco, steeling herself every time Coco goes underwater. Coco dives, flipping her legs up like a mermaid's tail. She's down for so long that

Kacy is about to go in after her—but then Coco surfaces, holding a sand dollar.

"Can you come in, please?" Kacy calls out, windmilling her arm. She knows she sounds like a mom, but the last thing she wants is for Coco to drown out here on her watch.

Coco rides the next wave to shore, shakes her short hair dry like a dog, and rubs at her face with a towel. "That was sublime," she says. "Now, what did I do with my wine?"

The first bottle of rosé goes quickly. Kacy opens the second bottle (Andrea gave her a look, but thank god she brought two). She pulls out the sandwiches, the chips, a cluster of frosty red grapes. The wine goes straight to Kacy's head; there wasn't a lot of day-drinking in the NICU. "So tell me about you," Kacy says.

"What do you want to know?"

"What was it like growing up in Arkansas? I can't even *picture* it. And the only things I know about the Ozarks, I learned from the show. What about your parents, do you have siblings, why did you go down to the Virgin Islands, what's on your bucket list, have you thought about the future?" Kacy takes a breath. "I know basically nothing about you."

Coco reaches for her wine. "Well, for parental figures, it's my mom, Georgi, and her live-in boyfriend, Kemp. Georgi works the deli counter at Harps, and Kemp owns a tobacco shop, which has become all about vaping. Both Kemp and my mother vape nonstop and will probably end up with popcorn lung. No siblings unless you count Kemp's daughter, Bree, which I don't. Their idea of vacation is survivalist camping. So when I was growing up, I learned how to make a lean-to, start a fire, track animals, shoot a bow and arrow, purify water—"

"You are *kidding* me," Kacy says.

"Forage for nuts and berries and wild greens, identify trees, stuff like that."

"That is so cool," Kacy says.

"Or so lame," Coco says. "My dream was to stay in a hotel with AC and a pool." She sighs. "A pool with a sliding board. As a kid, I was always reading—my mother used to make fun of me for it. Then in high school I became close with Ms. Geraghty, the town librarian. My mother approached her at my high-school graduation and accused her of corrupting me by giving me so many books, but books are what saved me. The only reason I've even heard of Nantucket is because Ms. Geraghty gave me *Moby-Dick*."

Kacy feels embarrassed that she's never read *Moby-Dick*. Like all the other nurses on her unit, she reads Colleen Hoover.

"What about now?" Kacy says. "What do you want to do? You're going to work for the Richardsons this summer and then…what? Go back to St. John to bartend?"

Coco shrugs. "I guess if things don't work out, yeah."

"Work out how?" Kacy asks.

Coco hesitates. She has been keeping her script a secret; like making a wish on birthday candles, she fears that talking about it will jinx it. But now that the script is finished and she has somehow managed to score a job with a movie producer and she seems to have made an actual friend, why not? "I've written a screenplay."

"Oh my god!" Kacy says. "You're kidding! What's it about?"

"It's about growing up in Rosebush, Arkansas," Coco says. "It's basically my life story."

"Would you let me read it?" Kacy asks.

"Would you want to?"

"Are you kidding me?" Kacy says. "I'll be able to say I knew you when."

Coco lets herself get swept up by Kacy's enthusiasm for a second, though she's terrified. Kacy will be her first reader. What if she hates it? Worse, what if she *pretends* to like it?

A bank of clouds rolls in, and the wind picks up. "Should we head home?" Kacy asks.

"Already?" Coco says. "We drove all the way out here. And I could use a nap."

Kacy is feeling dozy as well. If Coco isn't complaining about the weather, Kacy shouldn't either. She's the native Nantucketer, hale and hearty. She lies down on the blanket next to Coco and closes her eyes. But the wind whips sand into Kacy's face, which feels like ten thousand tiny needles.

"Let me move the Jeep," Kacy says, "so that it blocks the wind."

Coco has her eyes closed and doesn't answer.

Kacy climbs in the Jeep and throws it into reverse, but it won't budge. She senses she's about to face a reckoning. She hits the gas a little harder; the tires spin, chewing deeper into the sand. She shifts the car into drive, though she has to be careful because the front of the Jeep is dangerously close to the water. Was she really that careless, or has the tide come in? *Both,* she thinks. The Jeep edges forward a few inches and Kacy is heartened. She moves up a bit more, thinking, *Forget the wind block, I just need to get the Jeep on firmer ground.* But she succeeds only in putting her front two tires into wet sand, which is very bad. She tries to back up — nope. She turns the wheel, but this takes her closer to the water.

No! she thinks.

Coco is now on her feet. "Can I help?"

Kacy says, "I've got it," and her voice is still sort of cheerful because she'll figure it out. Let's not forget, she grew up driving on this beach! Her father taught her that if she ever got stuck, she should let more air out of the tires. Kacy does this only in the back because the front tires are in a sucking wet morass. Her only hope is to back up.

She throws the car in reverse with her teeth clenched. Her tires spray sand all over Coco, who shrieks and jumps out of the way. The car doesn't move.

Kacy climbs out and gazes down the beach. There's normally a ranger making sure that nobody hangs out in the delicate ecosystem of the dunes or lights an illegal bonfire or gets herself stuck at the water's edge like a person who has never driven on a beach before. But it might be too early in the season for a ranger. Kacy grabs her cell phone, thinking she'll call her father and he'll contact the gatehouse, and Pamela can come to their rescue. Kacy will have to eat a big plate of *Look at Miss Smarty-Pants,* but fine, whatever.

Kacy's phone has no service.

"Do you have service?" she asks Coco.

Coco checks her phone. "No. Why, are we in trouble?"

The Jeep is stuck in soft sand and the tide is rolling in. Yes, they're in trouble.

"Someone's coming," Coco says.

Sure enough, in the far distance, Kacy sees a truck trundling up the beach, probably settled in the tracks Kacy blazed. Kacy hopes the truck drives all the way out here instead of turning off to Coatue or Coskata Pond. She's tempted to jump up and down and wave her arms. Then she does—because what are their options? Walking the three miles back from the beach? Hoping a boat comes close enough to notice them?

"Hey!" Kacy shouts, but the wind carries her voice out to sea. Coco joins her, the two of them flailing their arms. Suddenly the truck flashes its lights and speeds up.

"He sees us," Coco says.

"Or she," Kacy says. "It's probably Pamela."

But it's not Pamela. The truck is a black F-150 pickup with a couple of casting rods sticking out of a PVC pipe rack on the front grille. Behind the wheel is a guy, and not just a guy, but…Kacy blinks… Lamont Oakley, who was her date for both the junior prom and senior banquet in high school. What is *Lamont Oakley* doing here? Last Kacy heard, he was off sailing in places like the Whitsunday Islands and Capri.

Lamont jumps out of the truck. He has…wow, definitely changed—matured, grown up, gotten smoke-show hot. He's completely ripped; his white polo strains over his broad chest and biceps, and his jeans fit perfectly. Ha! Kacy can't believe Lamont Oakley is now giving leading-man when all through high school he was a math nerd. He was also the best sailor the island had ever seen, though ironically, hardly anyone at Nantucket High School cared about sailing. They'd all taken free lessons in second grade but for the most part, it was viewed as a pastime for summer people. Lamont's sailing commitments kept him very busy and regimented; he was, therefore, the perfect match for Kacy. They'd gone home early from the junior prom because Lamont had a regatta in Newport the next day. The following year they went to the senior banquet together, but it was just as friends. At that point, Lamont was dating the skipper for the Georgetown sailing team, a woman he'd met on a recruiting trip, and Kacy was relieved because that meant she didn't have to worry about kissing him.

"Kacy Kapenash!" he says. When he hugs her, he lifts her off the ground, which is sort of thrilling. "You're the last person I expected to see out here. I thought you lived in California."

"I do," Kacy says. "I did. Long story."

"Hey," Coco says, extending a hand. "I'm Coco. Nice to meet you."

"I'm Lamont." He smiles, and Coco thinks, *Definite swipe right.* She feels like a Jane Austen character when the heir to the neighboring estate enters the drawing room. Lamont has tawny skin, close-cropped black hair, and a shredded body. He's wearing Ray-Ban Wayfarers and a belt with a brass buckle shaped like an anchor. He's part Michael B. Jordan, part JFK Jr.

"So what's happening here?" he asks.

"We're stuck," Kacy says.

Lamont strides over to check out the situation with the Jeep. "You mean you don't want to be featured in tomorrow's *Nantucket Current* because your car got swallowed by the sea?" He laughs. "I got you. I have a tow rope."

Oh, thank god, thank god. Kacy doesn't deserve this stroke of luck; whatever price karma exacts from her later, she will happily pay.

Lamont knows what to do. *It's almost as if he grew up driving on this beach,* Kacy thinks. He backs up his truck, attaches one end of the tow rope to his trailer hitch and the other end to Kacy's bumper.

"Get in," he says. "Put it in reverse. I'll tell you when to hit the gas."

Five seconds later, the Jeep is out of danger, back in established tracks, and pointing in the right direction.

"I'm not sure how to thank you," Kacy says.

"You just did," Lamont says. "Will you ladies be hanging around for a while?"

Kacy is about to say, *No, we have to get home.* They avoided disaster, her adrenaline high is fading, and a headache from the wine is setting in. But Coco jumps in: "Yes, we just got here. Are you hungry? We have extra sandwiches, right, Kacy?"

Kacy blinks. "We do. BLT or chicken salad? Don't say no, it's the least we can do."

"Chicken salad would be great, and a very generous payment for services rendered." Lamont opens a cooler in the bed of his truck. "Would either of you like a beer?"

"I'm good, thanks," Kacy says. She needs to sober up before she drives home.

"I'd love one," Coco says.

Lamont hands Coco a frosty can of Whale's Tale and joins them on the blanket. At that moment, the sun decides to come back out. Lamont Oakley is working all the magic.

He takes a swallow of his beer and asks Coco, "Are you a friend of Kacy's from California?"

"No," Coco says. "Kacy and I met on the ferry. She's graciously letting me stay with her and her parents —"

"The Chief," Lamont says to Kacy, "and your wonderful mother."

Kacy rolls her eyes.

"—until Monday, when I start my new job as a personal assistant."

Is it Kacy's imagination, or is Coco blossoming right before her eyes? Her body is turned toward Lamont; her expression is bright and engaged. She's...glowing.

"What are you doing back, Lamont?" Kacy asks.

"My mom has health issues," he says. "Her eyesight is failing, she has high blood pressure, she's on oxygen, yada yada. She's at the top of the list to enter the Homestead, which will be great, all her friends are there, but I'm not sure how long that will take, so I decided to come home. Some random couple just bought a huge house on island and they also bought a hella sailboat. They hired me to be their captain."

"Really?" Kacy says. "What's their name?"

"The Richardsons?" Lamont says. "Bull and Leslee?"

Coco spills her beer all over the blanket but barely seems to notice. "I'm working for the Richardsons too! On Pocomo Road?"

"No way!" Lamont says. "Seriously?"

"Seriously!" Coco says.

Kacy leans back on the blanket, face to the sun, head resting on her beach bag, and listens to Coco and Lamont chattering, swapping stories about how they met the Richardsons. Kacy has already heard about how the Richardsons walked into the bar where Coco was working and offered her a job on the spot. In Lamont's case, someone from Northrop and Johnson recommended him when Bull admitted, after he bought the boat, that he didn't know the first thing about sailing. Lamont has met the Richardsons only over Zoom.

"I can't believe that you of all people are the one who saved us," Coco says. "And that you also know Kacy."

"Kacy and I went to our junior prom together," Lamont says.

Kacy rolls onto her side. "And our senior banquet."

"Stop it!" Coco says. She raises her beer. "Well, here's to the summer ahead."

Lamont laughs. "Let's hope we survive it." He stands. "I'm going to cast a few lines."

"Oh!" Coco says. "Would you teach me?"

"Of course," he says. "Come on."

Kacy watches as Lamont takes his fishing rod out of the rack, and he and Coco walk to the water's edge. Kacy can no longer hear what they're saying but she can tell plenty from body language. Lamont shows Coco the reel, flips back the bail, and holds the line with his finger. Then he executes a gorgeous cast and starts reeling. Coco watches him with an expression of awe.

Kacy misses Isla. They'd gone to the beach together only once, at Half Moon Bay, on a weekend when Rondo was away at a conference. It had been overcast and chilly but they'd rolled up the bottoms of their jeans and strolled along the water holding hands until their feet were numb. They were, Kacy thinks now, like lovers in a movie. Then they ventured into the little town and ate sunchoke soup at the Moonside; they kissed across the table, marveling at being out in the world together, two tourists in a place where nobody knew them.

It's Coco's turn to try casting. She flips the bail and holds the line, but when she goes to cast, the line jerks and gets wrapped around the rod. Kacy tries not to laugh. She's a pretty skilled surf caster herself—her father and brother saw to that—and for a second, she considers showing Coco how it's done. But she won't be that person. She will be the person who watches as Lamont steps behind Coco, wraps his arms around her, and shows her how to bring her arm back, then fluidly arc it forward, almost as if she's skipping a stone across the water. This works: Coco's line sails out over the waves with a satisfying whiz. Kacy sighs. The sun makes it look as though both Coco and Lamont have been dipped in gold.

10. Field and Oar

The Field and Oar Club allows members to bring two guests at a time, but for lunch on Monday, Phoebe Wheeler brings three. Will anyone challenge her? She breezes past the reception desk with a wave, and the young person Sam (they/their, though the old guard at the club pretend not to understand nonbinary) says, "Good afternoon, Mrs. Wheeler. Here for lunch?"

"You know it, Sam," Phoebe says. Sam won't question her guests; Phoebe helped Sam get their job here.

It's only noon but the patio at the club is popping. It's the first glorious week of summer, when every day feels like Friday. Diane is playing the piano—"Building a Mystery" by Sarah McLachlan—and nearly all the wrought-iron tables under umbrellas are occupied. There's a table of women in tennis whites; one of boarding-school bros in polo shirts and loafers with no socks; one with a mother and daughter poring over a seating chart. Beyond the brick patio, guests can see a manicured green lawn, the giant iron anchor sculpture that children have climbed on for decades, the flagpole flying not only the American flag but the Field and Oar's burgee, and the brilliant blue water of Nantucket Harbor.

As Phoebe approaches the hostess stand, she sees Busy Ambrose sliding her lightship basket up her arm and rising from her table. Busy is the Field and Oar's commodore, and she's a stickler for the rules; if she sees that Phoebe has brought three guests, she'll make a comment. Phoebe believes she should be allowed to bring as many guests as she wants. She not only sits on the membership committee but chairs the scholarship committee, which means reading dozens of student essays on the topics of character and integrity, a thankless job. But Phoebe would like to avoid trouble, especially since it's early in the season and one of today's missions is to introduce Leslee Richardson to the club and the club to Leslee Richardson.

"Let's take a quick tour," Phoebe says to avoid a run-in with Busy. She leads the three women through the formal dining room and up the stairs. Leslee is right on Phoebe's heels, wearing a sundress printed with yellow poppies. Behind her is Andrea, in white capris and a lavender tunic, and bringing up the rear is Delilah, who is decked out in what Phoebe thinks of as one of her "Field and Oar–aspirational" outfits—a kelly-green shirtdress with a stiff upturned collar and a bubble hem. Phoebe wishes Delilah wouldn't try so hard; her own natural style would have been better. Delilah has paired the dress with matching green Jack Rogers sandals and a wicker purse with faux-tortoiseshell handles.

Phoebe acknowledges then that the reason she feels uncomfortable isn't that she has too many guests. It's that Delilah, who is Phoebe's best friend in the universe, has been trying to get into the Field and Oar for years with no success. Phoebe, although she is on the membership committee and is in the room when the vote is taken, has no idea why. Other couples just have more support, and the Drakes are perennially passed over. Each time, Phoebe expresses her ardent endorsement of Jeffrey and Delilah, but she always gets the feeling that the other committee members are just waiting for her to finish.

Phoebe invited Andrea and Delilah along today so they could meet Leslee, but she knows that Delilah is watching like a proverbial hawk to make sure the Richardsons don't leapfrog over her and Jeffrey to Field and Oar membership. *Would that ever happen?* Phoebe wonders. She dearly hopes not, but she admits that it might—Leslee Richardson presents well. On an island where you see the same faces year after year, she's a breath of fresh air. She's attractive, stylish, and a social butterfly; she's already talking about a housewarming party and the first sunset sail on her new yacht.

"This is the Governor's Room," Phoebe says, showing off the classic lounge where she hosted her son's thirteenth birthday party. They move out to the deck, which has an unimpeded view of the tennis courts; a group of kids are heading out for a sailing lesson. "And this is the jewel in our crown." Phoebe opens a door with a brass porthole window. "The Burgee Bar."

Delilah loves everything about the Field and Oar. It's an old-school club where understatement is key. The decor is outdated, but there's history in the faded chintz, the scuffs in the woodwork, the thick white paint. The walls boast plaques naming the winners of every regatta and tennis tournament since time immemorial. It's easy for Delilah to imagine women coming for lunch in dirndl skirts, pearls, and white gloves sixty years ago. The club seems determined to keep the twenty-first century at bay; cell phones are forbidden, and therefore you won't see the Field and Oar appearing on TikTok or Instagram or even Facebook. It can only be experienced in person.

Delilah's favorite part of the Field and Oar is the Burgee Bar. Burgees from clubs across the country flutter from the ceiling. The bar is made from oak salvaged from the original club floor; the leather stools are comfortably worn; and they famously serve Bugles as a bar snack. Nothing about the Burgee is fancy or sleek, but it exudes the rarefied feel of members-only.

"*This* place could use a makeover," Leslee says. "It's a bit…tired."

Delilah gives Phoebe a pointed look—*Leslee Richardson doesn't get it*—which Phoebe ignores. "Shall we go down to lunch?" she says.

They're seated at the best table—the one closest to the water that receives a welcome breeze—and Delilah feels like everyone in the place is whispering about her. Delilah and Jeffrey have been languishing on the wait list of this club for years. They can't seem to get in, even with Phoebe on the membership committee. Jeffrey doesn't give a rat's ass, and that's probably half the problem. He's not good at schmoozing; his idea of cocktail-party chat is talking about aphids and organic fertilizer.

But there's a part of Delilah that worries *she's* the problem. For years, she was the hostess at the Scarlet Begonia on Water Street, a place known for its spinach-artichoke dip and its wild after-hours scene. Delilah hasn't worked at the Begonia in over a decade, but she wonders if any of the members here saw her drinking bourbon at the bar at two in the morning, hair frizzed out, blouse undone one button too far, when she had two little children at home. There was one fateful night when Delilah left the Begonia and mistook another Jeep Wagoneer for her own. The keys were in the console, right where Delilah left hers, and she drove it all the way home; it was only in the morning when Jeffrey woke up and went out to the driveway that she learned of her mistake. They returned the Wagoneer to town without anyone knowing, but Delilah found out later that the other Jeep belonged to Talbot Sweeney, a longtime member of the Field and Oar.

Their server appears wearing a name tag that says MEAGHAN and, below that, her hometown: ANNANDALE, VA. Phoebe orders a bottle of Sancerre and Leslee says, "Thank god you're not a chardonnay drinker." Delilah clears her throat; her go-to wine by the glass is the Chalk Hill chardonnay; is there something *wrong* with that? Meaghan leaves to fetch the wine, and Andrea, who is seated to Delilah's left, goes straight into interview mode.

"So, Leslee, what made you want to come to Nantucket? Do you have friends here, did you come as a child, did you read a novel with Nantucket as the setting?"

Multiple choice, Delilah thinks. B would be the best answer, although Delilah's own answer would have been D, none of the above. Delilah had run away from home, gone as far east as she could, and ended up here. (Maybe some of the Field and Oar members have heard this story and disapprove?)

"My only friend here so *far* is Phoebe," Leslee says. She reaches over to squeeze Phoebe's hand. Delilah cranes her neck; where is Meaghan with their wine? "Bull and I have spent time in Palm Beach, in Aspen, and, most recently, in the Virgin Islands. We tried the BVIs first. We stayed at Oil Nut Bay—"

"Addison and I love Oil Nut Bay!" Phoebe says and Delilah nudges Andrea's knee under the table. Addison and Phoebe's extravagant vacations are a *topic.*

"Then we spent a few weeks in St. John. We've never really done summer on the East Coast—we've always gone to Europe."

Please, Delilah thinks, *say something* more *obnoxious.* What are they *doing* with this woman?

"But this past year we decided we wanted to give up our

wandering ways and put down roots. Buy a house, make it a home. Lucky for us, Triple Eight Pocomo was on the market."

"*So* lucky," Phoebe says and again Delilah bumps Andrea's leg. Is it *so* lucky that in a few years, the Richardsons are going to be living in a pineapple under the sea?

Meaghan arrives with the wine. *Hallelujah,* Delilah thinks.

They raise their glasses and Phoebe says, "Welcome, Leslee!"

Delilah smiles but says nothing. Leslee hasn't done anything *wrong* but Delilah (stubbornly? childishly?) doesn't want to welcome her. She doesn't like the way Phoebe is fawning all over her, and is it not obvious that this woman is glomming on to Phoebe because she wants something? She's a social climber, and the three of them are the rungs.

"What made you decide on that *particular* house?" Andrea asks. *Ha!* Delilah thinks. Andrea is tough with the questions today; Ed should put her in the interrogation room.

"The view, obviously. And the history. When we googled it, we saw it had been featured on the cover of *Architectural Digest.*"

It was Town and Country, *actually,* Delilah thinks, *but why split hairs?*

"But the thing that really *sold* me was the upstairs party room. You've heard about it? It was designed by Jennifer Quinn, the last Nantucket project she did before she started *Real-Life Rehab* and became a celebrity."

"I have," Phoebe says. "There was an article in the *Wall Street Journal* a few years ago about Nantucket homes with bars in them, and Triple Eight was featured."

"We are going to host *so* many parties," Leslee says. "And you're all invited."

"We love parties," Phoebe says.

They do love parties, especially Delilah. Back when all the kids were growing up, Delilah's house was where everyone gathered. At the end of every summer, she threw a lobster-and-rock-anthem party;

the counter of her kitchen island was reinforced with steel plates so Delilah and her friends could dance on it. She hosted everyone during hurricanes and blizzards. She concocted signature cocktails and popped popcorn on the stove and made hot chocolate from scratch.

But now that Drew and Barney are grown, the parties have slowed down. Way down. It might be nice, Delilah thinks, to let someone else entertain for a change. Especially at Triple Eight Pocomo. Delilah thinks buying the house was foolish, but the fact remains that it's a beautiful house. Delilah has seen it only from the water, though she's dreamed of standing at the railing of that octagonal deck, champagne flute in hand.

When Meaghan comes to take their order, Leslee says, "I'd like the bacon cheeseburger, rare, with fries and a side of mayo."

"Wow," Delilah says. "I had you pegged for a slutty vegan."

"Delilah!" Phoebe says.

Leslee laughs. "It's a joke. Slutty Vegan is a restaurant chain. I've been to the one in New York." She winks at Delilah. "You guessed wrong—I *love* meat."

Delilah warms to Leslee just a bit—but no, she won't be seduced. She isn't *easy,* like Phoebe, who in an obvious attempt to change the subject asks Leslee if she plays pickleball.

Yes, Leslee plays pickleball. In fact, she's played with "Julie, the over-fifty champion." Bull isn't much for the game, and he's too busy besides. Delilah wants to ask what Bull's business is (would this be rude?) but she can't get a word in edgewise because Leslee is exclaiming about how she would *love* to be their fourth. She pulls a tissue from her Goyard bag and dabs away happy tears. She's just so touched; she can't believe how lucky she is to be making such wonderful friends.

Delilah nudges Andrea's leg again. *Is this an act?* She's on her third glass of Sancerre, so she can't really tell.

Delilah leans forward and says, "So where are you and Bull *from*?"

Leslee laughs like an audience member on a late-night show and says, "Bull comes from the Land Down Under, which is obvious the second he opens his mouth." She looks around the table. "I've barely asked you ladies anything about yourselves."

This, Delilah thinks, *is true.* She wonders what kind of advance billing Phoebe gave them. Did Phoebe define them by their husbands? (*Delilah's husband, Jeffrey, owns Sea View Farm. Andrea's husband, Ed, is the chief of police.*)

Andrea clears her throat. "Delilah serves on the board of the Nantucket food pantry."

"Nantucket Food, Fuel, and Rental Assistance," Delilah says, though everyone calls it the food pantry.

Leslee brings her hands together as if in prayer. "You're a *do-gooder!*" She makes it sound like she's opened her front door to find Delilah in a Girl Scout uniform selling Thin Mints. "Phoebe has my email. Just send me the link. I'd be happy to read up on your cause and donate."

"I used to do a ton of philanthropy before I had Reed," Phoebe says. "I'll have more time for it next year once he goes to boarding school."

"Oh," Leslee says. "Where is he looking?"

"The usual places," Phoebe says. "Middlesex, St. George's, Milton. But the one he has his heart set on is Tiffin Academy."

"Tiffin!" Leslee shouts. "We know at *least* half the board at Tiffin." She waves a hand. "We'll see to it that he gets in."

At this, Andrea bumps *Delilah's* leg.

Phoebe, who never loses her composure, completely loses her composure. Her composure, Delilah thinks, is rolling around somewhere under the table. "You'd do that?" Phoebe says. "Put in a word when the time comes? Obviously you can't guarantee admission—"

"I'll pull every string," Leslee says. "It's the least I can do to thank you for writing our nominating letter." Leslee sighs. "I would love to be a member here."

Delilah sets her wineglass down on the wrought-iron table harder than she means to. "Nominating letter?" she says. "That was sweet of you, Phoebes." The legs of her chair scrape against the brick patio as she pushes it back from the table. "Excuse me a moment."

"Delilah," Phoebe says.

Delilah slams into the women's lounge. Phoebe is writing the Richardsons a *nominating letter*? She's known them five minutes! Back when Delilah and Jeffrey were applying, Phoebe said she'd rather not write the nominating letter because she didn't want to be accused of trying to get her friends in. She'd ended up writing a seconding letter, which had apparently done nothing.

The lounge has a seating area with a sofa upholstered in cheerful pink and white stripes and two pink Ultrasuede armchairs. This has never made sense to Delilah—who would want to hang out in what is essentially the ladies' room?—but now she collapses in one of the armchairs and thinks how nice it is to have a comfortable place to sit while she processes her best friend's betrayal.

Delilah realizes she's being petty, even ridiculous. Everyone else in the world has a problem bigger than not getting into a private club. But even so…if the Richardsons get into the Field and Oar, Delilah will never speak to Phoebe again.

Nominating letter!

The women's lounge, as far as Delilah can tell, is empty, but even if it weren't, she can't hold her frustration inside, not after three glasses of wine and two hours in this hideous dress. "Bahhhhhhh!" she cries.

A toilet flushes, and Delilah hears water running in a sink; the bathrooms are around the corner. She closes her eyes, praying that whoever it is will leave the lounge without comment.

No such luck.

"Are you okay?" a voice asks. Then there's a gasp. "Delilah?"

My life, Delilah thinks, *is officially over.*

It's Blond Sharon.

When Blond Sharon finished reading her character-study scene to her creative-writing class over Zoom, there was a lengthy silence.

Pow! Sharon thought. Her piece had rendered them speechless.

Lucky Zambrano cleared his throat. "Nancy, Willow, do either of you have comments for Sharon?"

Both women bowed their heads.

Lucky said, "Well, the physical description of Coco is quite vivid, although a bit of a stereotype, I'm afraid. Wearing black, the flamingo tattoo, the Joan Jett hair, the army duffel."

"She was a hell of a lot more interesting than the other woman, the one with the shiny hair and the whatever-brand blazer," Nancy said.

"Veronica Beard blazer," Sharon clarified.

"Sharon, please wait until the end to respond," Lucky said.

"I found it predictable," Willow said. "Like maybe Sharon used ChatGPT with the prompt 'Write a character study about two women getting off the ferry, one prep and one punk.'"

Sharon pressed her lips together to keep herself from shouting, *I did* not *use ChatGPT!*

"ChatGPT will be the end of writing as we know it," Lucky said. "And while I'm not suggesting that Sharon used this egregious shortcut, I would suggest starting this piece fresh with different characters."

"Different *characters*?" Sharon said, aghast.

"Sharon," Lucky said. "Have you ever heard the phrase *kill your darlings*?"

"Attributed to William Faulkner," Nancy said. Nancy was turning out to be kind of a pill. "It means you should delete anything that's not working in your writing, no matter how fond you might be of it."

"But my *characters*?" Sharon said. "*Both* characters?"

"Kill your darlings," Lucky said.

Sharon, dramatically, drew an X through her handwritten page.

"Let's move on," Lucky said. "Willow, you may read."

After class ended, Sharon called her sister, Heather. "I thought Walker leaving me for Bailey from PT was a hit to my self-esteem," she said. "It was nothing compared to the beating I just took in my creative-writing class."

"Mmgmmghbmm," Heather said. She was eating while they spoke, which they'd been brought up never to do, but Heather was so busy at work that the only time she could talk was during her desk lunch.

"You read it," Sharon said. "Did you think it was predictable?"

Heather slurped something through a straw.

"They told me to start over," Sharon said.

Heather swallowed. "So start over," she said. "If they thought it was predictable, then look around until you find something... unexpected."

What kind of crazy advice was that? If it was unexpected, how would Sharon know where to look for it?

The meaning of Heather's words lands on Monday at the Field and Oar Club. Sharon has just finished a tennis lesson with the new instructor, Mateo, who came to the Field and Oar from Buenos Aires. Mateo has the cheekbones and eyebrows of a luxury-brand model and he thought nothing of wrapping his strong arms around

Sharon in an attempt to fix her backhand. *A stranger comes to town, part three?* she thinks. However, even Sharon knows that lusting after her hot tennis instructor isn't exactly "unexpected."

In the ladies' lounge after her lesson, Sharon is mindlessly emptying her bladder when she hears a woman cry out. Not in fright or pain, Sharon doesn't think, but in frustration. Sharon pokes her head around the corner to find out what's going on—expressions of genuine emotion are rare at this club—and sees Delilah Drake squashed into one of the club chairs like a pea smashed into a rug.

"Delilah?" Sharon says. She doesn't quite consider Delilah a friend, though they've known each other forever and are connected through various filaments of the Nantucket web. Delilah is married to Jeffrey Drake; they own Sea View Farm, where Sharon buys her tomatoes and her corn. Delilah is close with Phoebe Wheeler and Andrea Kapenash, and their friend group has a name—the Outcasts? The Commitments? Sharon is guilty of making fun of the name, whatever it is, but that's just because she's envious. They are three smart, fun, accomplished women and Sharon has always wanted to know them better.

The other unexpected thing about finding Delilah here is that Delilah isn't a member of the Field and Oar Club. Sharon sits on the membership committee, and although she always votes to admit the Drakes, the motion never carries.

"Is everything okay?" Sharon asks. The answer is obviously no, but will Delilah spill the tea? Delilah sinks farther into the chair, her green dress billowing around her like a parachute.

Sharon sits on the sofa and props her sneakered feet up on the white wicker coffee table, pretending she needs to take a load off after an exhausting tennis lesson. Sometimes the best way to get people to talk is to be quiet.

Delilah says nothing for a moment and Sharon thinks, *Fair enough.*

Sharon isn't exactly known for her discretion. She wonders how to describe the color of Delilah's dress. It's not *lizard* or *haricot vert;* she considers *kaffir lime, shamrock,* and *emerald,* but all of those make the color sound more appealing than it is. *Traffic-light green,* maybe?

Finally, Delilah exhales. "Have you met Leslee Richardson?"

"No," Sharon says. Cautiously dropping her voice to a whisper, she adds, "But I've heard some things."

Delilah leans forward. "What have you heard?"

Delilah is turning the tables, but as Sharon knows, you must often give information to get information. "She and her husband bought Triple Eight Pocomo, and then a few days later, a yacht, *Hedonism.*" Sharon laughs. "Sounds like the name of a nudist colony. And I did hear...I can't say from whom...that she considers herself a 'party animal.'" The term is so ridiculous, Sharon uses air quotes. "I also heard she's *very* eager to become a member here."

Delilah takes a breath to speak, then hesitates. "This has to stay in the vault."

Surely she's being ironic, Sharon thinks. Everyone on Nantucket knows she is constitutionally unable to keep a secret. But maybe this once, to preserve the integrity of her character study, she'll try? "In the vault!" Sharon agrees.

Delilah starts to talk: Leslee Richardson is here having lunch with Phoebe, Andrea, and Delilah. She has managed to completely ingratiate herself with Phoebe, even offering to help Phoebe's son, Reed, get into his first-choice boarding school.

"Have you ever heard of anything so *transactional?*" Delilah says. "She offered because Phoebe is apparently writing the Richardsons a nominating letter to join the club."

"What?" Sharon says. She is offended on Delilah's behalf. "There's a *long* wait list." She nearly adds: *As you of all people know.*

"Leslee strikes me as one of these silky-smooth operators," Delilah says. "She's talking about all the parties she's going to throw at her house and on the yacht. She wants to be our fourth in pickleball."

Sharon nearly says, *I play pickleball if you're looking for a fourth,* but she doesn't want to sound like what her twins refer to as a "Pick-Me girl."

"The weird thing is how quickly she's infiltrated," Delilah says. "She and the husband, Bull, are out at the restaurants seven nights a week, making connections with every round of drinks they buy. They hired Lamont Oakley as their boat captain."

"That was a coup," Sharon admits. "Everyone loves Lamont."

"Exactly," Delilah says. "He's going to lend them legitimacy, but the truth is, nobody knows anything about these people."

"Where did they come from?" Sharon asks.

"We asked, but Leslee only said they've been bouncing around. She mentioned the Virgin Islands, Palm Beach, Aspen…"

"All the hot spots," Sharon says. "And now they've landed in the most exclusive place of all."

Delilah seems to relax a bit. "It's not like they have to provide references to live here," she says. "I just think it's odd the way they've decided to make Nantucket their forever home without any context. I feel strangely threatened, like I'm in middle school and Leslee is the new girl who shows up and steals away my friends. Though I do like her perfume. She smells like crème brûlée."

Now, that's a detail! Sharon thinks as she mentally writes the scene: Delilah's green dress reflects the jealousy she feels about this interloper; Phoebe succumbs to Leslee's sequined promises and her vanilla-and-burned-sugar scent. *How did Andrea react to Leslee Richardson?* Sharon wonders. She probably found some middle ground, reserved judgment; Andrea is known for being sensible and measured.

Suddenly Delilah stands, so Sharon does as well. "I'd better get back out there before they start talking about me," Delilah says.

Sharon laughs, though that's probably exactly what's happening. "Thanks for the warning about Madam Richardson." She wants Delilah to know that she can count on her as an ally—though maybe not *too* much of an ally because Sharon would like to get invited to the parties at 888 Pocomo Road and on the yacht.

"I'm sure she's not as bad as I've made her out to be," Delilah says. She tugs on the sides of her dress. "She's probably harmless."

"Well," Sharon says, "*that* would be a disappointment."

Delilah gives Sharon a hug before she disappears out the door. Sharon is tempted to poke her head out onto the patio so she can get a look at Leslee Richardson in person, but in the end, she decides to go straight home. She needs to start writing while it's all still fresh in her mind.

11. Thursday, August 22, 9:00 P.M.

When Nantucket's incoming chief of police, Zara Washington, and Sergeant Kevin Dixon do their preliminary questioning of the guests who were on the Richardsons' yacht, they find something odd: Most people know the Richardsons only slightly and some not at all.

"I was getting a pedicure next to Leslee at the RJ Miller Salon," a woman named Marla Sofia says. "We got to chatting, she seemed very nice, and the next thing I knew she was inviting me and my husband, Tony, on tonight's sail. But I wouldn't say I *know* them."

Sergeant Dixon talks to a couple who met the Richardsons while they were all singing at the Club Car's piano bar. They're tourists, here for three days.

A guest named Celadon Morse had taken the mat next to Leslee at a Forme Barre class and scored an invite. "I was thrilled!" Celadon says. "I've been hearing about these parties from everyone I know all summer long, but when I got here, I didn't recognize a soul." She pauses. "Except for that woman over there. She belongs to the Field and Oar Club. She has a funny name."

"Thank you," Zara says, and she approaches the woman, who is masked and giving Margaret Thatcher vibes — she has a severe bob and blue eyes that are watering from the smoke. When Zara asks her name, she lowers her mask and says, "Busy Ambrose."

"And you live here on Nantucket, ma'am?"

"I've summered on Nantucket since the sixties," Busy says. "I live on Ash Lane and I'm the commodore of the Field and Oar Club."

Zara is impressed that the yacht club here has a female commodore. "I'm Zara Washington, the new chief of police."

"Yes," Busy says. "I read about your hiring in the paper."

"Do you know the Richardsons, ma'am?"

"I do indeed," Busy says. "I befriended them earlier this summer."

"Do you know the missing woman?"

"Her name is Coco," Busy says. "She works for the Richardsons."

"Do you remember seeing Ms. Coyle on the boat?" Zara asks.

"Yes, she was serving drinks and passing hors d'oeuvres."

"What was she wearing?"

"Her uniform — a pink polo shirt and white shorts."

"At what point did you last see Ms. Coyle?" Zara asks.

"After Bull and Leslee renewed their vows, Coco handed out flutes of champagne for a toast."

"Wait a second," Zara says. "The Richardsons renewed their *vows* on the sail?"

"They did," Busy says. "It was a surprise."

"So you saw Ms. Coyle handing out the champagne," Zara says. "What time was that?"

"Maybe seven thirty?" Busy says. "The sun was just setting. We were out by Eel Point, getting ready to turn around, which was a good thing because a minute or two later, Bull got a call that their house was on fire."

Zara needs to parse this. "So Coco was still on the boat when you all learned the house was on fire?"

"She was on the boat while we were doing the champagne toast," Busy says. "After the toast, Lamont tacked and we were heading back, and right around that time, we learned about the fire. I can't say for sure if Coco was still on the boat then. Everyone was agitated; people had their phones out. I don't remember seeing Coco or not seeing her. I didn't see anyone go overboard. None of us saw that, obviously, or we would have *done* something."

"You said Bull Richardson got a call about the fire. Is that how you learned about it?"

"Yes," Busy says. "Then an instant later, I got an alert on my phone from the *Nantucket Current*. The *Current* reported that a house in Pocomo was ablaze and the Nantucket Fire Department was on the scene."

"Where was Mrs. Richardson during all of this?" Zara asks.

"I'm not sure," Busy says. "Leslee wasn't up front with the rest of us. Bull called out for her, then went looking for her."

"Was she below deck?"

"Either below deck or somewhere else on the boat. There were a few minutes when I don't remember seeing Bull or Leslee but then eventually we all saw Leslee crying. Bull told Lamont to lower the sails and motor back as fast as he could."

"Thank you," Zara says. "I'd like you to stay, if you don't mind. You're the only person who seems to know the Richardsons well."

"Yes," Busy says. "I'm the only one who's stuck by them this summer."

"Stuck by them?" Zara says. "Did something happen?"

Busy waves a hand. "Oh, you know how people gossip."

Zara had gone through a divorce from a public figure on Martha's Vineyard; she definitely knows how island people gossip. "Thank you. Please stand by in case we have further questions."

Mrs. Richardson's long white sundress is soaking wet and she's wailing about the things she's lost. "All those Urban Electric light fixtures!" she says. "The jukebox, my champagne coupes, the seashell fireplace! My Amalfi lemons!"

Amalfi lemons? Zara thinks.

"Leslee, stop," Mr. Richardson says. Zara is surprised to hear he has an Australian accent. "Coco is missing. She might have drowned."

"If she did drown, it would serve her right. She burned our house down!"

Oh, boy. Zara peers through a gap in the hedges at the remains of Triple Eight. She understands why they're upset—they've been left without a toothbrush, without a bathrobe or a change of clothes. The house is a charcoal briquette.

One good thing is that their garage is untouched, and it looks like there's a living space or a home office above. And they still have this garden, which is one of the most breathtaking outdoor spaces Zara has ever seen, with its lush hydrangeas and rosebushes along manicured cinder paths; the centerpiece of the garden is a mahogany hot tub. On the far side of the hot tub, Zara sees the Chief and his daughter talking to Lamont Oakley, the captain of the boat. She hopes the Chief hasn't started questioning Lamont without her present. When she said they would partner on this one, she meant it.

Dixon's talking to two men who met the Richardsons while

having dinner at the Languedoc. "Sergeant Dixon?" Zara says, trying to convey a sense of urgency. She looks at the gentlemen. "Would you excuse us a moment?"

"Did they find her?" one of the gentlemen asks. He turns to the group assembled behind him: "I think they found her."

Zara raises a hand. "Whoa, that's how rumors get started. The harbormaster has launched the search, and when we know more, we'll announce it." She beckons Dixon away from the party guests and nods discreetly in the direction of Lamont, the Chief, and his daughter. "I'll be questioning the principals alongside Chief Kapenash. Just so things are aboveboard."

Dixon squares his shoulders. "Ed is always aboveboard."

Zara is on slippery terrain here. Of course Dixon is loyal to Ed, as he should be, but not at the expense of the investigation.

"What I'd really like is for Chief Kapenash to step away from this investigation," Zara says. "His last day is Monday. He shouldn't be taking on the onus of this case, of these *two* cases, with only a few days left." She sighs, then blurts out, "It's like he wants some kind of swan song."

Dixon says, "There's no way Ed would walk away from this case. His daughter is friends with the missing woman, so Ed has skin in this game. He understands the connections between all these players better than anyone." Dixon lowers his voice. "He used to hang out with the Richardsons."

"He mentioned that," Zara says.

"He came to their parties. They were...friends, or friendly. But then I think something happened."

"What?" Zara says. "What happened?"

"Hell if I know. Ed doesn't gossip." Dixon pats Zara on the shoulder in the most patronizing way possible. "But you're right about one thing: This is a hell of a swan song."

12. Triple Eight

"I'm sure you'll love the job," Kacy says to Coco as they drive out to 888 Pocomo Road. "If you need anything, text me; if it's an emergency, call. Just because these people have money doesn't mean they own you. Stand up for yourself. Ask about your days off." Kacy raises her aviators to the top of her head. "Why do I feel like a helicopter parent dropping her only child off at a faraway college?"

Coco is glad Kacy is doing all the freaking out; it means she doesn't have to. There's a version of this summer where she just stays in the Kapenashes' guest room and bums around the island, jobless, with Kacy. The night before, as they ate fish tacos at the Oystercatcher, their feet in the sand, Kacy made a list of the Nantucket summer things they still had to do: There were at least a dozen beaches to lounge on, afternoons at Cisco Brewers with live music and food trucks, rainy days at either the Whaling Museum or the Dreamland Theater, oysters at Cru, a sunset cruise on the *Endeavor,* singing around the piano at the Club Car, and dancing at the Chicken Box, followed by a late-night Stubbys run. Of course, living that kind of life required an endless stream of cash, and Coco can't lose sight of her purpose: her script. She wants — needs — Bull to read it, to believe in it, then give it to the people who can greenlight it. Every night before she falls asleep, Coco imagines the announcement in *Deadline:* "Newcomer Colleen Coyle's First Script 'Rosebush' Sold in Competitive Three-Way Auction."

Kacy lets Coco play her music as they drive; she chooses Twenty One Pilots' "Stressed Out" and sings along under her breath.

When Kacy pulls into the long white-shell driveway of 888, Coco feels like she's standing on a precipice. What is it going to be like, not only working but *living* with the Richardsons? Will she hate it? Will she love it? She has no idea.

Once they park in front of the house, Kacy unloads Coco's army-green duffel and hands her the white eyelet dress from the Lovely, which is on a hanger, sheathed in protective plastic.

"Do you want me to stay until you get settled?" Kacy asks.

Yes! Coco thinks. "Oh, I should be fine," she says. She holds her arms out. "How can I ever thank you?"

"I'll see you in a couple days," Kacy says. "Just keep me posted." She gives Coco a hug, then gets in her Jeep, turns around, and heads back out the driveway, blaring "Summertime Sadness" by Lana Del Rey. Coco smiles. She must have planned that.

Coco climbs the steps to the front porch, feeling like a street urchin straight out of Dickens. She knocks on the door with a conviction she doesn't feel. She bluffed her way into this job by invoking the name of poor Ms. Geraghty; she's pretty sure the Richardsons are going to figure out she's a fraud. Coco might be calling Kacy within the hour to come pick her up.

Coco hears footsteps. She prays that it's Bull; Coco is better at handling men.

The door swings open—Leslee.

Shit, Coco thinks. She beams. "Hey!" she says. "I hope I'm not too early?"

In Coco's nightmares, Leslee responds in one of the following ways:

Who are you and what are you doing at my twenty-two-million-dollar home?

Or *The cutoffs–T-shirt–and–Chuck Taylors look is appropriate if you're working as a roadie for the Dirty Heads, but you're a personal concierge—you should be wearing a pencil skirt, heels, pearls.*

Or *Bull was drunk/just being polite when he offered you the job; neither of us dreamed you'd take it, but you snapped it up like a half-starved tiger with a T-bone, didn't you?*

Or *I saw right through your* I'm spending the summer on Nantucket too, actually *ploy. You're a scammer, Colleen. You're a parasite who lives off people who have money and connections.*

Or *I'm so sorry but we've offered the job to someone who knows the island a little better.*

But in reality, Leslee radiates serenity. She's wearing a white tank and white yoga pants; her long chestnut hair is piled on top of her head; her skin is dewy and glowing; her expression is placid. Coco must have caught her just after child's pose and a green smoothie. "Good morning, Coco, you're right on time. Just leave your bag on the porch for now. In a little while, we'll bring it over to the garage apartment where you'll be staying. But I'll hang your—dress?—in the hall closet so it won't get wrinkled."

Coco steps inside, closes the door behind her. The air-conditioning feels divine; it's a hot morning already.

And *wow*—this house.

The foyer is two stories with a sweeping staircase on either side and a view straight through the house to a screened-in porch and the water beyond. The floor is black-and-white checkerboard; the staircases have curved white railings, and the runners are printed with bright pink peonies and green leaves. In the center of the foyer is a round pedestal table that holds a huge arrangement of actual peonies in every shade of pink. Their scent suffuses the air. Coco stands for a moment, taking it all in, and Leslee says, "Welcome to Triple Eight."

Coco follows Leslee up the left staircase to the famous party room. It looks like the setting for a Slim Aarons photograph; every detail is midcentury perfection. There's a lounge area with a low serpentine white sofa that's scattered with throw pillows in candy colors; mirrored cigar tables; gooseneck lamps; an honest-to-god jukebox; and a parquet dance floor. But the showstopper is a fifteen-foot-long Lucite bar backed by bright pink lacquered shelves. The bar seems to float over the chrome-and-pink-leather stools. Behind the bar is a glass-fronted wine fridge filled with Laurent-Perrier sparkling rosé. Coco does a quick tally—there are forty-two bottles of champagne on display. Nice flex.

Wineglasses in a rainbow of colors line the pink shelves. The overall effect is "Willy Wonka after three martinis, but make it tasteful." Coco laughs. She can't *believe* she met these people at the Banana Deck.

Leslee leads Coco out to an octagonal deck that has views across Nantucket Harbor. *Sweeping* views, Coco supposes one would say. The golden stretch of Great Point is to the right, and the church steeples of town are in the distance. There's a majestic yacht on a mooring in front of the property's narrow beach, a sleek motorboat alongside it. Most of the speedboats Coco has seen are white, but this one has a navy hull and a gleaming mahogany deck. "The big one is *Hedonism,*" Leslee says. "Bull thinks sailing is elite, but I prefer to go fast, so over the weekend, I bought *Decadence.*" She points to the speedboat. "It's an Aquariva Super with dual two-fifties."

Coco nods like it's totally normal to impulse-buy a speedboat as though it's a lip balm by the register at Target. "I mean, yeah, you deserve something of your own."

Leslee swats Coco's arm. "You get me!" she says. "I knew it would be good for me to have another woman around! Come on, let me show you the rest of the house."

Off the other side of the deck is the living room, which Coco can only think of as fifty shades of blue. There's Delft-blue grass cloth on the walls, a blue-and-white rug patterned to resemble the designs on a Chinese vase, a blue-and-white leopard-print bench, throw pillows in a dozen complementary blues, and an unexpected pop of color—an apple-green lacquered coffee table. Adjacent to the living area is a dining-room table big enough to seat thirty people, with a very cool glass-orb chandelier hanging above it. Finally, they enter the kitchen, and Coco jumps.

Sitting on a stool at the kitchen island drinking coffee is Lamont Oakley.

"Hey!" Coco says. She feels herself flush, partly from the surprise and partly because of Lamont himself, who's looking all hot and captain-ish in a white button-down and navy shorts. Coco loved her hang with Lamont at Great Point, even if she'd turned out to be the world's worst surf caster. On his final cast of the day, Lamont caught a striped bass. It wasn't big enough to keep, but it was his first bass of the season, and Coco was happy to witness it. She took twenty-two million pictures on her phone, then offered to send some to him, and he gave her his cell number. On the drive home, instead of appreciating the view like she probably should have, Coco went through the photos and chose the five best, which she texted to him the second she got a signal. He'd responded a while later with Thanks, it was fun hanging out, see you at 888. This had made Coco so happy that even Kacy noticed. "Why all the smiles?" she asked.

Coco had wanted to ask Kacy about Lamont, but she worried that would be insensitive since Kacy was going through a breakup. Kacy had given Lamont's bass only a cursory glance, then started packing up.

Coco is about to tell Leslee the story of their serendipitous meeting and describe what a lifesaver Lamont was (*Thank god he came along or I might still be out at Great Point*) when Lamont strides over to her, hand extended, and says, "Lamont Oakley. Nice to meet you."

Coco stares at him for a second. Is he kidding?

Leslee tells Lamont, "This is Coco, our new personal concierge."

Coco shakes Lamont's hand more aggressively than she typically would have. "Yes, hi there. Lovely to meet you, Lamont."

"Lamont is our boat captain!" Leslee says. She slips her arm around Lamont's shoulders and squeezes. "I can't believe how lucky we got!" The tranquil, centered woman who greeted Coco at the door has vanished, and in her place is the person Coco remembers from the Banana Deck. Coco pictures Leslee's hand resting on the WAPA dude's thigh.

Lamont widens his eyes to telegraph, she supposes, that she should keep her mouth shut.

Fine, she thinks. *Weird, but fine.*

"Coco and I have some business to tend to this morning," Leslee says. "Would you like to get the boat ready?"

"Of course," Lamont says. "Pleasure meeting you, Coco."

Coco can't help rolling her eyes.

As Leslee takes Coco down to the primary suite, Coco lags a few steps behind, afraid that she's going to come across Bull in his boxer shorts. Leslee shows off the bedroom: It's bigger than Coco's entire house in Rosebush and has sliding glass doors that lead outside to the front lawn and the beach beyond. Leslee opens a door that turns out to be a walk-in closet. There are more clothes in this closet than there were in the Lovely. And there's an entire wall of shoes— sandals and ballet flats, pumps and strappy stilettos. Has Leslee seen the cobblestones on this island, the brick sidewalks, the deck boards that surround her own house?

Leslee opens a door next to the shoe racks and they step into a dressing room with a bench and floor-to-ceiling mirrors. "I haven't had sex in here yet, but that is definitely happening," she says breezily, and Coco thinks, *I did* not *need to know that, thanks.* On the other side of the dressing room is Bull's closet. He has so many beautiful colorful shirts, it's like that scene in *Gatsby.* "I'm showing you the closets so you'll know where to put the dry cleaning."

The last room Leslee shows off in the primary suite is the bathroom, which is as nice as a spa in a hotel. There are dual vanities, a two-person shower, a soaking tub, a water closet, a steam sauna, and a special area for Leslee to do her hair and makeup, on the counter of which are jars, pots, and tubes from La Mer and Valmont and an ornate bottle of Guerlain perfume. The fattest curling iron Coco has ever seen rests in its own ceramic stand; that must be the secret behind Leslee's impeccable barrel curls.

Out in the hallway, Leslee stops in front of a digital keypad. "This is the alarm system. Fire, flood, and there's a chime that goes off anytime someone crosses the threshold of the driveway. You can disarm the alarms with the code eight-eight-eight. I'd like you to turn them off whenever we have a party, of course. If the caterers are making cherries jubilee, I don't want the fire department showing up. Then after our parties, you'll have to remember to turn them back on."

"Very important," Coco says. She makes a mental note to look up cherries jubilee.

Next they poke their heads into Bull's study, which has a maritime-museum feel; there's an enormous model ship in a glass case. Coco peeks at the plaque under the ship: J-BOAT *SHAMROCK.*

"Is this boat special to Mr. Richardson?" Coco asks.

Leslee laughs and waves a hand. "All this stuff was here when we moved in. The only shamrock that's special to Bull is the one in his Lucky Charms."

This gives Coco an opening. "Where is he this morning?"

"Indo," Leslee says.

Indo? Coco thinks.

"Indonesia," Leslee says.

"Oh." Coco had expected Leslee to say he was with his trainer or in town picking up breakfast. "How long will he be away?"

"He has stops in Bali, Lombok, and Irian Jaya, then a big meeting in Jakarta. They're trying to pass all this new *legislation,* which would be very bad for Bull's business, but I doubt it will ever come to fruition." Leslee winks. "I told Bull he had to get his ass home by Saturday. We can't let work get in the way of our social life."

"Obviously not!" Coco says. She's been here fifteen minutes and already she feels like she needs a shower.

Leslee leads Coco through yet another door into what turns out to be the at-home gym, complete with side-by-side Pelotons, a treadmill, and a full rack of free weights; the room smells like the rubber floor and is as cold as a meat locker. Then Leslee says, "Time to get down to business." Coco follows her along the hall and they enter a tiny jewel-box library with a fireplace made entirely out of seashells. This could look cutesy and crafty but here it's a work of art, a showpiece that belongs in a magazine. Coco immediately spies some of her favorite titles on the shelves — *This Is How It Always Is, Beautiful Children, Luster.*

"Are these your books?" Coco asks. She plucks *Fates and Furies* by Lauren Groff off the shelf. "How much did you *love* this?"

Leslee stares at her blankly and Coco puts the book back. Okay, never mind. The books must have come with the house too.

Leslee sits behind an antique escritoire and invites Coco to take the chaise in front of the fireplace.

"I have some things for you," Leslee says. She hands Coco a white paper shopping bag from, yes, Murray's Toggery. Coco pulls out a stack of peony-pink polo shirts, size small. Beneath the shirts are several pairs of white linen shorts. Coco blinks. She has never worn shorts made of anything other than denim. She has never voluntarily worn a polo shirt.

"I'm sorry about the uniform," Leslee says. "It was Bull's idea. He feels…well, he wants our household staff to wear uniforms. So people know who you are."

Coco is no stranger to jobs that require uniforms. She had to wear a green gingham dress and a white apron when she worked at Grumpy Garth's Diner. But for some reason, Coco is caught off guard. She assumed her own clothes would be fine (though who is she kidding; they wouldn't have been fine at all). While they were standing in Leslee's closet, Coco had a brief fantasy that Leslee was going to invite her to borrow anything she wanted—after all, Leslee has more clothes than a person could wear in a lifetime. Coco supposes it's the phrases *household staff* and *so people know who you are* that irk her. But what did she expect? She works for the Richardsons; she isn't their friend.

Leslee pulls a Moleskine notebook from the escritoire's drawer and hands it to Coco. The moss-green cover is embossed with the initials CC. "I didn't know your middle name."

"It's Marie," Coco says. She accepts the notebook—the monogram is a thoughtful touch. Leslee hands Coco a slender box that turns out to hold a Montblanc pen.

"Your database," Leslee says. "Bull and I are hopelessly old-fashioned. We love pen and paper."

Coco appreciates the heft of the pen; it is, she thinks, a *writer's* pen. The gifts have improved her mood.

"Write everything down, please," Leslee says. "Take notes, make observations, create lists, and check things off. Understood?"

"Understood," Coco says. "Do you have forms for me to fill out?"

"Forms?"

"Like a W-two?" Coco says. "For my paycheck?"

"No," Leslee says. "This is a cash job."

Coco nods slowly, considering this. Part of her is, naturally, thrilled. Cash! But another part of her worries about the IRS. Will they come after her for tax evasion? If Kacy were sitting here acting as Coco's counsel or conscience, she would disapprove. If the Richardsons aren't paying Coco properly, how can she be sure they'll treat her properly? They could, in theory, fire her at a moment's notice, and she would have no recourse. Does their failing to play by the rules with her salary indicate more widespread improprieties? Everything from the at-home bar to the mahogany deck of the Aquariva appears slick and glossy, but are the underpinnings rotten?

Coco fears that the answer is yes. She's about to open her mouth to protest when Leslee says, "I know Bull told you thirty-five dollars an hour back in St. John but we've decided that the complex and discreet nature of this job deserves a more robust salary, so we're bumping it up to fifty dollars an hour."

Coco feels faint. She immediately thinks of her favorite line from the movie *Blue Jasmine:* "It's not the money, it's the money."

It's the money, Coco thinks.

"I'd like you to start each day at eight," Leslee says. "Mornings will typically be busy with errands, afternoons a little lighter. We'll ask you to work in the evenings when we entertain, and for that, we'll bump you to time and a half."

Seventy-five dollars an hour! Coco struggles to keep a straight face, though the imaginary Kacy sitting next to her would like Leslee to clarify what she means by "complex and discreet."

"A cleaning team will come on Mondays and Fridays," Leslee says. "But we'll need you to do light housekeeping. You'll make our bed every morning, fold our pajamas, put dirty clothes in either the hamper or the dry-cleaning bag. You'll set up an auto-pay account at the dry cleaner; I'll give you my card to do that. You'll take care of all the provisioning: groceries, produce, alcohol, pharmacy, bakery, florist. You'll make our dinner reservations—and we always like to have a plan B, because our mood or the weather might change—you'll pick up our mail from our post office box, open our packages, and make regular trips to the dump with the cardboard because apparently our trash service won't collect it."

Coco is madly scribbling in her new notebook: *Make bed, pajamas, dry cleaning, alarm code 888, cardboard.* But in her head, there's a different kind of scribbling: *Make the Richardsons' bed? Fold their pajamas? Eww! They're two grown adults; can't they fold their own pajamas, and haven't they heard that making the bed when you wake up is one of the habits of highly successful people?*

"Which days will I have off?" Coco asks.

Leslee glances up. "You know, you remind me of myself when I was your age."

"Seriously?" Coco says. She takes in Leslee's polished countenance, her ease in this giant, beautiful home on the water. Coco thinks about the house she grew up in: vinyl siding the color of margarine, wall-to-wall carpet, the pond out back with its skin of green algae.

"Seriously," Leslee says. She studies Coco's face as though searching for something—traces of her younger self, perhaps. Coco is so unsettled that she forgets what they were just talking about. Something important...it was...

"Days off?" Coco says. The imaginary Kacy sitting next to her approves. *Stand up for yourself!*

"You won't have any days *off*, per se," Leslee says. "After all, we don't take days off from *living*. But I assure you, you'll have plenty of downtime. You can lie on the beach here, I'm having a hot tub installed in the new garden—"

"I'll be free to leave the property, though, right?" Coco has a vision of herself chained to Triple Eight like the Rawleys' Doberman back in Rosebush. "I'd like to see my friends."

"You've made friends here already?" Leslee says. "Are we talking about 'Susan Geraghty, the librarian'?" She uses air quotes and Coco breaks into a light sweat. Does Leslee know that Ms. Geraghty never set foot on Nantucket?

"I'm friends with Kacy Kapenash," Coco says. "Her father is the chief of police."

"How funny!" Leslee says. "I had lunch with her mother yesterday." She pauses. "How well do you know the Kapenashes?"

"I've been staying with them this past week."

Leslee's perfectly shaped eyebrows rise almost imperceptibly. "You have?"

There's a knock on the library door. "Entrez!" Leslee calls out like a character in a play.

Lamont pokes his head in. "The boat is ready to go," he says. "We have time to zip around for a while before our reservation."

"Wonderful," Leslee says. She beams at Coco. "I thought we'd go for a boat ride, then up to the Wauwinet for lunch on the patio."

"That sounds amazing!" Coco says. The Wauwinet is the bougie place she and Kacy passed on the way to Great Point. Coco doesn't have anything to wear to a lunch like that...except for her new dress. She hadn't planned on wearing it so soon, but oh, well. It might not be so bad not having a set day off if her job entails going on boat cruises and having elegant lunches.

"Just let me finish with Coco and change my clothes and I'll be right out," Leslee says.

"Take your time—I'm at your disposal," Lamont says, then closes the door.

Leslee looks at Coco and all but smacks her lips. "I love it when he says that."

Oh god, Coco thinks. She's not sure she can stomach watching Leslee throw herself at Lamont all morning.

"I should probably change as well," Coco says, looking down at her cutoffs.

"Absolutely," Leslee says. "I hope the shorts fit. I had to guess at sizes."

Is Coco supposed to wear her uniform to lunch?

Leslee pulls a cardboard box from behind the escritoire. "Your first priority today is to get these delivered."

Coco peers into the box. It's filled with peony-pink envelopes. (*The pink is becoming a lot,* Coco thinks.) The top one is addressed to Mr. and Mrs. Addison Wheeler on Polpis Road.

"I thought..." Coco nearly says, *I thought we were going on a boat ride and to lunch,* but suddenly she understands that the *we* doesn't include her. The *we* is Leslee and Lamont only. "I'll take these to the post office, then. I'll need stamps. How are we handling money for things like this?"

"For provisions, you'll have one of my credit cards," Leslee says. "I don't check the statements—I could care less—but of course Bull does."

Coco nods. "Of course." Does Leslee think Coco might take her credit card and go on a spending spree around town?

"If you want to buy yourself lunch while you're on the clock, please do," Leslee says. "That means a sandwich from Something Natural or a quick stop at NanTaco, not rosé and oysters at Cru."

Coco can't keep herself from giving Leslee a look. "I understand reasonable expectations for lunch."

"Of course you do!" Leslee says, holding her gaze. "It's just...we don't really know you. Bull said he checked the references you gave him, but sometimes he tells me he's done things just to make me feel better when he's really let them slide. It would be very easy for someone like you to take advantage of us."

Coco is glad Leslee has just come right out and said it, and what can Coco think but *Yes, I am hoping to take advantage of you.* Just as the Richardsons will take advantage of Coco: No days off! No reporting of taxes! She would love to tell Leslee that Bull never even *asked* her for references.

Coco is relieved when Leslee turns her attention back to the box. "No to the post office and stamps, though. I'd like you to deliver these invitations by hand."

"By hand?" Coco says, thinking, *How very Edith Wharton.* Coco will knock on doors in her uniform and hand the envelope to the lady of the house or someone on the staff. "All of them?" There must be a hundred envelopes in the box.

"Yes, all of them," Leslee says. "The party is on Saturday and I don't trust the U.S. Postal Service to get them anywhere in a timely fashion. People need to clear their calendars. So I'd like it done this morning." She stands up and Coco follows suit, picking up the box of invitations. "Come with me. I'll show you your apartment and your car, then you can get going."

My apartment. My car. This job is like a seesaw, Coco thinks. The lows: no days off, wearing a freaking uniform, and delivering a hundred invitations by hand like she's a character in *The Age of Innocence.* The highs: cash money (as long as she doesn't get in trouble with the IRS; do they bother with poor folks like her?) and the view.

Coco's new apartment—which is located above a separate two-car garage—is also a high. It's not as grand as the main house, but it is light and bright and has a coastal-grandmother vibe. The kitchen appliances are stainless steel, and there's a fresh bouquet of cosmos and black-eyed Susans on the counter. In the living room, there's a deep sofa in front of a huge television, and Coco has her choice of bedrooms. She takes the one with the water views instead of the one with the walk-in closet. Both rooms have a king-size bed (Coco has only slept in a king-size bed during one-night stands). They're sheathed in white linens and have a million pillows, like beds in a Nancy Meyers film.

"Who will be in the other bedroom?" Coco asks. A part of her wills Leslee to say "Lamont," but she's even happier when Leslee says, "Nobody. This place is all yours."

Coco can't believe her luck. She can spread out; stay up all night fine-tuning her script and watching *Housewives;* no one will bogart her hummus or finish her bag of pita chips; she won't be subjected to anyone else's stink in the bathroom or cooking smells or lovemaking noises. Coco has never lived alone. *This,* she thinks, *is the definition of* luxury.

She follows Leslee downstairs to the white-shell driveway. Off to the left, a backhoe is clearing out scrub brush. That must be the new garden where the hot tub will go. Leslee presses a button on a remote control; the door to the right garage bay opens, and honestly, it's like one of the reruns of *Let's Make a Deal* that Coco's mother used to watch on her days off. *What's behind door number one?*

In this case, it's a Land Rover Defender, probably early 1980s, baby blue with a tan top. Coco peers in the open driver-side window. The steering wheel is wood and chrome, the seats are buff leather, and in the back are two sets of jump seats facing each other. It's the most beautiful vehicle Coco has ever seen.

"Do you drive stick?" Leslee asks.

"I do," Coco says. She's afraid to ask if this is her car because this could be a fake-out like the boat ride and lunch.

"In that case," Leslee says, "meet your new baby."

If Coco is on a seesaw, this is the highest of highs. She knows all about vintage cars from living with Kemp. He kept issues of *Classic Motorsports* and *Auto and Design* the way other men did *Playhouse* and *Penthouse*. Coco wants to take a picture of the Rover and send it to him: *Look what I'm driving this summer!* He'd think she was bluffing or that she had a sugar daddy or that she'd stolen it.

"Hello, Baby," Coco says, and Leslee laughs.

"Bull told me we had to buy an 'island car,' but I didn't realize it would be so...basic."

Basic? Well, it's over forty years old and has a canvas top and the back seat is impractical unless you're looking for cheetahs on the Serengeti, but the vehicle is in pristine condition, and Coco wonders where Bull found it. He must have an auto broker with outstanding taste. This car is best in class, which should reflect on its owners, but it's clear Leslee doesn't get it. Coco turns around to check out the other car in the garage, a flashy black G-Wagon, brand-new.

"The keys are in the console," Leslee says. "Can I count on you to get those invitations delivered?"

"You can count on me," Coco says with new enthusiasm.

"Please change into your uniform before you go," Leslee says. "Oh, and there is one more thing."

Of course there is. Coco steels herself. "Yes?"

"Bull and I have a strict rule about our staff dating one another. We don't allow it. Work romances don't always end well, and a bad breakup will make it disruptive for everyone in the household, as I'm sure you understand."

"Yes," Coco says. "Who else is—"

"It's just you and Lamont, officially. Lamont has hired two part-time crew members, but they're teenagers."

So...Leslee is telling Coco she can't date Lamont. Which is why he pretended not to know who she was.

"Okay," Coco says. "I get it."

"Do you?" Leslee holds Coco's gaze and Coco tries not to let her disappointment show.

"I do."

"Good, great, perfect. Because we're strict about it. You'd both be replaced"—she snaps her fingers—"like that." She waits a beat for these consequences to sink in. "Have fun with the invitations. I'll check in with you later."

Coco heads back upstairs, her elation about the room of her own and the Rover popping like an overinflated balloon. The only person on Nantucket she's not allowed to date is the only person she might want to date. Is she bothered enough by this to quit? No—she's here for a reason, and it's not to find a boyfriend.

Coco changes into her uniform; she tucks her shirt into the high-waisted shorts that make her look like Steve Urkel. Through the window, she watches Leslee wade out to the speedboat holding a striped beach bag over her head. Lamont reaches out a hand and helps her aboard. He guns the engines and the boat careens away in a huge sweeping arc. *It's almost like he knows I'm watching,* Coco thinks. He's showing off.

She eyes the box of invites and calls Kacy, thinking that Kacy will at least know where all these addresses are.

Kacy answers on the first ring. "Is everything okay?"

"You busy?" Coco says.

13. Special Delivery

Blond Sharon is at home preparing ham and cheese sandwiches on an assembly line for her son, Robert, and the friends he's invited over to swim in the pool when there's a knock at the door. Sharon peers through the window and sees a gorgeous vintage Land Rover idling in the driveway. Even Sharon's soon-to-be ex, who likes to snark about all the Land Rovers on Nantucket ("Explain what a car designed to be driven on the African savanna is doing on an island thirty miles offshore"), would have to admit it's a good-looking car.

Standing on the porch is a young woman holding out a pink envelope. "My employers, the Richardsons, are hosting a party on Saturday, and they'd love for you to join them."

Gah! Sharon thinks. The Richardsons? She accepts the invitation thinking, *These Richardsons are certainly shaking up the status quo.* Who hand-delivers invitations? Sharon can think of no one but the royal family. And yet it's a nice touch and, in Sharon's case, a welcome one. She and Walker used to find their mailbox stuffed with invitations to cocktail parties and benefits; in more recent years, invitations came via Paperless Post or Mint. But so far this summer, even those have been lacking. Sharon has tried not to wonder if she's been taken off people's lists because of her impending divorce. Are her married friends gathering without telling her, rationalizing it as "giving her space" when really they're just afraid that divorce is a contagious disease?

At least the Richardsons aren't put off by her newly single status.

"Thank you," Sharon says to the young woman. "I'll check my calendar and RSVP." She notices the woman's short, punk-rock haircut. It's the girl from her character study, Sharon thinks. Coco!

When Coco strides back to the Rover, Sharon notices someone riding shotgun—Kacy Kapenash. Ha-ha-ha! They've become friends! That story had a happy ending, but of course no one in Sharon's creative-writing class wants a happy ending; they want conflict, drama, *nuance.*

A second later, Sharon's kitchen is invaded by half a dozen thirteen-year-old boys. One notorious troublemaker, Baxter Morse, walks right into Sharon's pantry and emerges with a bag of Fritos. Sharon wants to snatch the bag away. Baxter is Sharon's least favorite of Robert's friends; his mother, Celadon Morse, is insufferable.

"I'm making lunch for all of you right now," Sharon says. "I'll bring it out to the pool."

"Do you have any sodas?" Baxter asks.

"Robert isn't allowed soda because of his diabetes," Sharon says. "Now, shoo, all of you. You're dripping all over my kitchen."

"Your mom is mean," Baxter says to Robert on the way out. "And I can't believe you aren't allowed to have soda."

I'm not mean! Sharon wants to shout. *You're rude! And thanks very little for your diabetes-shaming!*

She turns her attention back to the envelope. The invitation is on heavy, cream linen stock with a pink border and pink print.

Pink and White Party at Triple Eight Pocomo
Saturday, June 22, 7:00 p.m.
Cocktails, Dinner, and Dancing
Regrets Only

Pink and White Party evokes Truman Capote's Black and White Ball—or is Sharon upselling this? Surely they're meant to wear pink and white, which will be easy for Sharon. She thinks of that young woman, Coco, in her pink polo and white shorts. Coco is working for the couple everyone on the island is talking about—and Kacy Kapenash was in the car. Maybe Sharon should resuscitate her "darlings," despite her class's nay-saying. It feels like the plot is thickening.

Sharon tapes the invitation to her fridge, and the whole kitchen seems to take on a pinkish tinge—or maybe that's because of the improvement in Sharon's mood. She finishes making the sandwiches and manages to resist the urge to put a spider in one and give it to Baxter.

Fast Eddie speeds out the Milestone Road like a man on the lam. He just received word that Jeanne Jackson has decided to sell off her six acres of waterfront land in Tom Nevers, the last parcel of its kind on the entire island.

Eddie pushes his Cayenne to sixty, then sixty-five. He fears being nabbed by the Nantucket police, but he fears losing this opportunity even more. He spoke to Jeanne, who is, thankfully, a realist and is just fine with dividing the property into three two-acre parcels. It will be easier to sell that way.

When Eddie pulls down Jackson Way (the family has owned the property so long, the road is named after them), he realizes he's too late. Addison Wheeler's Aston Martin is already parked at the beach access and Addison is deep in conversation with Jeanne Jackson.

Eddie hurries over. He's been flirting with a crazy idea, and Addison might be just the person to make it work.

An hour later, heading the opposite way on Milestone, Eddie is speeding once again, this time due to a pure adrenaline high. His crazy idea wasn't so crazy after all because it turned out Addison had been thinking the same thing. *They* should buy the three lots and build spec houses. Jeanne wanted to list the lots at three million apiece, but instead of telling Jeanne (who clearly hasn't looked at a Nantucket real estate listing sheet in the past fifteen years) that she could easily list the parcels at five or six million apiece, Addison and Eddie locked eyes and an unspoken understanding passed between them. They could buy the lots for nine million, spend another four million per lot on a house, guesthouse, pool, and pool house plus landscaping, then flip them for twelve to fifteen million apiece. It was easy money just waiting to be made by the two people who understood the island's real estate market better than anyone.

When Eddie climbed into his car, Addison sent him a text: Call me in the morning. It was as electrifying as a message from a lover.

Eddie's phone rings; it's his wife, Grace. Immediately, Eddie feels...caught. The truth is that Eddie did a deal similar to this ten years earlier and lost not only his proverbial shirt but his good name and his freedom as well. He'd been so desperate for cash that he started a prostitution ring on Low Beach Road, a scheme for which he'd gone to prison for three years. When Grace hears that he's thinking of getting back into spec houses, she'll call a divorce attorney. He'll have to reassure her that this time will be different. Maybe instead of taking out a loan from the bank, they'll find a deep-pockets investor, someone who considers eighteen million dollars Starbucks money, someone who likes a challenge, someone who would value Eddie and Addison's island connections. It would mean divvying up the profits but also the risk. Eddie likes this idea; he isn't sure a bank would lend to him again anyway.

"Hello?" Eddie says.

"You aren't going to believe who invited us to their party on Saturday!"

Is it someone who wants to fund my new real estate venture? "Who?"

"Bull and Leslee Richardson," Grace says. "They're throwing a pink and white party at Triple Eight Pocomo. The invitation is gorgeous and it was hand-delivered by their *personal concierge*." She pauses. "Why do you think we got invited?"

"They're networking!" Eddie says.

"So they're *using* us?" Grace asks.

"Networking is a two-way street, darling," Eddie says. *Especially in this case,* he thinks. He's so amped up about the invite—it's like the universe is telling him something—that he hits the gas even harder practically without noticing. But someone else notices.

"I caught Fast Eddie going eighty-one miles an hour on the Milestone Road," Sergeant Dixon tells the Chief. "That was fast even for him. And get this—his excuse was that he was excited about some party invitation he and Grace received."

Invitation, the Chief thinks. Must be to the Richardsons' house on Saturday. Andrea texted a couple of hours earlier instructing the Chief to get a haircut because they had a swanky party to attend. Andrea had sounded pretty giddy and Ed supposed he understood. They didn't get invited to a lot of parties; having the chief of police in attendance felt like a buzzkill.

Andrea texts Phoebe and Delilah: Did you guys get your invitations to the Richardsons' party on Saturday?

Phoebe texts back immediately. Yes! Let me know if you want to go shopping. This is a new-dress occasion!

Andrea rolls her eyes. Every occasion for Phoebe requires a new dress. But when Andrea checks her closet, she sees a lot of brown and gray. Her wardrobe could use a summer refresh. She needs pink and white.

She texts back: I'm helping Delilah at the food pantry at noon. I can meet you at Milly and Grace at one p.m. to shop. Immediately, she feels a wave of guilt. How can she volunteer at the Nantucket food pantry and then turn around and drop two hundred dollars (probably more) on a dress she's going to wear to a glamorous party? She reminds herself that Leslee Richardson expressed interest in donating to the food pantry. Delilah should circle back about that with Leslee at the party. Or is that tacky?

A text comes in from Delilah: Was the invitation sent by email? I don't see it.

Phoebe responds: It was a paper invite, pink envelope, hand-delivered.

Hand-delivered? Delilah texts back. By a footman with white gloves and fringed epaulets?

Coco delivered them, Andrea texts. Kacy offered to help her.

There's silence from Delilah.

Oh god, Andrea thinks. *Is it possible Delilah isn't invited to the party?* Delilah *was* thorny with Leslee at their lunch. Andrea and Delilah had been kicking each other under the table because some of the things Leslee said were, quite frankly, hard to take, and there was a little honeymoon moment going on between Leslee and Phoebe that bordered on nauseating. Andrea has always been better than Delilah at dealing with uncomfortable situations; Delilah has a short fuse. Did Leslee sense that Delilah didn't like her and not include her?

That would be awkward.

Delilah checks her front door, looks under the welcome mat, in the hydrangea bushes. Nothing. As she marches out to the mailbox, a sinkhole opens inside her. Leslee Richardson is throwing a party just like she said she would—and she didn't deem Delilah worthy of an invitation. At lunch it felt like Leslee was interested only in people who could be of use to her. People like Phoebe, because of the club; Andrea, because of Ed.

Delilah still worries, however, that the fault is somehow hers. She wasn't very welcoming or gracious to the woman; she'd left the table abruptly because she was angry and jealous and then bad-mouthed Leslee to Blond Sharon, of all people. Sharon might have repeated Delilah's words to anyone, to everyone.

Well, Delilah hadn't said anything she didn't mean. She took an instant dislike to Leslee, and yes, that was wrapped up in her best-friend attachment to Phoebe and to her and Jeffrey's inability to get admitted to the Field and Oar Club. But didn't Leslee Richardson have some good qualities? She'd laughed at Delilah's slutty-vegan comment. She'd asked for information about the food pantry. Didn't that reveal a generous nature? But from the moment Delilah met Leslee Richardson, she'd gotten a bad feeling. Since that's the case, shouldn't Delilah be *glad* that she hasn't received an invitation? Would she agree to go even if she *were* invited?

Yes! Delilah thinks. She wants to buy a new outfit, she wants to see the famous house, she wants to go to the party.

Delilah wonders if maybe Coco couldn't find her house—it's off a dirt road and can be tricky to locate, even with GPS. But Kacy was with her, and Kacy has been coming to Delilah's since she was a little girl.

That's it! Delilah thinks. Kacy never uses the front door; she uses the family door on the side of the house. Delilah hurries out and, whoa, the relief she feels when she sees the pink envelope gives her a head rush. Of course Leslee invited her; it would have been an egregious oversight not to. Delilah, Phoebe, and Andrea are a package deal. They're all supposed to play pickleball together.

Delilah reads the invitation: Pink and White Party; cocktails, dinner, and dancing. It sounds like so much fun!

She vows to try harder with Leslee. If she gives the relationship a genuine effort, by the time the summer is over, she and Leslee will be the best of friends.

14. Party Animal

We show up wearing flamingo, blush, salmon, magenta, fuchsia, and rose gold. We wear pearl, blanched almond, alabaster, polar ice cap, and cloud. Fast Eddie is in a pink-and-white seersucker suit — is this too much? Apparently not, because the dentist Andy McMann wears a neon-pink top hat and his wife, Rachel, is in swan feathers. Even Romeo from the Steamship has cleaned up his act: He's wearing a Bazooka-gum-pink bow tie and has traded in his usual cargo shorts for a pair of pink madras pants.

We park along the Richardsons' white-shell driveway and note that all the hydrangea bushes are pink.

"Yes," we overhear Benton Coe say. "Leslee wanted the hydrangeas pink, so I put lime around the bases."

Whatever Leslee wants, Leslee gets, Blond Sharon thinks.

Sharon picks up her pace, even though she's in heels, to meet up with Romeo. "You look dashing tonight," she says.

Romeo notices Sharon teeter as she crunches through the shells in her stilettos. *Impractical,* he thinks, though they make her legs look a mile long. "Can I offer you my arm?"

"Thank you." Sharon is grateful to Romeo, not only for his steadying presence but also because now she won't be entering the party alone. She imagines Walker hearing that she and Romeo from the Steamship were looking cozy together at the Richardsons' party. Ha! It would serve him right.

* * *

On Nantucket, the prevailing aesthetic for everything—even parties—
is understatement. The old society matrons pretend to go to no effort
when they entertain (and some of them aren't even pretending). One
infamous hostess sends out invitations on index cards that read, simply, *Drinks, 6:00 p.m.* Another hostess serves only two snacks: ham
and butter sandwiches on postage stamps of Wonder bread and
spears of pickled asparagus.

We're elated to find that the Richardsons' party gives maximum
effort. The entrance is a soaring arch of Juliet roses. (Members
of the Nantucket Garden Club inform us that Juliets are among the
most expensive flowers in the world and to have such a profusion
of them is unheard of. We pose for pictures under the arch—this
is something our friends on Facebook have to see!) On the far
side of the arch, servers hold trays of drinks: flutes of Laurent-
Perrier rosé champagne, a cocktail called the pink lady—made
with Triple Eight vodka, of course—and pink lemonade for the
teetotalers.

We saunter onto the front lawn, where a pink-and-white-striped
tent shades a full bar, a huge grazing board, and the guitar player,
Sean Lee, who at the moment is playing "Pretty in Pink" by the
Psychedelic Furs.

The Richardsons are leaning into the theme, we see.

The entire harbor is spread out before us like a banquet. The
water is spangled with golden coins of sunlight; we see the church
steeples of town in the distance; and the Richardsons' yacht, *Hedonism,* cuts an impressive silhouette against the horizon. In the center
of the lawn, halfway between the tent and the beach, Leslee Richardson receives her guests. She's wearing a vintage Hervé Léger
bandage dress in pink ombré stripes and pink metallic platform sandals; her makeup includes pink eye crystals.

Hello, thank you for coming, so lovely to see you. Most of us have to introduce ourselves because we've never actually met the Richardsons.

Blond Sharon and Romeo are standing with Fast Eddie and his wife, Grace. Sharon's heels are chewing into the Richardsons' lawn and she regrets not wearing flats. Sharon knows every single person at this party except for the people throwing it. A moment ago, she shook Leslee's hand and said, "I'm Sharon, thank you for having me."

"Nice to meet you," Leslee said. (Immediately, Sharon caught a waft of Leslee's vanilla perfume. Delilah was right; Leslee smelled as delicious as a French bakery.) "I've been told to stay on your good side."

Sharon laughed in the moment, although now she wonders if she has an intimidating reputation. (Would this be a good thing or a bad thing?) Well, Sharon won't worry about it tonight. Leslee probably meant that Sharon knows everything about everyone and isn't afraid to share.

Sharon soon discovers that Romeo has never met the Richardsons, and Eddie and Grace know them only slightly. Sharon's antennae rise. The Richardsons don't know, but they *do* know, she thinks as she scans the crowd. This is more than just a party to meet the neighbors. Everyone here is a Nantucket someone. How did the Richardsons figure out whom to invite? She watches Delilah Drake enter the party in a white halter and pink pants with pom-poms on the hems, and Sharon relaxes. If Delilah has given the Richardsons the benefit of the doubt, then Sharon will too.

Sean Lee segues into "Who Knew" by Pink. *Okay, we get it,* Sharon thinks with a bit of an eye roll. But she's delighted when the food starts to appear. There will be no white bread or stale cashews here—Zoe Alistair is catering! Her servers pass immaculately constructed bites, from tiny chicken and waffles that Sharon dips in maple syrup to vodka-spiked cherry tomatoes rolled in basil salt.

Romeo sees that Sharon's champagne flute is empty and procures her a full one, then they wander over to the raw bar. "Where's your husband tonight?"

"Haven't you heard?" Sharon says. "He left me for his physical therapist. We're getting divorced."

"What an idiot," Romeo says. He has never understood men who leave their wives for younger women. Romeo believes women get funnier, wiser, and, yes, sexier as they get older. He would never ask Sharon how old she is but he's guessing they're within a couple of years of each other. He likes her smile and her energy. She engages in life. Romeo bets she's dynamite in bed.

Sharon helps herself to an oyster with mignonette while Romeo chooses a cherrystone. When they both reach for a plump pink shrimp, their fingers brush.

"Allow me," Romeo says. He dips the shrimp in cocktail sauce and feeds it to Sharon while holding a napkin under her chin.

Is everyone at the party watching? Sharon wonders. Oh, she hopes so.

The Chief is wary of big parties like this—so many things could go sideways. For starters, every single car lined up along that driveway will presumably be driven home tonight, and from the looks of things, designated drivers will be scarce. Where there is drinking, there are accidents; someone could fall off the octagonal balcony or drown in the harbor. Then there are dangers of the emotional sort— arguments, fistfights, hurt feelings, affairs. The Chief has seen it all.

But it's a stunning evening, the most glorious of the year so far, and they're in a spot that's extraordinary even by Nantucket standards. In the car on the way here, Andrea praised the Chief for all the progress he's made with his health. That morning, he jogged three miles and did ten full minutes of meditation. "You deserve a night out," she said.

He does, he thinks. It's his last summer on the job; they've narrowed the search for a new chief down to two people — a young guy from Brockton and a woman from Oak Bluffs — and the Chief feels the heavy mantle of responsibility he's worn for the past thirty-five years lighten a bit. Enough for him to have a real drink, anyway. He chooses the pink lady.

Coco stays upstairs at Triple Eight, checking in with the catering staff and prepping all the surprises in the party room until the guests start to arrive, then she hurries outside. Kacy glides in under the flower arch with her brother, Eric, and his girlfriend, Avalon. (Coco had called Avalon earlier that day because Leslee wanted her to do an at-home massage — throwing the party stressed her out. Avalon said, "I don't think Leslee and I are a good match, but here are a couple of other names.")

Kacy comes over, glass of rosé champagne in hand, and gives Coco a hug. "This is un-freaking-believable."

Well, yes, Coco thinks. Nothing in Rosebush, Arkansas, or the barefoot paradise of St. John has prepared her for this kind of glamour. There's a lot more to come, though she's been sworn to secrecy.

"You look pretty," Coco says. Kacy is in a pink floral prairie dress, and Coco feels like a douche-noodle in her uniform. She wants to know why she has to wear it while Lamont, the only other Richardson employee, is allowed to wear his own clothes — a pink oxford and a pair of white duck pants.

"Thanks," Kacy says. "Can you hang, or..."

"I'm on the clock," Coco says.

"Maybe when the party ends, we can go into town?" Kacy says.

"If Leslee has her way, this party isn't going to end," Coco says. She eyes the champagne flute in Kacy's hand with longing. She should have sneaked a glass while Leslee was in the bedroom curling her hair, but instead Coco was running through her checklist.

She turned off the alarms—fire, flood, the chime announcing visitors—then set a reminder to turn the alarms back on in the morning. She was in charge of the tent guys, the caterers, the various musicians throughout the night. There had been no time for champagne.

Lamont approaches and gives Kacy a kiss on the cheek, but his eyes are fastened on Coco. "Do you need help with anything?" he asks her. "I feel like a squid out here schmoozing while you break your ass."

"It's fine," Coco says. This is how Leslee wants it: Lamont schmoozing, Coco breaking her ass. At that moment, Coco's phone buzzes. It's a text from Leslee: ICE!!!! One of Coco's duties is to replenish the ice at each of the bars and in the enormo wheelbarrow where they're chilling the champagne. Leslee is *obsessed* with the temperature of the champagne. This is what she wants people to be talking about tomorrow, apparently: *The champagne was so cold!*

Coco hurries to the ice maker, which is in the laundry room, to transfer the ice to crystal buckets. The ice has to make its own stylish entrance to the party.

When Coco enters the laundry room, she gasps. There's a man standing in front of the washing machine in his boxer shorts.

He turns around. "Hey, how ya goin'," he says.

It's Bull. Of course it's Bull, this is his house, and yet Coco is surprised. Bull was in Indonesia on business and was due back yesterday, but his meeting in Jakarta ran long and he missed his flight to San Francisco and the connecting flight to Boston. Coco knows all this because Leslee had become completely unzipped about Bull missing the party. *I've invited all these people! I need him here!*

"You made it back," Coco says now.

"A few minutes ago," Bull says. "I'm not going to lie, all I want to do is crawl into bed and sleep for three days."

"I bet." Bull's suitcase gapes open at his feet and the suit he must have been wearing is in a charcoal heap on the laundry-room floor. Coco immediately goes into concierge mode. "I'll unpack your suitcase, separate laundry from dry cleaning, and put your toiletries away," she says. "You should get dressed and join the party. Does Leslee know you're here?"

"Not yet," Bull says. "What am I supposed to wear to this thing?"

"Pink and white," Coco says. She only now processes that Bull is nearly naked in front of her. He's a big guy, so although he has a bit of a belly, he can pull it off; his shoulders are well defined, and he has just a shadow of silver hair across his chest. Ordinarily she might feel uncomfortable being so close to Bull when he's undressed, but he looks so exhausted, she feels sorry for him.

"Would you please help me pick something out?" he says. "I'm color-blind."

"Leslee left your clothes on the bed in case you got here on time," Coco says.

He laughs. "Of course she did." He gives Coco's outfit an assessing eye. "I can't believe she's making you wear a uniform."

"Oh." Coco nearly says, *She told me you were the one who insisted on the uniform.* But it must have been Leslee's idea; she just blamed it on Bull. "She thinks it looks more professional."

He shakes his head. "Would you please get me a bourbon? There's a Pappy thirty in the bar in the library."

"Happy to," Coco says. She didn't notice a bar in the library before; all she remembers are the shelves of books, the seashell fireplace, the escritoire. But behind the desk, Coco finds a tall cabinet, and in the cabinet is a cache of really expensive bourbon: Gentleman Jack, Buffalo Trace, Pappy Van Winkle 13, Pappy 20, Pappy 30. Coco pours two fingers of the Pappy 30 into a crystal highball, then makes her way to the Richardsons' bedroom. She finds Bull in the dressing room wearing Nantucket Reds and a white button-down. He's combed his hair and applied an aftershave that smells peppery.

"Here you go," Coco says, handing him the bourbon.

"You're an angel." Bull downs the entire drink in one swallow and gives Coco the empty glass. "If Leslee ever gives you trouble, if she makes you...*uncomfortable* in any way, I want you to come to me. Do you understand?"

Coco blinks. This isn't the guy she remembers from the Banana Deck; that guy was all bluster and baloney, all *Look at how rich and important I am.* This Bull is stripped down, travel-weary, and way more human. It sounds like he wants to be her ally, which is exactly what Coco hoped for. She wants him to like her, to care about her enough to champion her script. But Coco has learned that in this life, nothing worth having comes easily. This feels too easy.

She nods. "I understand." At that second, her phone buzzes. ICE! Where are u???

"I have to go," Coco says.

"I'll go with you," Bull says.

"I have to get the ice."

"Let me help," Bull says. He follows Coco to the laundry room and together they scoop ice into the crystal buckets. It's a pleasant moment—the ice cubes clink against the glass, there's a smell of detergent and dryer sheets in the air, and it's nice to have help, however unnecessary.

"How was your trip?" Coco asks. "Did everything go okay with the meeting in Jakarta?"

Bull looks up. "Leslee told you?"

Oops, she thinks. She's not sure how to backtrack.

Bull whistles out a breath. "Yeah, it's bad. I have to downplay it for Leslee because she immediately jumps to the worst-case scenario and we're living in a van down by the river." His phone dings. He checks the screen, then sighs. "I've been found out." He sets his shoulders back and says, "How do I look?"

Coco is close enough to pin a boutonniere on him.

"You look very handsome," she says truthfully, patting the front of his shirt.

He eyes her mischievously for a second. "I'm tempted to change into some blue and orange. *That* would make Leslee spit the dummy."

"Yes, it would, mate," Coco says.

Bull chuckles. "You're okay by me, Coco." He disappears down the hall.

Coco takes an ice cube and rubs it against her forehead. Her phone dings: ICE!!!

A spoon chimes against the side of a glass and we gravitate to the pink-and-white-striped tent, where the grazing board has been replaced by a dinner buffet: pyramids of lobster rolls and beef tenderloin sandwiches, platters of fried chicken, a colorful assortment of fresh salads. Standing before the food is Bull Richardson. Where did he come from? Has he been here all along?

He waits for us to quiet, then says, "Leslee and I would like to thank you all for coming to our new home. We look forward to making...well, at least a few summers' worth of memories before this place falls into the sea."

We laugh—the forbidden topic has been addressed. As the sun sets over the water and the waves lap up onto the Richardsons' sugar-cookie beach, as we reach for our second (or third) cocktail or bite into buttery lobster rolls while Sean Lee serenades us with "Pink Houses," even those of us who thought that buying the place was foolish have to admit that, on a night like tonight, it feels priceless.

Fast Eddie has been wondering all evening how he and Addison are going to manage to get a moment with Bull Richardson to discuss the Jackson property without anyone else around (for Eddie, *anyone else* means Grace). But Eddie needn't have worried. Addison Wheeler, whose nickname has long been "Wheeler Dealer," is as smooth as they come. He approaches Grace and Eddie just as they finish eating, puts a hand on Eddie's back, and says to Grace, "Can I borrow your boyfriend for a moment?"

"Of course!" Grace says. A flush the same color as her Laurent-Perrier rosé starts on her cheeks and cascades down her neck into the cleavage displayed by her dress. "I've been wanting to mingle." Grace heads over to the table where the landscape architect Benton Coe is sitting. Normally this would send Eddie into an apoplectic fit of jealousy because of Grace and Benton's long-ago affair, but tonight, this is exactly what he needs. Grace will be occupied long enough for Addison and Eddie to talk to Bull.

There's more good luck—when Bull sees them coming, he excuses himself from a conversation with his boat captain, Lamont Oakley.

"Hello, gentlemen, good to see you," Bull says. They all shake hands and pound backs, and Addison comments on how beautiful the spot is, incomparable, really. Then, wasting no time, Addison goes on to say that Bull obviously recognizes a good business deal when he sees one, which is why he and Eddie are coming to him with an opportunity that recently fell into their laps: six waterfront acres on the southeast shore, the last parcel of its kind, and the owner is fine with dividing it into three lots.

"She's priced the lots ridiculously low," Eddie says. "We were going to advise her to raise the price—"

"But then we thought we'd buy them ourselves, build, flip, and make buckets of money," Addison says. "Now, we could go to the bank—"

"Or I could be the bank?" Bull says. His tone of voice and facial expression are inscrutable and Eddie worries they've come on too strong. But it turns out there's no such thing with the Richardsons, because Bull says, "The idea intrigues me. Let's talk on Monday, shall we? Come up with a plan of attack?"

Yes! Eddie thinks. He practically skips back to the party, where people have started dancing. Eddie finds Grace still at Benton's side.

Eddie says, "Hate to interrupt, but I'd like to dance with my wife."

As Eddie leads Grace on to the dance floor, he says, "What did you and Benton talk about?"

"Oh," Grace says. "Nothing, really. What did you and Addison and Bull talk about?"

"Oh," Eddie says. "Nothing, really."

When Sean Lee slows things down and plays "Wish You Were Here" by Pink Floyd, Romeo asks Sharon to dance. He's been by her side most of the night and she's learned a lot about him. Such as he was in the Merchant Marine for twenty years before coming to Nantucket to work for the Steamship Authority. He's never been married though he does have one son, age twenty-five, who works on one of those fishing boats in Alaska that you see on the reality shows. Sharon is intrigued; everyone in her hometown of New Canaan worked in tech, VC, or private equity. It's arousing to talk to a man who knows about engines and water draw and weather patterns. He considers himself an amateur psychologist—half the battle of loading and unloading cars from the Steamship is dealing with the personalities behind the wheels.

Romeo is also an entrepreneur; he owns a whale-watching charter business up in Provincetown. It has made him enough money that he was able to buy his own twenty-two-foot Grady-White.

"It's nothing like that sexy beast," he says, pointing to the Richardsons' speedboat, *Decadence,* which has been hiding behind *Hedonism.* "But I'd love to take you out for a boat day sometime."

"Anytime!" Sharon says. "I'm free as a bird this summer."

Romeo spins her around—on top of all his other charms, he's a skilled dancer—and Sharon is left literally and figuratively breathless.

When Lee finishes the song, he says, "That's a wrap for me for tonight, folks. The Richardsons would like everyone to enter the door of the summer porch and head upstairs to the party room for dessert and dancing."

A murmur ripples through the crowd as we gather our things; it's time to see the inside of Triple Eight.

Sharon is tempted to whip out her phone and take a video for TikTok, but she won't be that person. (Someone who *is* that person, however, is Dr. Andy's wife, Rachel. She has her phone out and is narrating: "A rare peek inside Triple Eight Pocomo.") Sharon and Romeo move around Rachel, enter the octagonal screened-in porch, go down a hallway with a black-and-white floor, and walk up one side of a grand double staircase.

The party room is bathed in pink light. Glass canisters filled with pink candy are lined up along the Lucite bar. There's a pink-chocolate fountain with strawberries for dipping, and servers pass cones of pink cotton candy.

Sharon notices there are fewer guests; the people still here are those who like to have fun. DJ Billy Voss has set up in the corner and he's brought his drummer, Joe, with him; Joe will play along with every song, making it feel like there's a live band in the room. The first song is "Crazy in Love," and all the women—and Romeo—hit the dance floor. Sharon loves that Romeo is secure enough in his masculinity to dance to Beyoncé.

Just then, Sharon's watch sounds an alert. It's her Dexcom app, which monitors her son Robert's glucose levels. Robert's blood sugar is spiking.

No! Sharon thinks. Robert is, unfortunately, spending the night at

Baxter Morse's house, and although Robert knows better, he's probably had not only soda but candy. Baxter's mother, Celadon, keeps baskets of Snickers and Twix around the house as though every day is Halloween.

Sharon sends Robert a text: Your sugar! He may have to give himself an insulin shot, something he hates doing.

"I have to call my son!" Sharon shouts to Romeo over the music. She twirls her finger. "I'll be right back!"

Romeo follows Sharon outside to the octagonal deck. It's quiet here, and cool, with a breeze coming in off the water. There's a crescent moon in the sky. It would be the most romantic spot on earth if Sharon's son weren't in the middle of an urgent health situation.

When she calls Robert, it goes straight to voice mail. Next, she calls Celadon. Voice mail. Robert's blood sugar is at 280; Sharon won't be able to relax until she talks to him.

"I'm afraid I have to go," she tells Romeo. "My son has type one diabetes, he's at a sleepover, his blood sugar is through the roof—"

"I'll go with you," Romeo says. "Let me drive. I'll take you wherever you need to go."

Sharon knows she should decline this offer. Surely Romeo wants to stay—this is the party of the summer and it's just getting started! But he looks at her earnestly, and before she can say, *It's fine, I'll go alone,* he's made a decision. "We're leaving right now."

On the other side of the deck, Sharon sees Kacy Kapenash, Lamont Oakley, and that girl, Coco, who works for the Richardsons. Sharon approaches them and tells Coco, "Would you please tell the Richardsons that Sharon and Romeo had to leave but that we loved every second of this grand soirée and we're so grateful to have been included."

"I'll tell them," Coco says. "And don't worry. There will be a *lot* of parties this summer."

* * *

A few of us notice Sharon and Romeo leaving and we think, *Sharon, what are you doing? The best is yet to come!* Sharon bumps into Rachel McMann on the stairs and explains about Robert's blood sugar. Of course we understand, and we think how sweet it is that Romeo is going with her. We've never thought of him as a lover before—but then again, his name *is* Romeo.

When DJ Billy Voss plays "Hot in Herre," Leslee makes her entrance. She's wearing a new outfit: a skintight metallic-pink jumpsuit and a pink wig. We all scream our delight, then notice Leslee's personal concierge, Coco, handing out pink wigs. In the next moment, Coco steps behind the bar and starts mixing up shots of something called tickled pink. Those of us who throw the shots back wonder if there's something in them other than alcohol because suddenly we're at an eleven on the dance floor. "Stacy's Mom" comes on, and Busy Ambrose, the Field and Oar's commodore and one of the most staid and proper women we know, is in the center of the dance floor, pink wig atop her matronly bob, shaking her booty because she has a daughter named Stacy and she has always secretly believed this song to be about her.

Fast Eddie throws back not one but two tickled pink shots and he doesn't protest when Grace fits a pink wig over his head, not even when he sees Rachel McMann taking videos of everyone on the dance floor. Eddie and Grace sing out to Icona Pop, *"I don't care! I love it!"* They're pogoing around like a couple of crazy kids in a mosh pit. This is exactly what their marriage needed and they didn't even know it.

The Chief lets Andrea pull him onto the dance floor when Billy Voss switches to an '80s medley, though he turns down the offer of a tickled pink shot (he's the chief of police, after all) and he will not wear a wig. Addison is wearing a wig; he's always been the life of the party. Jeffrey, however, is stuck to the curvy white sofa like a straight pin in a cushion; he's drinking ice water and probably thinking of how he has to get up in six hours and tend the fields. Phoebe is smack in the middle of the dance floor, her long pink wig swaying as she dances with Leslee Richardson. The Chief blinks—Phoebe is wearing a new outfit as well, a white leather minidress. When did she change? Billy Voss plays "American Girl" by Tom Petty. Phoebe and Leslee shriek and throw their arms around each other. Another woman in a pink wig—the Chief belatedly realizes it's Delilah— storms off the dance floor. Or maybe she needs the ladies' room.

Delilah rips off her wig and tosses it down the stairwell. Her head instantly cools (wigs aren't meant for people with as much hair as she has) but her temper is still blazing. She slams into the Richardsons' powder room, irate at how fabulous it is (dove-gray wallpaper patterned with pussy willows; a silver glass column sink that glows from within), and collapses on the toilet.

She's drunk, yes, but that's not the problem. The problem is that Phoebe has become Leslee Richardson's... *groupie!* At dinner, Delilah, Andrea, and Phoebe were looking for a place to sit, but then Phoebe peeled off and took the open seat next to Leslee. When everyone else went upstairs to the party room to dance, Leslee invited Phoebe—and only Phoebe—downstairs to the primary suite to, she said, "change." When Phoebe reappeared, she was wearing a dress she'd borrowed from Leslee and she stank of weed.

"Were you *smoking* down there?" Delilah sounded judgy, but in reality, she was jealous.

Phoebe giggled and followed Leslee onto the dance floor.

Then "American Girl" came on, and, while it might sound juvenile, that had long been Phoebe and Delilah's song. Delilah went looking for Phoebe so they could dance and found her basically making out with Leslee.

As Delilah sits on the toilet with her face in her hands, there's a knock on the door. She hears Jeffrey say, "Delilah, let's just go home."

But Delilah doesn't want to go home. This is, hands down, the best party she's ever been to.

She exits the powder room, sidesteps Jeffrey, says, "Let's stay for one more quick drink, babe," and heads to the bar. Coco is nowhere to be found, so Delilah fills a rocks glass with club soda. She pours the entire thing into the pot holding a pink-and-white orchid in the dining room. It's a silent revenge; the worst thing you can do to orchids is overwater them. Delilah feels a little better.

"Okay," she says when she finds Jeffrey morosely skulking in the doorway, watching Dr. Andy and Rachel McMann bump and grind. "We can go."

Billy Voss ends his set at one in the morning with "Last Dance" by Donna Summer.

The room is still pretty full and Coco is impressed — these old people can hang! — though she's relieved it's over. Everyone will go home now, right?

She's a little confused because there are still delicious aromas coming from the kitchen, Zoe Alistair's staff are somehow still here, and at that moment, a gentleman in a tuxedo comes walking up the stairs. His hair is slicked back; he has blue eyes.

"Party room?" he asks.

"Who are you?" Coco asks.

"Frank Sinatra," he says.

The Chief and Andrea are back out on the dance floor swaying to "You Make Me Feel So Young." The Chief realizes he must be either dreaming or drunk because it appears to be Frank Sinatra who's singing. Ol' Blue Eyes! He's not only still alive, he's here at Triple Eight!

Whose idea is it to go skinny-dipping? Some might say it's a natural next step. The after-party singer finishes; the caterers pass around cheeseburger sliders and paper cones of hot, crispy French fries that we scarf down like we're drunk high-schoolers at the McDonald's drive-through.

It's nearly three in the morning. Coco has been on the clock for nineteen hours and this, she decides, is enough. She follows every-one else down the stairs and out the doors of the screened-in porch. People are stripping off their clothes all over the lawn, and because Coco is still in concierge mode, she pulls a stack of beach towels from the porch closet.

She reaches the beach in time to see Leslee, naked, dive into the water, followed by her new sidekick, Phoebe, also naked. Eddie the real estate dude is there; he goes into the water in his boxers, but his wife goes in naked, and so does Benton Coe the landscaper, still in his pink wig. Coco averts her eyes.

Kacy comes up behind her. "Come on, let's go in." She's fiddling with the side zip of her dress.

Coco was already planning on it. She shucks off her polo and her shorts—it feels good to be out of her uniform—then her bra and her underwear, and she and Kacy charge into the water. This is far from the first time Coco has gone skinny-dipping—it was a full-moon tradition at Hawksnest Beach on St. John—but it's the first time she's done it sober. The water shocks her weary brain and bones into alertness, clarity. The crescent moon vamps above them.

"Thanks for everything tonight," Coco says. Kacy had helped clear the abandoned drinks; she collected the crumpled napkins, replen-ished the strawberries for the chocolate fountain, and fetched more tequila for the tickled pink shots. She took a selfie of the two of them on the deck with the Richardsons' yacht behind them and one of the two of them in the kitchen stuffing leftover lobster rolls into their mouths.

"I can't believe how crazy this party is," Kacy says. "Leslee is Her."

Coco understands how Kacy might think that, especially after Leslee reentered the party in her second outfit of the evening, a jumpsuit so tight you could see her religion.

Kacy gazes over at the other guests, who are swimming at the opposite end of the beach. "But ugh...I did not need undeniable proof that Addison has a flat ass."

Coco laughs and floats on her back, nipples pointing to the sky. *This is how people drown,* she thinks. Swimming when they're as tired as she is.

There's a disturbance in the water and Coco freezes, thinking it's a fish (or a shark!). A head breaks through the surface right next to her and she shrieks.

It's Lamont.

He laughs. Coco splashes him, and soon they're tussling. He grabs her ankle and pulls her under; she surfaces and jumps on his back and—what possesses her?—nibbles on his ear. He responds by reaching around underwater and grabbing her ass cheek (out of Kacy's line of sight), and Coco feels a surge of desire. She wraps her thighs around him. If Kacy weren't here, they would start making out. Coco would stroke his erection and get him up to her apartment as fast as she could. She doesn't care about Leslee's stupid rule.

How, she wonders, *can they get rid of Kacy?* Will Kacy pick up on the nature of their roughhousing and head for shore? She will not. When Coco turns, she sees Kacy only a few feet away, treading water.

Shit, Coco thinks. Whenever she bumps into Lamont around the Richardson compound, he's polite and friendly but nothing more.

147

Leslee has clearly given him the lecture: No dating the other staff member or you'll both be replaced *like that*. Snap. But right now they have a chance to sneaky-link. Who knows when another opportunity like this will come along?

A voice cuts through the inky air. "Lamont!"

Coco looks in the direction of the voice and sees Leslee in all her daily yoga-practice perfection on the bow of *Hedonism,* windmilling an arm. *Leslee is Her,* Coco thinks unhappily.

Lamont loosens his grip on Coco, dumping her back into the water. He starts swimming toward the boat. "Have a good night, ladies."

The Chief is still dancing to Frank Sinatra, who's currently singing "The Way You Look Tonight." This is the song he and Andrea danced to at their wedding. Andrea comes from a large Italian family; her uncles had approved. In the next instant, Frank Sinatra has changed his outfit (that seems to be a trend tonight). Instead of a black tuxedo, he's now wearing a *pink velvet* tuxedo. Ed is about to ask Andrea if she noticed this—except it isn't Andrea he's dancing with, it's Leslee Richardson.

The Chief startles awake. He's lying on the curvy white sofa in the Richardsons' party room. Andrea is next to him. The Chief looks around—everyone else is naked, or nearly so. What is going *on*? Addison wears only a towel; Phoebe is snoring under a throw blanket. Eddie Pancik is wearing boxer shorts and a pink wig. Busy Ambrose from the Field and Oar Club is lying on the floor, her head on a turquoise pillow. She isn't wearing a stitch of clothing—and neither are Dr. Andy and Rachel McMann. (The Chief can't unsee a naked Dr. Andy; he may have to change dentists.)

There's pearly light coming through the windows; the birds are singing. Ed checks his phone; the battery is at 3 percent, but there are no missed calls, no texts. There were apparently no party-related crimes or misdemeanors last night, which is a darn good thing since the Chief was dead to the world and couldn't have responded. It's a quarter past four in the morning. His head aches.

Gently, he nudges Andrea. Her eyelids flutter open and she too gazes around the room like she can't believe what she's seeing. Was there some kind of orgy that they missed—or (god forbid) took part in?

Delilah and Jeffrey are nowhere to be found; they probably acted like responsible adults and left when people started taking their clothes off. Ed gets to his feet. He considers waking Addison but decides it's better to make a clean getaway.

He offers Andrea his hand. "Let's go," he whispers. "Party's over."

15. Thursday, August 22, 9:15 P.M.

A welcome breeze has cleared some of the smoke from the air; Stu Vick and his team are investigating the fire site. Zara strides over to where the Chief is standing with his daughter, Kacy, and Lamont Oakley.

She offers a hand to Kacy. "I'm Chief Washington," she says, hitting the word *Chief* hard for Ed's benefit. "I'm sorry about your friend. We're going to find her. Right now we need to ask Lamont some questions."

"Yeah, of course, okay," Kacy says. She sinks down onto the low granite wall that encircles the garden. "I'm going to keep calling her."

Ed takes an intentional breath. Kacy no doubt realizes now that

Coco missing is a thing, it is real, they are not watching a movie, this is happening. He once attended a seminar about missing persons and learned that, in some ways, it's more challenging for people to grapple with loved ones' disappearances than their deaths. *Missing* causes one to feel equal parts despondent and hopeful. It nags: *What happened? Where is she?* The mind craves an answer. *Missing* is a special hell—and *missing at sea* feels worse than just *missing.*

Ed squeezes his daughter's shoulder. "We'll just be a minute," he tells her.

Zara and Ed settle with Lamont on a wooden bench in the middle of a circle of hydrangea bushes, which affords them all a bit of privacy. "Walk us through the evening," Ed says. "How did Coco seem?"

"Normal?" Lamont says. "She was working, she wore her uniform, she served the welcome cocktails, she served the hors d'oeuvres. I didn't really pay attention; I was sailing the boat. I normally have two crew members, Javier and Esteban, but it was their abuela's birthday so they weren't working. I had no problem handling the boat alone but I needed to give it my full attention."

"When was the last time you remember seeing Coco?" Zara asks.

"She passed around the champagne right after Leslee and Bull did their vow renewal."

"Did you know about the vow renewal?"

"I did," Lamont says. "But it was a surprise for the guests."

"Coco knew about it?"

"Yes," Lamont says.

"Can you run through the timeline from there?" Zara asks.

"Bull and Leslee renewed their vows just as the sun was setting," Lamont says. "Leslee was very particular about the angle of the sun and how they'd look in pictures. They did the vows themselves, without an officiant—they just read some stuff that they'd asked Coco to pull off the internet."

"Romantic," Zara says.

"Was Coco present during the renewal of the vows?" the Chief asks.

"Yes." Lamont pauses. "She was standing next to me in the cockpit."

"So after the Richardsons renewed their vows…"

"Coco passed around glasses of champagne, we all toasted Bull and Leslee, then Coco collected the glasses."

"Was Coco drinking at all?"

"No, she never drinks on the job. She never eats either. She's always conscientious about that."

No alcohol is good news, Ed thinks. If she didn't eat or drink then she probably wasn't drugged either intentionally or accidentally. But they can't rule it out.

"And then what happened?"

"I turned the boat around and we headed back."

"When did you hear about the fire?"

Lamont's eyes, Zara notices, are red from the smoke or from emotion. "Are they out there looking for her now? Is the Coast Guard looking for her right this second?"

"Yes," Ed says. "Lucy has two boats out and she's asking for a helicopter from Woods Hole." He pauses. "They'll find her."

Zara doubles down. "Lamont, this is very important. We need to know where Coco was when news of the fire broke. We need to know who the last person to see her was." Zara pauses and softens her tone. "Was it you?"

"Doubtful," he says. "She was cleaning up, coming and going. There were guests everywhere. I lost track of her."

"Another guest told us she saw Coco clearing champagne glasses right before they heard about the fire," Zara says. "Was Coco still on the boat when that news broke?"

"I assume so, though it was chaos. Bull ordered me to lower the sails and motor back to Pocomo. I wasn't thinking about where Coco was." He takes a breath to say more, then stops.

"What is it?" Zara says.

"Nothing," he says. "Not important."

"We understand Bull Richardson was on the bow when he heard about the fire," Zara says.

"Yes."

"Where was Leslee Richardson?"

"I don't remember," Lamont says. "Bull was calling for Leslee, so she must have been somewhere else on the boat."

"Below deck?" Zara asks. "On the stern?"

"She might have been using the head?" Lamont says. "I have no idea. Their house was on fire, I needed to get back to Pocomo, that was my focus. I wasn't thinking about anything else. I figured Coco was down in the galley washing glasses or maybe helping Bull locate Leslee. Coco had a lot of responsibilities." He shakes his head. "It never occurred to me, not for one second, that she'd gone overboard. She'd been on the boat plenty of times; she was sure-footed. The only thing…"

"Yes?" Zara says.

"There's a spot in the back of the boat where people can dive off, and there's a swim ladder. That area is secured by a gate, and the latch of the gate doesn't work properly. It closes, but not firmly with a click. I ordered a new part but it hadn't arrived, and when I told Bull and Leslee that, they said not to worry about it, just go ahead with the sail."

"Ah," the Chief says. He's surprised the Coast Guard didn't mention this, but then again, they were looking for the girl, not inspecting the safety of the boat.

"So possibly Coco fell," Zara says. "Can she swim?"

"Yes," Lamont says. "She's a strong swimmer. That's the only reason I'm even halfway sane right now. She can swim."

Lamont reminds Zara of one of her nephews. He's clean-cut and earnest—but Zara herself is the mother of two and she gets the distinct feeling Lamont is holding something back.

"Is there something else you want to say, son?"

Lamont looks from Zara to the Chief. "You're questioning the Richardsons, right?"

16. Morning Buns

Talk of the Richardsons' Pink and White Party is everywhere. Baxter Morse's mother, Celadon, is dying for the details. She bumps into Dr. Andy and Rachel McMann at Tupancy Links while they're walking their dogs and Rachel shows Celadon the videos she took: "Here are the pink cocktails, here's the crowd on the dance floor wearing pink wigs, here's the Frank Sinatra tribute band at the after-party, here's a blurry one of everybody skinny-dipping at the Richardsons' private beach under a crescent moon."

The videos, Celadon thinks, do not disappoint.

The Richardsons instantly become the island's sweethearts. They routinely double-book at restaurants, reserving tables at both Ventuno and Lola 41 for eight p.m. on a Friday and then deciding at the last minute which they'd prefer, which is a huge no-no that would normally result in a couple being placed on the naughty list—but the Richardsons are forgiven. When we see them out on the town, we jockey to introduce ourselves and explain our relevance: Megan manages the ERF boutique in town; would Leslee like a private shopping experience, and can Megan gift her a few items? Thaoi delivers for UPS; have Leslee's packages been arriving on time? The Winslows are summer residents from the Main Line—would Bull and Leslee like to join them at their home on Eel Point Road for cocktails?

As the commodore and chairperson of the membership commit-tee at the Field and Oar Club, Busy Ambrose receives the nominat-ing letter for the Richardsons from Phoebe Wheeler. Busy decides to write a seconding letter herself. She's certain the Richardsons will have no problem finding three other members to write letters, and maybe as soon as the August vote, they can admit the Richardsons to the Field and Oar. It will be such a coup, snapping them up before any other club does.

Fast Eddie is thrilled when Bull Richardson emails him and Addi-son on Monday afternoon and invites them out to Triple Eight for a breakfast meeting the next morning so they can discuss the poten-tial of the Jackson lots. Eddie and Addison decide it would be best to drive together, present a united front, yada yada, so Addison swings by in his Aston Martin convertible to pick Eddie up. As they cruise out the Polpis Road, they talk about what kind of cut they should offer Bull. A significant one, they decide, since he's fronting the money. All Eddie can think is: *This deal could change my life.* If it works out, he'll be back on top. He and his wife could finally move out of the tiny cottage on Lily Street (which was all they could afford after Eddie's disgrace) and buy a waterfront property similar to the one they lost. He wonders what Addison dreams of. Addison already has a pile of money, a beautiful home, and a lovely family. He's in this deal only for the sport of it, Eddie suspects, and

Eddie tries to convey the same kind of sexy indifference. What has he learned? The person who needs the least will always have the power.

When Addison pulls into the long white-shell driveway of Triple Eight, Eddie can't help but flash back to Saturday night. He has clear recollections of cocktails, dinner, and dancing to DJ Billy Voss and drummer Joe; he even remembers throwing back the pink shots and donning the pink wig. After that, things get hazy. According to Grace, there was a Frank Sinatra impersonator and trays of cheeseburgers, and Eddie vaguely remembers tipping a paper cone of French fries down his gullet, but how that led to him waking up in the Richardsons' living room in a soaking-wet pair of boxer shorts with Grace buck naked beside him is something of a mystery.

"Skinny-dipping," Grace told him. "We all went skinny-dipping — don't you remember?"

Does he?

The Richardsons' house, which only three days earlier was the site of a debauchery this island had never before seen, is now giving clean-and-sober weekday-morning vibes. The sprinklers are gently misting the pink hydrangea bushes, and Eddie sees one of Benton Coe's landscaping trucks parked in front of the garage. There's some kind of garden installation going in. Eddie is relieved Benton's personal truck isn't here; he's the last person Eddie wants to see on any given day, but especially after Saturday night. When Eddie asked Grace who, exactly, went skinny-dipping, she said, "You and me, Leslee Richardson, Addison, Phoebe, Benton, and some of the kids, I think."

"Benton?" Eddie said, and Grace mmm-hmmed as though seeing Benton naked was no big deal. *Well,* Eddie thought, *it was nothing she hadn't seen before.*

Eddie hasn't mentioned the skinny-dipping or the party in

general to Addison because, frankly, Eddie feels a bit ashamed that he was part of it. He remembers Rachel McMann taking videos of them on the dance floor; he should have insisted that Rachel delete them. Grace would no doubt tell Eddie he's being paranoid; everyone they know was at the party, including Ed Kapenash, the chief of police! Grace views their invitation as a badge of honor. Eddie overheard Grace talking about the party with their daughter, Allegra, on Sunday afternoon. "We didn't get home until five in the morning and I was missing a shoe! Yes, I'm serious!" Grace sounded delighted with herself.

Bull answers the door looking fresh and clean-shaven with a hearty "G'day!" He leads Eddie and Addison upstairs to the kitchen, which smells richly of coffee. On the counter is a colorful fruit salad and a platter of morning buns from Wicked Island Bakery.

"Help yourself to breakfast, gentlemen," Bull says. "Would anyone like a coffee?"

"I'd love one," Addison says. "Black, please."

"Eddie?"

Eddie normally takes his coffee very light and very sweet—Grace teases him that it's more dessert than coffee—but he senses this will telegraph fussiness. "Yes, please," he says. "Black." He loads up a white café plate with a generous scoop of the fruit salad—it includes ripe mangoes and huge, juicy blackberries—and a cinnamony, buttery morning bun.

"Please eat!" Bull says, though Bull takes nothing and Addison pats his midsection and says, "One morning bun would negate the PR I had this morning on the Peloton."

"Ah! I did a ride with Cody this morning," Bull says. "Leslee thinks I have a crush on him."

"You do you, Boo," Addison says, and they both laugh and Eddie holds his plate of food feeling like an idiot because he isn't in on the Pelo-speak and why is he the only one eating? He's failed some sort of test by showing his working-class background—when food is offered, Eddie eats. This is clearly one of those instances where the food is a prop. The buns and the elite fruit salad are here so Bull can check the box marked *breakfast meeting,* but neither he nor Addison actually eats because they both know better.

They head down to Bull's study. Addison points to the shelf of Patrick O'Brian novels. "He's a terrific author."

Eddie, who hasn't read a book for pleasure since his Encyclopedia Brown days, shoves the entire morning bun in his mouth.

"Ah, yeah?" Bull says. "Wouldn't know. Those were here when we moved in."

Bull sits behind his desk; Addison and Eddie take the leather chairs. In the car, they agreed that Addison should be the one to pitch.

"We can buy the three lots for nine million," Addison says. "Then, through the relationships Eddie and I have with local design-and-build firms, we can create three unique and dazzling estates for about four million apiece, and when they're finished we'll list them at fifteen million apiece, for a profit of approximately twenty-four million."

"Fifteen million seems low for a waterfront property," Bull says. "After all, I paid twenty-two million for this place."

Well, Bull, Eddie thinks, *you overpaid.* The house had been sitting on the market since November of 2019 for a reason. Rising harbor aside, the place just isn't worth twenty-two mil. The bones are old, there has been no structural work done since the eighties, and it isn't winterized; once temperatures start to drop, the house will have to be drained and put into hibernation mode until next spring. There's no pool and no proper guesthouse, only the garage with the apartment above. The sellers were two adult children who'd inherited the house and wanted nothing to do with the island. They were content to wait until they got their price; they seemed confident someone would offer the full amount, though Eddie begged them to lower their asking price to twenty or, even better, nineteen. But they were right in the end. Eddie couldn't believe it when Addison said he had a couple not only willing but eager to pay as long as they could close in thirty days and enjoy the house for the summer.

The wife loved the party room, Addison said. Had to have it.

Eddie says, "You bought the most fascinating property on the island."

"Classier than One Ocean Avenue," Addison chimes in. "Statelier than Seventy-Five Main Street."

Neither of these things is true, but Eddie watches Bull nod in satisfied agreement.

"We're calculating at fifteen million to be safe," Eddie says. "We may list at twenty."

"And you're positive construction costs won't run over?" Bull says.

"Our relationships with the contractors are rock solid," Addison says. "That's where we add value. We'll get the fairest bids, and the projects will be done on time."

Addison sounds confident but Eddie knows that every construction project on this island runs over in both money and time. The wrong custom tile is ordered for one of the seven bathrooms; the light fixtures have a six-month lead time; the automatic pool cover breaks; the only guy who does granite countertops on the island is notoriously impossible to get hold of. Eddie emits a soft cinnamon burp; his heartburn is flaring up. Now that he's back in the real estate development game, he supposes he'll start popping cherry Tums again.

"So you'd like me to front the twenty-one million?" Bull says. "Why wouldn't you go to a bank?"

One reason, which Eddie is not eager to disclose, is that after what happened nine years ago, no bank will lend to him. And Addison confided he's not okay with taking on twenty-one million in debt by himself. "It all comes down to timing," Eddie says. "Banks take forever, and the paperwork for construction loans is byzantine. We'd like to move quickly on this. Close on the properties as soon as possible, break ground in early fall, finish by May first, and sell on May second, if not before."

"Eddie and I have a long list of rental clients who will be bidding against one another to get their hands on these properties," Addison says.

"Brilliant," Bull says. "I love a gamble, and I'm not going to lie, fellas, I need a win. Gotta keep the wife happy. So I front the cash, you two work your magic, and we split the profit three ways."

Addison clears his throat. "Is that what you envision? A third for each of us?"

"What else would we do?" Bull asks.

"That's precisely what we were thinking as well," Eddie says, though this isn't at all true. They were hoping Bull would agree to 40 percent while they each took 30, although they decided they would entertain the idea of him taking 50 percent while they each took 25. But Bull sees their value as equal to his, even though they aren't investing a dime of their own money. "A third for each of us."

Handshakes all around. Bull suggests that Eddie and Addison choose the attorney, whoever they feel most comfortable with.

"Val Gluckstern," Addison says. "She's the best."

When Bull walks them out to the driveway, Eddie can't help asking about the landscaping project.

"Leslee wants a round, hedged-in garden for the octagonal hot tub she's custom-ordered. Benton Coe is doing the work."

Eddie takes a breath. He nearly says, *I'd watch Benton Coe around your wife. Take it from someone who knows.* But no, Eddie won't get into it. He needs to let go of the past, especially now that his future is looking so bright.

Kacy wakes up to a text from Isla: Good morning, Bun. I miss you.

Part of Kacy swoons; another part is furious. Isla can miss Kacy all she wants but it means nothing until she leaves Rondo.

Kacy scrolls through her phone to the pictures from Saturday night and finds a selfie of her and Coco. The picture is good; their faces are side by side, Kacy's glass of champagne is in the frame, and the sun hits Coco in a way that makes her blue eyes pop.

Don't do it, she thinks. It isn't fair to Coco.

But Coco seems pretty into Lamont, and if Kacy asked Coco if she could use the pictures to make Isla jealous, Coco would probably say yes. (Kacy would never ask; it would be too mortifying.)

She sends the photo.

Even though it's three in the morning in San Francisco, there's an immediate response from Isla.

Are you two together?

Kacy decides not to respond.

Another text comes in: I want to jump on a plane right now.

Please forgive me, Coco, Kacy thinks. *This is working.*

17. Amalfi Lemons

In the days following the Pink and White Party, Coco expects life at Triple Eight to quiet down, but she's busier than ever.

One of her duties, which wasn't mentioned earlier, is applauding Leslee as she congratulates herself.

"I heard multiple people saying that Saturday night was the best party they'd ever been to. Like, in their *lives,*" Leslee says.

"Everyone had a great time," Coco says.

"Rachel McMann, the dentist's wife, is leaking all kinds of videos," Leslee says. "You know what that gets her?"

"Followers?" Coco says.

"Blackballed," Leslee says. "Bull and I loathe social media. We prefer to experience our lives in person."

Right. Coco checked for both Bull and Leslee online and came up empty, which she finds strange. Leslee loves attention and could easily cultivate a devoted following on Instagram in the aspirational-lifestyle space. Coco nearly mentions this—but why feed the beast?

"Lots of people reached out to thank me," Leslee says. "And I'm keeping track of the ones who didn't. I haven't heard from the Kapenashes. I haven't heard from Delilah Drake, but that tracks because I'm pretty sure she hates my guts. I haven't heard from Blond Sharon." Leslee pauses. "She's apparently a vicious gossip. I need to know what she thought."

Blond Sharon? Coco thinks. *That's a person's name?* Then she remembers. "Oh, she and the Steamship guy had to leave during the dancing. She said she had some kind of emergency at home, but she made a point of telling me she had a fabulous time."

Leslee winds her long dark hair around her wrist and forearm. Coco has learned this is a nervous tic, but it's actually kind of fetching, so much so that Coco is considering growing her hair out.

"Someone killed my Rothschild's slipper orchid," Leslee says. "It was fine before the party, and the morning after I found it wilted."

"Maybe it drank too much," Coco says.

Leslee offers a vague smile. "Do you think the skinny-dipping took things a step too far?"

"That was the best part," Coco says. And it was, right up to the moment Lamont swam away.

"Oh, yes," Leslee says. "I thought so too."

Coco's other tasks are more straightforward but also more frustrating. The first pages of her Moleskine notebook are filled with lists, notes, and instructions; she also keeps a detailed log of her productivity in case Leslee ever asks her to account for her time. On Monday afternoon, Leslee informs Coco that Bull is hosting a breakfast meeting the next day and he'd like coffee, a fruit salad, and a dozen morning buns from Wicked Island Bakery.

"He likes mango in his fruit salad," Leslee says. "We had it every day on St. John."

Right, because St. John is a *tropical island* where mangoes grow on *trees,* Coco thinks. On Nantucket, thirty miles out in the Atlantic, she has to go to four places before she finds a mango that isn't as hard as a rock. However, the mango is a breeze compared to the morning buns.

To get the morning buns, Coco has to rise at five thirty in order to be standing in line at six when the bakery opens, and then she learns the limit per customer is six, and no amount of bribery (Coco offered to pay double; she offered a hundred-dollar bill) can persuade the girl behind the counter to give her a dozen.

In the end, this doesn't matter. The breakfast goes largely uneaten.

On Tuesday night, Kacy texts Coco that Eric had a fishing charter cancel for the following day and he has offered to take Kacy and Coco out on the boat. Coco says: I wish I could but I'm too busy. Kacy texts back: How do two people create so much work?

Coco wonders this as well. On Wednesday morning, she provisions for the household. She buys steak tips and salmon fillets from the Nantucket Meat and Fish Market, then heads down the street to Pip and Anchor for a wedge of Savage cheese (sourced from the von Trapp family farm in Vermont) and a certain organic rosé that Leslee likes. Coco selects tomatoes, lettuce, and herbs from Bartlett's Farm. ("Don't you want to use Sea View Farm?" she asked Leslee. "The owners, Jeffrey and Delilah, were at your party." "Go to Bartlett's, please," Leslee said. "As I mentioned, Delilah never thanked me.") Next it's off to 167 Raw for bluefish pâté, jumbo shrimp, and a key lime pie. Then Coco heads into town—where finding parking is like an episode of *Dude, You're Screwed*—to procure a loaf of sourdough, sliced thin, from Born and Bread. Leslee has requested a growler of Wandering Haze IPA from Cisco Brewers as well as Tanqueray and a bottle of Flor de Caña 18 rum (something else Bull developed a taste for in St. John) from Nantucket Wine and Spirits. Coco rounds out her errands with a trip to the mid-island Stop and Shop (with her cart and her list, she thinks, *It's official—I'm a mom*) and a visit to Dan's Pharmacy, where she picks up prescriptions for Leslee (Ambien, Ativan) and Bull (Viagra, *eww*).

Coco is about to text Kacy: Today I ran all over hell's half acre. She realizes she sounds like her mother, deletes this, and writes, Provisioning today required nine different stops! Surely Kacy will think this is hyperbole. It's not.

When Coco arrives back at Triple Eight with all the goods, she groans: There's a package waiting by the front door. The UPS and FedEx trucks pull in several times a day (setting off the alarm both coming and going; the chimes are starting to trigger headaches), and Coco is responsible for opening the packages, saving the return slips, and breaking down the boxes. She layers them in the back of Baby like some kind of cardboard mille-feuille awaiting her next trip to the dump out in Madaket, twenty-five minutes away.

Most of the packages are clothes for Leslee from places like Cult Gaia, Rat and Boa, Retrofête. Others are linens and home goods, some from Serena and Lily, some from Ban Ban Studio in LA. But this box, she sees, has been shipped from Italy. It's marked PERISH-ABLE. Coco imagines a craggy chunk of Parmesan, a loop of exotic salume, a whole black truffle. But once Coco gets the box—along with all her other bags and packages—upstairs, she slices through the top and finds a wooden crate filled with straw and, nestled within the straw, a dozen *limoni*. Lemons.

"My Amalfi lemons!" Leslee cries. She lifts one out of the box with cupped hands as though it's a baby chick. She holds it out for Coco to see, to smell. It's the roundest, most fragrant lemon Coco has ever seen or smelled. It's a lemon worthy of a van Gogh painting. Each lemon is swaddled in a little white jacket.

"These are the best lemons in the world," Leslee says. "The most flavorful. The juiciest."

"Will you use them in a recipe?" Coco asks, though she has yet to see Leslee cook. The provisioning and specialty ingredients are all for Bull—he'll grill up the steak tips for lunch, cut the salmon into tartare for a late-afternoon snack. Leslee eats sourdough toast, some-times with a slice of tomato on top, sometimes with the Savage cheese from Pip and Anchor. Bull and Leslee go out for dinner every single night. But maybe the arrival of the Amalfi lemons warrants an evening at home—a scampi with the shrimp Coco bought, perhaps?

"They're to display," Leslee says. She disrobes the lemons, places them artfully in a white ceramic bowl, and sets the bowl on the kitchen island.

Coco checks the packing slip. One dozen Amalfi lemons cost Leslee two hundred and twenty-four euros, plus sixty euros in shipping. Two hundred and eighty-four euros for lemons that—if Coco has to guess—will sit in that bowl until they soften and grow spots of green mold.

This gives Coco pause. She thinks of her mother, Georgi, slicing Black Forest ham behind the deli counter at Harps. Georgi's job is not glamorous, but at least it has a purpose. Then Coco thinks of schoolteachers, police officers, brain surgeons, fishermen, accounts receivable staff, customer-service reps, public defenders, third-shift factory workers, and bus drivers. What would they make of a woman who spends two hundred and eighty-four euros on lemons just because they look pretty on the counter? Coco has often been appalled by the waste in this house—Leslee wants things just to have them; most of the food never gets eaten, half the outfits never get worn—but this is the first time Coco wants to speak up.

But…she has become seduced by the luxuries of her new life— waking up in her king bed, driving Baby down the Polpis Road, ordering lobster salad sandwiches from Something Natural. Instead of making a big deal about the lemons, she decides, she will express her disapproval by leaving the kitchen without putting the groceries away. Leslee has two hands; she can do it.

Coco says, "I'll take these prescriptions down to your bathroom."

Leslee isn't listening. She's too busy fondling her lemons.

Downstairs, before she puts away the prescriptions, Coco pops into the library, which has become her refuge. She finished *A Spark of*

Light by Jodi Picoult last night and is ready for something new. She pulls out *Pachinko* by Min Jin Lee, which she has long wanted to read.

As she's heading down the hall to the primary suite, she hears Bull shouting. Coco nearly drops the book and the bag of pills.

"We should goddamned well be grandfathered in!" This is followed by more profanity—and then what sounds like Bull's phone hitting the wall.

Coco hesitates, terrified that Bull is going to storm out of his office and realize she heard him. But she's where she's supposed to be, doing what she's supposed to be doing. She keeps going, averting her eyes as she passes Bull's office; she can see the door is ajar.

"Coco!" Bull calls. His voice sounds improbably cheerful.

She backs up a few steps and pokes her head in. "Hi?"

"Come on in," he says. "Sit down."

Coco doesn't want to go in—she's holding a book she took from the library without permission and also Bull's Viagra. But what choice does she have? She steps inside but remains by the doorway.

"Close the door," Bull says.

This is it, then, Coco thinks. The moment when Bull does the predictable thing and tries to seduce her. *I've wanted you since the moment I saw you at the Banana Deck, your ass in those cutoffs, your tits in that T-shirt, your eyes, your eyes, your eyes.* Coco desperately wants to get her screenplay into the hands of Bull's contacts. But is she willing to sleep with him?

She closes the door and takes a seat across from him.

He comes out from behind the desk and leans against it, facing her. "How's everything going?"

"Great," she says.

"I thought we had an agreement," he says. "I'm here for the airing of grievances. I've got your back. I know working for Leslee isn't easy." He tilts his head. "Is it?"

Coco isn't sure what to say. This could be a trick, a way of evaluating her loyalty. "This job is pretty much what I thought it would be. Leslee makes her expectations clear and I try to exceed them."

Bull laughs. "God, you're good." He lowers his voice and says, "Can we agree the things in this office stay between us?"

Coco is certain now that this is a trap. "Sure."

"We really want to make Nantucket work," Bull says. "The other places we've tried...well, let's just say things got uncomfortable. Leslee has a tough time making female friends. No, let me correct myself—she *makes* friends easily, she just can't keep them. Other women are threatened by her. She's beautiful, she's fun...and she's naturally flirtatious, that's just her nature. But she's a complex creature, which is why I want to check in periodically and make sure you're okay."

"I'm okay," Coco says. She really wishes she weren't holding the man's Viagra.

"You probably heard me yelling."

Coco shrugs. "I was just passing—"

"I've built my beverage-distribution business from the ground up," he says. "My parents owned a shop on the Nullarbor Plain—do you know where that is? It's a desolate stretch of nowhere in the Australian outback. We used to sell to all the coaches and long-haul lorries that came through. Snacks, drinks, hot meals. I got to know the blokes who delivered our supplies and when I turned eighteen, I went to work for one of them. I rose up in the company, then left and started my own company, and I expanded outside of Australia. Now I distribute to all of Indo. But freaking snowflakes are everywhere, whinging about *ecosystems*..." He trails off. "I don't mean to unload on you, I just don't want you to think I'm a bad guy if you overhear me using some salty language."

"Not a problem," Coco says.

Bull notices the book in her hand. "Are you a reader, then?"

"I am. I borrowed this from the library. I'll put it back when I'm finished."

"No worries. I'm glad someone's taking advantage of that room."

"Are *you* a reader?" Coco asks.

"Used to be, a bit. These days I mostly read scripts."

Coco freezes. Is now the time? Can she tell him she has a finished screenplay entitled *Rosebush*? *No,* she thinks. *It's too soon.* Somehow, she senses this.

"I should get back to work," Coco says, standing. "Leslee was excited to receive her lemons."

"It's appalling, right?" Bull says. "Spending so much money on lemons." He gives a dry laugh. "And yet I've done crazier things to try to make that woman happy. Speaking of which, I heard the party got pretty wild at the end? I conked out right after dinner."

"It was just the right kind of wild," Coco says. "I'm actually still exhausted. I worked nineteen straight hours on Saturday."

"You'll be paid," Bull says. "Plus a bonus."

"I was wondering if I could have a day off, or even an afternoon?"

"Of course!" Bull says. "Why don't you finish up whatever you're doing now and take the rest of the day for yourself? Leslee has pickleball this afternoon, then we're going to the Field and Oar Club with Madam Busybody."

Ha-ha, Coco thinks. Busy Ambrose. "Would that be okay?"

"Go," Bull says.

Coco delivers the prescriptions to the bathroom and heads back upstairs to finish putting away the groceries because she's certain Leslee didn't do it. She's right; Leslee is nowhere to be found, and the groceries are all in their bags on the counter. Coco's mood is lighter now, and she takes great satisfaction in separating produce by color, pouring dry pasta into plastic containers, making sure the edges of boxes are lined up. Coco craved this kind of attention to detail when she was a kid. There was always enough food in her house but everything was shoved into the cabinets willy-nilly; cans routinely fell to the linoleum floor, the flour got weevils, Bree and her kids used to leave bags of chips open, so they went stale. Coco can admit now that while she never dreamed of the kind of extravagant plenty the Richardsons enjoy, she did long for things to be… nice.

When Coco is finished her "home editing," she brings one of the Amalfi lemons to her nose and inhales. *Ahhh,* she thinks. She's free.

She gets a text from Kacy: We're leaving now, are you sure you can't join us? We can cruise over and be there in twenty.

Coco gnaws on her bottom lip. She hates to lie, but oh, well: Wish I could! Leslee wants me to detail her car. Have fun!

She springs into action. Bikini, cutoffs, an old Soggy Dollar T-shirt, her straw bag that looks cute as long as you don't get close enough to see the fraying fibers and the holes. She waits at her apartment window until Leslee pops out of Triple Eight wearing a white tennis skirt and visor, gets into her shiny G-Wagon (Coco took it to the car wash the day before), and crunches off down the shell driveway.

There are some things Coco wants from the big house. Is she brave enough to take them?

Yes. She snatches a bottle of Tanqueray and a bottle of champagne. From the kitchen, she swipes sugar packets and…two of the Amalfi lemons. Her straw bag is sagging with the weight; the bottles clink against each other, making what can only be described as a *pilfered-alcohol* sound. But it's fine; Leslee is gone, Bull is back to yelling on the phone, this time in a foreign language. The man contains multitudes, and Coco makes a mental note to look up the Nullarbor Plain.

She heads out to the beach, whistles, and waves her arms. *Sorry, Kace,* she thinks. She has another kind of fishing in mind.

18. Whale Island

When Romeo leaves Blond Sharon at her house on Saturday night after the Richardsons' party (and after they dragged Robert home from the Candyland that is Baxter Morse's house), he tells her he'll call her about going out for a ride on his boat.

"I'd love it!" Sharon says.

Sunday he doesn't call—it's too soon anyway. Monday he doesn't call—he's probably working at the Steamship. On the way to the Field and Oar Club for her tennis lesson with Mateo, Sharon is tempted to swing through the ferry parking lot just to say hello. She can't stop thinking about how handsome Romeo looked in his bow tie and madras pants. Images of all the times over the years that Romeo directed Sharon's car on and off the ferry come flooding back. How had she never noticed his animal magnetism? Well, most of those times she was in the car with Walker and her children. Of course she wasn't going to lust after Romeo from the Steamship! In the end, she doesn't turn into the Steamship parking lot, though it pulls at her like a magnet.

Tuesday he doesn't call, and Sharon tries not to pine—but once Sterling and Colby are at their internship and she's dropped Robert off at Strong Wings bike camp, she thinks, *Of course he won't call.* Romeo can have any woman he wants on this island. Why would he choose Sharon, who has three children and a fussy lifestyle? Still, Romeo was so sweet and attentive at the party. He'd insisted on coming with Sharon to the Morse house and he was so cute and funny with Robert in the car, talking to him about MrBeast, who apparently they both watch on YouTube (should Sharon be concerned about this?), that Sharon became what can only be described as *enamored.*

On Wednesday morning, Sharon is awoken by a text. It's Romeo: Boat this afternoon? I finish work after the noon ferry leaves.

Ahhh! Sharon jumps out of bed. Should she answer right away or play it cool and wait?

She answers right away: I can make that work.

Great! Let's meet at the town dock at 12:30. I'll grab sandwiches.

Sharon shrieks with joy. Suddenly she's the heroine in a story about second chances!

Speaking of stories... Sharon realizes that if she goes with Romeo, she'll miss her online writing class. Is she going to sacrifice her newfound interest in the literary arts for... a man? Didn't she do enough of that in her marriage?

Sharon has printed out the last two lines of Mary Oliver's poem "The Summer Day" and once again taped it to her bedroom mirror. *Tell me, what is it you plan to do / with your one wild and precious life?*

The lines taunt her. Would this day be better spent sitting in front of her laptop discussing Nancy's character study set at the Registry of Motor Vehicles — or going boating with Romeo?

No contest, Sharon thinks. She hurries to her closet to pick an outfit.

There have been no more texts from Isla, and Kacy worries that she's pushed things too far. She wants to make Isla jealous enough to leave Rondo; she doesn't want Isla to give up because she thinks Kacy has moved on.

She won't text Isla, but she does indulge her second-worst impulse and checks Rondo's Instagram. There, she finds a picture of Isla and Rondo in Napa Valley at the Round Pond Estate vineyard. They're seated at a rough-hewn wooden table with a grand charcuterie platter in front of them and rows of grapes behind; they hold their wineglasses as though they contain liquid gold. Isla is breathtaking in a simple black tank dress that deepens her summer tan. She's wearing red lipstick; her diamond ring glitters on her finger.

Kacy aches with love.

The caption reads: *We've decided on Round Pond sauvignon blanc for our reception!* Followed by the wineglass emoji.

The Round Pond sauvignon blanc is Kacy's favorite, as Isla well knows.

Now Kacy just aches.

Her mood sinks even lower when she learns that Coco can't come out on the fishing boat—but it's a gorgeous day, and Kacy won't waste it.

Eric's fishing boat, *Beautiful Day,* is nicer than Kacy expected (she's never been on it; it's amazing how much you miss when you live on the opposite coast for seven years). She heard *fishing boat* and thought of a floating piece of machinery with rigging and nets. But Eric's boat has a glossy green hull and white leather cushions. There's a fighting chair up front and outrigger lines, but there's plenty of space to lounge as well, which is what Kacy wants to do. She strips down to her bikini and lies across the long bench in the stern next to Avalon.

"Please make yourself at home," Eric jokes. "I take it Coco couldn't come?"

"She has to detail Leslee's car today," Kacy says.

"Does she ever say what it's like working for the Richardsons?"

Avalon asks as she tears open a bag of Flamin' Hot Cheetos. (Avalon eats like a stoned frat boy — her favorite foods are meat lovers' pizza and anything you find in a vending machine.)

"Don't *you* know what it's like?" Kacy asks. "Aren't you Leslee's masseuse?"

"*Was,*" Avalon says. She pops open a Gripah, which is Cisco Brewers' idea of a breakfast beer. Kacy helps herself to one as well and tries not to let her mind wander to the NICU, to all the preemies fighting for their lives while Kacy is in the sun drinking before noon. "She called me to do an at-home massage, but I said no."

"I thought you did at-home massages all the time," Kacy says.

"Oh, I do!" Avalon says. "But the Richardsons give me the creeps. This one night, Eric and I were at the Box and Leslee Richardson started grinding with me, and then in the ladies' room she asked if Eric and I wanted to come back to their hotel room."

"Whoa!" Kacy says. Eric is standing at the ship's wheel, his expression inscrutable behind his wraparound sunglasses. Eric is cut from the same cloth as their father — he's a man of few words, but steady, straight, and true. "You mean to tell me you aren't the swinging type, E?"

"That," Eric says, "I am not." They cruise out of the harbor, and he cranks up the horsepower. "Billy told me the stripers are biting over by Tuckernuck, so that's where we're going. Not that either of you care."

"So anyway," Avalon says, licking nuclear-orange cheese dust off her fingers, "that's why I won't work on her."

"Wow," Kacy says. These are the first negative words she's heard about the Richardsons. Everyone else on the island is hopelessly in love with them.

Lamont appears on the deck of *Hedonism*. He waves at Coco on the shore and calls, "What's good?"

"I have the afternoon off," Coco says. "Finally."

Lamont gives her a thumbs-up. *Oh, come on,* Coco thinks. *Don't make me beg.* Coco has learned that Lamont gets paid regardless of whether the Richardsons use the boats. Lamont keeps them clean and maintained and performs safety and equipment checks. When all that is finished, he's allowed to do whatever he wants.

He disappears below deck. She must have misread what happened when they were skinny-dipping; he'd been drinking, it was just horsing around. She heads back up to the house thinking she'll drive Baby out to one of the ocean beaches, Cisco or Surfside. But then she hears the putter of a motor and she turns to see Lamont coming to shore in the dinghy.

Coco squints at him. "Do you want to hang?"

He moves his Wayfarers to the top of his head so Coco can see his eyes—brown with flashes of copper. "Didn't Leslee tell you the rule? We aren't allowed to date."

"But we're allowed to be friends," she says.

Lamont eyes the house. "Where are..."

"Leslee went to play pickleball and Bull is in his office, working. Bull gave me the rest of the day off. He said they're going for dinner at the Field and Oar tonight."

"Leslee will be home between pickleball and dinner?"

"I mean, yeah, but I doubt they'll need the boats."

Lamont checks his phone. "I'll take you out," he says. "But this has to stay under the radar. I have a very sweet situation here and I don't want to jeopardize it."

"I feel exactly the same way."

He still seems hesitant, and Coco thinks about how she's never been with anyone she would describe as *principled.* It's sexy.

She crosses her heart, locks her lips, tosses an invisible key over her shoulder. Finally, he smiles. "Do you want to sail or speed?" he asks.

"Speed," she says.

* * *

Blond Sharon waits on the town dock, smoothing her blue eyelet cover-up from Cartolina and adjusting her straw hat. She checks her phone: 12:28. Her heart is bouncing around in her chest like a hyper child on a trampoline. She ended up dashing off a quick email to Lucky Zambrano: *I'm sorry I have to miss class this week. Unexpected plot twist.*

I have a date! she thinks.

At that second, she sees a boat approaching. Yes, it's a Grady-White with a cute bimini top over the back. Romeo is behind the wheel, shirtless, in a pair of striped board shorts. Gah!

He pulls up to the dock, and one of the kids working catches his line and wraps it around a cleat. The name of the boat is written in script on the side in glittering letters: *Golden Girl.*

Sharon removes her flip-flops and accepts Romeo's hand as she steps down into the boat. She sees an open cooler filled with ice, seltzers, and a bottle of Domaines Ott rosé, which happens to be Sharon's favorite. There's a bag of sandwiches from Provisions. Did Romeo read her mind and order her a Turkey Terrific?

"Who's Golden Girl?" Sharon asks teasingly.

Romeo doesn't miss a beat. "You are," he says.

Coco has been on her share of boats, from flat-bottomed pontoons on the Lake of the Ozarks to catamarans in the Virgin Islands, but none of these compare to *Decadence,* the Aquariva 33. Coco has googled it—the deck is grain-matched maple with twenty layers of varnishing, sanding, polishing. It's floating elegance.

Coco sets her disintegrating straw bag on the leather banquette in the stern and picks at the strings of her cutoffs. She probably should have taken the afternoon and gone shopping for new clothes. On Monday, Leslee had handed Coco her week's pay in an envelope: thirty-six crisp hundred-dollar bills.

"Come on up here," Lamont says, patting the seat next to him. Coco moves up. She's officially a Bond girl.

"Hold on," he says. They navigate out of Pocomo Harbor and then he pulls back the throttle and they go flying. There are twin 380 Yanmars hiding beneath the aft; it's a Lamborghini on the water.

"Woo-hoo!" Coco says, raising her hands over her head. But then they hit the crest of a wave and she's jolted clear out of her seat. *Okay, okay,* she thinks. She'll hold on. She doesn't want to end up overboard.

Lamont slows down. Coco bumps her thigh against his and he presses back and she thinks, *Forget the rule, this is on. This is happening.*

They cruise along the north coast of the island. Lamont names each beach and adds some color commentary: Steps is where his mother taught him to swim, 40th Pole is where he went to bonfires in high school. They reach the western tip of the island and Lamont shows Coco Esther's Island and Smith's Point. Their thighs are still touching.

People on the beaches wave at them but Coco looks away. She doesn't want to call attention to herself.

"Where are we going?" she asks. "Do you have a plan?"

"I always have a plan," he says.

A second later, they've left Nantucket behind, but there's land ahead.

"Another island?" Coco asks.

"Tuckernuck," Lamont says. It's privately owned, he says; there are thirty-two houses run by generator. Lamont used to spend one weekend every August at a place called the Tate House—his mother babysat for the children of the caretaker, Barrett Lee, and they worked out a barter. Those Tuckernuck weekends were all about riding a rusty no-speed Schwinn around the sandy roads, surf-casting, grilling striped bass over a fire on the beach, taking rainwater showers.

"I would like that," Coco says, although who is she kidding? She's gotten used to six-hundred-thread-count sheets, central air, and four kinds of sparkling water ice cold in the fridge.

Looking at the stars on Tuckernuck, Lamont says, was how he became interested in celestial navigation. "Yes, I know the names of all the constellations. Yes, I can figure out where I am on planet Earth just by looking at the night sky. I am that nerd boy."

"Well, Nerd Boy, I am Nerd Girl. I can survive in the wilderness for a week with just a workman's tool and a canvas tarp."

"Were you a Girl Scout?" he asks.

"No," she says. "I had parental figures with a weird sense of fun."

"That's cool," he says. "You have layers!"

Coco laughs and feels brave enough to let her hand land lightly on Lamont's thigh.

He covers her hand with his own just long enough for her to know it's okay, then he grabs the wheel and directs them to a spit of golden sand.

"I thought you said it was privately owned."

"All except this beach, which is called Whale Island," he says. "It's the only part of Tuckernuck open to boaters. No one is ever here during the week."

Ten minutes later, they're lying on a blanket pulled from the cabin of *Decadence.* Lamont brandishes a couple of champagne flutes— *Decadence* is the kind of boat that comes with crystal stemware— and Coco slides into bartender mode.

"French Seventy-Fives," she says. The drink is a relic from the bartending course she took back in Arkansas; she remembers the recipe only because her instructor told the class they would probably never have the occasion to make one. *They're highfalutin,* he'd said.

Now here she is, living her best highfalutin life.

Coco makes the drinks—gin, champagne, sugar, the exquisite lemon juice—and they toast to Coco's first afternoon off.

Lamont takes a sip. "This is banging."

It's the best cocktail Coco has ever made and maybe ever tasted. The first round goes down quickly, and she makes another. "These aren't just regular lemons," she says. "They're Amalfi lemons. They arrived at the house in a straw-filled wooden crate wearing little white robes. Guess how much they cost?"

"I'm afraid to ask."

"Two hundred and eighty-four euros," Coco says. "It's not like I expect the Richardsons to buy their produce on sale, but you have to admit, that's outrageous."

"I think Leslee probably just likes the fact that she can afford them," Lamont says. "She comes from a pretty modest background."

"Leslee, modest?" Coco says. "Don't tell me—she's from Connecticut."

"Nope."

"Do you actually know where she's from?"

"I do," Lamont says. "But you can't let her know I told you. It isn't something she shares about herself."

"I won't tell."

"She's from a town called Pahrump, Nevada," Lamont says. "Her family owned a gun range and an ammunition warehouse. People would go there to shoot AR-Fifteens."

Coco knew some folks from Rosebush who would have loved that kind of place. "I have a pretty good imagination but I can't picture Leslee on a shooting range in Nevada."

"She moved to Vegas after she graduated from high school," Lamont says. "She worked as a crepe chef at the Bellagio to put herself through UNLV. Then she got a job on the casino floor serving cocktails. She said she did that for almost ten years, good money, but she hated it. She finally got a regular bartending job at what she said was the coolest place in Vegas. She told me the name but I forget. Pepper something? And that's where she met Bull."

You remind me of myself when I was your age, Leslee had said. Leslee also grew up in a place she wanted to get the hell out of. Leslee was also a bartender. Maybe that's why Leslee agreed to hire her.

"How do you know all this?" Coco says. "Obviously you two are...close? Is there something going on between the two of you that I should know about?"

"Leslee likes attention," Lamont says. "When Bull offered me the job, he told me I'm supposed to treat her like the only woman in the world. She talks; I listen."

"Why can't *Bull* just give her attention?" Coco says. "She's always all over you. It's weird."

Lamont studies his champagne flute. "I need this job, Coco. My mom is losing her eyesight, we have medical bills — and for someone with my skill set, this is the best job on the island. I'm capable of being Leslee's friend."

"Is that all you are?" Coco asks. "Friends?"

"It sounds like you're jealous," Lamont says. "Are you jealous?"

She lies back on the blanket. "I might be."

"Oh, yeah?"

Coco swats his arm. "Remember the night of the party? In the water? I had you in a leg lock."

"I do remember that," he says. "Fondly." He reaches over and traces one of Coco's ribs, which tickles. Coco squirms away and a second later, they're wrestling on the blanket. Lamont moves above her so that his knees are on either side of her hips and they stare at each other. Coco's entire body is vibrating with desire. Then he bends down and kisses her. His lips taste like sugar, his tongue like the finest lemons in the world. Coco can't get enough; she wants every part of her body touching every part of his body. Has she ever in her life been this aroused? She used to laugh when people came into the Banana Deck and ordered sex on the beach shots. *What, she wondered, could be worse than sex on the beach?* Nothing about it sounded appealing; even the scene in *From Here to Eternity* made it appear scratchy and uncomfortable. But right this second, sex on the beach is all Coco wants. She wants Lamont to untie the strings of her bikini, lightly brush her nipples, then bring them to his mouth while he pushes his erection into her quivering thigh.

Is this going to happen?

Coco hears the purr of an approaching motor and looks up to see not one but two boats headed their way. One is a white runabout with a couple aboard; the other is a fishing boat. Coco quickly sits up and puts on her sunglasses. "I thought you said nobody ever comes here during the week."

She hears a woman is calling her name. It's Kacy—she's on the fishing boat with Eric and Avalon, the same boat Kacy invited her on, an invite Coco turned down because she told Kacy she had to detail Leslee's car, only now here she is making out with Lamont Oakley on Whale Island.

"No," Coco whispers. "No, no, *no.*"

Lamont grabs his head and groans.

"Looks like someone beat us to it," Romeo says with a chuckle. He's directing *Golden Girl* toward the shore at Whale Island, and Sharon is thrilled. In all her years on Nantucket, she has never once been to Tuckernuck.

"Beat us to what?" Sharon says, then she sees the couple on the beach kissing. That's exactly what Sharon wants to be doing! She's so distracted by this idea that it takes her a moment to notice the boat—it's *Decadence,* the speedboat that belongs to the Richardsons. Sharon blinks. Who is that on the beach? Once she gets closer, she sees it's the Richardsons' assistant, Coco, and their boat captain, Lamont Oakley.

Ahhhhh! Sharon thinks.

An instant later, Sharon hears shouting. There's a third boat approaching, a fishing boat called *Beautiful Day*—and the person yelling is none other than Kacy Kapenash. "Coco!" she says. "Coco!"

Sharon can't believe that she is once again stumbling across these two. It's almost as if some unseen force keeps bringing them together. Sharon's notebook is in her beach bag and she's tempted to reach for it now. What is going to happen?

When Kacy sees Coco and Lamont making out on the beach at Whale Island, she thinks, *Is this a joke?* Has another woman Kacy trusted lied to her so she could be with a man? And why? Coco could have said she had plans with Lamont; Kacy would have understood. This is...disappointing.

"I thought you told us she had to work," Eric says.

Avalon says, "Looks like she's working on Lamont."

Kacy hands Avalon her beer and dives off the side of the boat.

"Whoa!" she hears Eric say. "A little warning would be nice."

A little warning would *be nice,* Kacy thinks as she swims to shore.

Romeo seems indifferent to the scene taking place on the beach. He's all business as he drops the anchor and makes sure Sharon climbs down the ladder safely into the thigh-deep water. Sharon holds her bag over her head; she can't let her notebook get wet.

"You pick a spot," Romeo says. "I'll bring the towels and the picnic."

Romeo is handsome and thoughtful—and seafaring. Sharon loves watching him move around the boat, testing the lines. But Sharon can't shed her natural curiosity. When she chooses a place on the beach, it's close enough to Coco and Lamont that she can eavesdrop.

Sharon drops her bag, unbuttons her cover-up, and wades back into the water, acting like a person who is interested only in the vista of Nantucket in the distance.

"It's fine," Coco says. "She didn't see anything."

Lamont's mouth is set in a grim line as he watches Kacy swim ashore. Coco throws back the rest of her French 75 as though the situation is casual. Friends bumping into friends. What a happy coincidence!

Kacy emerges from the water, squeezes out her hair, and smiles at Coco and Lamont.

Coco exhales. It's fine.

"Hey, guys," she says. She looks at Coco. "I can't believe you're here."

"I know," Coco says. "I unexpectedly got the afternoon off. I know this probably looks bad..."

"Bad?" Kacy says.

Coco swallows. "I told you I had to work, and I did, but then Leslee went to play pickleball—"

"In a dirty car?" Kacy asks.

Coco deserves that. She lied; she got caught. Kacy is the first real friend she's had in a long time and she's out of practice at friendship.

Kacy looks at them. "You know it's fine with me if you guys hang, right?"

It should be fine. But Coco broke the girl code. She almost wishes Kacy would be angry so she could accuse her of overreacting, but of course she's as cool and gracious as ever.

"Would you like me to make you a French Seventy-Five?" Coco says, holding up the remaining Amalfi lemon. "They're really good."

"Actually," Lamont says, "we have to go."

"But—" Coco says.

"Now," Lamont says. He tosses what's left of his cocktail into the sand, and Coco nearly cries out for the wasted lemon juice. To Kacy, he says, "We were never here."

"Understood," Kacy says. "Rain check on the cocktail."

"Why don't I just go with Kacy now?" Coco says. She puts all the drink ingredients back into her bag, then looks at Lamont. "That would be best, right?"

"Yes," he says, and he visibly relaxes. "That would be best."

Romeo wades ashore carrying the cooler, the sandwiches, and a stack of towels. He cocks his head. "Hey, Golden Girl," he says. "What do you say we head farther down the beach so we have some privacy."

"You read my mind," Sharon says, but she lingers to watch Kacy and Coco wade back to the fishing boat.

Farewell, my darlings, she thinks.

19. The Kitchen I

When the women gather at the pickleball courts off the Polpis Road, the first thing out of Leslee Richardson's mouth is "I'm on Phoebe's team."

It's Andrea who speaks up. "Phoebe and Delilah are a team. You can play with me."

Leslee unsheathes her paddle. Delilah isn't surprised that it's a top-of-the-line Encore, though she is surprised that it looks like it actually gets some use. "Is that a hard-and-fast *rule*? Are you two sponsored or something?"

"No," Phoebe says. "We just always play together because I suck and Delilah is great and we balance each other out."

Delilah is glad Phoebe said it.

"Well, I'm here to shake things up!" Leslee says. "Phoebe and I will play together."

Delilah opens her mouth to speak, but what can she say? *We invited you to play with us! You aren't allowed to shake things up!*

Phoebe shrugs. "Sounds good," she says. "Sorry in advance."

Delilah is heated—both physically (the court they're playing on is in full sun) and emotionally (*Is this happening?*)—and decides to take her aggression out on the court. They flip a coin to see who serves first; it's Leslee and Phoebe. Fine, fine. Let's go.

Leslee serves, Delilah returns, then it's tit for tat until Delilah does the predictable thing and hits to Phoebe's weak side.

"I told you I suck," Phoebe says. It's now Delilah who serves and Leslee who returns. There's a little volley, and again, Delilah hits it to Phoebe's weak side. *Candy from a baby,* she thinks. One, nothing.

The game could go on that way—Delilah knows how Phoebe will handle any given shot—but where's the fun in that? Delilah lightens up, lets Andrea take some shots. Then there's a volley where Leslee gets dangerously close to the kitchen; in fact, in one shot, her right foot is squarely *in the kitchen* while she's volleying, and as Delilah is wondering if she should call her on it, Leslee aims a shot right at Delilah's face.

Whoa! Delilah raises her paddle and deflects the ball, but they lose the point. Leslee and Phoebe tap paddles. Everyone realizes that was dirty, right?

Phoebe serves; Andrea returns, and again Leslee smashes the ball, aiming for Delilah's face. "What the hell?" Delilah says, but Phoebe and Leslee have their backs turned and are walking toward the baseline.

"Easy," Andrea whispers, which only serves to infuriate Delilah more. How about some team solidarity? Why does Andrea have to talk to her like she's an ill-behaved kindergartner?

Delilah will *not* take it easy. The game gets way more aggressive; the volleys are intense, and Leslee *really* pushes how close she comes to the kitchen when she volleys. Delilah has to admit that Leslee is a good pickleball player. Delilah had half suspected her of posing.

The score is 8–8–2, then 9–8–1. Delilah is drenched in sweat but she is bound and determined to win. Andrea and Phoebe are just furniture; this is a game between Delilah and Leslee. Delilah charges into the kitchen to return a ball; she needs the serve back, but the ball goes wide. Out.

Now it's 10–8–2. Match point.

Leslee serves, Delilah returns, there's a volley. Leslee hits it to Andrea, Andrea cupcakes it over to Phoebe, and, in a rare show of skill, Phoebe hits it to Delilah, who wallops it at Leslee, who is standing in the kitchen, but instead of letting it bounce, she volleys it back, and Delilah lets it sail past her.

"Our serve," Delilah says to Andrea at the same time Leslee says, "We win!"

Delilah turns around. "What? No. You aren't allowed to volley from the kitchen."

"I wasn't in the kitchen," Leslee says.

"You most certainly were," Delilah says. She looks to Andrea for backup but Andrea is already walking toward the net to tap paddles with Phoebe. "It's our serve."

"Let's just call it a game," Phoebe says. "It's hot. Who wants to come swim in my pool?"

"Me," Andrea says.

"That sounds heavenly," Leslee says. "Thank you for inviting me to play today." She reaches across the net to tap paddles with Andrea. Delilah is standing in the middle of the court, hands on hips, feeling as indignant as John McEnroe at Wimbledon in 1981. *You cannot be serious!* Delilah let the other infractions go—they were ambiguous; was one of Leslee's feet in the kitchen? Hard to say—but during match point she blatantly volleyed while she was in the kitchen. It's *cheating*!

Never again, Delilah thinks. *Never again are we inviting this woman to play pickleball with us.*

"Delilah?" Phoebe prompts. "Swimming?"

Delilah would love nothing more than a dip in Phoebe's pool but she won't voluntarily spend one more second with Leslee Richardson. As she's about to decline, Leslee says, "You can all help me plan our Fourth of July fireworks party aboard *Hedonism.* I want it to be smaller than the Pink and White Party. More exclusive."

Delilah is about to inform Leslee that they always watch the Fourth of July fireworks on Steps Beach, but she knows that will be futile. Leslee is throwing a party aboard her fabulous yacht, and of course the others will want to go. Of course Delilah wants to go. She has long dreamed of watching the fireworks from out on the water.

"Swimming sounds good. I need to cool down," Delilah says as, grudgingly, she taps Leslee's paddle. Apparently, they're stuck with this woman.

20. Thursday, August 22, 9:30 P.M.

The Chief's phone rings — Lucy Shields, the harbormaster.

"I've ordered the chopper out of Woods Hole," she says.

"Thank you, Lucy." He turns to Zara and Lamont. "Coast Guard is sending out a chopper."

Lamont looks skyward. "I wish they would take me with them. I could find her; I know I could."

The Chief looks at Zara. Is she thinking what he's thinking? "We should probably go talk to the Richardsons," the Chief says. Maybe Zara is right and he should step away from the investigation, he thinks. He had hoped never to speak to Leslee Richardson again.

"I have another idea," Zara says. She takes the Chief's arm, leads him away, lowers her voice, and says, "Let's talk to Kacy first."

"Kacy?" he says. "She wasn't on the boat."

"But they were friends. Close friends, Dixon said."

"True."

"A woman tells her girlfriends everything," Zara says.

Ed flashes to Andrea whispering with Phoebe and Delilah at Ventuno. "Good point."

They find Kacy right where they left her, but her facade has cracked — tears stream down her face, her hair has slipped from its chignon, her nose is running. Ed considers calling Andrea and asking her to come; this is a girl who needs her mother. Kacy looks up, wipes the tears from under each eye with a manicured fingernail, and sniffs. "She's somewhere. That's the thing. She's *somewhere.*"

Zara takes a seat next to Kacy, lightly touches her shoulder. "The best way you can help Coco now is to fill us in on a little background. I know you don't want to break Coco's confidence, but you're going to have to give us all the gory details so we know what we're dealing with here."

Please, Ed thinks, *don't let them be* too *gory.*

Kacy sits up straighter and focuses on Zara. "What do you want to know?"

Zara asks Kacy how she met Coco ("On the ferry") and what she knows about Coco's life before Nantucket. Kacy leans in, tells Zara that Coco grew up in a small town in Arkansas. She had been working in the Virgin Islands, which was where she met the Richardsons. They had dinner at the restaurant where Coco was bartending and they invited her to follow them up here.

Zara lifts her eyes to Ed. "These people have a thing for inviting perfect strangers into their lives."

Oh, do they, Ed thinks.

"Most of what I learned about Coco came from reading her screenplay," Kacy says.

"Her screenplay?" Zara and Ed say together.

"It's really good," Kacy says. "It's Coco's dream to get it produced."

Ed is impressed by how much information Zara is able to pull from Kacy without even seeming to try. She definitely has a way. Ed knows only the bare bones about Zara's personal life: She's forty-four years old, divorced from the minister of the Old Whaling Church in Edgartown, whom she once referred to as "the most popular man on Martha's Vineyard, especially with his lady parishioners." Ed had just raised his eyebrows and asked if they had children. Yes, two girls, one a freshman at Tufts, the other a sixteen-year-old, who would be transferring to Nantucket High School this fall for her junior year.

Zara's maternal instincts are helping here, though Ed knows better than to say this.

"What about Coco's romantic life?" Zara says.

Kacy immediately pulls back a few inches. *Oh, boy, here we go,* Ed thinks. *What is she going to say?*

"Do you have any water?" Kacy asks. "The smoke is irritating my throat."

"There's a cooler filled with waters in the trunk of my squad car," Zara says. She reaches into her pocket and passes Ed the keys. "I'm sure we all could use one."

Ed gets it—he's the errand boy now. Though he has to admit, bringing cold waters to a house fire was something he never would have thought of. Zara Washington is good.

21. Firecracker

News of the Richardsons' upcoming Fourth of July party aboard *Hedonism* sets the cobblestone telegraph ablaze. Once again the invitations are hand-delivered—square red envelopes this time—but the guest list has been trimmed by more than half. Dr. Andy hears about the party from Busy Ambrose while Busy is in for a cleaning, but when Dr. Andy checks with his wife, Rachel, he discovers they didn't make the cut.

"You shouldn't have taken so many videos!" Dr. Andy says.

"You shouldn't have passed out naked in their party room!" Rachel fires back.

"Everyone was naked," Dr. Andy says. "*You* were naked."

"Should we send them flowers?" Rachel asks.

"Nobody died," Dr. Andy says. "Why don't we invite them for dinner?"

"I'd have to redecorate the whole house before Leslee Richardson sets foot in it," Rachel says.

"Should we offer to take them out?" Dr. Andy asks. "I have a contact at Cru."

"They go out every night," Rachel says. "They can get into Cru on their own; they practically have their own stools at the back bar."

"So—what? We just give up?"

Rachel can put a positive spin on nearly any situation, but now she feels like one of those sad freshman girls who didn't get bids from their chosen sororities. Maybe Andy is right, she thinks. Maybe she shouldn't have taken all those videos.

Delilah peers out her window looking for Coco in the baby-blue Land Rover. The more Delilah thinks about her behavior during the pickleball game, the more ashamed she feels. Why did she act like such a poor sport? Yes, Leslee volleyed while standing in the kitchen, but who cares? (Delilah cares; it's not winning if you cheat.) At Phoebe's pool afterward, Delilah tried to smooth things over but Leslee frosted her out, addressing her comments to only Phoebe and Andrea. Delilah gave up and thought, *I can't stand this woman, why am I pretending?*

But even so, later, when she gets home from the Stop and Shop and sees the red envelope tucked into the corner of her screen door, she feels weak with relief.

* * *

Both Sharon and Romeo receive invitations but Sharon is in a quandary: Her sister, Heather, will be visiting over the Fourth. "I notice these invitations don't include a plus-one like the Pink and White Party did," Sharon says to Romeo over the phone. Since the day of the boat ride, they've been in constant communication, texting every few hours, talking on the phone each night before bed.

"Thank god my plus-one is already invited," Romeo says.

That's sweet, Sharon thinks. But what will she do about Heather? She calls Leslee Richardson. "My sister, Heather, will be visiting," Sharon says. "Is there any way I might bring her along?"

"I'm so sorry," Leslee says. "Numbers on the boat are limited."

"I completely understand," Sharon says.

"Will you not be able to make it, then?" Leslee asks. "I'm sure you want to spend time with your sister."

Sharon pauses. She knows she should offer her regrets and hang out with Heather, but the idea of missing the party — with Romeo — is too much to bear. "Don't be silly," Sharon says.

Eric and Avalon are invited on the sail, but they decline. They're going to drive out to Coatue and grill clams on their hibachi.

"Do you want to join us?" Avalon asks Kacy.

"Coco wants me to come on the sail," Kacy says, "and I think it sounds like fun."

"Well," Avalon says evenly, "if it's anything like the Pink and White Party, I'm sure you'll have stories for us."

The theme of the sail is American Summer, and those of us invited dress accordingly. We board *Hedonism* on Swain's Wharf and each of us is immediately handed a cocktail called the firecracker, which is a layered drink: red on the bottom (grenadine), white in the middle (vodka and lemonade), and blue curaçao on top.

Has any cocktail that includes blue curaçao ever tasted good? Coco believes the answer is no, but Leslee insisted on this drink for the wow factor, and people seem to be slurping them right down. Coco will have to handcraft another round, but because space on the boat is limited, she's in charge of passing the hors d'oeuvres that Zoe Alistair's team dropped off: pigs in a blanket, classic shrimp cocktail, and corn and lobster fritters with a seeded mustard dipping sauce.

Kacy says, "Do you want help?"

"I'll find you during the fireworks," Coco says.

"What's good with you and Lamont?" Kacy asks. "Are you linking?"

"No," Coco says truthfully. Since they were caught on Whale Island, Lamont has been avoiding her. Coco texted him to ask if everything went okay getting the boat back; he responded that it was fine—neither Leslee nor Bull noticed the boat had been missing—but they shouldn't try that again.

It was poor form. The Richardsons aren't paying us to hang.

Right, Coco thought. They broke "the rule," and bumping into Kacy spooked him; news of their adventure could easily have gotten back to Bull and Leslee.

Can we hang out off-property sometime? she texted. There's an entire island past the end of the driveway.

Three dots arose; he was typing. She waited for his response, but none came.

Coco hasn't seen Lamont except in passing since then, but she thinks maybe tonight, they can reconnect. When she finishes making the first tray of drinks, she offers one to Lamont. "Firecracker?"

"You're kidding, right?" he says. "I'm the captain, Coco."

"Okay," she says. "Sorry."

Fast Eddie boards the boat with a new confidence. Their offer for Jeanne Jackson's property was accepted and signed. In a few weeks, they'll sign the purchase and sale agreement; Bull will wire the money, and they'll break ground. Grace was initially livid that Eddie was getting back into real estate development, but she calmed down when he told her that Addison Wheeler was involved and that Bull Richardson was financing the entire thing as an equal partner. In Grace's eyes, the Richardsons can do no wrong.

Grace is wearing a new dress to the party, a slinky red thing with a low back and a slit up the front. Eddie would like to believe Grace wants to look good for him, but when he sees Benton Coe over on the port side holding a cocktail and talking with Leslee Richardson—who is, frankly, fawning all over the guy—Eddie wonders if Grace knew he would be here. Oh, how Eddie wishes Benton were one of the people who'd gotten axed from the Richardsons' guest list. No such luck.

Sharon and Romeo arrive at the party together, and the first person who notices is Busy Ambrose from the Field and Oar Club. "Are you two an *item,* then?" she asks. Instead of looking happy for Sharon, she appears perplexed. Busy is a terrible snob, and Romeo, "the Steamship guy," falls beneath her consideration.

"We are!" Sharon says. "And we're very happy, thanks."

Sharon is wearing snug white pants, a navy-and-white-striped halter, and the cutest red jean jacket that she'd asked her sister, Heather, to pick up from the Saks in Chevy Chase. "You look adorbs," Heather said in the minutes before Romeo arrived. "And very on-theme." Sharon had worried that Heather might be miffed about Sharon going to the party without her, but Heather was thrilled to have a night at home. Sterling and Colby were going to a bonfire, so Heather and Robert planned to order from Pi Pizzeria and "hang out"—which meant, Sharon knew, that Robert would watch MrBeast on YouTube and Heather would work.

"What's the name of the couple throwing the party again?" Heather asked.

"The Richardsons," Sharon said. "Bull and Leslee."

The name Bull Richardson sounded familiar to Heather, though she wasn't sure why.

Delilah tries to resist having fun, but that's impossible. She helps herself to a firecracker cocktail and joins a tour of the living space below deck. The boat is glamorous—so much creamy leather and gleaming mahogany, so many king beds sheathed in navy and white linens, so many huge bouquets of lilies and Dutch hydrangeas from Flowers on Chestnut. Back on deck, Delilah pops a crispy corn and lobster fritter into her mouth and feels a surge of excitement as the motor starts and the Valladares brothers, Javier and Esteban, who are crewing tonight, gather the lines and push them off the dock. She sees Leslee across the way talking to the Chief and Andrea, but as soon as Delilah approaches, Leslee says, "I have to check on the buffet, and the music should be louder, don't you think?" and disappears with a wave.

The Chief turns to Delilah. "I heard you were a real bulldog at pickleball the other day," he says.

Lamont Oakley and the Valladares brothers raise the sails as we exit Nantucket Harbor. The only sight more majestic than the sails billowing against the setting sun as seen from below might be *Hedonism* in full sail as seen from a neighboring boat.

Blythe Buchanan and her wife, Linda, have motored over from Cape Cod in their thirty-eight-foot Regal, *Dawg Daze II,* to watch our fireworks as they do every year. As *Hedonism* sails by, some people wave, and Blythe and Linda wave back. But a second later, Blythe nearly chokes on her spicy margarita.

"Did you see who was on that boat?" she asks.

Linda is a step ahead of her, using the MarineFinder app to figure out who owns *Hedonism.* "Lord have mercy," she says. "Bull and Leslee Richardson bought it." Linda and Blythe met the Richardsons in Palm Beach, and oh, boy, do they have stories.

Blythe groans. "Nantucket better watch out."

Back at Blond Sharon's house, Heather is working on a case, but she takes a quick break to google the couple throwing the party. Neither Bull nor his wife seem to be active on social media, though Heather finds Bulfinch Richardson's LinkedIn profile. He owns Sweetwater, a beverage-distribution company that's somehow also a Hollywood production company. (There are credits for movies Heather has never heard of.) When Heather digs a little deeper, the name clicks—the SEC did a preliminary investigation into Sweetwater Distribution. The company owns a bottling plant and a plastics factory that manufactures the bottles. A whistleblower called them out for environmental infractions and for misleading greenhouse-gas-emissions disclosures. But had anything come of it? Heather is going to check when she returns to the office.

Heather sends Sharon a text: How's the party? Heather needs to be careful. Her sister is the biggest gossip on the island and anything Heather tells Sharon about Bull's business will be all over Nantucket quicker than you can say *Vanderpump Rules.*

It's divine! Sharon texts back. Then another text comes in, a photo of Sharon with a red carnation clenched between her teeth and Romeo in an Uncle Sam hat. They're both holding sparklers.

Bull's company must have been cleared of any wrongdoing, Heather thinks. Just because he was investigated doesn't mean he broke the law. The Richardsons are allowed to have fun; as the sound of the first fireworks remind Heather, it's a free country. She won't say anything to Sharon about the Richardsons, she decides. After all, they're not *dangerous.* It's not like they're going to hurt anyone.

* * *

Hedonism anchors off Jetties Beach, where those of us not invited to the Richardsons' party have gathered to watch the fireworks. We hear the music pumping: "Born in the USA," then Katy Perry's "Firework." Everyone on board is whooping and dancing; we hear the distinct pop of a champagne cork.

Dr. Andy McMann and his wife, Rachel, are hunkered down in the sand eating takeout sushi and drinking a very nice white Bordeaux, but even so, Dr. Andy sees Rachel staring at *Hedonism* with longing. "Don't look," he says.

But it's like worrying a loose tooth (a behavior Dr. Andy knows only too well). Rachel can't help herself.

Eric and Avalon can see *Hedonism* from their spot on the second point of Coatue. Eric pulls clams off the grill, and Avalon drags the smoky gems through melted butter. She washes the clams down with a cold beer, then lies back on the blanket next to Eric and counts the emerging stars.

She hears music—the entire island is being treated to the Richardsons' soundtrack—and snuggles against her boyfriend, digging her feet into the cool sand. The first firework whistles, pops, and explodes in a burst of silver and gold above them. A chorus of happy screams goes up from the boat. Avalon is so glad she's not on it.

Coco can't wait for this party to be over. She's in charge of setting up the buffet—fried chicken, ribs, potato salad, coleslaw, baked beans, homemade pickles, and biscuits with honey butter—and then cleaning it all up. While she's collecting plates and trash, she finds a sparerib sticking out from between two of the cushions of the ivory sofa in the living area. Who does something like that? She moves on to setting up the miniature pies—cherry, blueberry, peach, pecan, and banana cream—that Leslee had flown in from a place called Peggy Jean's in Columbia, Missouri.

Coco hears the fireworks begin and thinks, *Thank god, the end is near.* When she goes above deck, her Leslee radar kicks in. Coco likes to know where her boss is at all times. First she checks the captain's wheel because, as she's learned, Leslee tries to stay as close to Lamont as possible, but Lamont is talking to his crew, Javier and Esteban. Javier is a senior at Nantucket High School, Esteban a junior; they're both on the sailing team. Just like Lamont was, Javier told Coco when she met him. They're listening to Lamont like he's Captain America.

Coco spies Bull in the bow talking to Fast Eddie and Addison Wheeler. Andrea, Delilah, and Phoebe are chatting amongst themselves. Sharon and the hot guy from the Steamship are all cozied up. Where is Leslee? Coco wanders the boat until she sees her boss with Benton Coe in the stern, leaning against the back gate. Leslee has opted for a different look tonight: a pair of skinny blue jeans and a tight Budweiser T-shirt with a red bandanna woven through her braid. Bright red lipstick. Coco has to admit, Leslee looks adorable (and far more comfortable than, say, Fast Eddie's wife, who came in a red silk gown). Benton obviously appreciates Leslee's look because the two of them are standing hip to hip, and when Leslee reaches up to rub Benton's neck, he lolls his head back and groans with delight.

Coco feels like she's spying. This is none of her business, she should be working; with thirty-five people on board, someone will need a drink. Kacy is sitting by herself on the starboard side. Coco should spend a few minutes with her, let Kacy take a selfie of them the way she likes to (knowing Kacy, she's probably making a Snapfish album that she'll give to Coco at the end of the summer; she's thoughtful that way)—but Coco can't tear her eyes away from Leslee and Benton. Benton sits on the back bench and Leslee moves behind him to give him a full-on back rub. After a moment, she bends down and whispers in his ear.

Is anyone else seeing this? Coco wonders.

The Chief is restless. The Fourth is one of his least favorite days of the year. It starts with all of the antics out at Nobadeer Beach—girls going topless, guys doing flips off the dunes, idiots using empty beer bottles as projectiles, the entire Boston College offensive line getting into a scrap with half the Morgan Stanley trading floor. Every year the Chief's officers write over a hundred tickets for underage drinking. This segues right into fifteen thousand people cramming onto Jetties Beach with their hibachi grills and open containers. Talk about a public-safety nightmare. Then there are the bozos who have bought fireworks out of state and choose to set them off from their buddy's widow's walk. There are noise complaints, people losing fingers, yards catching on fire.

As the Chief, Andrea, and Kacy were driving to Swain's Wharf to meet the Richardsons' boat, a car zoomed by, passing them illegally on Washington Street.

"Whoa, buddy," the Chief said. It was a silver Range Rover with the license plate BEAST. The blond kid driving eyed Ed in his rearview mirror and flipped him off. *You again?* Ed thought.

"Pull him over, Ed," Andrea said.

Ed wanted to, very badly, but they were in Andrea's car, he had no lights or siren, and they were already running late. He didn't want the boat to leave without them.

Now, Ed regrets his decision to come. What the hell is he doing on this boat? He should be on the ground with the rest of his department. The Fourth is an all-hands-on-deck occasion and here he is, aboard what is essentially a floating nightclub.

He takes a breath. He's not drinking tonight, Coco was kind

enough to bring him a seltzer with lime, and he has his phone in case of emergencies, but it's been quiet. Will this luck hold? The Chief has been listening to Jeffrey talk about how the dry summer has helped the corn crop while their wives gab away and Addison schmoozes with Bull and Fast Eddie. The Chief pushes himself to his feet.

"Are you getting one of those pies?" Jeffrey asks.

Oh, how he'd love to, but Andrea lectured him about not letting summertime sabotage his healthy routines, so no—no pie. "Just taking a stroll," he says. The fact is, he can't sit still. He wants the fireworks to be over, he wants to get back to Swain's Wharf. He wants to put out an APB for the jackass in the silver Range Rover.

Ed feels better once he's moving and catches the breeze. He circles to the back of the boat, reminding himself to *breathe;* the biggest threat to his health isn't cherry pie, it's stress.

He should have waited until next summer to attend parties like this—but Andrea is gung ho about the Richardsons. Eric and Avalon managed to wiggle out of this; the Chief should have done the same. Everyone would have understood.

He reaches the stern of the boat, hoping to be alone to reflect, but there's a couple on the back bench, the woman standing behind the man with her hands on his shoulders.

"Oops, sorry," Ed says. He's interrupting—but then the woman turns and he sees it's Leslee Richardson with Benton Coe. She's . . . what? Giving him a back rub? Benton hops to his feet, shakes out his arms, and says, "I feel much better, thanks." Then he offers Ed a lopsided smile as if to say, *This isn't what it looks like.* Ed isn't there to judge, though he's made uncomfortable by the memory of Leslee Richardson appearing in his dream. They were dancing together. This thought is enough to propel Ed right back to the front of the boat.

He shouldn't be here.

* * *

During the fireworks, Coco approaches the empty seat next to Lamont. "Mind if I sit?"

Without looking at her he says, "I would prefer it if you didn't."

He can't be any clearer than that. What happened on the beach was a fluke, then—except Coco knows it wasn't. She knows Lamont likes her. So...he's worried about the rule. As if Leslee isn't breaking all kinds of rules herself.

Coco moves closer to the bow and sits with Kacy. She considers telling Kacy about Leslee and Benton but the whistles, pops, and bangs make conversation impossible. Kacy snaps a selfie of the two of them—their faces are luminous with a rose-gold glow.

After what seems like an interminable wait—one rocket soars and explodes, then the next, at a leisurely pace—the fireworks start to overlap, unfolding one on top of the other.

This, then, is the finale. Coco turns around to sneak a peek at Lamont—and feels like she's been slapped. Leslee has taken the empty spot next to him; she has her arm snaked around the back of his seat, and one of her blue-jeaned legs is flung across Lamont's lap.

Kacy turns to look as well. "Jeez, poor Lamont."

What had he said on Whale Island? *When Bull offered me the job, he told me I'm supposed to treat her like the only woman in the world.* But sorry, this is beyond inappropriate. Coco checks to see if anyone else has noticed. Bull is up in the bow with his real estate bros, and the other guests' gazes are all aimed skyward. Those who have noticed are probably turning a blind eye because they're thrilled to have been invited on this sail and they may even believe that the way Bull and Leslee Richardson conduct their marriage is their own business.

Coco's rage glows like a hot coal in her chest. Leslee is *abusing* Lamont, taking advantage of his service and employment. She probably thinks he finds all the touching and flirting harmless, maybe even flattering.

Does he? Coco wonders.

When the sky finally goes dark, everyone on the boat and back on shore cheers.

Yankee Doodle Dandy, Coco thinks. *It's over.*

Bull stands in the prow and raises his champagne flute. "Where's my wife?" he calls. "Leslee?"

Leslee peels herself off Lamont and weaves among her party guests until she reaches Bull. The music starts back up — "American Woman" by Lenny Kravitz. Leslee grabs Bull around the waist and hugs him close, then they do some hokey dance steps to prove what a cute couple they are.

Bull beams. Coco supposes that to the casual observer, he must seem like the luckiest man in the world.

It's well after ten when Eddie and Grace get back to their car, but Grace says, "I thought the party would go on much longer. I thought maybe we'd be invited back to their house."

"This is just as well," Eddie says. "I have a showing at nine tomorrow."

Grace sniffs. "Did you see? First Leslee was all over Benton Coe, then she threw herself at Lamont."

"Wow," Eddie says. "She's a real firecracker on the Fourth, huh?"

Grace scowls, leaving Eddie to laugh at his own dad joke.

There's a knock on the door of Coco's apartment. She sits straight up in bed, though half her brain is still asleep. She's dreaming? There's another knock. No, she's awake, and someone is here. She checks her phone — it's a quarter past twelve. Nobody has come up to Coco's apartment since she moved in.

Another knock.

Well, she thinks, *it's either Bull or Leslee.* Maybe Bull realized he was being cuckolded at his own party on his own yacht and wants to get even by trying to seduce Coco. Maybe it's Leslee because she needs someone to listen while she feels herself: *Tonight was so fabulous, the best Fourth of July party this island has ever seen!* Maybe she thinks Coco didn't do a thorough job cleaning up (she did a very thorough job and found another barbecued rib stuck inside the Kleenex box in the guest bathroom; someone was out to make a point). Maybe she thinks Coco didn't separate the trash and recycling correctly (Coco is fastidious about the trash and recycling after being schooled by the women who work at the town dump).

Whatever the reason, Coco doesn't want to see either of the Richardsons. She will pretend she's asleep.

Her phone pings with a text. She reads it and then lies back in bed, blowing air at the ceiling. *Ignore it,* she thinks. But she can't.

She opens the front door. "Hey," she says.

"Hey," Lamont says. He leans against the doorframe like one of the Abercrombie models from Coco's youth. He's wearing his crisp white captain's shirt; Coco's eyes are drawn to his neck and the pulse visible beneath his smooth brown skin.

"You do realize that showing up here in the middle of the night comes *dangerously* close to breaking the rule?" she says.

"Yes." His eyes narrow at her. Has she ever been looked at so intensely? "My attraction to you is more powerful than my fear of breaking the rule."

"Is it?" she asks. Her nipples harden beneath the white tank she wears to bed. She moves one inch closer to him but does not touch him. She wants him to be the one to cross the line.

"It is." His voice is husky. He traces a finger along her exposed clavicle, dipping into the hollow at her neck. His touch is feather-light, more a tease than a touch, and it's working. Coco feels a pulsing between her legs. She wants to undo his brass anchor belt buckle, but she stands perfectly still.

"I don't want you to treat Leslee like the only woman in the world," she says. "I want you to treat *me* that way."

"Why do you think I'm here?" Finally, he bends down. His lips hover over hers for a second, then he kisses her and she pulls him inside.

22. The Summer Day

Falling in love, Sharon thinks, *is even better in her fifties than it was in her twenties.* Sharon and Romeo are adults. They don't have to worry about first-time home ownership or raising kids or establishing careers. They have learned how to be present and enjoy a moment.

Romeo loves making romantic gestures. He appears at Sharon's house with bouquets from the wildflower truck on Main Street; he brings Sharon a bunch of fresh mint from his garden and teaches her how to make mojitos. He picks Sharon up in his truck and they drive out to 40th Pole to watch the sunset with a bottle of wine, two sandwiches from Walters, and an '80s playlist. Once it's dark, they make out in the front seat like a couple of teenagers.

Sharon's twins, Sterling and Colby, are surprisingly supportive of their mother's new relationship. Sterling helps Sharon pick her outfits; Colby does her makeup.

"You look hot, Mom," they say. "You're a queen."

Of all the kids, Robert is the most enamored with Romeo. Robert and Romeo watch MrBeast videos together, laughing their heads off, and Romeo plays Fortnite with Robert. (*How does he know how to do this?* Sharon wonders. It seems as esoteric to her as playing the bagpipes.) Romeo even gives Robert a driving lesson on the sandy roads that crisscross the moors behind Sharon's house.

As July unfolds, Sharon and Romeo spend more and more time together—soon it's every night except Fridays. Sharon reserves Fridays for her children, and Romeo catches up with his buddies at the Anglers' Club. Taking one night apart feels healthy and normal—they're each maintaining their own lives!—and it also makes them crazy to see each other. One Saturday, they go to the movies at the Dreamland and have dinner at the Boarding House bar. After dinner they stroll on Main Street, stopping to listen to a guitar player, then an a cappella group; they peek in the window of Stephanie's, where Sharon sees a pair of shoes she likes, and they linger outside Fisher Real Estate and gawk at the picturesque estates in Shawkemo and Quaise. Do they imagine buying a home together? Sharon admits that it has crossed her mind. She'll get the house on North Pasture Lane in the divorce but she has agreed to let Walker use the house for two weeks of the summer (when she made this concession, she'd imagined herself on one of the Mediterranean cruises Heather has since advised her to avoid). Romeo owns a cute saltbox on Hooper Farm Road that has a nice lawn he keeps mowed; there's a basement apartment he rents out to servers from the Lobster Trap. Maybe next summer when Walker is in residence, Sharon will move in with Romeo.

She pulls him away from the real estate listings; she's getting ahead of herself.

They pass the Gaslight, where there's already a line forming; they can hear the strains of live music spilling out the open windows.

"Should we go in for a nightcap?" Romeo asks. "Maybe dance a little?"

Sharon has never been to the Gaslight, mostly because she's worried she'll feel like everyone's mother. "Let's save it for another night. I'm kind of tired."

Will Romeo think she's an old fuddy-duddy or that she lacks spontaneity? No. He pulls her close. "The sooner I can crawl into bed with you," he says, "the better."

On Wednesdays, Romeo gets off work at noon, and one day—is it already the seventeenth of July?—Sharon invites him to meet her at the Field and Oar Club for lunch. He hesitates, then says, "I won't be dressed for it," but Sharon tells him to bring a change of clothes to work; the club is just around the corner, he can walk.

"I want to show you off," she says.

"If you want to get lunch on the water," he says, "let's go to the Brant Point Grill."

"Don't be silly," she says. "The club is much nicer." What she means is that the club is private and exclusive—and it's only after Romeo sets foot in the foyer that she realizes he might be intimidated by this. When they take their table for two on the patio, Sharon feels like all conversations pause for one brief second. Maybe that's because Diane, the piano player, is between songs. Sharon pretends not to notice, though she supposes Romeo's presence is a big deal—this is the first time Sharon has brought a date to the club.

Diane, maybe as a wink, launches into "Changes" by David Bowie.

"Let's order a drink," Sharon says.

Once they sip on a couple of mind erasers—a Field and Oar specialty—Romeo visibly relaxes. He's dressed perfectly, in a forest-green polo and khaki shorts and the driving moccasins he calls his "fancy shoes." He's much more appealing than the other men at the club, all of whom seem a bit effete in their pink oxfords and needlepoint belts, their tidy tennis whites, their painfully close shaves. Sharon could stare at Romeo all day; his profile belongs on a coin. His hair curls up at the collar of his shirt, and there's just a touch of gray around his ears. When he puts on his reading glasses to peruse the menu, Sharon nearly dissolves into a puddle.

Romeo orders the steak sandwich with onion rings and Sharon the Cobb salad. While they're at it, they order another round of mind erasers. The first one has made Sharon feel like she's a soap bubble floating across the club's impeccable lawn toward the harbor.

This bubble, however, threatens to pop when Busy Ambrose approaches the table.

"Sharon!" Busy says. "I see you've brought…a guest."

Well, yes, Sharon thinks. That's the only reason Busy would come over. If Sharon is alone or with the kids, Busy ignores her.

"Busy, you remember Romeo," Sharon says. "It's his first time to the club."

"I imagine it would be," Busy says. "He's a very lucky man, finding someone like you, Sharon. Very lucky indeed."

Does Busy not realize Romeo is sitting right there? Any slight is intentional; Busy knows better.

"*I'm* the one who's lucky!" Sharon says.

Busy waves a dismissive hand. "The summer I turned seventeen, I had a steamy romance with one of the short-order cooks who worked at the snack bar here. My parents were distraught about it, of course, but they needn't have worried. It was over the second we said goodbye at the ferry on Labor Day." She turns to Romeo. "You *work* at the ferry, don't you?"

Romeo leans back in his chair and graces Busy with his gorgeous smile. "I do, thank you for remembering."

Busy's expression is one of bland amusement, as though a child has spoken. "Sharon," she says, "we have our membership committee meeting on August fourteenth. I'll send a reminder to your email."

"Mmm," Sharon says. "I think I have a commitment that day. I'll check and let you know." She pulls off a frosty tone but Busy will know she's bluffing. Sharon wouldn't dare miss the annual membership committee meeting.

"I'll see you there," Busy says, "if not before at one of the Richardsons' magnificent soirées. You seem to be on their permanent guest list."

"Yes," Sharon says. "Romeo and I are *both* on their list."

"Ta, then," Busy says. "Good to see you, Roman."

"Romeo," Sharon says, but Busy has moved on to her next victim. Sharon takes Romeo's hand. "She's awful. I'm sorry." She feels like an ass for suggesting lunch at the club.

But Romeo seems unbothered; in fact, he looks amused. He leans in, brings his mouth to Sharon's ear, which sends a thrill right through her. "Subaru Legacy, New York plate BUSY-B," he whispers. "She's on the standby list back to the mainland September second, but I have a feeling she's not going to make it on the ferry that day. Or the next day, or the day after that, poor thing. She might be very inconvenienced."

Forget the Cobb salad, Sharon thinks. She wants to take Romeo home and eat *him* for lunch!

On Wednesday afternoon after Leslee leaves for her pickleball game, Kacy comes over to Triple Eight to hang with Coco on the beach. Bull is in his study working; Coco has her cell phone in case he needs anything, but he's more self-sufficient than Leslee. Leslee can't seem to change the toilet paper roll or toast a piece of sourdough without Coco's help.

Kacy loves the private beach. The sand is clean and groomed with a sprinkling of pebbles and shells at the waterline. Two chaises rest side by side, swathed in Turkish cotton towels; between the chairs is a cooler table. Coco lifts the top and pulls out two ice-cold seltzers.

Coco is reading *A Separate Peace* by John Knowles. "The real tragedy of this book," she tells Kacy, "is that there isn't a single woman in it." Kacy is paging through *Vogue* when, unfortunately, she sees an ad for Grand Soir, the perfume Isla wears, and this immediately dampens her mood. She and Isla haven't texted since the Fourth of July, when Isla messaged her at midnight with Let us be lovers, we'll marry our fortunes together, the first line of "America" by Simon and Garfunkel. It brought back memories of rainy Tuesday nights, the two of them lying in Kacy's bed, indulging their shared love of '70s soft rock. But when Kacy checked Rondo's Instagram, she saw a picture of Isla and Rondo with Dr. Dunne and his wife, Totally Tami, on a roof-deck in Nob Hill where they were watching the fireworks.

Kacy responded to the text by sending the selfie of herself and Coco aboard *Hedonism,* and Isla sent back a one-tear crying emoji. But more than two weeks have passed and there's been nothing else—no texts from Isla, no posts on Rondo's Instagram.

Kacy is tempted to reach out now—the ad for Grand Soir feels like a sign—but then she hears a motor and looks up to see Lamont puttering in from *Hedonism* in the dinghy. Kacy isn't sure where things stand between Coco and Lamont, but once Lamont pulls up on shore, he ambles over, grinning.

"Look at you two, living your best lives," he says.

"Take our picture," Kacy says, holding out her phone.

Coco and Kacy hoist their drinks and Lamont snaps a few photos.

"Thanks," Kacy says. "Why don't you join us?"

"I'm going home to check on my mom," he says. "You ladies have fun."

"We will," Kacy says. When he's out of earshot, she turns to Coco. "He's so wholesome. That's exotic."

"He likes spending time with his mother," Coco says. "*That's* exotic."

They've reached the point in their friendship where they can enjoy a companionable silence, and Kacy feels herself drifting off to la-la land until Coco says, "Can I ask you a question?"

Her tone can only be described as *portentous,* and Kacy thinks, *She's going to ask about the selfies.* "Sure," Kacy says. She has to stop sending the selfies to Isla. It's not fair to Coco. It's worse than not fair, it's gross.

"Why haven't you said anything about my screenplay?" Coco says. "If you hated it, I want you to tell me."

Kacy feels like a fish released from a hook. Not the selfies after all—the screenplay! "Oh, Coco, I haven't read it yet." Though this, she realizes, might be an even greater infraction. Kacy asked Coco to let her read the script, Coco dutifully sent it, and Kacy has allowed it to molder in her inbox. Kacy has all day free, so what's her excuse? She isn't quite the reader Coco is—Coco is reading a classic while Kacy snacks on *Vogue*—but that's not the reason. Kacy belatedly realized that she wouldn't know what to say if she didn't like it. She would have to fall back on *I'm a nurse, what do I know about writing?* Or she could lie and say she loved it regardless, but what if Coco sensed she was patronizing her? *Don't do business with friends* is a rule for a reason, and another one should be *Don't offer to be the first reader of your friend's screenplay because it could end awkwardly.* "But I'll read it tonight, I promise. I'll start it as soon as I get home."

"Will you?" Coco says. "I'd really love some feedback before I... send it out."

"Where are you sending it?" Kacy asks. "Do you have any connects?"

"I have one," Coco says. "But I'm keeping it a secret because I don't want to jinx it."

Kacy is true to her word. When she gets home, she takes her laptop out to her parents' back deck and clicks on Coco's attachment: *Rosebush,* an original screenplay by Colleen Coyle.

An hour and twelve minutes later, she's wiping tears from her eyes with the back of her hand. The script is...breathtaking. It's raw and honest and poignant. It's very clearly about Coco's life growing up in Arkansas (the main character is named Coco), but Kacy wonders if everything in it is true or if Coco embellished. The overall arc is Coco's desire to escape her small town: Can she do it? Coco the character yearns for the world outside of Rosebush, but everything conspires to keep her there, especially her narrow-minded mother and the family's lack of resources. Kacy wants to know if Coco really robbed the cash register at the diner where she worked; she wants to know if her mother teased her for bringing home library books. The most powerful scene is Coco's senior banquet. The senior banquet at Rosebush High School includes a father-daughter dance. Coco is supposed to dance with her mother's boyfriend, Kemp, but the day before the banquet, Coco's mother picks a fight with Kemp and kicks him out (the viewer learns that she does this with some regularity). The scene follows Coco as she climbs into a pickup in her banquet dress and drives to each of the remote camping spots that Kemp frequents when he's been banished, but she can't find him. She ends up missing the banquet and the next day accuses her mother of intentionally sabotaging her big night. Her mother says,

"You act like you have some right to be happy when the rest of us are miserable."

Kacy can't in a million years imagine either of her parents uttering anything so hurtful. How did Coco make it out of that life with any self-esteem intact? Kacy wants to drive to Triple Eight and give Coco a hug, but that would be weird, and Coco wouldn't want Kacy feeling sorry for her, so Kacy calls instead.

"I loved every word," Kacy says. She doesn't have to make her voice sound persuasive because she's telling the truth. "It's brilliant, Coco. You're a genius."

There's a pause, then: "Really? *Really*-really?"

"Really-really," Kacy says.

Coco isn't sure when, why, or how, but at some point in the middle of July, everything clicks. She learns to go to the Stop and Shop at seven in the morning when it's been freshly restocked; she discovers a secret parking spot in town that's a stone's throw from the Born and Bread bakery; she becomes friends with Chris from Pip and Anchor, and he texts her when they have sandwich specials so that she can combine her marketing and lunch stop.

After she pays off her Visa balance, she has sixty-two hundred dollars in the bank, a veritable fortune. She returns to the Lovely and buys a few things from gorgeous Olivia—a tank, a skirt, a couple of dresses, a pair of cute sandals, a new beach bag. She makes an appointment at RJ Miller, even though the idea of spending a hundred dollars on a haircut kills her when she can simply do it herself. She tells the stylist, Lorna, that she wants to grow it out. Lorna is so skilled with her trimming and shaping that Coco vows never to cut her own hair again.

The Richardsons have also hit something of a sweet spot. The Fourth of July sail solidified their position in Nantucket society—they have invitations every night. Leslee is now a regular fourth at pickleball with Kacy's mother and her friends, and Leslee confides in Coco that she and Bull have secured a nominating letter for the Field and Oar Club from Phoebe Wheeler and four seconding letters, including one from the commodore herself, Busy Ambrose.

"If all goes according to plan, we'll be members as soon as next month," Leslee says.

"Great," Coco says—but this response isn't enthusiastic enough for Leslee.

"The Field and Oar was founded in 1905," Leslee says. "Its membership includes Nantucket's oldest and most established families. You can't just buy your way in; you have to be accepted based on personal merit. This is a very big deal."

If it's true that the Richardsons can't buy their way in, then this *is* a very big deal. It'll lend Leslee and Bull legitimacy. Leslee is obsessed with fitting in, with stature, with who's who, and she's critical of people she calls wannabes. She shows Coco an invitation she received from the dentist Andy McMann and his wife, Rachel. They're throwing a summer cocktail party with a *Preppy Handbook* theme.

"They're copying us," Leslee cries, thrusting the invitation at Coco. "I'm surprised Rachel didn't hand-deliver this, but I'm sure even she knew that would be a step too far. As it is, she's stealing our idea for a themed cocktail party." She sounds offended but also sort of delighted.

"A *Preppy Handbook* theme feels redundant," Coco says. "It's Nantucket in the summer."

Leslee beams. "I could hug you," she says—and then she does hug Coco, and Coco gets a full inhale of Leslee's Guerlain Double Vanille perfume and a mouthful of her barrel-curled hair.

"So will you go?" Coco asks. "To the party?"

"Absolutely," Leslee says, "not. Dr. Andy and Rachel are imitation crab. I could smell their weakness the moment I met them. Besides, I hear Jessica Torre is a far better dentist."

Coco recalls that the McManns were the first people struck from Leslee's invitation list for the Fourth of July. Cutting the invite list by half was a strategy that has made the Richardsons' stock rise. It's classic supply and demand: Everyone wants what they can't have.

Everyone, that is, except for Coco, who relishes each second of her new life. She throws her head back as she cruises along the Polpis Road in Baby. The top is down, the sun is shining, she's playing her favorite song: "I Wanna Get Better" by the Bleachers. But everything is already better, she thinks, because Lamont Oakley is her sneaky-link.

He comes by her apartment at the literal crack of dawn when both Bull and Leslee are fast asleep (they are not early risers). He parks all the way out on the Wauwinet Road, then jogs down Pocomo. (Coco has disabled the driveway alarm, with Leslee's blessing—they both agree the chiming is obnoxious—but even so, Coco checks daily to make sure Leslee hasn't turned it back on.) Lamont sprints along the grass on the side of the driveway so his footsteps don't make noise on the shells. When he arrives, breathless, at her door, Coco feels like they're working for the CIA. But the last thing either of them wants is to get caught breaking the rule now.

They've perfected the art of acting cordial-bordering-on-indifferent when they bump into each other at work. "Hey. S'up." There are no winks, no lingering looks; it drives them both crazy.

When Lamont enters Coco's bedroom in the apricot light of dawn each morning, Coco rolls over, warm with sleep, and instantly starts glowing with desire. Lamont kisses just beneath her ear; he nibbles on her hip bone. She cannot get enough of him.

The best part of the morning isn't even the sex, it's the talking afterward. One morning, Lamont tells Coco that every child on

Nantucket is eligible to take free sailing lessons through Nantucket Community Sailing. Lamont showed a talent for it right away; he had the adaptability, the patience, and the independence. "Plus, I love being on the water," he says. "I love weather, I love wind, I love the sound of the sails, I love tying and untying knots, I love the boats, especially the very simple Optis we learned on."

When he got older, members of the Field and Oar asked him to crew. It was at that point he realized there weren't a lot of Black people in the sailing-verse. "I was usually the only person of color at the Field and Oar," he says. "Which prepared me, I guess, for the whitewashed world of sailing. When I was in college, most of the teams we sailed against were all white."

"Did you feel like a trailblazer?" Coco says.

"Sort of," Lamont says. "But then the kids behind me in school— like Javier and Esteban, for example—saw what I did and their parents heard about all the places I've been able to travel. The Nantucket sailing program is way more diverse now."

Coco tells Lamont about her home growing up. "Nothing in our house was ever correct," Coco says. "I don't know how else to explain it. Something was always breaking—the porch light would go out, the downstairs toilet would overflow, the battery of my mother's Accord would die. My mother would wash our clothes and hang them on the line, but she never folded them or put them away; we'd all just pull stuff crumpled from the laundry basket. Even my mother's name, Georgi—that's her whole entire name, on her birth certificate—it's just not *finished*. Like, why not add the final *e* or *a*?" Coco sighs. "I remember this one time, my mother brought home steaks for dinner, these thick rib eyes that the butcher at work gave her. She mashed potatoes and boiled up some broccoli, and I made brownies for dessert. I was so excited to have a family dinner like you'd read about in a book and it was one time when Bree and her kids were in a good mood—no one was crying, no one was fighting. Just when everything was ready, my mother's phone rang. It was Kemp, saying he'd forgotten that darts league started that night and Bree's boyfriend, Larch, was meeting him at the bar and they wouldn't be home until late. Georgi got so mad they were missing dinner that she carried the platter of steaks out back and threw them into our pond for the snapping turtles. She just tossed everyone's dinner. I ran into my room with the tray of brownies, and I invited Bree's kids in, and we locked the door and ate the brownies straight out of the pan sitting on the floor." Coco tears up. She had been fourteen years old when this happened. She remembers because she wrote a "personal narrative" about it for a ninth-grade English assignment, and the teacher, Mrs. Buckwalter, asked Coco to stay after class. Coco thought Mrs. Buckwalter was going to report their family to child protective services—in a way, Coco *wanted* this to happen—but instead, Mrs. Buckwalter told Coco that she was a "very talented writer."

Coco laughs. "I'm sorry that story doesn't have an inspirational ending like yours. I didn't triumph; I only survived."

"But you did triumph," Lamont says, kissing her eyelids, her nose, then her lips. "Because you're here."

Every morning when Lamont gets up to leave, Coco longs for him to stay.

"Why can't we go to dinner one night? I know where Bull and Leslee have reservations. If they go to the Galley, we can go to the Sconset Café."

"If anybody sees us . . ." Lamont says, and Coco realizes he's right. The Richardsons know everyone now.

There is one place Lamont is willing to take Coco: to his house to meet his mother, Glynnie. At first, Coco can't believe it. "You're sure?" she says. It feels like they skipped a step.

"She wanted to know why I suddenly seemed so happy all the time. And I can't lie to my mama, so I told her about you. She asked to meet you."

Coco and Lamont arrange to go to his house at nine o'clock on Saturday morning. Coco has a little more leeway with her errands on the weekends because the Richardsons tend to sleep in even later than usual. Lamont lives in a saltbox cottage on a cul-de-sac over by the Miacomet Golf Course. The house is neat and tidy, with hydrangeas on either side of a yellow front door. As they approach, Coco hears a dog barking.

Lamont opens the door. "Molly!" he says to an English cream golden retriever who is as white and fluffy as a polar bear. "Molly, meet Coco. Coco, Molly." He ushers Coco inside to a mudroom that is giving Martha Stewart vibes—there's a rainbow of foul-weather jackets hanging on wooden pegs, and beneath a tastefully weathered bench are a row of boat shoes and flip-flops. They step into a bright kitchen with white glass-fronted cabinets and a white marble island with a bouquet of lilies in a green glass vase and a bowl of peaches and plums sitting on it. There's a pie underneath a glass-domed cake stand. On the far side of the kitchen is a breakfast nook with windows that open to the backyard. And at the round table sits a petite woman wearing earbuds with her phone in front of her. Her eyes are closed behind the lenses of her glasses, but her posture is as straight as a ballerina's.

"Mama?" Lamont says.

Lamont's mother opens her eyes in surprise. She presses the screen of her phone and removes her earbuds. "Darling!"

"I brought Coco," he says. "Coco, this is my mother, Glynnis Oakley."

Coco steps forward and offers her hand. "It's nice to meet you, Mrs. Oakley."

"Dear girl, call me Glynnie," she says. She scoots out from behind the table and gets to her feet. She's wearing white capris and a blue-and-white-gingham sleeveless blouse with a ruffled collar. Her skin is the same light brown as Lamont's and she has a few pronounced freckles on her cheeks. Her nails, Coco notes, are perfect ovals polished to look like milk glass. "My eyesight isn't what it used to be so I can't get a good look at you, but you sound just beautiful."

"Thank you for inviting me over," Coco says.

"Lamont will make coffee. I was just listening to my audiobook — it's quite gripping."

"What's it called?" Coco asks.

"Oh..." Glynnie says. "I forget the title, it's one of those...you know. You sit down here next to me and tell me all about yourself and about this crazy couple you're both working for. All the girls at church want the inside scoop. You wouldn't believe the rumors that are flying around this island. All anyone wants to talk about is the Richardsons, but Lamont won't tell me a thing about them."

Coco looks to Lamont, who shakes his head. Coco takes the seat next to Glynnie. "Well," she says, "I'm from a place called Rosebush, Arkansas."

"Rosebush, Arkansas!" Glynnie says. "That sounds made up."

If only, Coco thinks.

The best way to avoid gossiping about the Richardsons (though Coco is tempted to tell Glynnie about the Amalfi lemons; that would incite a spicy riot among the girls at church) is to ask questions about Lamont. Once Glynnie gets talking about him, she can't stop. She tells Coco that Lamont nearly quit sailing after his first lesson at age seven because there was a bully on his boat. Coco mentions that she's friends with Kacy Kapenash, and Glynnie leads Coco into the living room so she can show off Lamont and Kacy's pictures from the junior prom and senior banquet. Coco wants to scream, it is just so cute;

they're so young, they're *babies*. She studies Kacy's dresses: a dusty-rose sheath for the junior prom, a black strapless gown for the senior banquet. Kacy had impeccable taste even then.

"I always secretly hoped something more would happen between them," Glynnie says. "But for some reason, it never did."

From there, Glynnie shows Coco Lamont's school pictures starting in first grade, when he was missing his two front teeth, all the way to his senior portrait in his cap and gown. Next, it's on to his sailing trophies and the collections of postcards he's sent her from around the world. Coco keeps turning to see how Lamont is taking all of this, but he's just chilling on the sofa with his coffee, playing with Molly, smiling and rolling his eyes.

Finally he stands up, washes out their mugs, and fixes Glynnie a ham and cheese sandwich that he covers with plastic and puts in the fridge. "We have to get back to work, Mama," he says. "I'll see you tonight."

"Can't you leave Coco behind?" Glynnie says. "We've barely gotten started."

Lamont walks Coco out to Baby. "She loved you."

"I loved her. She's so proud of you. I know you take that for granted, but..." *But what?* she thinks. Should she tell him that her mother never ordered Coco's school pictures because she thought it was a rip-off? "You shouldn't."

Lamont takes a step closer to Coco, and Coco stage-whispers, "Are you going to kiss me in broad daylight?"

"I'm not," Lamont says. "But I want to, very, very badly." He comes in even closer; his hips bump against hers and she moans softly. Then he steps away and says, "I'll see you back at the base. Thank you for doing that with me."

Lamont gets into his car, and Coco takes a moment after he drives away. She desperately wants to text Kacy and say, *Lamont just took me to meet his mother. He must like me!* But she's not sure she can trust Kacy to keep it secret. What if she slips and tells her mother, then her mother tells Phoebe, and Phoebe tells Leslee? It would be all over.

Coco is eager to give her screenplay to Bull, but Kacy has had it for weeks and hasn't said a word about it. When prompted, Kacy admits she hasn't read it. But she will, she promises. She will!

At dinnertime the same day, Kacy calls to say: "It's brilliant. You're a genius."

It's brilliant, Coco thinks. *I'm a genius.*

The next morning, she prints out the script (the Richardsons are pen-and-paper people) and knocks on the door of Bull's office.

"Come in!" he says.

Coco takes a breath. *This,* she thinks, *is it.* This is why she's here. She remembers back to the night at the Banana Deck—the paradise playlist, Harlan from WAPA, *Give us all the appetizers*—and thinks how astonishing it is that, only two months later, she lives on Nantucket and is indispensable to Bull and Leslee. Everything has gone exactly as she planned. Bull is going to agree to read her script, she just knows it.

She steps into the room. Bull is behind his desk, looking tan and relaxed in a navy polo shirt. He isn't on the phone, isn't screaming in English or any other language. In front of him is a green juice from Lemon Press that Coco procured for him earlier that morning, and he's working the *New York Times* crossword.

" 'Actress Ellen in *Same Time, Next Year,*' " he reads. "Seven letters."

"Burstyn," Coco says, and spells it for him.

"You're a whiz," he says. He looks up. "Everything okay?"

For a second, she can't speak.

He notices the script in her hands. "Is that a…did that come for me?"

"It's a screenplay," Coco says. "It's called *Rosebush*."

He waves his fingers and she sets it down on his desk. "Who wrote it?" he asks.

"I did," Coco says.

It takes him a second to process this, but then he reads the cover page, lifts it to inspect the second page. He raises his eyes to hers. "You wrote a movie?"

"I've been working on it for a while but it's finally finished and I thought you might want to read it."

He's searching her face, but what is he thinking? Does he realize she's his assistant solely because she wanted *access*? He could shut her down, say he's too busy, say, *How dare you.* But he's not going to. She can tell he's intrigued.

"Well," he says. "This is certainly unexpected, but not unwelcome. I can't wait to dig in."

"Okay," Coco says, and she leaves the study, trying to act natural. Before she closes the door, she peeks back in and sees that he's already started to read.

Coming to Nantucket is the best thing she's ever done.

23. Thursday, August 22, 9:35 P.M.

Once Kacy has downed a bottle of water, she says, "There are a few things you should probably know."

"Such as?" Zara says.

"Coco and Lamont are seeing each other."

Zara and Ed exchange glances. Not a complete surprise, considering Lamont wants to go up in the Coast Guard helicopter to look for Coco.

"How long has this been going on?" Zara says.

"You'd have to ask him."

Zara wishes Lamont had offered up this information himself. "Why wouldn't he have..."

Kacy drops her voice. "It's a secret."

"Because?"

"The Richardsons have a rule. Their staff isn't allowed to date."

"But Coco and Lamont did anyway?" Zara says. "Without the Richardsons knowing?"

"Yes," Kacy says.

"And was everything okay between them at the time of the sail as far as you know?"

"As far as I know?" Kacy says. "Coco and I haven't talked much the past couple weeks. We kind of had a falling-out."

"Did the falling-out have anything to do with Lamont?" Zara asks.

"No, no, it was over something completely unrelated. But we were still texting." Kacy pulls out her phone. "So you should probably know...I have a text Coco sent a few days ago that says Leslee was trying to kill her."

"*What?*" Ed says. "May I see that, please?" He pulls his reading glasses from his shirt pocket and enlarges Kacy's text messages. There it is, from Coco: I can't make the dinner. When I asked, Leslee tried to kill me. Literally nearly crashed us both in the car.

"What does this mean?" Ed asks. "What dinner?"

"Your retirement dinner," Kacy says. "Tonight. I invited Coco, and when she asked Leslee if she could go, they were in the car together. Leslee hit the gas until she was going eighty-five miles an hour. On the Polpis Road."

Even the Chief, who has seen his fair share of egregious speeding on this island, whistles. "It's a miracle they didn't crash."

"Did Coco ever share how she felt about the Richardsons?" Zara says. "How she felt about her job?"

"You're asking if I think Coco set the Richardsons' house on fire," Kacy says. "The answer is absolutely not. Coco wouldn't do that."

"You feel this because..."

"Because she's a normal person, not an arsonist. Did she like the Richardsons? No, but she accepted them for the screwed-up people they are."

"From what I saw firsthand," Ed says, "I agree with this assessment."

"Thank you," Zara says. "This is helpful."

"I'm not leaving," Kacy says. She looks at Ed. "I'm not going anywhere until they find her."

"Of course not," Ed says. He and Zara step away. "Talk to Lamont again, then Leslee?"

"Read my mind," Zara says.

They find Lamont pacing in front of the garage. When he sees the Chief and Zara, he says, "Any news?"

"You and Coco are seeing each other?" the Chief says. He can tell Lamont is deciding whether to deny it. "Let me save you the trouble. We know you and Coco are—or were at some point—involved."

Lamont nods. "Yes. It doesn't matter now anyway."

"What doesn't matter now?" Zara asks.

"If the Richardsons know. They had a rule...we didn't want to lose our jobs..."

"Understood," Ed says. "When did this relationship begin?"

"Fourth of July."

That long ago? Ed thinks. *And they managed to keep it secret?* "Leslee never found out? Never *suspected*?"

Lamont sighs. "I think she figured it out yesterday, actually. She came upstairs to Coco's apartment unannounced, which she'd never done before. She didn't see me, but I'm pretty sure she knew I was there."

"Did she say anything later?" Zara asks. "Did she act any differently?"

"No," Lamont says. "We thought maybe she was okay with it. That's why I did what I did on the boat."

"Meaning?"

"Right after the Richardsons renewed their vows, when everyone was raising their champagne glasses, I kissed Coco."

"You kissed her," Ed says.

"Yes. We were in the cockpit, and no one was looking at us—all the guests were focused on Leslee and Bull—so I kissed Coco. And I told her I loved her. I whispered it."

Zara considers this information. She pictures the sun setting, the romance of the moment. "What did she say?"

"She said she loved me too."

"Did anyone overhear you?" Zara asks. "Did Leslee Richardson hear you, or Bull? Did either of them see you kiss?"

"There's no way they heard us. Did one of them see us? Maybe. In the moment, I didn't care. After that, Coco collected the glasses and went below to the galley. I turned the boat around, which required all my attention. Then Bull found out about the fire and asked me to take down the sails and motor home, so I did. When we got back to the mooring, Coco was gone."

"Is it possible Leslee confronted Coco about her relationship with you but Coco didn't tell you?" Ed asks.

"It's possible," Lamont says. "Why?"

"Maybe Leslee told Coco she had to stop seeing you and Coco was so angry that she burned the Richardsons' house down."

Lamont gives Ed an incredulous look. "Seriously? No. That did not happen."

"Maybe Leslee was angry about the two of you breaking the rule," Ed says. "She confronts Coco on the boat, she's been drinking, she's emotional from the vow renewal, and maybe it gets physical, maybe Leslee pushes her or backs her up against the gate that you told us doesn't latch properly—"

At that moment, the Chief's phone rings. It's Lucy Shields.

24. Big Swing

Delilah and Andrea are in the car headed to the pickleball courts. "I'm not sure how much longer I can bite my tongue," Delilah says. "Every single time we play, she volleys from the kitchen. It's like she doesn't know the rule."

"It's a game, Delilah," Andrea says.

"A game with rules," Delilah says. "When you break the rules, it's cheating."

"You know what annoys me about Leslee?" Andrea says, and Delilah perks up. Andrea rarely says a negative word about anyone. "She doesn't put her hair up. It's always down and always perfectly curled. How is that even possible?"

Delilah has less than no interest in Leslee Richardson's hair. "Basically the *only* rule in pickleball is that you can't volley from the kitchen."

"Think of it as exercise in the fresh air and sunshine," Andrea says. She pauses. "If it weren't for Leslee, we wouldn't be able to play at all."

* * *

The teams are always Delilah and Andrea versus Leslee and Phoebe, though when they arrive at the courts today, Delilah suggests mixing it up. "Phoebe could be on my team."

Leslee scoffs. "Why mess with perfection?"

Exercise, Delilah thinks. *Fresh air. Sunshine.* It's nice for the first twenty minutes or so; the game is evenly matched, Leslee doesn't commit any egregious fouls, and at one point, the four of them have a spectacular rally, the kind you see on Instagram. It eventually ends with Delilah hitting a shot that gets past Leslee, but they've all played so brilliantly, they give a collective cheer.

Andrea's right, Delilah thinks. *It's a game, it's fun, and we're all becoming better players, even Phoebe. We're lucky we found a fourth.* Delilah will stop complaining.

Delilah and Andrea win the next point, and the next. Delilah's relaxed attitude is paying off—they might actually win!

The very next point, Leslee volleys from the kitchen; it could not be more blatant. Delilah looks at Andrea, but Andrea just wipes sweat off her brow with the bottom of her shirt. The serve goes to Leslee. It *is* annoying how perfect her hair is, Delilah thinks. It's long and shiny with round barrel curls; her visor keeps the front pieces out of her face and the rest cascades down her back.

Leslee serves; Delilah returns; Leslee hits it to Andrea; Andrea hits it to Phoebe; Phoebe smacks it to Delilah; Delilah hits it to Leslee, who charges into the kitchen to volley it back. Delilah drops her racket to her side and lets the ball go.

"Our point," Leslee says.

Finally, Andrea speaks up. "You know it's a rule that you can't volley from the kitchen, right?"

Leslee looks astonished. "Obviously. Why, was I in the kitchen when I returned that?"

Delilah waits for Andrea to say, *You were, actually, yes.* But Andrea says, "It doesn't matter, it's all in good fun," and she returns the ball over the net so Phoebe can serve.

The next point, Leslee volleys with one foot squarely in the kitchen, and Delilah keeps playing because she realizes that protesting is useless; Leslee is never going to play by the rules. Delilah considers volleying from the kitchen herself—but no, she won't sully the game that way. Instead, she'll transform her fury and indignation into skill and power. She doesn't care about exercise! She doesn't give a rat's ass about fresh air and sunshine! She and Andrea and Phoebe could easily find someone else to be their fourth. Why does it have to be this woman?

She has good hair, Delilah thinks. *So what?* She has the house, the boat; she throws parties, she's fun. She is probably the most popular woman on Nantucket right now. In record time she has somehow become an integral part of the community.

It's match point and Delilah doesn't have to guess what will happen because she knows. Andrea serves; Phoebe returns; Delilah volleys from well behind the line, and Leslee charges into the kitchen and volleys back. Delilah lets the ball go and briefly closes her eyes.

"That's game," Leslee says.

Both Andrea and Phoebe are still, waiting for Delilah to react.

Delilah jogs to the net, smiling even though sweat is dripping into her eyes. "Good game!" she says, tapping Leslee's racket.

"I think that was our best game yet," Leslee says. "You played *well*, Delilah."

"Thanks," Delilah says. "You were incredible, as always."

"And I sucked!" Phoebe says, which makes everyone laugh.

Delilah zips up her racket and drinks deeply from her water bottle, thinking, *I'm not walking away empty-handed.* "Hey, Leslee," she says. "Are you free tomorrow at ten?"

"Free as a bird!" Leslee says. "What do you have in mind?"

"Do you remember I told you I sit on the board of the food pantry?"

"I do!" Leslee says. "I've been meaning to make a donation."

"Well, you're in luck. I'm meeting with the executive director tomorrow morning and I'd love for you to join me."

"It's a very important nonprofit," Phoebe says. "There's a lot of food insecurity on this island."

"Forty-four percent of school-age children on Nantucket qualify for a school lunch," Delilah says.

Andrea says, "That's a lot of hungry children."

"Say no more!" Leslee says. "I'll be there tomorrow at ten. What's the address?"

Delilah is curious to see what Leslee is like one-on-one. Leslee pulls in right next to Delilah on Main Street and Delilah feigns joy: What a coincidence, now they can walk to the food pantry together! Leslee has dressed simply in khaki capris, a white T-shirt, and, hmm, Chanel slingback flats that retail for more than it costs to feed a family of four for a month. But even so, Delilah grudgingly approves; at least there's no ostentatious Hermès or Goyard bag.

Does Delilah catch the faintest whiff of cigarette smoke masked by the mint that Leslee is crunching and her usual miasma of exotic vanilla perfume? Delilah matches her steps to Leslee's as they stroll down the brick sidewalk. Yes, definitely cigarettes. Delilah flashes back to her own era of secret smoking when she worked at the Scarlet Begonia. She was so overwhelmed back then with her late-night job and two little kids to entertain all day that she would smoke on her way home at two or three in the morning, blasting Amy Winehouse. She put the car windows down even in the winter, but Jeffrey could always tell and would bow his head, conveying his deep disappointment.

"Are you a smoker?" Delilah asks.

Leslee whips her head around and gives Delilah an incredulous look that melts into a conspiratorial smile. "I sneak one from time to time."

"Me too," Delilah says. "Or I used to, anyway." This could be what bonds them, she thinks. Phoebe and Andrea put cigarettes in the same category as heroin and Miracle Whip: bad.

Delilah wonders why Leslee smokes—is it a habit left over from a misspent youth or is it to combat stress? What, Delilah would like to know, does Leslee have to stress about? Nothing, that's what. *Must be the misspent youth,* then, Delilah thinks. But before Delilah can explore the topic further, Leslee changes the subject to . . . the weather. "It's been beastly hot for the past ten days," she says, plucking her T-shirt away from her body. "And yet it refuses to rain."

Delilah says, "I have to pay more attention to my perennial bed than I do to my husband."

"Oh, are you a gardener?" Leslee asks. "I'm having a circular garden installed on our property, but it's taking forever. Benton promised it would be done by now, but it's not even close to finished. The custom octagonal hot tub I ordered is collecting dust at the storage center. I want to have a crazy hot-tub party once the garden is completed, but Benton never shows up. It's almost like he's avoiding me."

He wasn't avoiding you on the Fourth of July sail, Delilah thinks.

They reach the food pantry, where the executive director, Corwin Moore—one of the kindest, most thoughtful human beings Delilah has ever known—is waiting for them.

There was a moment, right before Delilah left the house, when she wondered if this meetup was a good idea. Corwin does god's work. Delilah imagined Leslee ignoring him—checking her phone, filing her nails—or making the organization seem cute or quaint. Or, worse, hitting on Corwin because he's tall and *quite* attractive.

Delilah needn't have worried. The second Leslee steps into the food pantry, she transforms into someone else. She greets Corwin warmly and listens earnestly as he explains that the need on Nantucket has increased from sixteen thousand bags of groceries per year to twenty thousand. Then he tells her about the food pantry's relationships with local farms ("Delilah and her husband, Jeffrey, provide a farmers' market bounty as well as fresh eggs to our clients").

Leslee says, "I had no idea there was such a large underserved community here. I thought Nantucket was all rich people."

"A common misperception," Corwin says. "We have lots of families in need." He pauses. "Lots of children in need."

"I want to make a *substantial* donation," Leslee says. "I'm thinking a hundred and fifty thousand dollars."

Delilah and Corwin exchange a quick glance. In their text conversation, they had bandied about a five- or ten-thousand-dollar ask.

"That's incredibly generous," Corwin says. He passes Leslee the annual report and the information packet for donors.

"In fact, make it a hundred and seventy-five," Leslee says. "Any more than that and my husband might curtail my shopping budget."

"You're an angel," Corwin says. He takes Leslee's hand. "How can I ever thank you?"

Leslee inspects his thick black wedding band. "I could think of some ways," she says. "But it looks like you're taken."

Maybe Leslee isn't a completely *different person,* Delilah thinks.

"I am," Corwin says. "My husband, Nick, and I are celebrating our one-year anniversary tomorrow."

"Well, Nick is a lucky man," Leslee says. "I'll drop off a check this week."

Thank you, goodbye, goodbye. Delilah and Leslee leave the food pantry. Delilah—who feels like she just stood in a tornado of hundred-dollar bills—says, "Do you want to go up to Lemon Press and get a coffee?"

"I've had three cups already," Leslee says. "Bull is going overseas tomorrow, so I should get home."

Delilah feels rebuffed but also relieved. "Thank you for that pledge. It's incredibly generous."

Leslee studies Delilah for a moment, then half smiles. "Anything for you," she says.

After Delilah watches Leslee get into her G-Wagon and head up Main Street, she gets a text. It's from Corwin: Job well done!

Sharon turns in a second character study. This one is so personal that she's not sure what she'll do if her class tears it apart. But it turns out she didn't need to worry about that.

"It's so much better," Nancy says.

"Agreed," Willow says. "These two people are intriguing."

"I think you've found your muse," Lucky Zambrano says. "Go with these two—they feel vulnerable and authentic."

The second Sharon clicks Leave Meeting, she shrieks with joy. They liked it! She has found her muse! The first person Sharon wants to tell is Romeo, but she worries that he'll ask to read it, and she can't let that happen, so she calls her sister, Heather.

It's three o'clock on a weekday and Heather is working a big case, but Heather's assistant, Melodie, says, "She's been wanting to talk to you," and she patches Sharon through. That, Sharon thinks, is the definition of *sisterhood*.

"I have the greatest news!" Sharon says. "My online creative-writing class *loved* my character study. They called it intriguing and authentic."

Heather doesn't respond right away. Sharon hears her shuffling papers, so she decides to embellish a little. "My instructor said it was brilliant and that I'm on my way to becoming a published writer."

"The next Charlotte Perkins Gilman," Heather says, and Sharon thinks that, no, *this* is the definition of *sisterhood*—the older sister showing off. (Sharon isn't sure who Charlotte Perkins Gilman is, and Heather knows it.)

Heather says, "She wrote 'The Yellow Wallpaper,' a story about a Victorian-era housewife who slowly loses her mind because her life is so boring and purposeless."

Sharon hopes Heather isn't insinuating that Sharon's life is boring and purposeless. It's definitely time to change the subject. "Melodie said you've been wanting to talk to me?"

"Yes," Heather says in a serious tone—and Sharon's guard immediately goes up. "Are you still hanging out with the Richardsons?"

"I've seen them in passing," Sharon says. The other day, she spied Leslee Richardson having lunch at the Field and Oar Club with Busy Ambrose, but Sharon was so miffed at Busy for how she'd treated Romeo that she did not go over to say hello.

"But you haven't been to any of their parties or gone out to dinner with them?"

"No," Sharon admits. Every time the pool-cleaning crew pulls into the driveway, Sharon wishes it were Coco in her baby-blue Land Rover with another hand-delivered invitation. As for dinner, Sharon has heard the Richardsons prefer to go out alone and eat at the bar, where they can introduce themselves to even more people. "Why do you ask?"

"I didn't tell you this earlier because it's really none of my business, but I recognized the name Bull Richardson because..." Here, Heather draws out a long pause as though *she's* the writer creating suspense. Sharon has to admit her interest is piqued. She knows nothing about the Richardsons, really, which is odd, since she's been inside their home and aboard their boat.

"Yes?" Sharon says.

Heather sighs. "Well, we investigated him for a whistleblower complaint about some environmental fraud."

Oh my god, how dull, Sharon thinks. But what was she expecting? Heather works for the federal government. "I didn't realize you investigated private companies."

"Of course we do," Heather says. "Theranos. Ring a bell?"

The know-it-all comments are starting to irritate Sharon. "And that's what you wanted to tell me?"

"I mentioned the name to Skip," Heather says. Skip, Heather's longtime (dare Sharon say *long-suffering?*) boyfriend, has a job that's even more boring than Heather's: He works for the IRS. He's pretty high up—not the top-top job, but close.

"And?" Sharon says.

"He *intimated*—because of course he can't come right out and tell me—that Bull Richardson and Sweetwater Distribution might be in their crosshairs as well."

Environmental fraud and taxes. Sharon is practically asleep.

"I know you're enamored with the Richardsons," Heather says.

"I wouldn't say *that,*" Sharon snaps. "Leslee throws fun parties."

"You said she's shaking up Nantucket and that she and Bull have basically become the grown-up version of prom king and queen."

Did Sharon say that? She'd had at least three firecracker cocktails on the Fourth of July as well as some champagne, so she was pretty tipsy when she got home, but did she use that phrase—*the grown-up version of prom king and queen?* She might have.

"Just be careful, please, Sharon," Heather says.

Sharon doesn't like it when her older sister tells her what to do; she has never liked it. Sharon is about to toss a snide-adjacent *Will do!* when she hears a beeping. Heather has already hung up.

She considers what Heather told her. She would never betray her sister's confidence by going into specifics, but the old Sharon would have called Fast Eddie and intimated that maybe the Richardsons weren't quite what everyone thought—and Eddie might have mentioned this to his brother-in-law Glenn Daley, and Glenn might have called Rachel McMann, and Rachel would naturally have said something to Dr. Andy, and Dr. Andy would tell his dental hygienist Janice, and the next time Sharon bumped into Celadon Morse at Sea View Farm, Celadon would ask her if it was true that Bull Richardson was a drug lord with connections to the Mob.

Sharon doesn't call Fast Eddie; Sharon doesn't repeat what Heather said to anyone. Has the world turned upside down? Sharon has no interest in speculating about Bull and Leslee Richardson. Sharon has become the kind of woman she never understood before—someone who doesn't need to talk about other people to make her days more interesting because her days are interesting enough as it is.

When Coco gets home from her errands in town, she lugs bags of groceries and a handle of Tito's up the stairs without crushing the loaf of sourdough and finds Leslee and Lamont in the kitchen; Leslee is making crepes with whipped cream and peaches.

"Oh, hello," Coco says. There's a bottle of Laurent-Perrier lounging in an ice bucket. Lamont has a full flute in front of him; Leslee is drinking hers at the stove.

"Hey," Lamont says.

"Did you remember to get the bread sliced thin?" Leslee asks as she pours crepe batter into a pan sizzling with butter.

"I did," Coco says. There are so many things assaulting her senses that she's not sure where to start. First off, Leslee never cooks, yet here she is, whipping up *crepes*? (Then Coco remembers: Leslee used to be a crepe chef in Vegas. Apparently, a true story.) Second, why are she and Lamont day-drinking together on a weekday? Third, Coco has never failed to get the sourdough sliced thin, so why must Leslee check? "Are you two celebrating something?"

"I just dropped Bull off at the airport," Leslee says. "He'll be gone for a week."

"He…what?" Coco is confused. Neither Bull nor Leslee mentioned another trip.

"That thing in Indo is blowing up," Leslee says. "He needs to be there in person. Then he's going to the Philippines afterward to try and drum up some new business."

Coco made the Richardsons' bed this morning and folded their pajamas, and she didn't see a suitcase. It feels like this trip was kept secret from her.

"What about all the dinner reservations I made?" she says. "The tickets for the White Heron Theatre? The passes for the silent disco at the Dreamland? I thought you guys wanted to go to that. Should I cancel?"

Leslee slides a golden-brown crepe onto Lamont's plate. "Cancel?" she says. "Why would you do that?"

Coco hopes this doesn't mean what she thinks it means. She tries to catch Lamont's eye but he's intent on the bowl of sugared peach slices and ignores her, just as they agreed to do.

Coco puts the groceries away with military precision; she tucks the sourdough into the bread box, folds the reusable shopping bags, and takes the vodka into the party room. Who is Coco kidding? Of course it means what she thinks it means. Bull is away; Lamont will slide into his place. Did Lamont know Bull was leaving? He made love to her earlier that morning; he ran his thumbs over her eyelids, nibbled her earlobe, fell asleep for a few precious minutes spooning her. He'd been extra-sweet, she noted, extra-attentive. He knew he was about to be called in from the bullpen. *Or maybe,* Coco thinks, *he just walked into a full-on champagne-and-crepes ambush.*

Coco needs to vent her anger. Should she do a shot from the bottle of vodka? Two shots? Should she take the cue ball off the pool table and hurl it through the plate-glass window?

She wanders over to the jukebox, searches the selections. One song jumps out at her. She presses J12 and after the record drops, it's as though Linda Ronstadt is there in the room. *You're no good, you're no good, you're no good, baby, you're no good.* Coco sits on the curvy white sofa and belts out the lyrics; in her mind, she's a karaoke queen, perfectly in tune. Can Lamont and Leslee hear her, and if they can, do they care? When the song is over, Coco goes back out into the hall and hears Lamont and Leslee's easy banter and Leslee's laugh, extra-girlish today.

Coco hurries down the stairs and enters Bull's study. Where is her screenplay? It's not on his desk. Is she brave enough to venture *behind* his desk? Yes. She checks the piles on either side of Bull's desktop computer—financial documents, loads of them. Taped to the top of Bull's keyboard is a slip of paper that says *Email password: SweetH2O888.* What kind of idiot leaves the password to his email taped to the computer? *No, it's not stupidity,* Coco thinks. It's that he feels safe here. It's his home, his office. He trusts anyone who might see it—Leslee, the cleaning staff, Coco.

She's almost chastened enough to leave without checking his desk drawers. Almost. She rifles through them but doesn't find her manuscript. She checks the trash. It's (thankfully) not there either.

She sneaks into the primary suite. Her manuscript isn't on Bull's nightstand or on his dresser or in his closet. The library? She looks, but it's not on the escritoire, the chaise, or any of the shelves; it's not in the hidden bourbon bar.

He took it with him, she thinks.

Coco imagines Bull at that very moment, tucked into his luxurious pod on Singapore Airlines. He's got a glass of Dom Pérignon, a tiny bowl of warm, salted nuts. The flight attendant has hung up his sports coat; he's removed his loafers and put on his slippers. He peruses the menu, chooses the black cod in ginger sauce, then scrolls through the movies on offer. Does he want to watch *Oppenheimer* again? What about *Caddyshack*? Both feel like a waste of time. He reaches into his briefcase and pulls out Coco's script.

He begins to read.

Coco keeps track of how much time Leslee and Lamont spend together. The crepes and champagne are followed by a ride on *Decadence*. Coco watches them zip off as she washes the frying pan and their whipped-cream-smeared plates; she is Cinderella before the fairy godmother shows up. When they return in the late afternoon, Leslee is golden from the sun; her hair is piled on top of her head in a messy bun. She strolls past Coco, who is in one of the beach chaises reading *Life After Life* by Kate Atkinson, and says, "We had such a magnificent day. Lamont took me to a place called Whale Island over on Tuckernuck."

Coco, who has been visiting the English manor of Fox Corner in her mind—thank god for books!—opens her mouth, but no sound comes out.

"Did you confirm at Proprietors?" Leslee asks. "I'd like a table for two tonight, not the bar, and not that communal table, please. Something tucked away."

"Confirmed," Coco says, though she feels a snarky satisfaction because she did confirm for two at the bar and she won't change it. "Who's joining you?" She holds out a filament of hope that it's Benton Coe, though Benton hasn't shown his face around Triple Eight since the Fourth of July sail.

"Who do you think?" Leslee says. She gazes back at *Decadence*, where Lamont is wiping down the upholstery.

My boyfriend, Coco thinks. *You're taking my boyfriend out for dinner.*

Later, after she watches Lamont and Leslee drive away in the G-Wagon—Lamont in a striped button-down and jeans and his boat shoes, Leslee in a long lavender jersey dress that shows off her smoking body—Coco is tempted to text him: *Bull is gone, so now you're the husband?* She wants to call him a gigolo. But then she thinks about his mother, how Glynnie has to feel her way from the kitchen to the living room, how she has to listen to books rather than read them, how Lamont makes her lunch. He needs this job, and Leslee is his boss; this is work, there's nothing going on. Coco needs to take the high road, conduct herself with quiet dignity.

But the next morning at a quarter to five when Coco hears Lamont's tapping, she doesn't rise from bed. She hears him trying the knob; for the first time, she has locked the door.

He texts: You awake?

He texts: Coco?

Leslee and Lamont go out on *Decadence* every day; Leslee even skips her pickleball game. At night, they go to Languedoc, to Oran Mor, to the freaking Galley, where Leslee asked Coco to reserve them a table out in the sand. They go to the White Heron Theatre to see a production of *The Bald Soprano.*

A dozen roses are delivered to Triple Eight from Flowers on Chestnut. Coco assumes they're from Bull for Leslee—but the name written on the envelope is *Colleen Coyle.* Coco blinks. *For me?* She reads the card, which says, *I miss you.* It's unsigned.

Coco hasn't texted Lamont or left her door unlocked all week, but as she carries the roses up to her apartment, she considers relenting. This is the first time a man has sent her flowers (Carnation Day in high school, she decides, does not count). The roses are the color of ripe apricots or, more relevantly, of the sunrises that normally accompany her and Lamont's lovemaking.

But when Coco returns to the kitchen for a vase, she finds Lamont and Leslee preparing to go out on the boat—only this time, they both have overnight bags.

"Coco!" Leslee says. "We'll need you to hold down the fort until tomorrow."

High road, Coco thinks. *Quiet dignity. Princess Diana, Grace Kelly, Sidney Poitier.* "Are you taking a trip?"

"We're sailing *Hedonism* over to the Vineyard," Leslee says. "I've never been!"

"And you're spending the night?" Coco asks. She feels her coffee threatening to come back up in a hot, stinky stream.

"Leslee is staying at the Charlotte Inn," Lamont says. "I'll stay on the boat."

"I might stay on the boat too," Leslee says.

"Are the boys going?" Coco asks. "Javier and Esteban?"

"They can't get away overnight, unfortunately," Leslee says. "They're breakfast servers at Black-Eyed Susan's and can't miss a shift on short notice."

Behind her, Lamont shakes his head. The expression on his face is one of abject misery, but Coco doesn't care.

"You two have fun!" she says, then she marches out of Triple Eight and over to her apartment. She opens the window in the second bedroom, the one that looks down on the future circular garden but that is still just furrows of dug-up earth, hillocks of pea gravel, and pale slabs of granite awaiting placement. Coco holds the roses out the window, but she can't bring herself to dump them.

She ducks back inside, closes the window, sets the roses in the sink, and texts Kacy: We're going out tonight.

25. Single Ladies

After nearly three weeks of radio silence, Kacy receives a text from Isla: There's something going on with Dave.

Dave is Rondo; Kacy sometimes forgets he has a first name.

Something going on? Kacy thinks. What does that mean? She realizes the text is being used as bait; Isla wants her to ask. Kacy clicks on Rondo's Instagram—nothing new. His last post was on the Fourth of July, the picture of him and Isla and Dr. Dunne and the wife, Totally Tami, with her centerfold breasts and caterpillar eyebrows.

There's something going on with Dave. Kacy considers the options: Rondo has gotten cold feet. Rondo is having professional trouble; he lost a patient; he has a staffing issue; he's butting heads with the hospital administration. (Kacy can't imagine Rondo butting heads with anybody; he's not a butter.) Maybe Rondo is sick. Does he have terminal cancer? Although Kacy wants him to disappear, she doesn't wish for this.

While Kacy's deciding if she should text back—part of her wants to know; part of her doesn't care; part of her wants to engage with Isla; part of her thinks it's better to ignore Isla—a text comes in from Coco: We're going out tonight.

Yes, Kacy thinks. Where do you want to go? she asks.

Everywhere, Coco says.

* * *

When Kacy pulls into the driveway at Triple Eight and sees Coco waiting, she whoops. Coco is wearing the white eyelet dress from the Lovely and a pair of sandals that lace up her slim calves. She's grown her hair out to chin length and she tucks it behind her ears. She's gotten some sun on her face, which makes her ice-blue eyes even more arresting.

"You're a total smoke-show," Kacy says when Coco climbs into the car.

"I'm so happy to be out of my uniform," Coco says. She points ahead. "I know this is the most overused phrase of our generation but...let's do this."

Kacy doesn't need to be told twice; she peels out of the Richardsons' driveway so fast that white shells fly into the air like confetti.

Their first stop is the Oystercatcher for buck-a-shuck. This is, in Kacy's opinion, the best way to spend the golden hour. They order two glasses of rosé and a dozen fifth points from their bartender Carson Quinboro (a legendary Nantucket badass), who directs them to two stools overlooking the scene on Jetties Beach—striped umbrellas and sandcastles, mothers chasing after little kids with bottles of sunscreen. A cover band called Cranberry Alarm Clock plays an acoustic version of "Single Ladies," which is a little weird but also sort of charming. And, in their case, it's appropriate. Kacy raises her glass. "To all the single ladies."

After the first sip of her rosé, Coco explains her get-out-of-jail-free card: Bull is away on a business trip and Leslee and Lamont have sailed to Martha's Vineyard overnight.

"Overnight?" Kacy says. She doctors an oyster with mignonette and tosses it back. "They're sleeping together, right? There's no way they aren't."

Behind her sunglasses, Coco squints in the direction of the lifeguard stand.

"You saw them on the Fourth of July?" Kacy says. "She was practically lying on top of him. And at the Pink and White Party, they were skinny-dipping, remember? She was naked on the boat and he swam out there, Coco."

Coco sips her rosé, though she would like to chug the glass. "They're not," she says. "Leslee just flirts."

Um . . . okay? Coco sounds defensive, and Kacy wonders if she still has a thing for Lamont. She hopes not — Lamont is definitely getting with the boss lady.

"What are the sleeping arrangements for this overnight trip?" Kacy says.

"Lamont is staying on the boat," Coco says. "Leslee is staying at the Charlotte Inn."

Gah! Kacy is *dying* to stay at the Charlotte Inn. Back when Kacy and Isla used to talk about coming to Nantucket on vacation, Kacy imagined a weekend trip to the Vineyard — staying at the Charlotte Inn, hanging out at clothing-optional Lucy Vincent Beach, drinks at Nancy's, dinner at the Red Cat, dancing at the Ritz, breakfast at Morning Glory Farm. "How much is that place per night?"

"I have no idea," Coco says.

"Didn't you make the reservation?"

Coco did *not* make the reservation, a detail that hasn't occurred to her until this very second.

"They can't get into too much trouble," Kacy says, "because the boys on the crew will be there, right?"

Coco's head falls back. "They couldn't go."

"Oh, honey," Kacy says. "Leslee is definitely staying on the boat."

Kacy might as well be sticking the three-pronged oyster fork into Coco's heart. "I don't care," Coco says. "I just feel sorry for Bull."

"They must have some kind of agreement," Kacy says.

Kacy's right, Coco thinks. *They must.* She feels naive, duped, out of her league. There weren't a lot of open marriages in Rosebush.

Kacy hands her phone to the bartender, Carson. "Would you take our picture?" she asks.

The next stop is Lola 41, where they order hibiscus blueberry margaritas. Kacy says, "I'm going to have my parents come get my car and we'll walk. Because we are getting drunk!"

Drunk sounds good to Coco. As she's tasting her margarita, she recognizes two dudes at the end of the bar. "It's Addison," she says to Kacy.

Kacy glances over. "This island is too small. He's with Fast Eddie."

Eddie Pancik, Coco thinks. *Married to Grace, residing at 1313 Lily Street.* She's delivered invitations to their house twice now; it *is* starting to feel like a small island. "Should we go say hello?"

"Absolutely not," Kacy says. "I want to enjoy myself."

When Addison notices Kacy at the bar with the Richardsons' personal assistant, he lowers his voice: "Bull priced out the difference between on-island contractors and off-island contractors for our project," he says to Eddie. "Off-island contractors came in twenty percent cheaper. Which, I hardly have to tell you, is a savings of nearly three million dollars."

Eddie takes a beat. *Why did Bull reach out to only Addison with this information?* he wonders. This feels like something that should have been written in an email to them both. Are Addison and Bull intentionally sidestepping Eddie? Is he expendable on this project? (He fears the answer is yes, but they have a deal.)

"We know off-island contractors are cheaper," Eddie says. "We also know we have to add in the cost of transportation over and back every day, which adds up. We have to factor in bad-weather days when the boats and planes are canceled and they can't work or they get stuck on the island and we have to put them up at a hotel. If there's an issue after the homes are built, is the off-island contractor going to show up? No! But most important, the on-island contractors *are the ones we have the relationships with.* They'll show up. They'll get it done."

Addison spins his Aperol spritz. He persuaded Eddie to order one as well—the drink is having a moment, Addison said—but to Eddie, it tastes like the toothpaste they use at a dental cleaning. He ordered a second one anyway, hoping the drink will telegraph that Eddie, too, is having a moment.

"I told him that," Addison says. "But he still wants to go with off-island contractors and I told him it was okay."

"You..." Eddie feels himself about to lose his cool. "The three of us are partners, are we not? Why wasn't I privy to this conversation?"

"Well," Addison says, and for the first time ever, Eddie sees him squirm. Addison Wheeler is to the manor born; he has an ease in the world that Eddie envies, a combination of pedigree, education, and charm. But right now, Addison looks like he's holding in a fart. "It came up in a conversation about something else."

"Which was..."

Addison sighs. "Bull is helping Reed get into his first-choice boarding school. Tiffin Academy. Bull knows several people on the board, and apparently it's an old-fashioned place where strings can still be pulled."

"And in exchange for him doing you this favor, he wants you to concede on the off-island contractors."

"Yes," Addison says. "But also, Eddie, it's a lot of money. Three mil, a million dollars apiece. You can't sneer at that."

Eddie pushes away what's left of his Asinine spritz. "I have to go," he says and then he does, in fact, sneer. "And for the record, that drink sucks."

At Cru, which is perched on the very end of Straight Wharf, Kacy and Coco order the Crucomber, which is icy cold vodka, cucumber, lemon, and toasted sesame. It's served by a bartender named Shawn, who is so fine, Coco forgets about Lamont for a moment. She thinks Shawn might be checking her out as well because when he sets down their drinks, he says, "You have zombie eyes."

Coco laughs. This is a new one. "Is that a good thing?"

"Yeah, they're otherworldly," he says.

Coco raises her glass to him. She's terrible at flirting.

The woman on the other side of Kacy is holding a tiny baby, Kacy would guess only three or four weeks old; she can see the pulsing of his anterior fontanelle. She's whisked right back to the NICU—the beeping of the monitors, the whoosh of the respirators, the squeak of the nurses' sneakers. In the midst of all this, Kacy suddenly hears Isla's voice. She would address every baby formally—"Good afternoon, Mr. Defazio." "Good evening, Ms. McQuaid"—in a way that lightened the mood in the unit but also indicated a future where these teeny-tiny babies would become adults. Isla is such a good doctor that she inspires every NICU nurse to be just like her. This brings Kacy to the question she's been asking herself since she left San Francisco: How can a person so impeccable in her professional life have such a messy personal life?

She has reached the conclusion that this must happen all the time.

Kacy hands Shawn the bartender her phone. "Would you take our picture?"

Shawn obliges and when Kacy gets the phone back, she laughs. "I think he's into you." She shows Coco the picture: It's all of Coco and just a sliver of Kacy.

"Here, I'll take it," says a pretty, dark-haired girl who has just popped in between them. "Shawn takes terrible pictures. Trust me, I know — he's my brother."

Coco recognizes this chick. "You're Olivia from the Lovely," she says. "You're the one who sold me this dress!"

"Oh, hey!" Olivia says. She looks from Coco to Kacy and back. "Yes, I remember you."

Because Coco and Kacy are four cocktails in, bumping into Olivia seems like the world's most insane coincidence, and they order shots of Fireball all around.

"We need food," Kacy says. They're now too drunk to sit down at anyplace respectable, so off to the Strip they go. Coco says she might want Steamboat pizza or a Reuben from Walters but Kacy calls her an amateur and yanks her into Stubbys. Ten minutes later, they're across the street on a bench scarfing down double cheeseburgers and a pile of hot waffle fries. *Has food ever tasted this good?* Coco wonders. A stream of cars passes them, people just off the ferry.

"The August people are arriving," Kacy says.

The vehicles are mostly Jeeps and luxury SUVs; they're filled with kids who point at the Juice Bar and golden retrievers that hang their heads out the windows. One car has boogie boards strapped to the top; another one has three bikes hanging off the back. Coco sees lacrosse sticks, golf clubs, Provençal-print duffel bags. She can't help but think back to how bewildered she was the day she arrived — and now look at her!

"Let's take a selfie," Kacy says.

Thank god she met Kacy, Coco thinks. And she smiles.

Coco feels like she's entered the cantina in *Star Wars,* but really, it's the Club Car. Instead of aliens, Coco finds a woman in a lime-green linen sheath and pearls and a gentleman wearing a bow tie embroidered with watermelons. Kacy weaves through the crowd until they're standing by Mike the piano player. He's singing "Rich Girl," and everyone singing along agrees that she's gone too far but they know it don't matter anyway.

Kacy says, "You stay here, I'll get drinks. What do you want?"

Coco wants Lamont to call her and confirm that Leslee is staying at the Charlotte Inn, where she's seduced the bellman, and Lamont is heading back to the boat alone. She wants him also to say that he misses her and wants their romance to be public, that he'll tell Leslee in the morning, come what may. "Whatever you're having," Coco says.

Mike the piano player glissandos an end to the song and calls out, "Requests?"

A dude in a navy polo and a pair of dusty-pink Nantucket Reds (not only can Coco identify the pants now; she also knows if they're authentically weathered) puts a hundred-dollar bill in the tip jar. "Would you play 'Just Like Heaven'?" he says. "And dedicate it to Sharon?"

Mike's eyes light up when he sees the blue Benjamin drift down on top of the fives and tens in his jar. "Sharon!" he calls out. "This song is for you!"

Blond Sharon and Romeo are enjoying a tequila cocktail called the Mr. Brightside and a plate of light, cheesy gougères at the Club Car bar when Sharon hears Mike the piano player say, "Sharon! This song is for you!"

"Ha!" Sharon nudges Romeo. "There must be another Sharon here." She and Romeo have already planned to request "Hooked on a Feeling" once they finish eating.

"Show me, show me, show me how you do that trick," Mike sings.

Good god, she thinks. *It's "Just Like Heaven."* That used to be her song with Walker.

It was the early nineties. At a bar called the Mill on the Upper

East Side, Sharon and Walker danced to "Just Like Heaven" and ended up making out on the dance floor with all their friends watching. When the lights of the bar came up, Walker asked for Sharon's number, which she wrote on a cocktail napkin; Walker shoved the napkin in his back pocket. Sharon figured the napkin would end up lost or go through the wash, but — surprise, surprise — Walker called the very next day. He invited Sharon to a West Side pub crawl with the rest of his Columbia MBA classmates. (Sharon almost didn't go because she hated taking the crosstown bus.) During the pub crawl, they stopped at a bar called Wild Life, and Walker asked the DJ to play "Just Like Heaven." Then he said in Sharon's ear, "We'll dance to this song at our wedding."

And they did.

Romeo lifts the plate of gougères. "Do you want the pope's nose?" This is what Sharon's mother used to call the last remaining hors d'oeuvre on the platter. Sharon told Romeo this at the Richardsons' Pink and White Party, and it's cute that he remembered. She pushes thoughts of Walker from her mind and pops the last gougère into her mouth. That one warm, cheesy bite while sitting next to Romeo is *just like heaven.*

Sharon feels a hand on her back. The Club Car bar is narrow — it was originally one of the Pullman cars on the old Nantucket railroad — and hence there's no such thing as personal space. All night, people have been jostling Sharon and Romeo and saying, "Vodka soda, close it," right between them. But Sharon and Romeo don't mind; singing at the Club Car is a Nantucket tradition.

The hand presses; someone wants Sharon's attention. She turns just as Mike sings her favorite line: *"Why won't you ever know that I'm in love with you?"*

Standing there is . . . Walker. It's as though she conjured him.

Sharon is so stunned, she can't speak. She looks past Walker for a person who might be Bailey from PT. Did he have the gall to bring the little vixen to the island? It doesn't appear so. In the next instant, she understands that *she's* the Sharon this song is dedicated to. Walker appeared on the island unannounced, found her at the Club Car, and requested their song as some kind of...grand romantic gesture?

"What," she says, "are you doing here?"

He holds a hand out. "Dance with me."

Sharon is immediately swept back four and a half months to the Day Her Marriage Fell Apart.

It's a typical March day in Connecticut—dreary, raw, raining sideways—and Sharon is parked in front of Centrality Physical Therapy and Wellness, waiting for Walker to emerge from his final appointment. Sharon mindlessly scrolls through her phone, but she's also recalling how reckless Walker had been on their Christmas vacation in Breckenridge—he's nowhere close to the skier he thinks he is—and how he'd torn his ACL ten seconds into a run down George's Thumb. Sharon doesn't have anything planned for dinner, so after they pick up the twins from debate and Robert from basketball practice, the whole family can go to Tequila Mockingbird to celebrate Walker's healed knee. This improves Sharon's mood; she could use a margarita.

When Walker gets into the car, his expression is a tragedy mask. Has someone died?

"Are you okay?" Sharon asks. "Did they add another week? Two weeks?"

"I'm in love with Bailey," he says. "My physical therapist." He swallows. "I love her, Sharon, and I can't believe I'm saying this, but I'm leaving you."

In Sharon's mind, the windshield wipers stop, the car's engine cuts out, the rehabilitation center crumbles. She feels like a block of ice despite the seat heater toasting her bottom. She has heard all about Bailey: twenty-seven years old, a graduate of Fairfield University, hands of a healer, brought chocolate eclairs from the Silvermine Market every week so she could reward Walker for his hard work. Sharon had thought, *Cute, he has a crush on Bailey.* She supposed that was typical at their age, and their marriage was strong enough to withstand a crush; it made things a little spicy, even.

Sharon knows Walker is serious by how devastated he seems. He knocks his head against the car window, saying, "I just cannot believe this. I am such a douchebag!"

Sharon gets a text from Colby: Where u at? She starts to drive toward the high school, saying nothing. Walker brushes his tears away, takes a shuddering breath, and manages to collect himself before the twins pile into the car, both of them so deep into their phones that Sharon and Walker could be on fire—they *are* on fire, Sharon thinks—and they wouldn't notice. She asks a desultory question about debate that receives no answer. She proceeds to the middle school and picks up Robert, and when he's settled in the car, jockeying for space with his sisters, who won't budge, Sharon makes the big announcement: They're going to Tequila Mockingbird for dinner!

Sharon is shocked at how normal—even pleasant—their dinner is. She allows herself to believe that Walker was experiencing a moment of temporary insanity earlier, that all it will take to right the ship he seems so desperate to capsize are some sizzling fajita platters.

But when they get home, Walker packs a bag. He leaves that very night to stay at Bailey's one-bedroom apartment in a sketchy section of Norwalk.

"Are you crazy?" Sharon says to Walker now. "I'm not going to dance with you." The song has come to an end anyway; a few people cheer, and Mike launches into "Philadelphia Freedom."

Romeo spins around on his stool and offers Walker his hand. "Hey there," he says. "I'm Romeo, from the Steamship."

Walker looks from Sharon to Romeo and back and belatedly grips Romeo's hand. "Hey there, I'm Walker, Sharon's husband."

"Ex-husband," Sharon says.

"The divorce isn't final," Walker says. "Legally, I'm still your husband."

"What is this all about, Walker?" Sharon asks. She's pleased to note that Walker looks awful. He's pasty and bloated, and there are some long hairs sticking out of his nose that Bailey from PT must have been too timid to tell him about.

"I'd like to talk to you," Walker says. "I made a big mistake, an *epic* mistake, and I want you back."

Sharon blinks. How many times in the days and weeks following Walker's departure had she envisioned this moment?

"She isn't coming back to you," Romeo says. He stands up so he can face Walker, and Sharon tenses.

Walker huffs. "This is none of your business."

Sharon has to stop this. The last thing she wants is a *scene* in the middle of the Club Car; there isn't room for a confrontation and she doesn't want to go viral for being part of a Gen X love triangle. Walker is right that this is none of Romeo's business, but Romeo is right about something too: Sharon has repeatedly told Romeo that she would never, ever, *ever* go back to Walker.

But now that she sees the two men together, she feels like she has known Romeo for only fifteen minutes. She has never used or even thought the word *rebound,* though she can understand how the term might apply. Sharon and Walker have thirty-plus years of history, routines, habits, inside jokes, memories; they have a community, neighbors, couple-friends; they have relationships with each other's families; they have their *ways;* and, most important, they have their children.

Sharon puts a hand on Romeo's right biceps. (If there's a fistfight, Romeo will break Walker in half.) "Let me just go talk to him."

Romeo's expression is incredulous; his eyes are wounded. "Really?"

She nods, and Romeo retakes his stool, throws back what's left of his drink, then throws back what's left of Sharon's.

Sharon grabs her purse and follows Walker out the door. There are so many people trying to get in that getting out takes longer than she expects. When she reaches the cool air at the entrance, she hears Mike saying, "This one is for Sharon!" And he launches into "Hooked on a Feeling."

Coco sees Romeo from the Steamship standing in the crowd on the other side of the piano, and where Romeo is, Coco has learned, Blond Sharon is sure to be as well. Coco and Kacy sing along gamely to "Hooked on a Feeling," but when it ends, Coco wants to go. Everywhere they've been tonight, they've seen the Richardsons' friends.

As if Coco needs one more reason to leave, Mike the piano player starts singing "You and Tequila." *No,* Coco thinks. *No Kenny Chesney for me.* She grabs Kacy's hand and pulls her out the back door.

Every good night out on Nantucket ends at the Chicken Box. Kacy hasn't set foot in the place since a Christmas break during nursing school, but it never changes—it still smells like beer and lust. The place is crammed with the beautiful people lucky enough to be on Nantucket tonight. There's a cover band playing the Backstreet Boys and everyone on the dance floor is scream-singing the words: *"I! Want! It! That! Way!"*

"I'll get beers," Coco says, and she dives straight into the crush at the bar.

Kacy heads over to the pool tables, where it's less crowded, and rereads Isla's text. There's something going on with Dave.

It sounds like Isla wants Kacy to give her relationship advice. How unfair is that? Kacy would like to respond: *I don't care about Dave!* She wants to say: *If you'd just left Dave like you said you would, you would be here at the Box with me!* Any issues that Isla has with Rondo are her own problems.

Kacy knows she should continue to wear Isla down with silence, but she's had just enough to drink that she decides to throw gasoline on the fire instead. She texts Isla three pictures: one of her and Coco at the Oystercatcher, one from Cru, one from Stubbys. She captions this with the two-girls-with-heart emoji and then four dots meaning "end of discussion."

Coco brings back four Coronas—two for her and two for Kacy—and they enter the fray to dance to "The Sign" by Ace of Base. It couldn't get any cheesier, but Coco seems to love it. A super-hottie breaks into their bubble. It's Shawn from Cru! Coco hugs him like they're long-lost lovers and she turns to Kacy. "Take our picture!"

Kacy snaps a bunch of photos, thinking that Coco is the happiest drunk she's ever seen. Kacy would like to be a happy drunk too, but she's too preoccupied with waiting for Isla's response. It's midnight here, only nine on the West Coast; Isla is definitely still awake.

"Text me those pics," Coco says as she spills beer down the front of her white eyelet dress. Kacy notices one of Coco's sandals is missing. Coco has peaked; now she's on the downslide and getting sloppy. Kacy should get them both into a cab. Shawn is draped over Coco like a fur coat. In her mental crystal ball, Kacy sees Coco going home with Shawn and having forgettable, regrettable sex.

Kacy hears someone calling her name. She peers into the crowd and sees her brother and Avalon. *Oh my god,* she thinks. The Chicken Box really is the center of the Nantucket-verse.

Kacy tries to make her way to Eric and Avalon, but Coco yanks on her arm, saying, "Text me the pics!"

"I will when we get home," Kacy says, but Coco plucks Kacy's phone out of her back pocket. "I'll just send them to myself real quick."

Fine, Kacy thinks, hoping Coco doesn't drop her phone onto the beer-sticky floor. When she finally gets to Eric, she says, "You have to help me get Coco out of here." The band is now playing "Poison" by Bell Biv DeVoe and people are going bonkers. In the midst of this chaos, Eric is a stanchion, a pillar; he is the image of their father.

"We're leaving anyway," he says. "Avalon doesn't feel well."

Kacy turns around to find Coco, but she's vanished into the crowd.

At first Coco isn't sure what she's seeing on the screen of Kacy's phone. She forces herself to focus. There are texts sent to Isla—that's the woman that Kacy broke up with back in San Francisco. In the stream are...pictures of Kacy and Coco. Coco scrolls back. So many pictures—three from tonight alone, plus one of the two of them on the Richardsons' beach, one from the boat on the Fourth of July, one from the Pink and White Party, one from their trip to Great Point, a couple from their first lunch together at the Nantucket Pharmacy counter when they barely knew each other. Kacy has sent Isla literally *all* the pictures. Coco reads one of Isla's responses. I'm sick with jealousy. Now I won't sleep. Thanks.

Jealousy? Coco thinks. Kacy has been making it seem like she and Coco are...*together?*

No. Please, no. What can Coco think but that all this time, Kacy has been using her? Maybe since the moment they met in the line for the ferry. Is that why Kacy bought her a chowder? Because she thought Coco was pretty and looked vulnerable? Was their so-called friendship premeditated so Kacy could make Isla jealous and win her back?

Coco's eyes sting. Lamont has left her, and now Kacy maybe isn't her friend after all. Is this possible? Coco is sober enough to realize she's drunk, drunk enough to let Kacy grab her by the arm and lead her through the crowd and out the door to the cool, fresh air of Dave Street.

Kacy waves over a cab. "Let's get you home," she says.

The morning after their big night out, Coco is so hungover that she messes up her errands. For the first time ever, she forgets to ask for the sourdough at Born and Bread to be sliced thin and by the time she realizes her mistake, it's too late—she has to go to the back of the long line and order a second loaf. She puts regular unleaded instead of premium unleaded into Baby and she skips Nantucket Meat and Fish altogether because the idea of staring at raw salmon and halibut makes her want to puke.

When she turns into the driveway at Triple Eight, she notices a black Lincoln following her. Her first thought is that she's in some kind of trouble, maybe for cutting off the chick in the Mini at the rotary. She pulls into the garage; the Lincoln heads straight to the front of the house. A uniformed driver gets out and opens the back door.

Bull climbs out. He's home.

The Lincoln leaves; Coco hurries over. "You should have texted, I could've picked you up."

Bull waves. "It's fine, you have other things to take care of." He strides past the garage to inspect the garden site. "Are you kidding me? This still isn't finished?"

Coco winces. "No one has been here the entire time you've been gone."

"I'm going to have to break some legs," Bull says. He nods toward the house. "It's good to be home."

Coco wishes she'd known Bull was coming back today; she wouldn't have blown off the fish market. She'll unpack his bag, separate laundry from dry cleaning. He may want a bourbon; it's only ten o'clock in the morning here, but on Bull's clock, it's ten o'clock at night.

When they step inside, he calls, "Leslee!"

"Oh," Coco says, putting down the groceries. "She's not here."

"Pickleball?"

"No," Coco says. She focuses on the arrangement of lilies on the pedestal table in the foyer. Leslee has instructed Coco to remove all the pollen from the stamens with a wet paper towel, but one of the lilies has just opened; Coco will have to take care of that. Her head is as heavy as a bowling ball. She woke up in her own bed that morning but she has no recollection of getting home. When she checked her phone, she saw pictures of her and the bartender from Cru, whose name she's forgotten, sent from Kacy's phone. "She's . . . well, she and Lamont sailed over to Martha's Vineyard."

"When will they be back?"

Coco shakes her head. "I'm not sure."

Bull smiles at her. "Come to my office. I want to talk to you about your script."

Oh my god, Coco thinks.

Bull sits behind his desk and Coco takes one of the leather chairs. He brings Coco's screenplay out of his briefcase. It's battered-looking, which means . . . he *read* it. Coco's stomach squelches. *This is it,* she thinks. *The moment.*

Bull pats the title page. "You're talented," he says. "The writing in this is *extremely* good."

"Thank you," Coco says. Her headache is miraculously gone, replaced by a sparkling clarity.

"I thoroughly enjoyed it," Bull says. "I learned a lot about you?" He ticktocks his head. "Maybe, maybe not?"

"Maybe," Coco says. "Maybe not."

"Well, I very much look forward to reading your next effort."

"My *next*?" Coco says. "What about this one? You just said you enjoyed it."

"Oh, I did," Bull says. "But ultimately, it's too…small."

"Small," Coco repeats, and suddenly she feels herself shrinking. "I realize it's about a small town—"

"No one will ever make this," Bull says. "Maybe back in the nineties it could have been picked up as an indie, but those days died with Kurt Cobain."

Coco flinches. "What about *Hillbilly Elegy*?" she says. "What about *The Glass Castle*?"

"Both of those were bestselling memoirs first," Bull says. (Coco is impressed he knows this.) "Though you're right, if I were to pitch this, I'd say it's *Hillbilly Elegy* meets *The Glass Castle* with a dash of *Ozark* thrown in—and nobody would buy it. You've been to the movies, you know what sells—Marvel, DC, Barbie."

He's right; she knows he's right. He read the script, he praised it, she can't fault him. But neither can she accept his death sentence. She worked too hard. She suffered through the first eighteen years of her life, believing her miserable existence would be worth it when she turned it into art. Her metaphorical blood is all over those pages.

"Doesn't anyone want to make a movie about people with actual feelings and struggles?" she says.

"There is no story here, Coco. Hollywood loves mystery, suspense, drama. This script doesn't have any of that." He comes out from behind his desk and Coco stands to face him.

"There must be someone else you can send it to." She thinks but does not say: *A real producer.*

"If I send this to my people, they'll never take me seriously again," Bull says.

Coco sucks in her breath. "You could pitch it as the next *Winter's*

Bone," she says. "Small, yes, low budget, but we could cast an emerging talent the way they cast Jennifer Lawrence—"

"Calling it the next *Winter's Bone* isn't going to change anyone's mind," Bull says. He clears his throat. "Besides which, this *isn't* the next *Winter's Bone.*"

"Are you even a real producer?" Coco says. "Do you have *any* influence or are you just the person they come to for money to make you feel like you're part of something important? I watched *Snark,* you know. It was dreadful."

"Agreed," Bull says. "Dog's breakfast." He pauses. "And it bombed and I lost my shirt. Which is why I need the next script I invest in to be a big winner."

"Please?" Coco says. She can't have this be the end. That script is not only her goal and her dream, not only her reason for being here—it's her reason for being, period. She takes a step closer to Bull, which is officially too close. She gazes up at him and considers snaking her arms around his neck, pressing her body against his. Is she that desperate? Would that change his mind? *They must have some kind of agreement.*

Bull takes a step back. "Come on now, Coco. You don't want to ruin everything. I'm not going to let you. I'm a married man."

"Married?" Coco says. "Leslee has been playing house with Lamont the entire time you've been gone, which can hardly surprise you because she throws herself at him every chance she gets. And what about the little massage she was giving Benton Coe on the boat on the Fourth of July? He hasn't come to finish your garden because he's afraid of your wife!" She takes a breath. "That night I met you at the Banana Deck? She had her hand on that guy Harlan's thigh."

Bull nods slowly. "I love her," he says. "And she loves everybody."

Right, Coco thinks. It's their kink. It's what makes them the

Richardsons, that along with the Amalfi lemons and the crazy parties and the boats they know nothing about.

"My advice," Bull says, "is to give yourself five or even ten years, until you've lived a little and you have something more to write about, then try again."

Coco feels tears blur her eyes. Five or ten *years*? Is he *joking*? She flees Bull's office before she either flips him off or says something she can't take back. Out in the hallway—of course, of course—Coco rams right into Leslee.

"Hey!" Leslee says, giving Coco an assessing look. "Are you all right?"

Coco smiles through her tears. "Bull's home," she says.

26. Thursday, August 22, 9:45 P.M.

"Hey, Lucy," the Chief says when he answers the phone. *Please,* he thinks, *tell me you found her.*

"Hey, Ed," she says in a weighted tone that lets him know the news isn't good. "One of my track-line patrol found what we believe to be Ms. Coyle's clothes, a pair of white shorts and a pink polo shirt, both size small, washed up on the beach at Smith's Point. That matches the description of what Ms. Coyle was wearing?"

"We can't be sure until we see them, though that sounds right." Ed pauses. "They didn't see anyone?"

"There were still a couple of picnickers out," Lucy says. "And one couple banging in the back of a Bronco, which was pretty brazen, since the top was down. But nobody who matched Ms. Coyle's description. The picnickers and the lovers said they hadn't seen anyone."

"She may have taken her clothes off in the water," Ed says.

"Or she may have swum ashore, ditched the clothes, and made a run for it," Lucy says. "If she was the one who set the fire."

The Chief checks his watch. The last ferry of the night left five minutes earlier. "Call the Hy-Line and see if she's on the boat." *If she is,* Ed thinks, *she'll have some explaining to do.*

"Copy that," Lucy says. "I'll have someone run the clothes out to you in Pocomo to ID."

"Thank you, Lucy." Ed hangs up and tells Zara the news.

"I tend to think the former," Zara says. "She stripped down to have a better chance of making it to shore. Don't you think?"

Ed isn't sure what to think.

"Let's talk to Leslee," Zara says, and Ed swears under his breath.

Leslee Richardson is a hot mess. Her dress is soaked—she clearly waded ashore—and her makeup is smeared down her face, and yet somehow there isn't a hair out of place; it's still long and flowing in barrel curls, and all Ed can think is how much this would annoy Andrea.

The Chief knows how he has to start. "I'm sorry about all of this, Leslee."

She snarls at him. "No, you're not. Your daughter's little friend set our house on fire. She tricked us into hiring her and now she's destroyed everything we have."

"Tricked you into hiring her? What do you mean by that?"

Leslee waves him off. Ed doesn't believe a word that comes out of the woman's mouth, but if Leslee thinks Coco tricked her, did Leslee take her revenge on the boat?

"Why would she want to burn down your house?" he says. "This is where she lives."

"*She* lives in the garage!" Leslee says. "Which you'll notice is *still standing!*"

Yes, Ed notices the garage is unscathed.

"She has the codes to the alarms," Leslee says. "She probably turned them off before we left so the house would be sure to burn to the ground."

"I still don't understand what reason she would have—"

"She was jealous that Bull and I were renewing our vows," Leslee says.

"Jealous because—"

"Coco is in love with Bull. She was always in his office talking to him about books and movies. Once I caught her coming out of his office and she'd clearly been crying. They must have had a lovers' spat."

"You're saying they were involved? Did you ask your husband about this?"

"Of course I asked him, and of course he denied there was anything going on."

"So there's no proof, no corroboration that they were together?" the Chief says. Again, Leslee waves a hand, which isn't an answer. "It's my understanding that Coco was involved with…someone else."

"She and Lamont are sleeping together. They think I don't know, but I know. Coco is the kind of person who isn't satisfied with only one man."

Hmmm, the Chief thinks. *Sounds like someone is projecting.* "How would you describe your relationship with Coco?" the Chief asks.

"We treat her like family," Leslee says. "Coco has a two-bedroom apartment all to herself. She has the Land Rover at her disposal—Baby, she calls it. We pay her generously."

"You said you think Coco is jealous of you," Zara says.

"Very jealous."

"Did this ever affect the way she did her job?"

"No," Leslee says. She sniffs. "Coco was good at her job. She was incredibly competent; she followed detailed instructions and never made a mistake. She used common sense when she hit roadblocks, she didn't complain, she was discreet."

"She sounds like a dream," Zara says. "What would make you think she was jealous of you?"

"I know when someone is jealous of me," Leslee says. "Most women are." Leslee eyes the Chief. "Like your friend Delilah."

The Chief can feel Zara's gaze on him.

"Let's get back to Coco," Zara says. "Can you describe specific behaviors that made you believe she was jealous?"

Leslee's eyes suddenly fill with tears. "The thing is…the last week or so? Coco and I bonded. We reached a new level of intimacy, or so I thought. I took her into my confidence, I treated her like a friend. And then she goes and does *this*!"

"Where were you when news of the fire broke?" the Chief asks. "Bull was on deck, and more than one guest said he was calling for you. Where were you?"

Leslee wraps her long hair around her wrist. "I was sneaking a cigarette."

"You smoke?" the Chief says.

"It's not in my official bio," Leslee says. "But I do occasionally sneak one, yes."

"Were you smoking on the back of the boat?" Zara asks. "By the broken gate?"

"That gate isn't broken," Leslee says. "It latches, but it falls open if we hit any kind of wake. And no, I wasn't in the stern, I was on the port side of the boat so that the wind would blow the smoke away from my guests."

"Do you ever smoke inside your house?" the Chief asks.

"Eww, no," Leslee says. "How disgusting."

"Did you see Coco while you were sneaking this cigarette?" Zara asks.

"I did not."

"When's the last time you remember seeing her?"

Leslee seems to seriously consider this. "She was collecting empty champagne glasses after the toast to our vows," she says. "I didn't see her when I was smoking. Then Bull yelled for me, told me about the fire, and we motored back. By the time we got to our mooring, Coco had vanished." Leslee snaps her fingers. "Into thin air."

27. Day-Drinking in Denpasar

The next Richardson party is a spur-of-the-moment event. Instead of getting hand-delivered envelopes, those invited receive a text: Day-Drinking in Denpasar! Cocktails and Asian-inspired buffet. See you at 888 Pocomo Road tomorrow at two p.m.

Busy Ambrose is overjoyed. The forecast for the next twenty-four to thirty-six hours is driving rain, and Busy dreads nothing more than a summer Sunday at the Field and Oar Club without tennis or sailing. Busy was being pressured to organize a bridge tournament in the ballroom, but now she can delegate that onerous task to Talbot Sweeney because she is going to pull her silk kimono out of mothballs and go to the Richardsons'.

* * *

"Day-Drinking in Denpasar," Delilah says to Jeffrey. It's ten o'clock on Saturday night and Jeffrey is already under the summer-weight blanket. "Party tomorrow at the Richardsons'."

"You go," Jeffrey says. "I don't do day-drinking."

"It's supposed to pour rain," Delilah says.

"I'm well aware," Jeffrey says. "I'm a farmer. I'm doing paperwork tomorrow."

Fine, Delilah thinks. She'll go alone. She's been meaning to talk to Leslee anyway. Corwin at the food pantry has not yet received the donation Leslee promised. He doesn't feel comfortable pestering her, so Delilah volunteered to follow up, which she'd meant to do during pickleball, but last week Leslee had been strangely unavailable, so they'd had to cancel.

Delilah texts Phoebe: Jeffrey not going to 888. Can you pick me up?

Phoebe texts back: We're Ubering. Followed by the cocktail emoji.

Delilah texts Andrea, who says yes they're going, Ed will drive, he's not planning on drinking. *Thank god for the Chief,* Delilah thinks.

Eric shows the invitation text to Avalon, who still isn't feeling well. ("It's like I got bitten by a tsetse fly," she said, whatever that means.) "Do you want to try to go to this?" he asks.

"Hell no," she says. "Why is that woman still inviting us to things? Can she not take a hint?"

Eddie calls out to Grace, who is in the bathroom brushing her teeth, "We got invited to another Richardson party tomorrow. The theme is Day-Drinking in Denpasar." He pauses. "What's Denpasar?"

Grace pokes her head out. "The capital of Bali."

"Really?" Eddie says. "How did you know that? Did you just google it?"

"No, I didn't just google it," Grace says. "I'm brushing my teeth." She flashes Eddie her pearly whites. "I read *Eat, Pray, Love.*"

Sharon hasn't heard from Romeo in days, despite the fact that she has called three times, left two voice mails, and sent half a dozen texts, including one with a lengthy apology.

Sharon's fantasy about reconciling with Walker lasted only a matter of hours. The act he put on inside the Club Car was just that, an act. Once they were out on the cobblestones, Walker's contrition turned into amusement that Sharon was actually dating *Romeo from the Steamship.*

"I thought it was a rumor," Walker said. "I had no idea you were that desperate."

"Speaking of desperate," Sharon said, "how's Bailey from PT?"

Walker spilled the beans: Things with Bailey had been "magical" and "incandescent" until the middle of July, when Bailey left New Canaan for a share house in the Hamptons. "She went to Surf Lodge every night, and some nights I heard from her at three a.m., some nights not at all. I know how much money she makes, and there's no way she was paying for her own drinks."

He got dumped, Sharon thought.

If Sharon had been smart, she would have hightailed it back to the Club Car at that point, but she clung to some romantic notion of saving their marriage and returning to their old life. She imagined being able to send a holiday card with the five of them smiling on the front. With this in mind, Sharon drove Walker back to their house, but the whole time in the car, he was texting on his phone.

"Who are you texting?" she asked.

"No one," he said. "Work."

Work? At ten o'clock at night? When they got home, Walker tried to kiss her but he was sloppy about it and his breath was sour, and

Sharon was distracted by the hairs in his nose and it felt disturbingly like kissing someone she was related to.

"You can sleep in the guest room," she said. Before Walker could protest— "A guest in my own home?"—Sharon went into the primary suite and closed the door. And locked it. Still, even then, she thought they might be able to make it work. She would learn to trust him again; she would ask him to tweeze his nose hairs; their sex life would resume. In the morning, Sharon knocked softly on the door of the guest room; she wanted to discuss how they would explain things to the kids.

"Come in," Walker said.

He was sitting at the desk with Sharon's laptop open. He was... reading her character study, which Sharon was working on turning into a story. She had the characters down; she just needed a conflict.

"Excuse me," Sharon said, slamming the laptop shut. "That's private."

"Hey, I didn't get to finish. That was good. You wrote that?"

"I did."

"Well, I'm glad you've found a little hobby," he said. "Other than gossiping."

So many things about this statement offended her, she wasn't sure where to begin. *It's not "a little hobby," I'm pursuing a lifelong passion for creative writing. It's what I plan to do with my one wild and precious life.*

What Walker would have her do with her life was cater to him— cook, clean, drive the children around, keep track of Robert's blood sugar (Walker didn't even know how to use the Dexcom app), handle the twins' applications to college. Sharon realized that she gossiped because her own life was so extraordinarily dull and unfulfilling.

Until this summer.

"Wake up the kids and take them to the Downyflake for breakfast," Sharon said. "After that, I'd like you to leave."

"Leave?" Walker said.

"It's over, Walker." Sharon texted Romeo: It's over with Walker. He slept in the guest room and will be leaving after breakfast.

There was no response. Sharon called Romeo and was dispatched to his voice mail. She thought she might see him when she drove Walker to the ferry, but Walker insisted on taking the Hy-Line, not the Steamship. "On principle," he said.

When Sharon gets the invitation to the Richardsons' day-drinking party—a party Romeo will likely attend—she decides she needs advice, so she calls Heather, who is in the office even though it's Saturday.

"You're married to your work," Sharon says.

"It's a blissful union," Heather says. "What's up?"

Sharon tells Heather how her own blissful union with Romeo was disrupted by a surprise visit from Walker. "He requested 'Just Like Heaven' at the Club Car piano bar and dedicated it to me."

"Dirty pool," Heather says.

"Now Romeo won't speak to me and I have to see him at a party tomorrow and I don't know what my approach should be. Should I plan to arrive right at two so I'm there when Romeo walks in or should I let him arrive first and wonder where I am?"

Heather takes a beat. "Who's throwing the party?"

Sharon doesn't like to lie to her sister, but she doesn't want to admit that she's still consorting with the Richardsons. "Dr. Andy and Rachel McMann," she says. "It's a *Preppy Handbook* theme."

"Isn't that redundant on Nantucket?" Heather says, and she laughs. "My perennial advice is to play hard to get. Show up late. Make an entrance, or as much of an entrance as you can make in a grosgrain headband."

Coco hates the Richardsons.

She hates Leslee for making Lamont her boy toy, and Bull for casually crushing her life's dream. She considers quitting her job. She can pack up her things and return to her rental in St. John, but the Caribbean is staring down the barrel of hurricane season, and the Banana Deck is closed, so where would Coco work, and can she walk away from the absurd amount of money she's making? Can she leave Lamont? Lamont comes to Coco's apartment at sunrise the day after he gets back from the Vineyard. When he knocks, Coco ignores him, but then she hears a whispery noise. She goes out into the hallway to see that he's slipped a piece of paper under the door: *I'm not leaving until you talk to me.*

Coco stares at the door, picturing Lamont's lean form on the other side, his coppery eyes, his beautiful, strong hands. The truth is, she's missed him. In her gut, she knows that when Lamont is with Leslee, he's working. He took Coco to meet his mother for a reason—he wanted her to understand.

She opens the door and pulls him inside and immediately his mouth is on her neck and she nearly falls to her knees, she wants him so badly. He picks her up and carries her over to the sofa, then lightly tongues her collarbone and starts working his way down, stopping every so often to look up at her. *Is this okay?* It's torture; she wants his mouth on her. She begs him and he goes slowly and then faster and faster until she's screaming, she doesn't care who hears her.

Later, she asks him, "Do you do this with Leslee?"

"I hope you're joking."

"Lamont..."

"Coco," he says. "I'm just her arm candy."

But Leslee acts like she wants Lamont to be *more* than arm candy. Leslee wants what Coco has, and even though Leslee doesn't know about Coco and Lamont, it still feels like a kind of revenge.

Coco could, she realizes, take her revenge against the Richardsons in other ways. She could poison their food; she could go into Bull's computer and screw with his emails—maybe alter the

Richardsons' application to the Field and Oar Club—she could take their dry-cleaning bags to the dump or shrink Bull's suits in the washing machine.

Leslee, she decides, is merely pathetic. Coco doesn't know much about Leslee's life growing up, but she can guess—her father was absent or died early, so Leslee never received the right kind of validation from him and has to seek it from every man she comes in contact with.

Coco's fury at Bull is more complex. He read the screenplay and admired things about it but found it unsuitable to pass on to his contacts in Hollywood. *There is no story here, Coco.* These are the words that crush her. She handed him a secret piece of herself and it wasn't enough. *It's too...small.* She's also mortified that she considered propositioning him; she can't believe she was that desperate. And after all that, he proved to be honorable. She hates Bull, she realizes, because if she doesn't hate him, she'll end up hating herself.

Coco gets a text from Kacy: Hey, I haven't heard from you in a couple days. You okay?

Coco loathes Leslee, despises Bull, is in danger of falling in love with Lamont—but her feelings about Kacy are the ones that trouble her the most. Coco is not only disgusted, she's hurt. All. Those. Selfies. How can Coco reconcile Kacy's actions with the smart, thoughtful person she believed Kacy was?

She doesn't respond to the text.

Bull brings Leslee a sarong from Indonesia. It's made of the finest silk, Leslee brags to Coco, it's the highest quality of batik. Coco has to admit the sarong is gorgeous, with swirling shades of green from jade to seafoam. Leslee googles six ways to tie it, all of which look fabulous on her.

But, she complains to Coco, she has nowhere to wear it. This combined with the forecast of rain on Sunday leads to the conception of the Day-Drinking in Denpasar party.

OMG, Coco thinks. *She's throwing another party.*

Leslee calls Zoe Alistair: Can she whip up an Indonesian feast for thirty people by Sunday?

Yes! It just so happens that Zoe vacationed on Senggigi Beach in Lombok the winter before. She can definitely make that happen.

Leslee takes the theme and runs with it. She unearths all kinds of treasures Bull has brought back from Southeast Asia over the years—carved masks and shadow puppets from Jakarta, strings of colorful paper lanterns from Hoi An in Vietnam—and she asks Coco to decorate the party room with them. She downloads Balinese gamelan music. She buys enormous bouquets of tropical flowers—birds-of-paradise, frangipani, hibiscus.

When Leslee sees what Coco has done with the party room, she gushes, "You're a genius!" Coco filled the room with pillar candles, strung the Vietnamese lanterns and Japanese parasols from the ceiling, and created a showpiece of the spirit house that Bull brought back from Bangkok. The spirit house is a small-scale temple intricately carved from teak, and Coco (after considerable research) fills it with traditional Buddhist offerings: incense, a dish of water and of food (Coco cuts up an Amalfi lemon from the brand-new shipment, sorry-not-sorry).

Leslee places a cool hand on Coco's cheek. "I don't know what I would do without you."

What is going on here? Coco wonders. Leslee has never said anything like this. Can Leslee read Coco's mind? Does she know that Coco has contemplated both desertion and murder?

"I want you to enjoy this party," Leslee says. "The cocktails are going to be extraordinary. Feel free to sample them."

After her big night out with Kacy, Coco can't imagine drinking again, but she's intrigued by this offer. "Should I still wear my uniform?"

"Yes, yes!" Leslee says. "Obviously, you'll still be *working*."

The rain starts late Saturday night as forecast and continues into a gray and dreary Sunday, and after a long, hot, humid string of days, it's the perfect morning to sleep in.

By the time all of us arrive at the Richardsons' house, the day has deteriorated even further. The sky is filled with ominous clouds, and the wind whips the harbor into a froth. We park our various vehicles along the white-shell driveway and navigate the puddles to the grand entrance of Triple Eight, where we shed our boots and jackets and hand Coco our dripping umbrellas.

"Welcome!" Coco says. "Head upstairs. Your hostess awaits."

Stepping into the party room is indeed like entering another country, Delilah thinks. The room glows with candlelight and colorful paper lanterns; the air smells of ginger and sandalwood. Lilting gamelan music plays over the speakers. Leslee's wearing a green batik sarong; she has pearls strung through her hair.

Andrea leans over to Delilah and whispers, "I can't believe I'm saying this, but I kind of want pearls in my hair too."

Delilah agrees. Her only nod to the theme was securing her bun with two takeout chopsticks.

"Selamat sore!" Leslee says. "Welcome, and please help yourself to a drink at the bar."

There are four large-format cocktails to choose from: lychee mai tais, mint ginger gin fizzes, lemongrass margaritas, and Singapore slings. Delilah wants one of each. It's better that Jeffrey isn't here; he can't monitor her intake, so she can drink as much as she wants, and Ed will drive her home. She starts with a margarita and garnishes it with a stick of lemongrass. She sees Phoebe and Addison arrive, Phoebe in a cute embroidered silk jacket and white palazzo pants. Delilah realizes she should have made more of an effort with her outfit. Busy Ambrose is wearing a kimono and has done something very interesting with her eye makeup.

Romeo from the Steamship joins Delilah in pouring a margarita. "Gotta love self-serve cocktails," he says with a wink. "I'm about to teach a master class in day-drinking."

Delilah sees Leslee coming toward them. Delilah should chat with her about the food pantry donation, but it turns out Leslee isn't interested in Delilah.

"Romeo!" Leslee says, standing on her tiptoes to kiss him on both cheeks. "I'm so happy you're here. Where's Sharon?"

"Sharon and I are no longer a thing," Romeo says and Delilah thinks, *Oh no! They were the cutest match.*

"In that case," Leslee says, "come sit by me."

Delilah rolls her eyes. Seriously? Delilah is on a mission, however, so she reaches out for Leslee's arm. "Thank you for the invite," she says. "Listen, before things get too crazy, I wanted to follow up on—"

"Hey there, Delilah," Leslee says, then laughs. "That should be a song." She takes Romeo's arm and leads him to the sofa, calling over her shoulder, "The buffet will be ready in a little while."

Blown off in Bali, Delilah thinks. But this might not be a bad thing. Delilah will wait until Leslee's looser, then ask about the money. Leslee will probably be so embarrassed that she forgot about her pledge, she'll pull out her checkbook on the spot, and Delilah will call Corwin tomorrow with the news.

Phoebe approaches and gives Delilah the up-down. "You didn't dress up?"

Delilah turns her head. "I put chopsticks in my bun."

"Leslee has pearls in her hair, have you seen? So fabulous."

Phoebe helps herself to a lychee mai tai. "I'm definitely having this. What is a lychee, anyway?"

Leslee has done it again, Delilah thinks. By next week, every woman will be wearing pearls in her hair and special-ordering lychees from Pip and Anchor.

Eddie, Addison, and Bull have convened at one end of the Lucite bar, Eddie and Addison with the mint ginger gin fizzes (*They go down way too easily,* Eddie thinks) and Bull with a Tiger beer. "I can't handle the hard stuff during the day, especially not as jet-lagged as I am."

"That's right," Addison says. "How was the trip overseas?"

Bull says, "It was mostly business but I did spend an afternoon spearfishing off Nusa Lembongan."

"Phoebe and I love Bali," Addison says. "People say Ubud is over-run but we can't get enough."

"My trip this past week was a little more bare-bones—I didn't want to run up the expense account or set off alarms with the IRS," Bull says. "But if you ever get a chance to stay at the Amandari, it will not disappoint."

Eddie has no frame of reference for any of this. Last September, he and Grace went to Italy. Grace pulled their entire itinerary off Instagram, which meant a lot of preposterously expensive alfresco lunches under grape arbors overlooking the Mediterranean and a lot of Italians giggling at Eddie's long, baggy swim trunks, but sorry, he wasn't about to wear a banana hammock. What the pictures didn't show was the stress Eddie felt about spending so much money and Grace's whining at the end of the week because she'd gained ten pounds.

Thanks to this trip, Eddie considers travel overrated, although he wishes he could contribute something to this douchey conversation. He finishes his gin fizz and says, "Addison tells me you priced off-island contractors for our project. I know they're less expensive, but for cost-value, the guys we use here on Nantucket are better."

Bull dead-eyes him. "Come on, mate, it's a party," he says. "Let's not talk business." Just as Eddie is feeling like a squid — it's a terrible habit of his to talk business wherever he goes — someone across the room snags Bull's attention. "I can't believe that bastard had the nerve to show his face here," Bull says. Eddie turns around to see none other than Benton Coe walk into the party room. The first person Benton greets (with a longer-than-necessary hug) is Grace. "Excuse me, gentlemen," Bull says. "That bastard isn't getting a step further until I have a little chat with him."

Eddie watches Bull clamp a hand on Benton's shoulder and lead him out of the room. The sight fills Eddie with glee. *Throw him out!* "What's all that about?" Eddie asks Addison.

"They're having a circular garden built," Addison says. "I guess Leslee custom-ordered an octagonal hot tub, and Benton hasn't shown up in weeks."

Addison certainly knows the particulars of Bull's life, Eddie thinks, but he pretends not to care.

Bull and Benton Coe leave the party room and thunder down the stairs, Bull saying, "I need a moment of your time in my office so we can review expectations," and Benton responding, "I asked for a deposit check. Leslee assured me she sent it, but I haven't gotten it." They pass Blond Sharon, who's standing at the bottom of the steps, wishing the house had an elevator. It took her a full fifteen minutes to reach the house from the car (thank god for her golf umbrella). The skirt of Sharon's red embroidered silk dress is so tight, she can take only mincing steps. How is she going to make it up the stairs? If she were still with Romeo, she thinks, he would offer to carry her.

She manages to hike the skirt, the hem of which is soaked from the rain, to mid-shin, then ascends one step at a time. When she reaches the top, she arranges herself. Her hair is in a chignon; her face is powdered; she's done a bright red lip. She enters the party room and hears a wolf whistle—it's Fast Eddie. Sharon beams. She can always count on Eddie.

In an instant, she's surrounded by Andrea, Phoebe, and Delilah. They love her dress! She looks a-maze-ing! They admire the cloisonné bracelets that Walker bought her when they were dating (she's pretty sure he got them from a street vendor in Chinatown). Sharon enjoys being the center of attention, though she doesn't quite get it. The dress is cute—she bought it on Amazon for a Chinese New Year party years earlier—but other people have dressed up. Busy Ambrose is in a kimono, Phoebe wears a silk jacket.

Delilah hands Sharon a cocktail. "This is a Singapore sling," she says. "You drink gin, right?"

"I do," Sharon says. Everyone is being so nice to her; she's been low-key fantasizing about something like this for years. "I should find Leslee to say hello."

An uncomfortable silence follows.

The room is lit only by candles and colorful lanterns, so it takes Sharon a few moments of shuffling and squinting to find Leslee. And then it all makes sense. Leslee is on the sofa, sitting close—too close—to Romeo. She has her hand on his thigh; her head rests on his shoulder.

Sharon wants to leave, but no, she won't. She walked out on Romeo, left him at the bar by himself when they were in the midst of a lovely evening, and this is her karmic payback.

She approaches the two of them. "Hello! Leslee, thanks for having me. Romeo, it's nice to see you."

Has she spoken? At first she isn't sure because neither Leslee nor Romeo look up; they're too focused on each other. Half a second later, Coco appears in her pink shirt and white shorts and says, "Leslee, the buffet is ready."

Leslee rises. She's wearing a green batik sarong and has seed pearls strung through the front pieces of her hair. She looks like a glamorous mermaid—her tanned shoulders are bare, her long legs peek through the folds of the sarong. Sharon missed the mark with her outfit; it's uncomfortable and overwrought. Why didn't she think of a sarong?

"Let's eat!" Leslee says. "Then we'll turn up the music and get this party started!"

Leslee told Coco to enjoy herself, so Coco does. She sneaks into the party closet, which is where they keep surplus liquor, table linens, cocktail napkins, toothpicks, drink charms, the box of pink wigs, rows of martini glasses, copper mule mugs, margarita glasses, milkshake glasses, pilsners, beer mugs, champagne flutes and coupes, bamboo utensils and plates. The best thing about this closet is that it locks from the inside. Coco lures Lamont in on the pretext that she needs him to help her find paper umbrellas for the drinks, but instead, she turns off the light and they make out. It's hot and sexy because it's so risky—kissing inside Triple Eight with everyone around. When they emerge with their lips swollen and red, their breathing shallow, they bump smack into Kacy.

"Hey, you guys," Kacy says, her eyes flicking back and forth between Coco and Lamont, no doubt registering their ravished appearance, their emergence from a dark closet. "What's going on?" She focuses on Coco. "I sent you a text a few days ago, did you not see it?"

The time has come, Coco thinks. "Can you help me with ice?" she asks.

"Of course," Kacy says.

Coco leads Kacy downstairs to the laundry room.

"Are there buckets for the ice or a cooler?" Kacy asks.

"Forget the ice. I want to talk about a couple of things." Coco lowers her voice. "First of all, Lamont and I are sneaky-linking."

Kacy nods. "I mean, yeah, I figured."

"Nobody knows and nobody can know," Coco says. "Leslee has a rule about her employees dating. We'll both get fired."

"So why do it?" Kacy asks. "Do you *like* him?"

"A lot," Coco says. "I think..."

"What? That you're in *love* with him?" Kacy asks.

Coco bites her bottom lip. "I'm not sure. Maybe. But, Kacy, you can't tell anyone — not Eric, not Avalon, not your mom, not Delilah or Phoebe." Coco holds Kacy's gaze. "And there's something else. When we were at the Box and I had your phone, I saw that you've been sending our selfies to Isla."

Kacy's mouth drops. "Oh my god. I am so mortified."

"You sent her *every single picture,*" Coco says. "I thought you were documenting our summer together so you could make me a photo album, but really, you were using me as ammunition."

Ammunition? Kacy thinks. She has messed this up so badly. "First of all, yes, I sent the selfies to Isla, and yes, I did it to make her jealous, and although I never specifically said we were together, that's what I implied." Kacy's eyes are glassy with tears. "Because I'm in love with her and she promised me... then didn't... but that doesn't make any difference. I shouldn't have used our pictures that way. It was gross, and I totally get it if you never want to hang with me again. I just need you to hear me say that I do genuinely care about you. You're the best friend I've had this summer, the *only* friend I've had. Sending the pictures wasn't calculated, Coco, I swear. It was something I did late at night during some desperate moments, and then, when it elicited the response from Isla that I wanted, I kept doing it." Kacy feels physically sick. It is absolutely the most hideous feeling, fighting with your best friend. She wipes at her eyes. "I'm sorry, Coco. I hope you can forgive me."

Coco isn't sure what to say. She's been away from the party too long; any second now, Leslee is going to text and ask where she is. "I have to go back upstairs," she says. And she does.

Kacy has to decide: Stay or go? Her parents are her ride, so she'd have to call an Uber and wait for it in the pouring rain. To leave the party, she feels, would be running away. She heads back upstairs to sit in her discomfort.

Kacy bumps into Leslee, who says, "The buffet is ready, please start." Kacy would really like another drink but Leslee ushers her into the dining room. There's a tower of glistening golden spring rolls; there are platters of satay—beef, chicken, pork—with velvety peanut dipping sauce; there are individual cast-iron skillets of nasi goreng, each topped with a fried egg; there are rows of Chinese takeout boxes containing lobster dan dan noodles; and there's a pyramid of shrimp burgers with sriracha mayo. The food is set up in tiers on top of banana leaves and garnished with tropical fruits and flowers, and all the guests start snapping pictures. Kacy would take pictures too except she's decided she's never taking pictures again.

She fills a plate and chooses a spot by herself on the curvy white sofa. A second later, Busy Ambrose plops down next to her.

"There you are, Kacy," she says. "I've been looking for you."

Busy Ambrose has been looking for her? Kacy barely knows the woman. They were introduced once by Phoebe, though of course Kacy knows who Busy is because everyone on the island knows who Busy is.

"You have?" Kacy says.

"My daughter, Stacy?" Busy says. She winds noodles around her chopsticks like a pro, and Kacy has to admit, she's impressed. Kacy herself took a fork.

Kacy bites into a crispy spring roll. "Mmm-hmm?"

"She's gay." Busy whispers this like it's a secret. Maybe it *is* a secret; Kacy isn't sure how homosexuality is perceived at the Field and Oar Club. "And she's coming for a visit next week. I thought maybe you two could meet."

Kacy coughs. Her spring roll went down the wrong pipe. Is Busy Ambrose trying to set Kacy up with her daughter? Clearly she is. Then Kacy wonders: *Is this such a bad thing?* Kacy is presently low on friends, and sending the selfies to Isla, in the end, wasn't that effective. Kacy hasn't heard from Isla since the text saying there was something going on with Rondo.

Maybe Kacy should meet Stacy. Kacy and Stacy—they'd be such a meme.

Kacy says, "Here, take my number." Then she excuses herself for the bar.

Delilah cleans her plate and considers going back for seconds. "Would anyone like more?" she asks.

Ed says, "I shouldn't."

"None of this food has any calories, Ed," she says.

"I'll have one more spring roll," Andrea says. "Actually, maybe another cocktail instead."

Ed clears his throat. He's *such* a police chief.

"Why shouldn't I?" Andrea says. "You're driving!"

Across the room, Delilah sees Leslee with Phoebe and Busy Ambrose. *Now is the time,* she thinks. She heads over. "Hello, ladies."

"Hi, honey," Phoebe says. "We were just taking about you."

There's no way they were saying anything good. But then, why would Phoebe bring it up? "Oh, really?"

Leslee says, "I was telling them how much I enjoyed meeting Corwin and spending time with the two of you at the food pantry."

Ahh! This is going to be easier than Delilah thought—and what a relief! Delilah can admit now that broaching the topic of money with Leslee at her own party felt a little tacky.

"But I'm afraid my support for your cause is going to have to wait a year or two," Leslee goes on. "I'm sending *significant* donations to Tiffin Academy"—here, Leslee beams at Phoebe—"and to the scholarship fund at Harvard that Busy established in her late husband's name."

"The Francis Ambrose Memorial Scholarship," Busy says, tightening the kimono over her bosom.

"Lovely!" Delilah says. In her mind, every strand of her hair is standing on end in horror. Leslee sent the money she pledged to the food pantry elsewhere? To Busy's husband's scholarship fund at Harvard? (Doesn't Harvard have *enough* money?) And to Tiffin Academy? Delilah stares hard at Phoebe. There's no way Phoebe *asked* Leslee to do this. Leslee must have offered to grease the wheels so that Reed could glide through the admissions process.

The food pantry provides twenty thousand bags of groceries to families with food insecurity, but that's not important to Leslee. Or rather, *Delilah* isn't important to Leslee.

"Lovely!" Has Delilah said this already? Her vision blurs with tears but no one notices. They're back to talking about a lunch at the Field and Oar Club that Busy wants to host in Leslee's honor. "We'll invite Talbot Sweeney," Busy says. "Talbot can be an old stick-in-the-mud, but you do need him on your side."

Of course, Delilah thinks. The Field and Oar Club. That's why Leslee donated to causes for Phoebe and Busy. They both sit on the membership committee.

At that moment, the room grows a shade darker. Outside, a mass of black clouds rolls in. Rain pelts the window, and a bolt of lightning splits the sky in front of them. As if this is a dramatic production Leslee has arranged, the dance music begins: "Knock on Wood" by Amii Stewart. Leslee pulls Phoebe onto the dance floor.

That's it, Delilah thinks. She's leaving. Can she persuade Ed and Andrea to go? Nope; Andrea is dragging Ed out onto the dance floor. Delilah will have to call an Uber.

She grabs two takeout boxes filled with lobster noodles—it's all going to waste anyway—and notices that dessert has been set out: coconut cupcakes and mango with sticky rice. Both look delicious, but nothing can make her stay in this godforsaken house one minute longer. What is this party but a gross example of cultural appropriation? Delilah pulls the chopsticks from her bun and stabs them through two of the cupcakes. One of the chopsticks trails a strand of Delilah's hair. Even better.

At the top of the stairs, Delilah bumps into Blond Sharon. "Are you leaving?" Sharon says.

"Yes," Delilah says. "You?"

"I can't get out of here fast enough," Sharon says.

This makes Delilah smile. Sharon has been an unlikely ally this summer.

"Would you mind if I held on to you so I don't take a nosedive down the stairs?" Sharon asks.

"Please do," Delilah says, and she offers an arm.

Coco hears the pop of a champagne cork and sees Addison Wheeler standing on the bar spraying a bottle of Laurent-Perrier all over the dancing crowd. Everyone cheers; they're jumping up and down chanting along to ABBA: *"Gimme, gimme, gimme a man after midnight!"*

Addison passes the bottle to Leslee, who tips her head back and drinks; champagne flows out the sides of her mouth and down her neck, dousing her sarong. Phoebe takes the bottle and drinks next. Addison pops another bottle—more spray. Outside, lightning flashes.

The song changes to "September" by Earth, Wind, and Fire, and Leslee grabs Romeo's waist from behind and urges him to start a conga line. Coco stands well out of the way. She dreads nothing more than a conga line.

Romeo leads everyone around the party room—across the dance floor, past the jukebox, around the pool table, then out the door to the landing. *If he goes into the kitchen, Zoe's staff will be pissed,* Coco thinks. But Romeo turns the other way and leads the line out onto the octagonal deck. In the pouring rain. Does anyone balk or protest? No! Everyone looks deliriously happy, raising their faces to the sky, drinking in the natural wonder that is a summer thunderstorm.

Coco sighs and heads downstairs to get towels.

Delilah and Sharon can hear the music as they make their escape; there are outdoor speakers all over the property.

"I'll drive you home," Sharon says. Sharon is holding her golf umbrella, which is keeping Delilah and her boxes of noodles dry.

As they approach the garage, Delilah notices the door of the left bay isn't closed all the way. She gets an idea. "Hold on." She looks at Sharon. "Are you up for a little mischief?"

"I am today," Sharon says.

Delilah pushes on the bottom of the garage door and it slides right up. There sits Leslee's G-Wagon, gleaming like Darth Vader's helmet. Leslee's driver-side window is half open. Because she's a smoker, Delilah thinks.

Delilah turns to Sharon. "Trust me when I say she deserves this."

"Preaching to the choir," Sharon says.

Delilah opens the takeout containers and dumps the lobster noodles all over the buttery leather of the driver's seat. Then she joins Sharon under the umbrella and the two of them splash in the puddles all the way back to Sharon's car.

28. Thursday, August 22, 10:05 P.M.

The Chief and Zara find Bull standing by the fire department's barricade, hands deep in his pockets, shoulders hunched, eyes red and watering. The Chief has never had a beef with Bull; in fact, he kind of likes the guy. Likes him but doesn't quite trust him. Ed would never, for example, have gone into business with him the way that Addison did.

"Bull," he says. "We have questions for you."

"I'm sure you do, mate," Bull says.

The Chief looks over at the garage. "There's an apartment on the second floor, right? Where Coco lives?"

"Yes," Bull says. "Two bedrooms, though she has it all to herself." He clears his throat. "We treat Coco very well. I have a hard time believing she did this."

"This?" Zara says.

"Burned our house down," Bull says. "Then disappeared into thin air."

Into thin air—Leslee's exact words. "Would you describe your relationship with Coco for us, please?" the Chief says.

"She was an excellent assistant—organized, responsible…"

"What about your personal relationship?" Zara says. "Did the two of you get along?"

"Of course," Bull says.

"Your wife seems to think that Coco has feelings for you," the Chief says. "Would you agree?"

Bull's nostrils flare like...well, like a bull's. "That's rubbish."

"Leslee told us Coco used to hang out in your office," the Chief says.

Bull runs his hand over his face. "Ahhh," he says. "She did come by my office a few times, but it wasn't like that."

The Chief and Zara wait.

"We used to talk. Listen, I know my wife isn't easy to work for. I used to check in with Coco to make sure she was okay and that she wasn't harboring resentments that would build up so that she felt like stabbing us in our sleep. Or burning our house down." He shakes his head. "I thought we were friends."

"Just friends?" Zara asks.

"That's what I thought. But I'm often clueless when it comes to the women in my life."

The Chief recalls the last time he set foot on this property, during the hot-tub party. He feels his dinner churning in his gut. "Just tell us what was going on between you and Coco, please, Bull."

"A few weeks ago she came to me with a script she'd written." Bull stands a little straighter. "I do some producing, which we told her when we met her down in St. John. I now think she might have manipulated us a bit. We hired her; she moved up here to work for us, and then she hands me this screenplay out of the blue. She'd never mentioned it before."

"So you think she was using you?" Zara says.

"*Using* might be a strong word," Bull says. "*Taking advantage* is probably more accurate. And I respected her for working the angle. Leslee and I do it all the time."

The Chief coughs. He's quite glad Andrea isn't here. Or Delilah. Or Addison. "So you read the screenplay?"

"I did," Bull says. "I gave her positive feedback but I couldn't pass the script on to anyone I knew. It wasn't viable. Which wasn't what she wanted to hear. She tried to persuade me otherwise—"

"Sexually?" Zara says.

"I think there was an implication of that, yeah," Bull says. "But I nipped it in the bud. I'm married, for better or worse."

For worse, the Chief thinks. Bull and Zara turn to stare at him. Did he say that out loud?

"I told Coco I'd read whatever she wrote next," Bull says. "The problem with these artistic types is that they get attached to their projects. That script was Coco's baby. But to me and the rest of the world, scripts are a commodity. And this one I knew I couldn't sell."

"When you turned Coco's screenplay down, did she leave your office in tears?" the Chief asks.

"She did, yes."

That explains the lovers' spat, the Chief thinks.

"Are you aware that Coco is in a relationship with Lamont Oakley?" Zara asks. "They've been seeing each other since the Fourth of July."

"Huh," Bull says. "I didn't know that, but then again, I'm not vested in the love lives of my employees."

"But Leslee is vested," Zara says.

"Oh god, yes," Bull says. "If she found out, she wouldn't be happy."

"Because..." the Chief says.

"Because she's fond of Lamont," Bull says. "My wife likes to exert power over every man in her orbit." He pauses. "You know a little about that, don't you, Chief?"

Zara gives Ed a startled look. *At what point,* he wonders, *will Zara regret taking a job on this island?*

"What is Coco and Leslee's relationship like?" Zara asks.

"It's fine."

"But there's a rivalry between them?" Zara says. "Either because of you or because of Lamont?"

"Maybe a bit," Bull says. "But is that a reason to burn our house down?"

"Leslee seems to think the vow renewal pushed Coco over the edge," Zara says.

"That doesn't sound right," Bull says. "Coco was the one who came up with the vows—she found them on the internet. Before we set sail, she seemed excited about the secret of it. Leslee didn't arrange for the vow renewal as a romantic gesture. She just wanted something to make the sunset sail memorable for our guests. Leslee likes our parties to be memorable." He nods at the Chief. "As you know."

"Would you give us five minutes, please?" the Chief says. "We'll likely send home all the guests except Lamont and my daughter. It seems like everyone else here is a relatively new acquaintance."

Bull nods sadly. "Total strangers."

The Chief and Zara step away, and the Chief checks his phone: There's a text from Lucy Shields. No one matching Ms. Coyle's description was on the last ferry.

Shoot, Ed thinks. It would have looked very bad for Coco if she'd left the island, but at least they'd know she was alive. She has now been missing for over two hours. "Coco and Leslee had issues," he says, "because of either Bull or Lamont."

"Bull has an alibi," Zara says. "He was on the bow all evening, and Lamont was sailing the boat. That leaves Leslee."

"Or Coco set the fire, then later jumped off the boat to escape," the Chief says. "Or did Leslee hear about the fire, assume Coco set it, and push her off the boat in anger?"

"Coco had motive to set the fire," Zara says. "Leslee was competition for Lamont and maybe Bull. Bull turned down her screenplay."

"So she either jumped or was pushed," the Chief says.

"Or it was an accident," Zara says. "She fell against the back gate, which is unreliable, at best, and everyone was too agitated by news of the fire to notice."

"We have to find her," he says, though of course what he means is they have to find her alive.

Zara cocks her head. "Do you hear that?"

She and the Chief stride past the ashes of the fire and reach the Richardsons' front lawn just in time to see Lamont speeding away in the Richardsons' motorboat. "Damn it," the Chief says. "There's already a search underway. I'm sure the last thing Lucy wants is a bunch of Lone Rangers out on the water."

One Lone Ranger can't hurt, Zara thinks. "He loves her," she says.

29. The Kitchen II

The Monday after the Richardsons' day-drinking party, the sky clears and the sun shines bright and hot. The roses of Sharon bloom and Sea View Farm harvests the first of their field tomatoes. It's the second week of August — where has the summer gone? — and Nantucket reaches its peak. Every hotel room is filled; each ferry is standing room only; it's impossible to get a reservation at Languedoc or Proprietors. The Oystercatcher is "fully committed" by six p.m., and don't get us started about the line at the Chicken Box.

It's on Monday that we see Zoe Alistair's Instagram photos of the spring roll tower and the shrimp burgers. We hear chatter about champagne showers and dancing in the rain.

"Leslee Richardson has done it again," Busy Ambrose announces to her lady friends at the Field and Oar Club. "That woman knows how to have fun. The club *needs* someone like her." Busy's lady friends nod and cluck. They wouldn't dare cross Busy in public — she's the commodore — though frankly the stories about Busy's own escapades at these parties are troubling. When Busy approaches Talbot Sweeney about having a lunch for Leslee Richardson, he flat-out refuses.

"I have no interest in Leslee Richardson's fribble," he says. "This club has standards of gentility and decorum. Not all of us are interested in joining the mosh pit, Busy."

Talbot's dismissal of Leslee Richardson could be a problem, Busy has to admit. But there are ways to work around him.

Coco is upstairs in her apartment when she hears Leslee scream. *What fresh hell?* she thinks. Leslee and Bull spent the day after the party in their suite eating fried rice in bed while Coco un-bedazzled the party room. She had to call in not only the regular house cleaners but upholstery and carpet cleaners as well. There was a sticky champagne residue all over the floor and furniture; Coco collected twenty-nine empty bottles of Laurent-Perrier.

Coco dutifully descends to see what Leslee is kerking about. The second Coco steps into the garage, she gags at the smell: a combination of rancid soy sauce and rotting fish.

"It was Delilah!" Leslee says. "She impaled the cupcakes with her dirty hair chopsticks, and now this."

Coco holds her nose and silently congratulates Delilah on a job well done, even though she is the person who has to clean up the mess. She wonders if Delilah was responsible for leaving the BBQ spareribs all over the boat on the Fourth of July and for murdering Leslee's orchid after the Pink and White Party.

"I'm taking Baby to pickleball," Leslee says.

"You're still going to pickleball?" Coco says.

"Hell yes," Leslee says.

Delilah prays that Leslee won't show up at the courts (oh, how Delilah would love to propose they find a new fourth!), but just as they're about to give up and go home, Leslee comes screeching into the parking lot in Coco's Land Rover.

Shit, Delilah thinks.

She hasn't told Andrea about Leslee reneging on her donation and she certainly hasn't told her or Phoebe about dumping the lobster noodles, which felt cathartic at the time but now seems childish.

Delilah steels herself for an accusation: *It was you or Sharon, it had to be, I know you two left early.* Benton Coe also left early; could Delilah get away with throwing him under the bus?

She's a terrible person. She'll confess and blame it on the lemongrass margaritas.

But Leslee is all smiles. "Hey, girls! Sorry I'm late—I had to do a little do-si-do with the vehicles. Phoebe, are you ready?"

Do-si-do with the vehicles? Delilah thinks. Maybe Leslee doesn't realize it was Delilah—but Delilah knows, and the guilt weighs her down. She plays like she has gum stuck to the bottom of her shoes. However, Andrea, for the first time all summer, plays like a beast. She scores three consecutive points.

Wow, Delilah thinks. Maybe Andrea has always been this good and Delilah is a ball hog.

The score is close, though Leslee and Phoebe maintain the lead—9–8, 9–9, and finally 10–9, match point. Leslee serves, Delilah returns, Phoebe volleys, and Andrea runs forward and hits a ball that passes right between Leslee and Phoebe.

Leslee raises her hands above her head. "Woo-hoo!" she says. "Good game!"

"What?" Andrea says. "That ball was in. It's our serve."

"Oops, no, sorry," Leslee says. "Your toe was over the line. You volleyed from the kitchen."

Delilah can't help herself; she brays like a donkey: "You're kidding, right? Her *toe* was over the line? First of all, no, it wasn't. Second, you have been volleying from the kitchen all summer long and we let it slide. Even though it's cheating."

Leslee goes to the sideline and zips up her racket. "I know it was you who vandalized my car, Delilah."

There's a second of stunned silence. The sun scorches Delilah's bare shoulders.

"What?" Phoebe says. "What are you talking about?"

Leslee removes her visor and fluffs her perfectly curled hair. "Why don't you ask Delilah."

"You promised the food pantry a hundred and seventy-five thousand dollars," Delilah says. "Then you backed out."

"I don't remember signing a contract."

"You made a pledge," Delilah says. "You told Corwin you'd stop by with a check. Of course, that was *after* you flirted with him."

Leslee shrugs. "Whatever. He was cute."

"It was offensive," Delilah says, though she isn't sure she should be speaking for Corwin. He might have been flattered. "But not as offensive as reneging on your donation."

"You don't like me," Leslee says. "You've never liked me. You asked me to meet you at the food pantry because you wanted my money. You were *using* me, Delilah. I recognized that right away.

I've met people like you before, people who are threatened by me because I'm friendly and outgoing and I entertain with pizzazz."

Delilah concedes this point: Leslee does entertain with pizzazz. "I'm not *threatened* by you," she says—though of course she is.

"I'll send you the bill for detailing my car," Leslee says. With that, she strolls off the court, climbs into the Land Rover, and drives off.

"Delilah?" Phoebe says.

"If you don't understand what just happened," Delilah says, "then you haven't been paying attention at all this summer."

"I understand," Andrea says, and she taps Delilah's racket.

It's this small act of solidarity that makes Delilah's eyes mist up. "I'm going home," she says. "I'll talk to you guys later."

30. Her

Kacy meets her blind date, Stacy Ambrose, in the unlikeliest of places: the Field and Oar Club.

When Stacy suggested the club, Kacy thought, *Is there a less sexy or romantic place on the island?* They'll be under a proper, staid, and very WASPy microscope. They're *gay*—are there any same-sex couples at the Field and Oar Club, any queer members? There's probably a closet full of them somewhere.

Stacy obviously holds out no hope for this setup, which lowers the stakes. If nothing else, it's a nice change for Kacy. She has hung out with only her family and Coco all summer.

They plan to meet in the Burgee Bar at seven o'clock for drinks.

Kacy has never been to the Burgee Bar, though she read somewhere that it's the best place for cocktails on the entire island (although you have to be a club member or be lucky enough to get invited by one).

Tonight, Kacy has been invited. She climbs to the second floor of the club and pulls open a door with a brass porthole window. The bar is nearly empty—all the Olds are downstairs finishing the dinners they sat down to at five thirty—but Kacy sees a young woman sitting alone at one of the two-tops by the windows. The woman glances at Kacy as she brings an icy martini to her lips.

Kacy's eyebrows lift. The girl has a Wednesday–from–the–Addams Family energy with her dark, structured bob and big brown eyes. She's wearing an outfit Kacy loves but considers a bit scandalous for the Field and Oar—an oatmeal-hued tube sweater, an ivory mini-skirt, and a wide beaded belt. Veja sneakers on her feet.

She sets down her drink and stands up. "Kacy?"

"Stacy?"

They both laugh. "We can't date unless one of us changes her name," Stacy says.

"I'm properly Katherine," Kacy says.

"Then it'll be you." Stacy smiles. "What would you like to drink? And yes, I am putting these on my mother's chit."

"I'll have what you're having," Kacy says.

"Hey, Ryan," Stacy calls to the bartender. "Another very dirty Grey Goose martini with extra olives for my very clean friend here, please."

Very clean? Kacy thinks. She finds herself wanting to protest. *I'm not very clean!*

Against all odds, Stacy Ambrose is cool. Yes, she has summered on Nantucket her entire life, and yes, she grew up climbing on the giant anchor on the lawn below them, but she seems almost apologetic about her privilege. "This place has an underbelly," she says. "Trust me."

Stacy is just a year younger than Kacy. How did they never meet? Stacy grew up in a big, ramshackle house on Hulbert with a bunch of cousins. They played sardines and a lot of Monopoly, badminton in the side yard. "We weren't allowed to go to the parties or the bonfires," she says, and Kacy admits that, as the daughter of the police chief, she wasn't either.

As Stacy is telling Kacy about her job—she's a guidance counselor at McDonogh, a private school in Maryland (yes, Kacy has heard of it; very fancy)—Kacy's phone rings.

"You can't talk on your cell here, sorry," Stacy says. "I break every rule at this club, but not that one."

"Right, no, obviously," Kacy says, reaching into her bag and turning off her ringer by feel. *"I'm* sorry." She takes a quick peek at the display: Isla.

Isla is calling for the first time all summer now? While Kacy is on a date?

"Everything okay?" Stacy says.

"Yeah, of course." Kacy turns her attention back to Stacy and their martinis and the dish of Bugles that has appeared between them. Stacy places a Bugle on each of her fingertips like little hats and eats them that way.

"So what do you do for work?" Stacy asks. She gives Kacy the up-down. "I'm thinking fashion or lifestyle influencer."

"Ha! Hardly!" Kacy says, though she's flattered. "I'm a NICU nurse. I've been living and working in San Francisco for seven years."

"And you took the summer off?"

"I came to a crossroads," Kacy says. "Something bad happened at work and then something bad happened in my—" Kacy's phone buzzes. Kacy should turn it all the way off, and she will, but first she peeks at the screen. Is this a joke? Does Isla have a sixth sense? Does she know Kacy is out with a woman who is normal, maybe even better than normal?

"Do you have to take that?" Stacy asks. "If you do, there's an old-school phone booth next to the ladies' lounge."

"No," Kacy says, but a second later a text comes in from Isla: Pick up, it's an emergency.

"Okay, yeah, maybe. I'll return this call real quick."

"I'll get two more martinis," Stacy says. She hops up and leans over the bar in a way that is undeniably appealing.

Stacy is Her, Kacy thinks.

Downstairs, tucked into a phone booth minus the phone, Kacy texts Isla back. What is it? I'm kind of in the middle of something.

Kacy's phone rings and Kacy thinks, *Okay, I guess we're doing this,* and picks up.

On the other end there's silence, then a breath, then a long, loud wail. Someone's dead, then. Isla's father? Her mother? Kacy has never been introduced to Isla's family.

"Hey," Kacy says. "What is it?"

"He's *sleeping* with Tami!" Isla shrieks. "He says he's in *love* with her! They've been screwing around for a year and a half!"

The first thing that strikes Kacy is Isla's voice. She forgot how much she loves it. "Calm down, I can barely understand you."

This is met with sobs, then Isla blowing her nose, then a deep breath. "Dave is having an affair with Tami Dunne."

"Dr. Dunne's wife? The chick with the ridiculous eyebrows and the fake tits?"

"They've been together since the fall before last."

So have we, Kacy thinks. She remembers back to the last time she saw Rondo—midday at the elevator bank, looking as though he'd just taken a shower. Kacy had thought *affair* then, but she never would have guessed Totally Tami Dunne, his best friend's wife. Apparently Rondo isn't Mister Rogers after all.

"It's going to be okay," Kacy says. "I know it feels bad now—"

"He lied to me!" Isla says. "He cheated on me!"

"Isla," Kacy says. "You have got to get a hold of yourself." Kacy isn't unhappy about this turn of events, though it's disheartening that Isla seems so destroyed about it and that she apparently forgot that she and Kacy were having their own affair. "Listen, I'm out right now—"

"I need you, Bun," Isla says and blubbers some more. "Please don't hang up."

Kacy sighs. "Okay, let me go say goodbye. I'll call you back in five, okay?" Kacy hangs up and texts Stacy: I'm sorry, I have to go. Rain check?

Stacy sends a picture of their two martinis side by side, looking as seductive as two drinks possibly could. *Go back upstairs!* Kacy tells herself.

But she can't forsake Isla. She exits the phone booth and leaves the club before her good sense can kick in.

31. The Third Eight

Coco has made it deep enough into the summer that she's confident she can take a few liberties. When she stops at Nantucket Meat and Fish, she gets the steak tips, the salmon, and the bag of Bull's favorite pretzels that are on Leslee's list, but she adds a slender bottle of truffle oil, a package of crisp rosemary flatbreads, and a pound of

Rainier cherries for herself (she's not even sure she'll like the cherries but they're expensive and she figures they should be something she at least *tries*). Down the street at Pip and Anchor, she buys Leslee's usual organic rosé and her Savage cheese, then goes on a spree in the jams and spreads section. She throws a bottle of homemade ketchup into her basket along with cider syrup and a jar of strawberry Italian plum rosewater jam (for the name alone). Leslee has never once asked Coco for a receipt, never questioned a charge, so why not indulge?

She opts to go to Sea View Farm rather than Bartlett's, hoping to "bump into" Delilah. She would like to speak in code so that Delilah knows that Coco, too, would have filled Leslee's G-Wagon from floor mats to dashboard with lobster dan dan noodles if she thought she could've gotten away with it.

Delilah isn't around, but no matter. Coco chooses a rainbow of heirloom tomatoes, six ears of Silver Queen corn, a dozen eggs that are still warm in their carton, and half a dozen lilies (at fifteen dollars a pop) to brighten up her own apartment.

At the register, she hands over Leslee's card and sets the eggs and produce gently in the canvas bags she brought from home (this is her own touch; Leslee doesn't care about reusable bags).

"I'm sorry," the cashier says. She's a teenager with a pale round face and one prominent zit on her chin that's hard not to stare at. "Your card isn't working."

"What?" Coco says.

"It's been declined."

Coco smiles indulgently. "Would you try it again?"

The girl feeds the chip into the reader. "Declined again. Do you have another card?"

Coco has only her own card and some cash, her own personal money. The total is a hundred and twenty-six dollars (for tomatoes, corn, eggs, and lilies!). There's no way Coco is paying for this. She wonders if Leslee blocked Sea View Farm on her credit card because she hates Delilah so much. Is that a thing you can do? There are three people behind Coco in line, and she has two choices: use her own money or humiliate herself by putting everything back. This, she thinks, is karma pinching her for her hubris.

Just buy it, she thinks. The lilies will look pretty on the counter and they'll smell nice; who cares if they cost ninety dollars? (Coco cares. *It's not the money, it's the money.*)

"I'm sorry," she says. "I think I should just..." She remembers the young mothers she used to see at Harps in Rosebush, asking the cashier to take off the six-pack of Mountain Dew (*We don't need it*) and the clementines (*I'm not even sure how they got in my cart*) when they spent more than they had on them. Coco feels the heat of the other customers' gazes at her back.

"Coco?"

Coco turns to see Delilah approaching. Which makes the situation a thousand times more awkward. Now Coco will *have* to suck it up and pay.

"Is there a problem?" Delilah asks.

"Her card—" the teenager says.

"My card," Coco says, "I mean *Leslee's* card was declined. But it's fine, I have cash of my own, I'll just—"

Delilah waves a hand. "Put it on my house charge," she tells the teenager.

"Oh, no, you don't have—"

"Coco, please," Delilah says. "I'm just so happy to see you somewhere other than Triple Eight."

Coco takes her bag and the lilies. Delilah strolls with her to where Baby is parked. Coco says, "Thank you, I'm sorry. The card being declined was...unexpected."

Delilah winks. "Leslee probably forgot to pay her bill because she's been so busy getting everyone on the island stinking drunk." She peers in the passenger window at the other parcels. "Do you ever splurge on treats for yourself?" she asks. "Because I know I would."

Coco lays the lilies across the seat and puts on her new sunglasses; she finally upgraded from the pink plastic pair she'd found at her bar. The new pair has polarized lenses that turn the whole world a clear, sparkling blue. "For myself?" Coco says, as though the idea never occurred to her.

Coco has one last errand — to fill Baby's tank with gas. Baby takes premium unleaded, which on Nantucket is a mind-blowing five dollars and sixty-five cents a gallon. But Coco doesn't get to spend ninety-five dollars on three-quarters of a tank of gas because, once again, Leslee's card is declined.

When Coco gets home, she finds Leslee in the library seated at the escritoire with — Coco blinks — two fingers of bourbon in front of her (it's a quarter past eleven) and her checkbook out.

"Hey," Coco says. She waves the card. "This was declined a couple of times this morning."

Leslee glances up. "Ridiculous."

Right, Coco thinks. *Except it's not.*

"It was declined at the farm. I had the girl try it twice." Coco will obviously not mention Delilah. "Then it was declined at the gas station."

"Well, I don't know what to tell you, and Bull's not here."

"He's not?" Coco says. "Did he go on a business trip again?"

"New York," she says. "Or DC. I can't remember which. He's meeting with lawyers about god knows what. He'll be back tonight."

"Do you want to look at your account online and see what the problem is?" Coco asks. "I can help you."

Leslee sips the bourbon. "No, I do not want to look at my account online," she says. She tears a check from the checkbook. "I have to pay Benton before he sues us."

There are two other checks on the desk, one made out to Tiffin Academy for a hundred thousand dollars and one made out to the Francis Ambrose Memorial Scholarship Fund for seventy-five thousand. Leslee takes pictures of each check on her phone.

"Would you like me to mail those?" Coco asks.

Leslee rips up both checks and lets the pieces float into the waste-basket. "No, I would not." She glances up at Coco impatiently. "Anything else?"

"What should I do about the card?"

"I have no idea, Coco," Leslee says, picking up Benton's check, which is still in one piece. "I have to deliver this so that he'll finish the garden so I can have my hot-tub party." She throws back the rest of the bourbon. "I need to go."

The next morning, Coco and Lamont eat the juicy, sweet Rainier cherries in bed. "Elite cherries," Lamont says. "The Amalfi lemons of cherries," Coco says. She's been considering getting a tattoo of an Amalfi lemon on her inner wrist.

"Do you think Bull and Leslee have money problems?" Coco asks.

"You're kidding, right?" Lamont says.

Coco tells him about the credit card (Leslee gave Coco a new card from something called ANZ, an Australian bank). Then she tells him about Leslee taking pictures of the two donation checks before ripping them up.

"I don't pretend to understand why Leslee does what she does," Lamont says. "And you probably shouldn't try either." He holds a cherry between his teeth and Coco leans in to take a nibble. Juice dribbles down her chin, leaving golden drops on her white sheets, but in the next second, the cherry is devoured and she's kissing Lamont and who cares about the sheets and who cares about Leslee?

In the days following, Benton Coe's crew work around the clock on the circular garden. (Twice, they arrive so early that they almost catch Lamont leaving Coco's apartment.) The progress they make in just a few days blows Coco's mind. She feels like she's on the sofa with her mother watching an episode of *Extreme Makeover: Home Edition. Where are you, Ty Pennington?* she wonders.

Leslee invites Coco for the big reveal and tells her to close her eyes. Leslee must not realize Coco can see straight down into the garden from her apartment.

But there is a certain amount of wonder once the arched wrought-iron gate opens and Coco steps inside. The boxwood hedges enclosing the garden are eight feet tall and too dense to see through; she feels like she's entering a room. A low stone wall topped with granite benching runs around the base of the boxwoods. There's a maze of cinder paths that wind around hydrangeas, rosebushes, a bed of cosmos and zinnias, a bed of snapdragons, pansies, and foxgloves; there's a gazing ball on a pedestal amid cool green hostas. The flowers are in full bloom, buzzing with fat bumblebees, aflutter with butterflies. In the center is an eight-sided mahogany hot tub with elegant copper ladders hanging off each side. The bottom of the tub is tiled cobalt blue. It's the bougiest hot tub Coco has ever seen.

Coco feels weirdly proud of Leslee for imagining such a lovely space. Leslee saw this in her mind's eye and now they're standing in it. "It's like something out of a storybook," Coco says. "Did you read *The Secret Garden* as a child?"

Leslee gives Coco a blank look. "It's a party space," she says.

"We're having a party." Later that morning, she gives Coco six ivy-green envelopes to deliver.

Only six? Coco thinks. She wonders if Leslee made a mistake, because a lot of people are missing. But Leslee doesn't make mistakes.

Heads, Coco thinks, *will roll.*

Please join us for a garden party on Tuesday, August 13,
at 6:00 p.m.
Cocktails and light bites
Suggested dress: Vintage Lilly Pulitzer
(Bring a swimsuit!)

When Sharon sees the baby-blue Land Rover pull into the driveway and Coco emerge holding an envelope, she hurries to her bedroom to hide. Robert, who is playing his video game in the family room, answers the door. (Poor kid; he probably thinks it's Romeo—if only!)

A second later, Robert shouts, "Mom, you got something!"

Sharon is tempted to throw the envelope away without opening it, but curiosity gets the best of her. *A garden party?* she thinks. *Vintage Lilly Pulitzer?*

"Vintage Lilly Pulitzer?" Grace says. "I have an entire closet filled with *new* Lilly Pulitzer. Is that not good enough?"

"Wear what you have," Eddie says. "The last thing we need to do is spend money on new clothes for the Richardsons' party."

"Not new clothes, Eddie. New *old* clothes. And yes, we do need to. Leslee will be able to spot the difference between vintage Lilly and new Lilly from In the Pink."

"What if we skipped this one?" Eddie says.

"*Skipped* it?" Grace says. "You can skip it, but I want to see Benton's work and use that hot tub."

Eddie thinks, *You are not going to a hot-tub party in a Benton Coe garden without me.* "See if you can find me some vintage Lilly too."

Delilah and Andrea are floating in Phoebe's pool when Phoebe comes out onto the deck waving a green envelope. "Hand-delivered by Coco," she says. "Leslee never stops."

"I'm sure I didn't get invited," Delilah says. "Hell, even I wouldn't invite me."

Phoebe says, "Didn't you apologize?"

Yes, Delilah apologized via text. She'd said she was upset about losing Leslee's support for the food pantry and that she'd been drinking. I acted like a freaking child, she wrote. Please forgive me. Then she Venmoed four hundred dollars for the car detailing and sent a bouquet of sunflowers from the farm.

Leslee texted back: Don't worry about it, lol.

Delilah thinks about telling Andrea and Phoebe that she let Coco put Leslee's charges on the farm's house account when Leslee's credit card was declined, but she's afraid it will sound like she's patting herself on the back or like she's hinting that the Richardsons have money problems, which is absurd.

Phoebe opens the envelope. "It's a garden party," she says. "Oooh, vintage Lilly Pulitzer."

"Oooh," Delilah and Andrea tease.

Phoebe laughs. "We mock what we don't understand."

The next day, when the Chief gets home from work — it was the first day of training for Nantucket's new police chief, Zara Washington, which means Ed can officially start the countdown: thirteen days to go — Andrea shows him the invitation from the Richardsons and says, "I'm staying home but you should go."

"What are you talking about?" The Chief studies his wife. She is still as beautiful to him as she was the first time he saw her — at the police station, standing in line to get a beach sticker for her Jeep. That day, she was wearing a white tank top, jean shorts, and flip-flops, and her hair was in a high ponytail. Ed had noticed her shoulders. He would later find out that she was a swimmer (and that she had just broken up with Jeffrey Drake, the farmer who is now one of their closest friends). Ed had introduced himself—he did this often back then because he was new—and when she smiled at him, Ed experienced a moment of recognition: *You are the one for me.* He'd offered to waive the fee for her sticker, and she said, "I'm not going to let you do that. I'll go out with you for free."

"Are you okay?" he asks now.

Andrea sighs. "Delilah and Jeffrey didn't get invited. There's a whole mess between Leslee and Delilah that you don't want to know about, trust me."

"I trust you," the Chief says. He kisses Andrea; she has long been the one protecting *him.* "But I'm not going without you."

"Will you please, Ed? Just make an appearance for an hour? I don't think it's wise to completely alienate the Richardsons."

Ed gathers her up in his arms. "If you come upstairs with me, I'll do whatever you ask."

Andrea nuzzles against his neck. "What has gotten into you?"

"I got my first taste of freedom. Zara started today."

"Well, I hate to break it to you, but Kacy's home."

Ed laughs. "I didn't picture still having kids at home during my retirement."

"Let's go upstairs anyway," Andrea says, "and pick your outfit."

Because there are only nine guests, Coco assumes the party will be low-key—but she's wrong. Leslee ordered five thousand white string lights that Coco hangs around the arched gate and near the stone benches. Zoe Alistair sets up a very cool curved bar and high round-top tables along the cinder paths.

"I'm going for a swingers-in-the-summertime vibe," Leslee tells Coco. "I wanted to put that on the invite but Bull didn't want people to get the wrong idea."

Presumably, Leslee means *swingers* like the movie, Coco thinks, that new-old Sinatra feel. The cocktails are retro: bourbon sidecars, raspberry mules, and, yes, French 75s made with juice from the Amalfi lemons (this was Coco's suggestion). They're serving only finger foods — appetizers and desserts — because Leslee claims people don't want to put on bathing suits when they feel full.

Coco thinks: *A swingers theme, strong cocktails, tiny bites of food, a hot tub — what could go wrong?*

Leslee wears a long halter dress printed with pink flamingos. It has white rickrack down the front that reminds Coco of icing on a Hostess cupcake. Leslee makes a point of mentioning that Beth from Current Vintage put this dress aside for Leslee the second it came in. (Beth apparently bought it from an estate sale in Palm Beach and thinks it might once have belonged to Lilly Pulitzer herself.) Coco makes the appropriate exclamations, then regards Bull, who is wearing hibiscus-orange pants with a bright turquoise linen shirt. (Coco reminds herself the man is color-blind, and Leslee clearly doesn't care what he looks like.) If Bull and Leslee walked down the street in Rosebush wearing these outfits, everyone would go to their windows and stare. Some might grab their shotguns.

The first guests to arrive are Addison and Phoebe, then Eddie and Grace. Addison is wearing a green and yellow Lilly blazer that matches Phoebe's A-line skirt. Do people have this stuff in their closets? No — the Wheelers also went to see Beth at Current Vintage. Grace is wearing a cute Lilly halter top — "It's not vintage, sorry" — and Eddie is wearing a tan linen suit and a panama hat. "I brought Lilly bathing trunks for later," he says.

Busy Ambrose shows up in a yellow and pink shift dress with a pink kerchief on her head. Romeo is wearing navy and pink Lilly pants, and the Chief shows up in a white shirt with a Lilly bow tie.

Leslee asks the Chief where Andrea is and he says, "She's had a little too much summer; she's taking a night off. And I can only stay an hour."

"Don't say that!" Leslee links her arm through the Chief's. "Let's get you a sidecar."

Sharon appears wearing green pedal pushers printed with white daisies and a white blouse knotted at her midriff. She's piled her blond hair on top of her head and done winged eyeliner and a hot-pink lip. Another surprise is that she enters the garden on the arm of Benton Coe, who is wearing jeans. Not on theme—but he's so hot it doesn't matter.

The music kicks in with "You and Me and the Bottle Makes Three Tonight," and at the same time all the lights in the garden come on. Coco passes out sidecars in coupe glasses, mules in copper mugs, and the French 75s in flutes. Addison and Phoebe say they want to try all three, then Busy says she does too. Zoe Alistair dropped off platters of deep-fried olives stuffed with sausage and tiny cucumber sandwiches, a chafing dish of grape-jelly meatballs.

Coco gets a text from Lamont. How's it going? He got a pass from tonight's party. Leslee told him to skip it, and Coco fears this is because Leslee has figured out they're seeing each other and she wants to keep them apart. Lamont thinks Coco is paranoid. Tonight he's chauffeuring Glynnie to her book group.

Coco watches Leslee insist the Chief have a drink and sees Benton show Sharon the hollyhocks. Busy is telling Romeo that her Subaru mysteriously disappeared from the Steamship's standby list, and is there anything he can do?

Calm and civilized, Coco texts back.

That's disappointing, Lamont says.

Check back later, Coco texts.

* * *

Sharon has pulled out all the stops: She got a mani-pedi, she had Lorna at RJ Miller style her hair in a cute updo, and her blouse shows off both her cleavage and her midsection. Even Sterling and Colby gave her a compliment: "Total smoke-show, Mom." But will she look as hot as Leslee?

As Sharon is walking down the driveway, she hears, "Hey, Sharon, wait up!" She turns to see Benton Coe jogging toward her.

"Well," Sharon says, "if it isn't the man of the hour."

Benton scoffs. "I can't believe I was invited. The Richardsons aren't happy with how long it took me to finish." He shakes his head. "I wasn't happy with how long it took them to pay me. If I had it to do over, I would have turned this job down."

"Oh, really?" Sharon says.

"Leslee is a lot," Benton says.

Isn't she just, Sharon thinks.

"I know you know what happened years ago between me and Grace Pancik—"

"Ancient history," Sharon says.

"It's hard to live something like that down on an island this size," he says. "And Leslee is such a touchy-feely person that I felt uncomfortable showing up here."

"Well, I think you're safe," Sharon says. "At the last party, Leslee moved on to someone new."

"Would you mind if we walked in together?" Benton asks.

"Not at all," Sharon says. "Don't worry, I'll protect you."

They reach the arched wrought-iron gate. "This is gorgeous," Sharon says. "Is it antique?" The gate looks like it came from an English manor or a French monastery.

"It's brand-new but fabricated to look authentic," Benton says.

Sort of like the Richardsons themselves, Sharon thinks.

There's nothing phony about the garden, however. Sharon admires the stone wall and benches, the bright bursts of color from the flower beds. And although she's prepared to be underwhelmed by the octagonal hot tub, she has to concede that it's magnificent. Can a hot tub be considered a work of art? It's deep mahogany with a glowing cobalt interior, and the curved copper ladders are divine.

Coco approaches them with a tray of drinks; Sharon selects a French 75 and Benton takes a mule garnished with mint and fresh raspberries. "Cheers," he says. "You look beautiful tonight, by the way."

"Thank you for noticing," Sharon says. Only after she takes a sip of her drink does she allow her gaze to wander to the other guests. She was right—Leslee *has* moved on to someone new, only it's not who Sharon expects. It's Chief Kapenash. Leslee has him by himself on the far side of the hot tub, her arm through his. Sharon spies Romeo locked in conversation with Busy Ambrose. *Serves him right,* she thinks.

Romeo looks up at Sharon. His eyes flick over to Benton and he frowns. It is, unmistakably, a frown of jealousy. Sharon beams at him and waves. He nods in her direction and glares at Benton. Sharon couldn't be happier.

The Chief decides to take advantage of Andrea's absence and eat whatever he wants. Leslee basically forces a cocktail on him—the bourbon sidecar—and it hits just the right way. After a few sips, he feels like he's floating. Zara Washington is going to excel as police chief, that's clear only a few days in, and Ed will be able to relax for the first time in thirty-five years. He swipes a cracker through the pecan-crusted cheese ball that's sitting on the bar, then indulges in a deep-fried olive stuffed with sausage. Andrea would definitely disapprove of these. Ed takes a second.

A server comes around with a platter of oysters Rockefeller, and the Chief remembers a party he attended as a teenager, his grandparents' fiftieth wedding anniversary. It was held at the Park Plaza in downtown Boston (his mother's parents, the Bryants, were a good deal fancier than the Kapenashes). Ed was introduced to oysters Rockefeller, the most delicious thing he'd ever tasted.

These are even better. The oysters, the server says, were harvested off the fifth point of Coatue that very morning.

The Chief helps himself to a second oyster. *Okay, that's it,* he tells himself. "I should go," he says to Leslee.

"You just got here," Leslee says. "And I went to a lot of trouble, so I can't let you leave. Come on, let's get you another sidecar."

Eddie, trapped in conversation with Grace and Phoebe, sees Bull and Addison chatting by themselves. Eddie needs to join them, but at that second, Benton and Blond Sharon approach. Eddie watches Grace brighten at the sight of Benton; naturally she gushes with praise for the garden.

Eddie can't keep himself from cutting in. "Congratulations on finally getting it done."

"Eddie!" Grace says. "Everyone knows genius can't be rushed."

Sharon can't believe the way Benton sticks by her side. He's a barnacle on her boat. Romeo hasn't taken his eyes off Sharon and Benton for even a second. Sharon thought she would have to battle Leslee for Romeo's attention, but the only person vying for his attention now is Busy Ambrose.

Sharon has to admit, this party is a home run. Coco holds out a tray of buttered, baked saltine crackers; Sharon nearly laughs at the sheer WASPy-ness of it. Sharon's own grandmother used to serve crackers like this to her bridge group. The music is snappy, and whatever they put in these French 75s is divine. Sharon hates to even think it, but when it comes to entertaining, Leslee Richardson has the magic touch.

Leslee has instructed Coco to keep the drinks flowing, but once everyone has a fresh cocktail Coco take a moment to observe. "These Boots Are Made for Walkin'" segues to "Big Girls Don't Cry." It's finally dark enough for Coco to light the tiki torches and press the button that brings the hot tub to life. The backyard is suddenly a vibe—everyone is drinking and laughing, the cheese ball has been demolished, the meatball dish is empty, colorful toothpicks are scattered across the high tables. Coco cleans up, then serves dessert: bite-size baked Alaskas and brownie cups that Leslee made herself. Coco heads back to the kitchen and gets a tray of brandy Alexander shots, meant to complement the sweets. When she returns, everyone is dancing to "Let's Twist Again"—even the Chief! (Coco nearly takes a picture to send to Kacy, but that feels invasive.) Benton swings Sharon around; the two of them are really good dancers. Leslee doesn't like anyone else taking the spotlight, so when the song ends, she calls out, "Hot-tub time!" She unties the strap behind her neck, and her dress falls to the ground. *Ta-da!* She's wearing a bikini in the exact same print as her dress. Everyone cheers! Coco exhales relief; she worried Leslee might not be wearing anything under it at all.

Leslee directs everyone to the main house to change into their suits. Grace pulls Eddie along even though he wants to stay in the garden where Bull and Addison are talking. Are they one-upping each other with all the fancy places they've stayed—Aman this, Auberge that— or are they discussing business?

"I'll be right back," Eddie says to Grace. "I forgot my..." But he doesn't have to tell her what he forgot because she's now ten feet ahead of him talking to Sharon and, yes, Benton.

Eddie races back to the garden and peers through the arched

gate. Leslee lounges in the hot tub with her arms outstretched, cocktail in one hand, her head lolling back. Bull and Addison are talking so intently that Leslee could slip beneath the surface and drown and they wouldn't notice.

There's a narrow path that curves around the outside of the garden. Eddie beelines down it, nearly tripping on an irrigation pipe, until he reaches the spot where Bull and Addison are talking on the other side of the hedge. He can barely see them in the gathering dark, but he can hear them perfectly. He feels like a character in an Agatha Christie novel.

Bull says, "If we cut him out, we can split the pot fifty-fifty. That's an additional four mil for each of us. Eddie just doesn't seem to be on the same page—"

"He has a valid point about hiring local contractors," Addison says. "After all, we live here year-round. A lot of the guys we're talking about raised their kids alongside Eddie's twins—and my son, for that matter."

"But your son is heading to boarding school at Tiffin."

Addison clears his throat. "Be that as it may, when it's Thanksgiving Day and your uncle Shep accidentally flushes his beer can down the toilet and the thing overflows, it's nice to have a local guy on speed dial."

"Eddie tries too hard," Bull says. "He's a bit...inelegant."

Inelegant? Eddie thinks. Bull is calling *him* inelegant? At least Eddie can match his top to his bottom; Bull is wearing a clown suit. Bull spills on himself, he shows off his money every chance he gets, and he lets his wife disgrace herself—and him—with other men.

"Doesn't he come from a working-class background?" Bull asks.

"Eddie is from New Bedford," Addison says. "He's very proud of that."

"He's redundant," Bull says. "You and I could do this deal without him."

"We could…" Addison says. "But we signed a contract."

"There's a clause at the end, didn't you see it? The terms of the contract can be changed right up until the purchase and sale is signed and I write the first check."

"What?" Addison says. "I did not see that."

Eddie didn't see the clause either. He holds his breath, wondering what he can do. Bursting through the hedge and knocking Bull to the ground comes to mind, but that won't help his cause.

"Just think about it," Bull says. "Fifty-fifty."

"I couldn't do that to Eddie," Addison says, and Eddie feels himself misting up. Addison has his back.

"Maybe you could, though," Bull says.

When Sharon pops out of the powder room — she's wearing a Lilly bikini, but it's not vintage and it doesn't match her outfit (advantage Leslee) — Romeo is waiting for her.

"Sharon," he says.

"Romeo."

They stare at each other. Romeo is wearing the same board shorts he wore when they went to Whale Island, which makes Sharon's heart ache. *Who's Golden Girl? You are.* She wants to jump into his arms, but he's got his tough-guy stance, the one he uses when some ass-clown from the city demands to skip the standby line in the height of summer so he can get his Tesla off the island.

Does he want to talk? Is he expecting an apology? Because Sharon has called him half a dozen times and sent an embarrassing number of texts, all of which went unanswered. If anything, it's now Sharon who deserves an apology.

At that second, Benton appears; he's bare-chested and in a pair of Billabong board shorts. "Ready to tub?" he asks.

Sharon holds Romeo's gaze one moment longer. Is he going to

fight for her? No—though he stabs Benton with the daggers in his eyes.

"Sure," Sharon says. "Let's go."

"It's an eight-sided hot tub, not an eight-person hot tub," Leslee says. "Come on, we can all fit. Coco, would you please make sure everyone has a fresh drink and then pass the brownie cups one more time?"

The Chief takes the last brownie cup and winks at Coco. "Don't tell Andrea."

"Everyone climb in," Leslee says. She shows people where she wants them; she's probably had the seating chart planned for days: Leslee, the Chief, Blond Sharon, Benton Coe, Grace, Romeo, Busy, Addison, Phoebe, and Eddie. Bull isn't getting in.

"Hot tubs aren't for big blokes like me," he says. "I'm sweating my balls off just looking at you all."

"I'd like to sit next to my wife," Eddie says. "Benton, what if you and I traded spots?"

"Spouses are always separated," Leslee says. "Keeps things interesting."

"Addison is next to *his* wife," Eddie says.

"Eddie," Grace says. "Stop being weird."

Is he being weird? Is it inelegant that he doesn't want his wife sitting next to the man she had an affair with nine summers ago? He doesn't want things to get "interesting." The hot tub is bubbling and steaming like a witch's cauldron—and it's pretty clear who the witch is.

Sharon leans her head back against the edge. "This is heavenly, Leslee."

There are murmurs of agreement, but not from Eddie. He would like to get out of this people soup and talk some sense into Bull.

Suddenly Romeo says, "Hands, Coe! Let me see your hands!"

Benton laughs and raises his palms. "Here they are."

Swingers in the summertime, Coco thinks.

"Sharon, let's get out of here," Romeo says.

Sharon sits bolt upright. Is this happening? It's a bit abrupt, maybe even rude, but she's not missing her chance. "Okay," she says. One of the copper ladders is directly behind her, so it's easy to make a quick escape.

"Stay!" Leslee cries out. "Sharon? Romeo? Please don't leave yet!" She sounds a little unhinged, even for her.

"We should probably go too," Eddie says. "Right, Grace?"

"Don't be silly," Leslee says. "The party is just getting started. Coco, what happened to the music?"

Coco is pretty sure Bull turned the music down when everyone went to get changed. She turns it back up—it's "Wouldn't It Be Nice" by the Beach Boys. Leslee says, "Something better!" Coco scans the playlist and settles on "I Want You Back" by the Jackson Five. She hands Romeo and Sharon towels and they disappear through the gate and into the dark night.

The party *is* just getting started, the Chief thinks, but he should leave. He's only had two cocktails and yet he feels funny, loopy. He's lost all track of time, doesn't quite remember getting changed—but wait, yes, he does. Leslee lent him a pair of Bull's swim trunks. Why did he agree to that? He has broken all kinds of rules tonight. He had one of the baked Alaskas and a brownie—no, two brownies. Leslee encouraged him to take a second, saying she made them herself. Phoebe and Addison are here, his oldest friends, and as long as they're here, he's fine, right? He likes the music; the water is delightful. He'll stay another five minutes. Busy seems to be asking him a question about Kacy: "Did she mention meeting my daughter?"

Did she? Ed wonders. He's about to tell Busy that he hasn't talked to Kacy in a day or two. And if he dug in, he would admit he hasn't talked to Kacy in any meaningful way all summer. He's not sure why she really left San Francisco.

Ed is jolted from these thoughts by a hand on his leg. Whoa! Is he imagining this or is it a trick of the water jets, the bubbles? No, there are human fingers stroking his thigh. He turns to see Leslee with her head back, her eyes closed. Her arm closest to Ed is beneath the water's roiling surface. Leslee is touching the Chief's leg.

Is there a split second when the Chief thinks maybe he'll just let this play out, ignore it or . . . even *enjoy* it?

Absolutely not. The Chief stands up, splashing Leslee in the process, but he doesn't care, he's leaving. He cheated on his diet tonight. But he hasn't cheated on Andrea—in mind, body, or spirit—since the day he noticed her waiting in line to get her beach sticker. And he never will.

As he clambers out of the tub, Addison says, "Ed, where are you going?"

"Home," Ed says. He takes a towel from Coco. God only knows what she thinks of him cozying up next to her boss in the hot tub; what was he *thinking*? Well, he wasn't thinking, or not clearly. Something is wrong with him.

The brownies—the ones Leslee made herself. They must have been pot brownies, and that's why Ed feels this way, so loose, discombobulated. He snatches up his clothes and goes. He doesn't bother saying anything to Bull and hopes never to see the man again, but if Ed were to leave Bull with parting words, they would be *Your wife needs help.*

He climbs into the back of his car and changes into his clothes, which is a tricky business, as he's soaking wet and still high. He finds his cell phone and calls Andrea.

"Please come get me," he says. "I can't drive."

"You're kidding," Andrea says.

"Not kidding," he says. "Bring Kacy with you, please, I need to get my car out of here."

"On our way," Andrea says. "I was wondering where you were. I worried maybe Leslee got her claws into you."

It's a little scary how on the nose she is. "No chance of that," he says. "I'm all yours. Now please hurry."

32. Thursday, August 22, 11:00 P.M.

When nobody is looking, Kacy sneaks up the stairs to Coco's apartment. She suspects this is against the law and that if she asked her father, he would tell her not to—potential crime scene, search warrants, detectives, yada yada—but Kacy can't continue standing around doing nothing.

There's a light on under the microwave that allows Kacy to find her way around. She checks the bathroom, pulls aside the shower curtain (a part of her hopes Coco has somehow made it back without their noticing and is now hiding up here). Empty. In Coco's room, the bed is neatly made. On Coco's nightstand are two novels: *Trespasses* by Louise Kennedy, *The Candy House* by Jennifer Egan. Sitting on top of these is the sand dollar Coco found during their trip to Great Point.

Kacy remembers Coco swimming that day, utterly fearless. Did Coco set the fire and then ditch? *Did* she?

There's a shelf on the opposite wall and on it is a framed photograph.

Kacy goes over to inspect it, and her gut twists. It's one of the selfies Kacy sent her: Coco and Kacy at the Nantucket Pharmacy, Coco happy with her frappy. Kacy's eyes burn. She was such a terrible friend and yet Coco went to the trouble of printing this picture out and framing it. She kept it in her room. So does that mean Coco has forgiven her? It must, right?

They have to find her. They have to.

There's a crumpled article of clothing peeking out from beneath the far side of the bed. Kacy bends down. It's a Nantucket Whalers Sailing T-shirt that looks like it's about fifteen years old. Lamont's. Kacy thinks, *Lamont came here, Leslee found out, Leslee confronted Coco on the boat, there was a tussle, Coco fell in, Leslee thought,* Oh, well, *and went to get herself another glass of Laurent-Perrier.*

Kacy goes to the kitchen, opens the fridge, sees a six-pack of grapefruit fizzy water, a plastic clamshell of fresh raspberries, half an avocado BLT from Something Natural. Nothing that suggests *I set my employers' house on fire and jumped off their boat to escape.* It looks like Coco planned to come home and finish her sandwich.

On the coffee table in front of the TV is Coco's laptop—but it requires a password. Kacy tries *Rosebush;* she tries *Lamont* and *Lamontishot* and *Lamontishotaf.* She tries *Colleencoyle27.* Coco mentioned she's a Scorpio but Kacy doesn't know her birthday. She's a horrible friend.

Under the laptop, Kacy discovers a green Moleskine notebook. Jackpot.

It's an enormous violation of Coco's privacy to open it, but under the circumstances, Kacy feels she has no choice.

The notebook contains addresses, phone numbers, and the hours of operation for Pip and Anchor, Born and Bread, Dan's Pharmacy. Following that is a log of sorts with dates lined up neatly on the left followed by notes on the errands Coco ran that day. *July 8:*

Nantucket Meat and Fish (they're out of Bull's pretzels, shipment coming Tuesday), Bartlett's Farm, post office. On another page, there's a record of what packages came to the house and what they contained: *Amalfi lemons, box of Bridgewater chocolates (thank-you gift from Rachel McMann), three bottles of Guerlain Double Vanille perfume from Neiman's, copper mugs engraved with the letter* R, *strings of white lights.*

Kacy pages forward until she finds August 22. *Sunset sail,* it says. *Print out Google vow renewal, Zoe A. will drop off appetizers 5:00 p.m., ice, change sheets in primary suite on* Hedonism, *twenty-five champagne flutes.* There's even a note for August 23: *Drop boxes at Hospital Thrift Shop, India Street, open 9 to 4.*

The rest of the notebook is all blank pages, or so Kacy thinks until she gets to the back and finds a...diagram. In the center are the words *The Personal Concierge,* and radiating out like spokes on a wheel are lines that end in circled names: Bull, Leslee, Lamont, Kacy.

Kacy flushes at seeing her own name. What does this *mean?* She doesn't think twice; she slides the notebook into her bag.

She realizes she hasn't checked the second bedroom. She opens the door slowly, feeling like a girl in a horror film, half expecting Coco to jump out at her, soaking wet and bedraggled, seaweed in her hair. The room is dark; Kacy wants to turn on the light but they'll see that outside, so she makes do with the glow from her phone.

The room is filled with cardboard boxes. *Okay,* Kacy thinks, *these must be the boxes Coco was going to take to the thrift shop.* Kacy opens one of them and finds jeans and cashmere sweaters; underneath that is the pink ombré Hervé Léger dress Leslee wore to the first party. This dress is going to the thrift shop? It belongs in a museum. The next box is filled with shoes—stilettos, platform sandals, Manolo Blahniks, Louboutins. Leslee is giving these *away?*

Kacy's phone dings with a text and she jumps, thinking that somehow the text is from Coco: *Stop snooping.* But the text is from her father: Where are you?

Kacy is busted. Bathroom, she types. Be right down.

Kacy's phone rings. It's her father. She declines the call and rushes out the door. The Chief waits at the bottom of the stairs. "You didn't touch anything up there, did you?"

"No," Kacy says. "I had to go. We've been here for hours."

The Chief has a roll of yellow police tape in his hands; he cordons off the entry to the stairs. "The Coast Guard is concluding its search for the night. They'll start up again at dawn. Lamont took the Richardsons' boat and went out to look for Coco on his own."

"He did?" Kacy has more faith in Lamont finding Coco than the Coast Guard.

"We'll stay until he gets back," the Chief says. "Then I'm taking you home."

Home? Suddenly Kacy feels like she's going to vomit. Should she turn over the notebook or offer to put it back? It could be evidence.

"Let's wait for Lamont on the beach," Kacy says. She strides across the Richardsons' lawn and the Chief follows. They hear a commotion and see Bull and Leslee down by the water; in her long white dress, Leslee looks like some kind of ghost bride.

"This is all your fault!" Leslee shrieks at Bull.

"Everything okay down there?" the Chief says.

"Fine, fine," Bull says. "Leslee's just upset. I was hoping to take the dinghy since we're going to sleep on *Hedonism* tonight, but it's already at the mooring."

"Lamont took the other boat to go look for Coco," the Chief says.

"Oh," Bull says. "Good, good." The Chief gets the feeling Bull only now realizes his other boat is missing. How did the Chief and

Andrea get mixed up with these people? Part of it was Kacy befriending Coco and part of it was Addison. A perfect storm of sorts.

The Chief hears a motor and sees running lights. A boat pulling
in. Lamont is back. *Please,* he thinks, *let him have Coco with him.*

Coco! Kacy thinks.

Bull wades into the water, cups his hands around his mouth: "Did
you find her?"

Lamont heads for the mooring, not the shore. The Chief's heart
sinks. He didn't find her.

Lamont cuts the motor, turns off the lights. As soon as the Chief's
eyes adjust, he can see that Lamont is alone in the boat. They all wait
in silence for Lamont to row in. When he reaches the beach, he
looks at Ed. "Do you have any news?"

"No," Ed says.

"I covered every inch of water," Lamont says. "She's not out
there."

33. Kill Your Darlings

The membership committee of the Field and Oar Club is Nantucket's own version of a secret society. There are nine members on the
committee, each serving a nine-year term with three terms allowed.
Some of the members on the committee—Busy Ambrose, Lucinda
Quinboro, and Penny Rosen—are in their third term, and one, Talbot Sweeney, is in his final year of service (much to his dismay).
Blond Sharon and Phoebe Wheeler are at the start of their second

term, which makes them relative newbies. The committee is rounded out by Helen Dunsmore, Larry Winters, and Rip Bonham.

They meet on the second Wednesday in August to vote so that the newly elected members can be welcomed at the Commodore's Ball on Labor Day weekend. The meeting is held, not up in the Governor's Room, as many believe, but in the club's snack bar at the unusual hour of eleven p.m. By that time, service has ended and the staff are gone, leaving the club deserted, dark, and locked up. The members gather around Busy Ambrose on the front porch like they're teenagers on a caper; as commodore, Busy is the only member with a key.

Blond Sharon has always loved the rituals of the membership committee meeting: the late hour, the hushed passage through the front hall and the ballroom to the snack bar, where they push two tables together and sit in white molded chairs. The meeting is BYOB. The past few years, Phoebe has brought a bottle of Sancerre, Talbot a bottle of Bushmills, Rip a cooler of Cisco beer. Busy traditionally serves as short-order cook (she learned a few tricks from her long-ago summer love). She prepares chicken strips and French fries that she serves in plastic baskets lined with wax paper.

Once Busy has served the snacks, she sits down to conduct the meeting. "Has everyone read the applications, the nominating letters, and the seconding letters?"

Everyone nods yes, though they all know Larry Winters never does the reading and Rip does maybe half (he recently took over his father's insurance business and has three little kids at home). Talbot does the reading but can't remember any of it. (Is it surprising that the weak links are all men? Not to Sharon.)

This year there are spaces for six couples, and there are five legacy couples at the top of the list. Legacies are always admitted unless there are problematic issues, and this year all five couples are from wonderful families in good standing at the Field and Oar; they all sail and play tennis and have three or four children apiece, ensuring a solid, vibrant future for the club. These applicants breeze through and are unanimously accepted.

Then it's on to the rest of the list. The list has long been misunderstood by club members and nonmembers alike, and the committee prefers it that way. It's common knowledge that the Field and Oar has a "ten-to-twenty-year" wait list—but the truth is, as soon as couples submit their full applications, they're eligible for admission. In fact, the committee does not start at the bottom of the list, with the people who have been waiting the longest, but at the top.

Busy clears her throat. "The first couple up for our consideration are Bull and Leslee Richardson." Busy beams. "I like them so much, I wrote their nominating letter. And Phoebe wrote one of their seconding letters."

Helen Dunsmore says, "They live out in Pocomo? Do they sail or play tennis?"

Does Helen Dunsmore live under a rock? Sharon wonders. Has she not heard about the Richardsons' parties this summer?

"Sail," Busy says. "They have a yacht called *Hedonism.*"

"*Hedonism*!" Larry Winters says. "Now, that's something I can get behind." Larry used to own a popular nightclub in Key Largo. He's the kind of eighty-year-old who always makes a point of checking out Sharon's cleavage.

"Where are these people from?" Lucinda Quinboro asks. Lucinda is also a member of the old guard. She and Penny Rosen both got married at the Field and Oar Club during the Kennedy administration. "It says here…Perth, Australia?"

"That's a mailing address," Busy says. "They've recently spent time in Aspen and the Caribbean, but they've made Nantucket their home."

"My company insures their house," Rip says. "They told me Nantucket would be their primary residence. Bull said he was planning on having the house winterized, though to my knowledge, he's made no move to do so."

"There's no *way* Leslee Richardson will be able to tolerate Nantucket in January," Sharon says. "Or, worse, March."

"These are the people who throw the parties?" Talbot says.

"Yes," Busy says. "They're very social and extremely philanthropic and I think they'll make a wonderful addition to the club. Shall we take it to a vote?"

Voting on non-legacy members has its own protocol. Busy must go around the table and get a yea or nay from each committee member, and the applicants must have a two-thirds majority, or six votes, to be accepted. Busy goes first: "Yea." Then, thankfully, she turns to her right, which means Sharon, to Busy's left, will go last. By then, Sharon is fairly certain her vote won't matter.

Lucinda offers an uninterested yea and Penny, who always votes as Lucinda votes, is also a yea. Helen Dunsmore is a yea; she's the least discerning (or, as she claims, the most inclusive) among them; she would let in someone who moved here yesterday. Talbot is a nay but Sharon could have predicted this; Talbot hasn't approved a non-legacy member in twenty-seven years. Rip is a nay—he always complains there aren't enough year-round families at the club and apparently the Richardsons' failure to winterize has rubbed him the wrong way. Larry Winters is a yea because he has a long-standing beef with Talbot.

There are five yeas and two nays when it comes around to Phoebe, and Sharon thinks, *This is over, the Richardsons are in.* But Phoebe drops her head into her hands and moans.

Busy says, "You can hardly be deliberating, dear. You wrote one of the Richardsons' seconding letters."

"I know," Phoebe says. "But..."

"Didn't Leslee tell me she donated to Tiffin Academy on your son's behalf?" Busy asks.

"That's not supposed to matter," Rip says.

"Membership at this club can't be bought," Talbot says. "Any idea how many bribes I've been offered over the years? And I'm proud to say I refused them all."

"You're right," Phoebe says. "Leslee didn't offer money to me personally; she donated it to my son's first-choice boarding school, but I believe that was as a favor to me." Phoebe spins the diamond stud in her ear. "I should abstain."

"Don't be absurd," Busy says. "Give us an answer."

"That is my answer," Phoebe says. "I'm abstaining from the vote."

"So the Richardsons have five yeas and two nays," Talbot says. "Sharon, it seems their fate lies with you."

Never in a million years did Sharon imagine she'd be the deciding vote. The good thing is, she doesn't even have to think about it. "Nay," she says.

"Sharon!" Busy cries. "You went to all their parties!"

Exactly, Sharon thinks.

"Wait!" Phoebe says. "Is it too late to change my vote?"

The technical answer is yes. Everyone at the table knows there is no changing your vote based on how other people have voted. But Busy says, with undisguised glee in her voice, "Because you abstained, I'll allow it. What's your vote?"

"Nay," Phoebe says. She lifts her plastic cup of Sancerre, and she and Sharon toast their good sense.

As Busy is huffing and puffing about how she just doesn't understand people sometimes, Phoebe leans toward Sharon. "Would you like to be our fourth in pickleball?" she asks.

"I'd be honored," Sharon says.

34. Dumped

"We'll have a big party at the Oystercatcher right after Labor Day," Andrea says. "But I think we should do something more intimate too. A dinner with just us and the Wheelers and the Drakes. What do you think about that?"

Kacy is at the kitchen island, staring at a text from Isla that reads I'm booking a flight to Nantucket. I have to see you.

"Kacy?" Andrea says.

Kacy looks up. Her mother is waiting for . . . some kind of answer? Kacy didn't hear the question. This whole thing with Rondo is real; Rondo is in love with Tami Dunne, he's leaving Isla. And Isla is flying out to see Kacy. Kacy has been dreaming of Isla realizing that she loves Kacy in a way she will never love Dave Rondo and leaving him despite the inevitable outcry from her family.

But this is a little different.

"Sounds good," Kacy says to her mother, hoping this is an appropriate answer.

"I'll let your father pick the place," Andrea says. "Do you think you'll bring a plus-one? Maybe Coco?"

"Um . . . yeah," Kacy says. Since the horrible scene at the day-drinking party, things between Kacy and Coco have cooled. Kacy texted her a few days after the party: Hey, again, I'm sorry. I hope you don't hate me. Coco had responded right away: I don't hate you. So that, at least, was good, but there has been nothing else—no invitations to hang out on the Richardsons' beach, no more nights out. "What is this for again?"

Andrea swats at Kacy's arm with a dish towel. "Your father's retirement dinner. Us, the Wheelers, the Drakes. We'll do it next Thursday, a week from today."

"Okay, sorry." This is the perfect opportunity to make things right with Coco. "I'll ask her."

She types: Hey there—Mom wants to know if you can join us for my dad's retirement dinner, a week from tonight.

Coco responds: Can I let you know? It's crazy around here right now.

That's a no, Kacy thinks, and she clicks out of her texts. Her mother is portioning skinless chicken breasts for her father's sad lunch salads but Kacy feels Andrea watching her. She has to get out of the house.

"I'm going to the beach," she says.

The south shore is foggy, which turns Kacy's introspective beach walk into a whole mood. She meanders along the water's edge as the waves crash, then froth around her feet. Seagulls cry out; sandpipers scurry along in a V formation. There's a guy surf-casting and when Kacy passes, he gives her an appraising look. If this were a rom-com he might say, *Why the long face?*

Kacy keeps going. What if she brought *Isla* as her plus-one to her father's dinner? That has long been the fantasy, that Isla would show up and declare her love and Kacy could introduce her to her parents, to Eric and Avalon. *This is my girlfriend, Dr. Isla Quintanilla.* They would be impressed with Isla—a brilliant neonatologist, so well educated, from an important Mexico City family.

Why has Kacy been keeping you from us? Andrea would ask.

Isla was engaged, Kacy would answer. *But her fiancé has fallen in love with someone else and taken down his wedding Pinterest page, so...here she is!*

It's wrong. Isla should have left Rondo, not the other way around. Isla wants to come to Nantucket now because she's been dumped. Kacy is her backup, her plan B, her second choice.

Kacy is getting what she wants, but not for the right reason. And the reason matters.

She pulls out her phone and texts Isla: Don't come.

Immediately, Kacy's phone rings. She declines the call.

When Eddie enters his office on Main Street, his sister, Barbie, gives him a wide-eyed-closed-mouth look. Something is up.

What? he mouths.

She points to the partition between their two desks. Eddie peeks around the corner and sees Bull Richardson sitting in the chair meant for clients.

Eddie is spooked. Everyone on earth has a cell phone; there's no excuse for showing up anywhere unannounced. This is an ambush. Bull is here to tell Eddie that he's out of the deal.

Eddie is about to back out of the office when Bull spins in his chair, cranes his neck, and sees Eddie. He jumps to his feet. "Edward!" he says, thrusting out a hand.

What can Eddie do but shake it? "To what do I owe this pleasure?"

"Please sit," Bull says and Eddie thinks, *This is my office, I'll sit when I'm good and ready.* Also, he hates being called Edward; it reminds him of his grandmother and his high-school principal, Dr. Lewicki.

Eddie takes off his panama hat and settles into his chair. *Sexy indifference,* he thinks. The original idea for purchasing Jeanne Jackson's property was his, but no biggie. Easy come, easy go. He'll be glad to be rid of the stress because, you know, in real estate development, there's always stress. It's almost worth the eight million he would have made to have it go away, ha-ha-ha. He'll handle this with grace. Bull will not be able to call him inelegant.

Bull leans forward in his chair and lowers his voice to a stage whisper. "I think we should cut Addison out of the deal."

Eddie blinks. "Addison?"

"There's something a little slippery about the bloke," Bull says. "Are you aware that his nickname around town is Wheeler Dealer?"

Of course Eddie knows this. It was Eddie's brother-in-law Glenn Daley who gave Addison the nickname a million years ago. These days, Wheeler Dealer is a term of affection and respect for Addison.

"What am I missing?" Eddie says. "Did something happen?"

"Phoebe and Addison just aren't the people I thought they were," Bull says. "Leslee and I made a large financial gesture that would benefit their son—"

"The donation to the boarding school," Eddie says, thinking, *See, Addison does tell me things.*

"Precisely," Bull says. "But when it came time for Phoebe and Addison to reciprocate, they didn't deliver. I'm sorry, but I don't want to do business with a fella like that."

Eddie isn't sure what the Wheelers promised the Richardsons and he doesn't care. "Addison and I are a package deal," Eddie says. "I heard you at the garden party last week telling Addison the two of you should dump *me.* I heard the things you said about me, Bull."

Bull says, "Well, then, I guess the person who's leaving the deal is me. Have fun financing this by yourself, mate. You can kiss my money goodbye." Bull gets to his feet so rapidly, his chair topples over behind him. *Inelegant,* Eddie thinks.

Barbie appears in the doorway, resting-bitch face in place. "I'll see you out, Mr. Richardson."

Eddie sets Bull's chair upright, then all but collapses into his own. Addison—he has to call Addison! They can get a loan from Nantucket Bank as long as they're partnered up. They should have done this in the first place; what were they thinking?

But before Eddie calls Addison, there's someone else he needs to talk to. He dials Blond Sharon.

"Hey, bae," he says. "Do you know what happened between the Richardsons and Phoebe and Addison?"

There's a pause. "It's confidential," Sharon says. Then she laughs. "But it's too good to keep secret. Sit down."

35. Cruel Summer

When Coco steps in the door from Meat and Fish with a pink drink for Leslee and a container of sesame noodles for Bull, she hears Leslee screaming for Bull, and not just screaming but crying.

Someone is dead, Coco thinks, and her stomach drops even though the last thing she wants to do is feel sorry for the Richardsons. Who could it be? Neither Bull nor Leslee has ever mentioned brothers, sisters, or cousins. Coco has mentally placed Leslee's family members on some dusty acres in Nevada with the sound of machine-gun fire reverberating in a tin building. Bull's family she pictures in a similarly dusty Australian outback, two elderly parents waiting for the tour bus to pass through. They don't talk about friends they grew up with, college roommates, work colleagues, people they've met on vacation. They've had no houseguests. The Richardsons seem to exist in a bubble, the here and the now, this house, the connections they've made this summer.

Has something happened to someone Coco knows? She moves to the plate-glass window and sees Lamont bent over the stern of

Hedonism; he's fiddling with the back gate, which he complains is janky. He ordered a replacement but it won't arrive for six weeks. The broken gate technically makes the boat unsafe, though Bull told Lamont not to worry about it. When Lamont told Coco that he was indeed worried about it, Coco said, "I know I should be a good girlfriend and commiserate. How about this—the Meat and Fish Market is once again out of Bull's favorite pretzels. They won't have more until Tuesday."

Lamont stared at her. "You just called yourself my girlfriend."

Coco tucked her hair behind her ears; it was finally long enough to do that. What she nearly said was that she liked him so much, she felt like more than a girlfriend. But because their relationship was secret, she also felt like less than a girlfriend. She almost *wanted* to get caught by Bull and Leslee. Would they really fire them? Coco doubted it. Bull and Leslee and Lamont and Coco were like a family, one no more dysfunctional than the family Coco grew up in.

Coco checks the *Nantucket Current* to see if there's any breaking news about an untimely death or accident—nope. She heads downstairs—she has books to switch out in the library—and hears Leslee sobbing and Bull murmuring, then Leslee lets out a blood-freezing shriek and Coco thinks, *I will not get pulled into their drama.*

In the library, she replaces *Life After Life* by Kate Atkinson and takes *May We Be Forgiven* by A. M. Homes, geniuses both, in her humble opinion. When she's back in the hall, she hears a door close. She turns around to see Bull leaving the primary suite.

"Everything okay?" Coco asks.

He shakes his head. "We didn't get into the Field and Oar Club."

That's why the world is ending? Coco thinks. *Spare me.*

Leslee doesn't come out of her room at all on Thursday; Coco reads on the curvy white sofa in the party room, listening for signs of life downstairs. She gets a text from Kacy asking if Coco can go to the Chief's retirement dinner. Coco is surprised at how happy the text makes her. Time is a miracle worker; Coco's feelings about the selfies have mellowed. But before Coco can say she'll go, she has to check with Leslee. Can I let you know? she texts back. It's crazy around here right now.

Friday, Bull leaves the house in the G-Wagon, and when he gets home, Coco is unpacking yet another wooden crate stuffed with straw that cushions yet another dozen Amalfi lemons.

"Those should cheer Leslee up," he says and Coco checks to see if he's kidding. "Listen, will you keep an eye on her, please? I have to travel for the next few days—a car is coming to get me in a minute."

Coco wants to tell him he can't just pawn his pathetic excuse for a wife off on her while he gets a hot-stone massage in Ubud. "When will you be back?"

"Tuesday night," he says. "I'm sorry. This situation in Indo is proving to be a sticky wicket." He claps Coco on the shoulder like they're best mates.

Leslee doesn't emerge from her room on Friday. *What is she doing about food?* Coco wonders. When Lamont sneaks up to her apartment early Saturday, Coco fully expects him to tell her that he's taking Leslee out on the boat. Coco steels herself for this news, but he says he hasn't heard from her.

Coco waits until noon and then taps on Leslee's door. "Hey," she calls into the dark bedroom. "Can I bring you anything?"

"Go away," Leslee says.

Oh, how Coco would love to take these words to heart so she can go out onto the beach and read, but she can't let Leslee continue her hunger strike. She thinks back to her own worst story: the time she stole money from the diner in Rosebush. Coco arrived in the pinkish-gray light before sunrise, let herself in with the keys Garth had entrusted her with, opened the register, and took what was there. She was pulling money out of the safe when Garth walked in and caught her. He could have called the police or fired her, but instead, he said, "Are you really that desperate to get out of this town?" And when she nodded, tears of shame rolling down her face, he made her breakfast.

Coco preheats the oven, lines a baking sheet with tinfoil, pulls out the waffle iron and gets it smoking hot, beats eggs with some heavy cream. She melts butter in a pan.

Twenty minutes later, she has scrambled eggs, a tray of bacon, and—thanks to some wizard on Instagram—golden hash-brown waffles. She's about to take a plate down to the primary suite when she hears a shuffling on the stairs. It's Leslee—or, maybe more accurately, the woman who used to be Leslee. Her skin is the color of putty; her hair is straight and frizzled at the ends; she's wearing a pair of hideous purple drawstring shorts and one of Bull's undershirts.

"I smelled bacon," she says.

Coco sets the plate down at the kitchen island. She pours Leslee a cup of black coffee and a glass of ice water.

Leslee digs into the food with such naked appetite that it feels almost indecent to watch her. She shoves a bite of one of the hash-brown waffles in her mouth, then mumbles something, and Coco pulls ketchup from the fridge. As Leslee is shoveling in the eggs, Coco toasts two pieces of sourdough, butters them, then replenishes Leslee's eggs. Half a pound of bacon is consumed in seconds. Leslee eats every bite of food down to the bread crusts, which she swipes through the remaining ketchup. She finishes the coffee and the water and burps.

Leslee's eyes, which resemble small dull pebbles in their swollen sockets, fill with tears. "Thank you."

"Bull told me about the Field and Oar. I'm sorry, I know how much you wanted to join."

"I can't believe we didn't get in," Leslee says. "I just don't understand it."

You don't? Coco thinks. Leslee masterminded all the debauchery at Triple Eight this summer; she shamelessly flirted with Lamont, with Benton Coe, with Romeo, and with the freaking chief of police! Everyone has been keeping receipts.

"Busy explained what happened at the membership meeting," Leslee says. "Sharon voted against me. People told me to watch out for her, you know. And then Phoebe voted against me."

"Phoebe?" Coco says with genuine surprise.

"I told her I'd donated a hundred thousand dollars to Tiffin Academy so they'd let in her son. I chose her as my pickleball partner even though she sucks so bad she shouldn't even be let on the court. I invited her boring friends to all my parties — except for Delilah at the end."

Coco thinks about the check to Tiffin Academy that Leslee ripped up and threw away. She *told* Phoebe she'd donated, but had she actually donated?

"We did everything right," Leslee says. "But everywhere we go, we fit in for a little while and then people shun us. Why?"

Because you aren't genuine? Coco thinks. *Because everything with you is transactional? Because you're an egregious social climber?*

"Bull tells me I shouldn't care. Easy for him to say—he's consumed with his work. He's always traveling, trying to keep his business from going down the toilet." Leslee taps her phone. "Come look."

Reluctantly, Coco positions herself behind Leslee's shoulder so she can see the screen. There's an article in the *New York Times* with the headline "Indonesia to Ban Single-Use Plastics (But Is It Too Late?)."

Leslee shows Coco the photographs that accompany the article. In a simple wooden hut on stilts over murky green water, a brown child pokes his head out a glassless window. Below the house, in the water, is—Coco enlarges the image because she can't quite believe what she's seeing—trash. Plastic bottles, hundreds, thousands of them. Leslee scrolls through picture after picture: flotillas of plastic bottles on rivers, clogging up canals, washing up on beaches. One picture shows a mountain of plastic bottles against a backdrop of verdant rice paddies. In another, a majestic white long-legged bird—an egret or a heron—picks its way among bottles floating in the reeds.

"I've been with Bull on his trips overseas," Leslee says. "It made me sick, seeing all the pollution. These new regulations are good for the Earth, but they'll ruin us."

"Ruin?" Coco says, thinking, *What does that mean, exactly?*

Leslee winds her hair around her forearm. "Bull's doing battle with the IRS now. They claim he owes millions in back taxes, which he's fighting since he makes most of his money overseas, but I think he hired a disreputable accountant, someone who tries to work the loopholes, which is fine until you get hanged."

"What about the movies he invests in?" Coco asks. "Do they make you money?"

"Ha!" Leslee says. "They've all lost money. The production business is a sinkhole for cash." She sniffs. "But Bull loves seeing his name in the credits. Whatever. We were still okay, since Bull's bev company has always been gangbusters—Indonesia has a population of two hundred and seventy million, not to mention all the tourists—but now it won't be legal for Bull to do business there. He's talking about pivoting to aluminum or paper containers, but we own plastics factories, Coco. Bottling plants."

This, Coco thinks, *is what Bull meant by a sticky wicket.*

"He has some real estate venture cooking that he claims will bring in some cash, but who knows how long that will take? Bull is a flagrant risk-taker, a shark jumper. And you know what? Every gambler loses at some point. I've only been with Bull when he's winning. I don't know what I'll do if he loses everything." She turns off her phone and the offensive images disappear. "Maybe I'll kill him. Switch out a cyanide pill for his Viagra. He's color-blind, you know"—Coco thinks of standing with Bull in the laundry room during the Pink and White Party: *Would you please help me pick something out?*—"so he'd never be able to tell." Leslee holds Coco's gaze for a second, then bursts out laughing. "I'm kidding!" She hugs Coco, then starts crying in her arms. Leslee's words are muffled by Coco's shoulder but she hears "So nice having another woman around" and "Didn't want to belong to that la-di-da club anyway."

When Leslee finally pulls away, Coco rips some paper towels off the roll so Leslee can mop her face.

"Thank you for listening," Leslee says.

Coco nods. Leslee isn't going to kill Bull. She's just really sad. For perhaps the first time, Coco sees Leslee Richardson as a human being with a point of view. *They're having a moment,* Coco thinks, and no one is more surprised than she is.

The new closeness with Leslee is thrilling and scary, like a toboggan ride down a steep hill. On Sunday, Leslee invites Coco to lunch at Cru and when Coco asks if she should wear her uniform, Leslee says, "Absolutely not. We're going as friends."

Friends? Coco thinks—and yet this is what it feels like once they're seated at a table by one of the open windows that overlook the boat basin. They order a bottle of rosé, oysters, beautiful salads topped with pan-roasted halibut.

"So how did you and Bull meet?" Coco asks. "I don't think I've heard the story."

Leslee cocks her head. "Oh. Well…it was many moons ago. I was bartending at a place called the Peppermill in Vegas and Bull came in."

"You were a bartender too?" Coco says. Lamont told her this, but she didn't quite believe it or believe Leslee would ever admit to it.

"I was."

Coco flashes back to her first day of work, sitting in the library with Leslee: *You remind me of myself when I was your age.*

"What made you notice him?" Coco asks.

"He sat down in front of me, middle of the day, the place was empty, and ordered all the appetizers." Leslee sips her wine and smiles. "Hard to ignore a man like that."

Their server comes by at the end of the meal with two coupe glasses of Pol Roger champagne. "Compliments of Shawn, the bartender."

"Who?" Leslee says. They look over at the bar to see the guy Coco met the night she was out with Kacy. Coco feels herself flush. She forgot all about Shawn.

"Oh god."

"Is he a love interest?" Leslee says. "I have to say, I've wondered about your romantic life. I thought maybe you and Kacy…"

"No," Coco says. She is now definitely bright red. "I'm straight."

"Well, Shawn certainly hopes so," Leslee says, and she waggles her fingers in his direction. "He's cute. I wonder if he'll come join us."

"He's working," Coco says. Although she's on the verge of complete mortification, she's relieved that Leslee has no idea about her and Lamont.

"I'm going over to say thank you," Leslee says. She walks over and takes a seat at the bar, probably assuming Coco will follow, but Coco is doing no such thing.

All three restrooms are occupied, so Coco waits in the alcove. A woman with short dark hair and cute glasses pops out of one of the doors and gasps when she sees Coco. She comes over, takes Coco's arm. Does Coco know this woman? Was she a guest at one of the parties? Coco isn't sure.

"My name is Blythe Buchanan," she says. "Did I see that you're having lunch with Leslee Richardson?" She makes it sound like Leslee Richardson is a celebrity and, well, isn't she, sort of?

"Yes," Coco says.

Blythe takes a breath. "I feel like I should warn you about her."

Oh no, Coco thinks. *That* kind of celebrity.

"We met Bull and Leslee in Palm Beach last winter. They were very eager to join the Bath and Tennis Club and we said we'd sponsor them, but Leslee made a spectacle of herself at the Coconuts New Year's Eve party. She lured our friend's *husband* into a dark gallery at the museum..."

Coco considers jumping in and saying, *That doesn't sound like Leslee at all.* But she couldn't pull it off.

"And that was the end of the Richardsons and Palm Beach, needless to say. How long have you two been friends?"

Coco would like to dart into the restroom, lock the door, and never come out.

"Friends?" she says. "Not that long. This is the first time we've had lunch together."

"This is what she does," Blythe says. "She finds new, unsuspecting people to seduce. I know she may seem great now, but trust me, you should run as far away from her as you can before she burns you."

Coco nods. "Thanks for the warning."

Blythe Buchanan smiles kindly and leans in to whisper. "Also? She cheats at pickleball."

Coco finds Leslee leaning over the bar, close enough to Shawn to take a bite out of him. She seems to have paid the bill in cash—good, they can make a clean getaway.

"Leslee," Coco says. "We have to go."

"Shawn just poured me another glass of champagne," Leslee says. "Sit down, we'll get you some as well."

"Hey, Coco," Shawn says.

"No," Coco says. She pulls Leslee to her feet and gives Shawn a close-lipped smile. "Thanks anyway. We're leaving."

On Monday, Leslee takes Coco to barre class at Forme on Amelia Drive. Coco doesn't like group exercise and, after being approached by Blythe Buchanan, the last place she wants to be is in a roomful of strangers—however, Leslee is in her element. She introduces herself around to the other women with their enormous diamond rings, their Cartier Love bracelets, their impeccable highlights. "I'm Leslee Richardson," she says. "And this is my friend Coco."

The woman on the mat next to Leslee says, "I'm Celadon Morse. Aren't you the woman who throws the swanky parties?"

Coco waits to see how Leslee will react to the word *swanky*. Favorably, it turns out. "I am!" Leslee says. "Give me your number and I'll invite you to the next one."

Later that afternoon, Leslee treats Coco to a pedicure at RJ Miller. She takes the number of the woman who's seated in the chair next to her, Marla.

"There are a lot of people on this island," Leslee says once they're back in the car with foam separators between their toes. "I don't need Phoebe or Delilah or Blond freaking Sharon."

Coco gets a text from Kacy. Have you asked if you can come to dinner on Thursday night? My dad chose Ventuno and my mom wants to make a reservation so she needs to know how many people.

They're driving down the Polpis Road toward home. Leslee taps the steering wheel as Taylor Swift sings, *I'm drunk in the back of the car, and I cried like a baby coming home from the bar.* It's been a cruel summer for Leslee, but right now she seems relaxed. Should Coco broach the topic? It's just dinner, and Coco so rarely ventures out at night, this won't be a big deal.

"Kacy invited me to dinner on Thursday with her parents," Coco says. "It's her dad's retirement celebration at Ventuno. Is it all right if I go?"

The car veers ever so slightly toward the center line, but Leslee straightens it out. "The Chief's retirement celebration?"

"It's just dinner," Coco says. Why the hell did she use the word *celebration*? "He's retiring. It's only family, I think."

"And yet you were invited."

"Family and close friends, I guess."

"Like Delilah and Phoebe, of course. And insufferable Addison and that overcooked potato Delilah is married to, I can never remember his name."

"Jeffrey," Coco whispers. She wants to stick up for Jeffrey—he's a steady, thoughtful, measured person—but she senses that now is not the time.

"I'll tell you who *wasn't* invited," Leslee says. "The Richardsons. Which is *insulting.* The Chief and his wife owe us, we've invited them to *everything,* all summer long."

Oh, dear, Coco thinks. She should never have said where she was going. *Out,* she should have said. *I'd like to go out.*

"But we're pariahs now," Leslee says. "Nobody wants us around."

She hits the gas, and the G-Wagon goes flying down the road so fast that the split-rail fence, the ponds, the cottages with their green lawns and snapping flags, become a blur out the window. Coco watches the speedometer needle: sixty, seventy, eighty-five. She grips the armrest, reminding herself that Mercedes builds cars for the autobahn, that going eighty-five, even on a winding road, is nothing, Coco is wearing her seat belt, the car certainly has excellent airbags. But Leslee shows no sign of slowing down. Coco thinks of how Leslee casually threatened to switch Bull's pills. Then she thinks of Leslee as a teenager, an AR-15 strapped across her chest, raining bullets into a target. They're going ninety. Coco hears a high-pitched whining in her ears—it's the sound of her own fear. This is the end of the toboggan ride, the part where they're going too fast to stop at the bottom of the hill so they'll either crash into a tree or go sailing off an unexpected ledge.

At the last minute, Leslee hits the brakes, puts on her signal, and turns left onto the Wauwinet Road as the tires squeal. They've slowed down but Coco's heart is still hammering in anticipation of her untimely death.

"I'm afraid you won't be able to make the Chief's dinner," Leslee says. "Because we're having a sunset sail that same night and I need you to work it."

"A sunset sail?" Coco says. She takes a moment to reset now that they're cruising along at a more leisurely pace. She texts Kacy: I can't make the dinner. When I asked, Leslee tried to kill me. Literally nearly crashed us both in the car.

Kacy texts back: WTF?!!? Are you okay?

Coco isn't sure how to respond. There isn't an emoji that will express how lucky she is to be alive.

"Yes," Leslee says. "It's a special occasion. Bull and I are renewing our vows."

Did Coco hear that right? "Renewing your *vows*?" she says.

"I'm going to invite all my new friends," Leslee says. "It's going to be so much fun."

36. Friday, August 23, 1:00 A.M.

When the Chief and Kacy get back to the house, Andrea is waiting up in the kitchen.

"I called Phoebe and Delilah," she says. "Everyone knows, everyone's praying." She opens her arms to Kacy.

Kacy lets Andrea hug her for only a second. "I can't talk about it," she says. "I'm so tired I feel like my head is going to topple off my body."

"Get some sleep," Andrea says.

"Will you—"

"The second we hear anything," the Chief says.

Andrea waits until she and Ed are in their bedroom before she says, "What the hell happened, Ed? Do you think Coco set the Richardsons' house on fire and then ran?"

"I'm not sure what happened," he says. "Is that a possibility? Yes. Is it possible Leslee heard about the fire and pushed Coco off the boat? Yes. Is it possible Coco fell? Yes. Who set the fire is a secondary concern. Nobody was hurt, although the house is a total loss. The garage is fine."

"Is that where the Richardsons are staying tonight?"

"They're sleeping on the boat." The Chief sighs. "Stu Vick will have an inspector there in the morning. My concern is finding Coco."

"Obviously," Andrea says.

Ed tries to pry one of his loafers off with the toe of the other while standing up and nearly falls over. Andrea takes his arm, leads him to the bed. "I can't believe this happened when you were so close to finished."

"Zara wants me to give her the case and just advise from afar."

Andrea laughs unhappily. "You'll never do that."

"I overheard Dixon saying that I'm looking at this as some kind of swan song." Ed finally kicks his loafer off. "That's not what this is. We *know* the girl. She stayed with us."

"You don't have to explain. I know you'd never walk away, nor would I want you to."

Ed is grateful he doesn't have to quarrel with Andrea on this point. He drops his head in his hands. He feels dizzy; his gut is churning up a cement of fritto misto and steak and cannoli. Does his arm tingle or is that his imagination? Did he set himself back six months with all the stress of the night? He takes a deep breath. Andrea helps him out of his sports coat, then kneels in front of him and unbuttons his shirt like he's a child. If this night had ended like it was supposed to, she would be unbuttoning his shirt for another reason.

Once Ed gets into bed, he makes sure his phone is plugged in and the ringer is on. The helicopter has returned to Woods Hole; the track-line searches will resume at first light. At Ed's behest, Lucy has agreed to keep one boat out searching for the rest of the night.

Andrea turns off the light, the Chief closes his eyes. A part of him thinks Coco *did* set the fire and then run—and that same part hopes she gets away with it.

37. For as Long as We Both Shall Live

Coco and Lamont lie naked and spent across the crisp white sheets of Coco's bed. Lamont's leg, which is maybe the finest she's ever seen on a man — long tapered thigh, defined calf muscle — is intertwined with Coco's leg, his tawny, hers alabaster. Sunlight streams in through the blinds; Coco hears birdsong and the gurgling of the coffee machine. It's set for six a.m., a fragrant alarm, but it means Lamont has to leave. Leslee has new friends, and Coco is afraid that might mean unexpected kinks in Leslee's daily routine; she might meet Celadon for sunrise yoga or Marla for a morning bun at Wicked Island Bakery.

"Before you go," Coco says, "I have to read you the renewal vows I got off the internet for Bull and Leslee. You're going to vomit."

"Exactly how I was hoping to start my day," Lamont says. He leans back into the pillows while Coco recites various lines: " 'I find myself falling more in love with you each day' . . . 'You are my best friend, my confidante, my one true love' . . . 'I promise to continue to practice patience, kindness, understanding' . . . 'For as long as we both shall live.' " Coco shakes her head. "I don't think I can keep a straight face. It's a good thing no one coming on this sail knows them."

"Leslee, I promise to keep you in Amalfi lemons for as long as we both shall live," Lamont says. "I will turn a blind eye when you throw yourself at any available man in your vicinity —"

Coco pokes Lamont in the ribs, where she knows he's ticklish.

"You can cut the word *available*—she doesn't care if a man's available."

At that second, they both hear it: a key turning in the lock, then the rubbery sucking sound of the apartment door opening.

"Coco!" Leslee calls out. "Are you awake?"

Lamont seemingly turns to liquid and oozes himself over the side of the bed and onto the floor without making a sound. He starts pulling on his clothes. Apparently, he's scripted precisely what he would do in these circumstances, but Coco, who considered this moment inevitable—Leslee was going to catch them at some point—is at a loss.

"Coming!" she says, though her voice cracks like someone is strangling her. She pulls on her shorts and tank, picks up her water glass and a book so she has something to do with her hands, steps out of the bedroom, and closes the door behind her with a definitive *click*.

Leslee is holding a huge cardboard box with DONATE written on the side in black marker. "I went through my closet last night," she says. "I have twelve boxes for you to take to Goodwill on Friday. Wait until then, please—this is just the preliminary load and I don't want you to make two trips."

"I'm not sure there is a Goodwill," Coco says. "But I can take them to the Hospital Thrift Shop."

Leslee drops the box in the second bedroom. "Whatever."

"If you leave the boxes at the bottom of the stairs, I can bring them all up," Coco says. She needs Leslee to leave. When she goes to pour herself coffee, her hand is shaking.

"That would be wonderful, thank—" Leslee stops suddenly and Coco whips around. Leslee is four feet from the front door, her eyes on the ground. Coco follows her gaze—and sees a pair of boat shoes, size ten and a half, with leather laces tied into corkscrews. Unmistakably Lamont's.

In what feels like slow motion, Leslee turns around. Her eyes stop briefly at Coco's bedroom door and Coco thinks: *Here it comes.* Leslee will search her room, find Lamont, there will be a scene, and they will both be fired.

However, instead of being afraid, Coco feels defiant. *Yes,* Coco thinks. *We're together. He hasn't said so yet but I know he loves me. He's mine, not yours.*

Leslee faces Coco head-on in a way that feels melodramatic. "Do you remember when I told you that I wasn't sure why people here haven't accepted us?"

Coco presses the soles of her feet into the wood floor.

"I've been thinking about it," Leslee says. "Bull and I are solid. People liked us; our parties were the most coveted invitations of the summer. Remember how that camel turd Rachel McMann and her skeevy dentist husband tried to throw a party of their own when they were cut from our list?"

Of course Coco remembers. It's a good thing Leslee and Bull haven't had a dental emergency because she's certain they're black-balled from Dr. Andy's practice.

"But Bull and I made some tactical mistakes. The first one was hiring you. You're a hick, Coco. Everything about you is shabby. You defiled your body with those budget tattoos, you dress like a hill-jack — *that* was the reason for the uniform, if I'm being honest — you reek of poverty. The reading you do is a valiant attempt at self-improvement, though it hasn't lent you even a shred of refinement. You lucked out befriending Kacy — if it weren't for that connection, I would have fired you in week one. Also, *Colleen,* I checked at the Nantucket Atheneum and nobody by the name of Susan Geraghty has ever worked there, so the little story about the librarian inviting you to Nantucket was a lie. You scammed your way into this job, and if you think I don't know why, you're wrong."

Leslee pauses long enough for Coco to wonder if she should

respond. The litany about how baseborn and unwashed Coco is doesn't faze her; she's been waiting for it all summer. But Coco would like to claim at least some integrity: She never said Ms. Geraghty *invited* her to Nantucket; she said Ms. Geraghty *introduced* her to Nantucket, and she had, in the form of *Moby-Dick,* one of the novels that has apparently not made a dent in Coco's inherent inferiority.

But Leslee isn't finished. "We also made a mistake in hiring Lamont. He came highly recommended, and Bull was charmed by the local-boy-makes-good story, but trying to show how *woke* we were backfired. We should have hired a more…*traditional* captain."

Coco blinks. "Do you mean *white*?" She suddenly feels a rage that's so pristine, she considers tackling Leslee or backing her out the open door and watching her fall down the stairs. "Is that what you mean, Leslee?" Is Leslee, on top of everything else, a *racist*? Or is she just so angry about Coco and Lamont's relationship that she reached into her bag of tricks and plucked the filthiest scrap from the bottom?

"I meant older," she says. "Thanks for your help with the boxes." She leaves the apartment. She wasn't brave enough to fire Coco, but then again, Coco wasn't brave enough to quit.

In the bedroom, Coco finds Lamont fully dressed, shirt and khakis somehow without a wrinkle—he irons every night before bed—his brass anchor belt buckle polished. Coco doesn't care what Leslee says or thinks about her; in a way it felt good to have her impostor syndrome confirmed. She *did* con her way into his job; if you're using the metric of pedigree, education, or sophistication, she *isn't* good enough for either this job or this island. But to malign Lamont, who has talent and a strong work ethic and so much basic human decency, is to incur Coco's fiercest wrath.

"I heard," Lamont says. "She didn't mean any of it, Coco, she's just angry. It's less than two weeks until Labor Day. We can tough it out."

Coco would like to call Lamont weak for taking Leslee's abuse, but she knows it's strength. He would never let something Leslee said in the heat of the moment bother him.

"Sure, yeah," Coco says. She has been nurturing an idea for revenge against the Richardsons, but it always seemed outlandish and beyond the scope of what she's capable of doing. Until now.

38. Thursday, August 22, 8:00 P.M.

It's Romeo's turn to plan date night and he chooses karaoke at the Rose and Crown.

Really? Sharon thinks. If he wants to sing, they should go to the Club Car piano bar, but when she mentions this, he says, "It's going to be a while before I can go back to that place." Sharon chastises herself for being insensitive. After the whole debacle with Walker, she wouldn't blame Romeo if he never went to the Club Car again. And so the Rose and Crown it is.

And guess what—karaoke is fun! Romeo and Sharon order beers and a plate of nachos. At the end of the bar, Sharon sees a girl named Woodlyn who used to babysit for the kids. Woodlyn, who has corkscrew curls and is wearing a top that is essentially a bra, buys Sharon and Romeo shots of Fireball. It's the jet fuel Sharon needs to propel her onto the stage. She and Romeo decide to sing "Reunited" by

Peaches and Herb, and they must sound okay because the crowd, urged on by Woodlyn and her bare midriff, chant for an encore, so they sing "Don't Go Breaking My Heart" by Elton John and Kiki Dee. After the song is over, Romeo sweeps Sharon up off her feet and carries her out of the bar, saying, "Always leave them wanting more."

They hold hands as they stroll down Water Street toward the car, but then Romeo stops Sharon outside the Pacific Club at the bottom of Main Street. He takes a breath. "I love you, Sharon."

Sharon, who at the beginning of the summer might have said she no longer believed in love, says, "I love you too." Then she presses her head against Romeo's chest and thinks, *I love Romeo Scandalous Steamship Guy!*

When they get home, Robert is awake playing a video game and Romeo tells Sharon, "I'm going to hang out with him for a little while if that's okay."

It's more than okay. Sharon is only one scene away from finishing the short story for her online class. She sits down at the laptop and the words flow right out of her.

Later, Sharon and Romeo reunite in the bedroom—*And it feels so good,* Sharon sings to herself. As she falls asleep, she realizes that for the first time in years, maybe decades, she doesn't know where her phone is and she doesn't care.

She is, therefore, *shocked* the next morning when she paws through her bag for her phone—she bookmarked a frittata recipe on Instagram that she wants to try—and finds she has one missed call from Delilah, one from Phoebe, and three from Fast Eddie, the most recent one only two minutes earlier.

She figures Delilah and Phoebe are calling about pickleball—they're going to play for the first time this week—but what is up with Eddie?

Then Sharon sees the alert from the *Nantucket Current* on her phone: Fire Destroys House in Pocomo, Woman Missing off Homeowners' Boat.

Sharon can't click fast enough. As she reads, she murmurs, "Oh my god, oh my god" — the Richardsons' house burned to the ground. Their personal concierge has gone *missing off their boat*! Leslee and Bull apparently hosted a sunset sail, where they renewed their wedding vows. When they received word about the fire, they motored back, and only when they reached the mooring in Pocomo did they realize Coco was missing.

Sharon calls Fast Eddie. He picks up on the first ring, his tone somber. "Hey."

"Is this a *joke*?" Sharon says. She realizes she sounds just like her twins. "The Richardsons' house burned down?" Sharon thinks about the dual grand staircases, the pink lacquered shelves above the Lucite bar in the party room, the iconic octagonal deck. It's all gone? That's a minor concern, of course, compared to the missing personal concierge. "What happened to Coco?"

"Nobody knows. Lucy Shields launched a search; a copter flew over from Woods Hole; they had a fleet of ATVs searching the south shore, and they found her clothes washed up out at Smith's Point. But they can't find her."

Tears sting Sharon's eyes. "I don't care about the Richardsons' house..."

"Nor do I," Eddie says. "As far as I'm concerned, the address of that place should be Six-Six-Six Pocomo Road."

"Coco has to be okay," Sharon says. "But what if she isn't?"

39. There Is No Story Here

She hits the water with a smack that disorients her. Her shorts balloon, and her phone falls out of her hand; she grabs for it but then realizes it's too late. The water is a green glass globe with a stream of translucent bubbles, her own breath escaping. Which way is up? For one panicked second, Coco isn't sure. She kicks her feet, feels instinctively that she's going down, not up, flips around, and pulls apart the water like she's opening a heavy curtain until she breaks the surface. In the twilight, Coco can see the sailboat, but it's cruising away from her, both motors churning.

She tries to swim toward the shore; the beach at Eel Point is probably only a few hundred yards ahead. But the water has other plans for her. The current carries her out; it's one stroke forward, two strokes back. She tells herself not to panic—she knows that in a riptide, you swim parallel to shore. She does this for a while. Is she getting closer? Yes, she thinks so. Her sodden polo shirt is weighing her down, and she's having trouble using her arms. She treads water for a second, though even this is a challenge. The water is muscular, insistent: *She will do what it tells her.* She wrangles off her polo, unbuttons her shorts, lets them both go. She's lighter now, but she's lost ground. She watches as the westernmost tip of the island, Smith's Point, recedes.

So what now? She turns and sees land behind her. Tuckernuck, Whale Island. It looks close but she knows this is deceptive; it's half a mile away. Her shoulders start to ache as she swims, and she can no longer feel her legs. She remembers swimming off Great Point, Kacy's warning about sharks. She moves in the direction she knows land to be, though now the dark land is nearly indistinguishable from the dark sky. She doesn't think about Leslee or Bull or Lamont or Kacy or her mother, Georgi, back in Rosebush, who is no doubt vaping at the picnic table out back of the house with Kemp. Or, rather, she does think about them but only to remind herself that she can't waste her precious energy thinking about anything other than getting to shore.

Is she going to die out here?

Coco kicks, scoops her arms forward. She can swim. She has swum not only in her murky, turtle-infested pond but also in the cobalt water of the Lake of the Ozarks, the turquoise water of St. John, clear to the white sandy bottom.

She hears a helicopter, but it's far away. Even so, she treads water, waves her arms, cries out. Someone is looking for her. She has to make it to Tuckernuck. There's nothing but ocean between here and Portugal.

Coco's arms grow heavy; she kicks with all her might just to stay above the surface. Waves smack her face, water goes up her nose, down her throat. She thinks she can still see the coastline but she's not sure, and then she sees—or thinks she sees—a pinprick of yellow light. A moment later, it disappears. What did Lamont say about Tuckernuck? No electricity, only generators. She gazes up in the sky and sees stars, but navigating by them is a pipe dream. She tries to remember where she saw the light and swims in that direction. She has to stop and tread water in order to catch her breath; she flips onto her back and floats but she feels the current carrying her in what she's certain is the wrong direction. She's out of gas, plain and simple. She can't move her arms; her legs are two lead weights pulling her down.

As Coco slips below the surface, she replays her favorite movie scenes in her head.

The hotel-bed scene in *Lost in Translation.*

Armageddon: The crew singing "Leaving on a Jet Plane" as they board the spaceship.

"O Captain! My Captain!" in *Dead Poets Society.*

Finding Nemo, the scene with Crush the turtle. Also the fish tank in the dentist's office. *Just keep swimming,* Coco thinks. Her lungs burn; she lets her breath go.

Rocky running up the art museum's steps.

All of *Barbie.*

And, of course, the final scene of *The Player,* which has long served as the touchstone for Coco's artistic vision. She has a purpose. She is a screenwriter.

Coco fights her way up, breaks the surface, gasps for air.

There is no story here, Bull said. But he was wrong.

40. Friday, August 23, 6:15 A.M.

"Kacy!" The Chief's voice booms and Kacy startles from a dream. She was in her apartment in San Francisco waiting for DoorDash. Alerts came onto her phone: Your driver is seven minutes away...Four minutes away...Your driver has arrived! Kacy opened the door, and a teenager handed over her food, and Kacy somehow intuited that it was Little G. He had lived, he had grown up. And when Kacy turned to Isla to say, *Look, Little G survived after all, he's here with our beignets from Brenda's!* she realized the person sitting at her kitchen table wasn't Isla. It was Stacy Ambrose.

"Kacy!" Her father is in the doorway of her bedroom, using his police-chief voice. She's in trouble, but why?

She opens her eyes. "Daddy?" Her father is in his pajama bottoms and a Cisco Brewers T-shirt; his hair is a mess. What time is it? Then Kacy remembers about Coco and sits up.

"They found her," the Chief says. "On the south shore of Tucker-nuck. Tate Cousins was out running and she saw something washed up on the beach. She thought it was a seal, but then she realized—"

"Dad," Kacy says. "Is she alive?"

"She's alive," the Chief says.

Coco is admitted to Nantucket Cottage Hospital and treated for dehydration and exhaustion. As soon as the Chief gets the okay from the nursing staff, he and Zara go in to question Coco about what happened.

"I'm not sure," Coco says. "I don't remember."

"Can you walk us through what you do remember?" Zara says. "Starting with when you all left to get on the boat. Who was the last one out of the house?"

"Leslee," Coco says. "I went out to the boat early with the trays from the caterer, like usual. The guests came in stages on the dinghy. Leslee was the last one out of the house. She was in her white dress, because the vow renewal was a surprise and she wanted to make a walking-down-the-aisle entrance. It worked. Everyone on the boat applauded."

"When you set sail, everything seemed okay at Triple Eight?" the Chief says. "There were no alarms going off?"

"Alarms?" Coco says.

"Triple Eight burned to the ground," the Chief says.

Coco's jaw drops; her eyes widen, then fill with tears. The Chief has been at this job so long that he considers himself a human poly-graph: He knows when someone is lying, when someone is *acting,* and his gut tells him Coco isn't. But maybe Zara is right, maybe he's too close to the situation to be a good judge.

"You didn't know this?" Zara sounds skeptical.

Coco shakes her head, wipes under her eyes with her free hand; her other arm is attached to an IV. "What happened?"

"The fire inspector is still investigating," the Chief says. He received a call from Stu Vick: *It looks like the fire started in the pri-mary suite. That house was a tinderbox, all that old wood, no insula-tion to speak of, just pockets of air that fed the beast. I'll let you know if we find an accelerant.*

"Once you were on the boat, what do you remember?" Zara says.

Coco was serving drinks, passing the hors d'oeuvres. She didn't know many people on the boat; they were mostly new friends that Leslee had made. Bull and Leslee renewed their vows on the bow, Coco served the champagne toast, the sun set, Lamont turned the boat around.

"He told us he kissed you," the Chief says. "He kissed you in pub-lic and Leslee saw."

"Yes, that's right." Coco's eyes brighten. "He kissed me."

"Then what happened?" Zara asks.

"After I cleared the champagne flutes, I took a moment in the back of the boat."

"Took a moment?"

"I went to the spot in the stern where the swimming ladder is. There's a safety gate...I was standing inside the gate. I took a pic-ture of the sunset on my phone. I wanted to remember the night because, after Lamont kissed me, he told me he loved me for the first time. Then the music on the boat stopped and I heard everyone yapping all at once. I remember thinking, *I've got to get back, fix the music, wash the glasses…* and the next thing I knew, I was in the water."

"Did someone push you?" the Chief asks. "Or did you slip and fall?"

"I have no idea," Coco says. "The gate was there, so I didn't slip. I guess it's possible someone pushed me…though actually, that gate wasn't latching properly, so maybe I did slip and fall in. Lamont told Bull and Leslee the latch was faulty; he'd ordered a new one but it hadn't arrived yet. They told him it didn't matter, they wanted to sail anyway." Coco offers the Chief a weak smile. "They don't like anything getting in the way of their fun."

"Believe me, I know," the Chief says.

"Do you know anything about how the fire in the Richardsons' house might have started?" Zara asks. "We learned that Leslee was a smoker—did she ever smoke in the house?"

Coco shakes her head. "I never saw her smoke, ever. She didn't smoke around me."

"Leslee and Bull both told us you all had a…thorny relationship at times," Zara says. "They seemed to think it was you who started the fire."

"Me?" Coco says.

Ed holds up a hand. "This isn't a formal questioning. You don't have to answer."

Zara says, "They told us you had the code for the alarm system and that you would have been able to turn the alarms off."

"I had the code, yes," Coco says. "Leslee instructed me to turn off the alarms anytime they had a party in case the caterers burned something or whatever."

Oh, dear god, Ed thinks. Did Coco turn off the alarms? Should he advise her to get an attorney?

Coco swallows. "But I didn't turn the alarms off yesterday. The party was on the boat, so why would I? I didn't touch the alarms. And I don't know anything about how the fire started. I didn't do it, if that's what you're asking." She pauses. "Do people think..."

"If the nature of this fire turns out to be suspicious," Zara says, "then we may have to bring you in for further questioning. And at that point, I would suggest you get a lawyer."

"A *lawyer?*" Coco says. She turns even paler, which Ed didn't think was possible.

He says, "For now, the important thing is you're okay. We'll let you get some rest. When they're ready to discharge you, Kacy can come pick you up. You're welcome to move back in with us for a little while until you figure out your next steps."

Coco sinks back against the pillow. "Thank you."

As Zara and the Chief walk out to the car, Zara says, "All along I liked Coco for setting the fire and Leslee for pushing her off the boat."

"That's where my mind went as well," the Chief says. When they climb into the Chief's Suburban, he pulls out Coco's green Moleskine notebook, which Kacy gave him that morning.

"Coco kept a list of her daily tasks," he says. "Thursday, August twenty-second: 'Change sheets in primary suite on *Hedonism.*'"

"Ahhh," Zara says. "It's almost as if someone knew they were going to be spending Thursday night on the boat."

"Could be a coincidence. Leslee and Bull had just renewed their vows, so maybe the plan was always for them to spend a romantic night on the water." The Chief points to the next entry. "But look at this. Friday, August twenty-third: 'Drop boxes at Hospital Thrift Shop.'"

"Boxes?" Zara says.

"Kacy went upstairs to Coco's apartment last night to use the bathroom and she told me there were at least a dozen boxes filled

with clothes to be donated. Kacy opened a box and said that everything in it was not only expensive but in perfect condition—
cashmere sweaters, party dresses, tennis dresses..."

"You think Leslee packed all her clothes up and moved them to
the other apartment to save them because she planned to burn the
house down?"

"It seems like a remarkable stroke of luck," the Chief says, "that
all her clothes were spared."

"Is it terrible of me to say I would not be sad to see that woman
charged with arson?"

Would it be terrible of Ed to say that he wouldn't be sad either?
Yes, he thinks, *terrible.* "Let's wait and see what the fire inspector
turns up," the Chief says. "The good news is that Coco is okay and I
can end my tenure with a win—or at least not a loss."

"End your tenure?" Zara says. "My calendar says it's only Friday.
You aren't finished until Monday. We have all weekend for something else to pop up."

As the Chief is going around the small rotary by the mid-island
post office, a silver Range Rover with the vanity plate BEAST cuts
right in front of him, the driver flipping Ed off as he does.

That's it, Ed thinks. *Third time's the charm.* He throws on his
lights and siren and pulls the kid over in full view of midday
traffic.

"License and registration, please. You failed to yield in a rotary.
The vehicles already in the rotary have the right-of-way," the Chief says.

"How do you expect me to know that?" the kid says, his blond
forelock falling into his eyes. Ed checks the license: Gryphon Dreck,
hailing from a town called Newmony. If Ed had made up a name
and a town for this tool, he couldn't have done a better job.

The Chief heads back to his car, calls it in, then issues the
maximum-fine ticket, which gives him enormous satisfaction. "I
expect you to know it because it's the law," he says when he hands

Gryphon the ticket. "The police are here for your safety. I hear about you flipping off any other officers, you're going to have a problem. Am I understood?"

Gryphon mumbles something to the affirmative, and the Chief watches as he checks the ticket fine.

"What the *hell*?" he says.

Ed smiles. "Have a nice day, Beast." He climbs back into the Suburban, looks at Zara, and says, "Now *that* was a swan song."

41. The Cobblestone Telegraph III

The news about Triple Eight burning to the ground and the Richardsons' personal assistant, Coco, going missing off their yacht nearly breaks the cobblestone telegraph. So many of us have a personal connection to the story that it's hard to remain impartial. What *actually* happened?

Fire chief Stu Vick calls Chief Kapenash with the inspector's report midday on Friday.

"It looks like the culprit was a curling iron left on in the primary suite," Stu says.

"A curling iron?" the Chief says. Then he thinks: *Leslee's hair. Wait until Andrea hears about this.* "So it's being ruled an accident?"

"Someone *wanted* it to look like an accident," Stu says. "But we found an accelerant. At first we weren't sure what it was. Not gasoline, not kerosene, not lighter fluid. A little research revealed that its profile matched certain kinds of perfumes. Practically the first thing the inspector said to me was that the site smelled like burned birthday cake. I joked that it would have been wedding cake." Stu pauses. "You know, because of the vow renewal."

"But you're sure there was an accelerant?" the Chief says. Which meant arson.

"Oh, yes," Stu says. "Also, I don't know if this matters or not, but one of the homeowners crossed the police tape and went up to the garage apartment and took a couple of boxes out of it. I told her she needed to leave everything up there untouched since that's where the girl was living." Stu clears his throat. "I won't repeat what she said back to me."

"What did she do with the boxes?" the Chief asks.

"She took them on the dinghy back out to the boat."

Presence of an accelerant is enough for the Chief to get a search warrant for not only the garage but *Hedonism* as well. The Chief checks Coco's notebook and sees that a few days before the fire, a package arrived for Leslee from Neiman Marcus containing three bottles of Guerlain Double Vanille perfume. Was *that* the accelerant? If so, was Leslee to blame, or—Ed's heart sinks—do they need to take another look at Coco?

By Friday afternoon, the Nantucket police are all over the garage apartment as well as the trash and recycling in the actual garage. They find little of interest; the boxes in the spare bedroom contain Leslee's clothes, the ones she supposedly intended to donate.

The Chief and Zara catch a ride with Lucy Shields, the harbormaster, out to *Hedonism*. They call Bull and Leslee up to the deck—Leslee is still in her white dress—and leave both the Richardsons under Lucy's watchful eye while they search the boat.

The Chief is the one who finds the boxes, shoved in the crawl space under the bunk in the crew's quarters, a blanket thrown over them. Someone did not want these boxes found. Ed gets down on his hands and knees, grunts as he pulls the boxes free. Blood pounds in his ears; he's short of breath. The universe is testing his endurance with all this heavy lifting in his final days.

"Chief Washington!" he calls.

Zara helps him bring the two boxes out to the living area. The boxes both say DONATE on the sides and they're bound up with packing tape; Zara searches for a knife in the galley so they can slice them open. Meanwhile, they hear Leslee up on deck giving Lucy a hard time: "I'm not sure what they think they're going to find, this is insane, our house burned down and you're treating us like *we're* the criminals!"

Inside the boxes is...Monopoly money? There are bricks of what appears to be cash, only it's in candy colors—orange, yellow, lime green. The Chief picks up a green brick and sees Queen Elizabeth II's face.

It's Australian money. A lot of it.

The money, totaling nearly half a million Australian dollars, is enough for Chiefs Kapenash and Washington to arrest the Richardsons for arson. But before their lawyer even arrives at the police station, Leslee Richardson confesses: She acted alone; Bull knew nothing about it. While everyone was waiting on *Hedonism,* Leslee placed her hot curling iron into one of the Amalfi lemon crates filled with packing straw and doused the whole thing with her perfume. After turning off the alarms, she created a trail of perfume-soaked rags down the hall to the library, where she hoped the books and the closet filled with bourbon would be enough to combust the rest of the house.

Her motive? Insurance money, of course. Bull's business is going belly-up, the IRS have his feet to the fire, he owes them millions, and the real estate deal that he planned to do with Eddie Pancik and Addison Wheeler soured. The Australian cash is theirs; Leslee has been skimming off their accounts for years so that she had an emergency fund.

"I would have burned down all of Nantucket if I could have," Leslee tells her attorney, Val Gluckstern, causing Val's eyebrows to shoot up. "I hate this island and everyone on it."

Curling iron, we think. *Perfume. Amalfi lemons and hidden cash.* Leslee Richardson is one hell of a glamorous arsonist.

But will she be charged with pushing her personal assistant, Colleen Coyle, off the back of her boat? Aggravated assault, perhaps even attempted murder?

Colleen "Coco" Coyle was discovered on the south shore of Tuckernuck, exhausted but alive. She has no recollection how she ended up in the water. She realizes that she could easily claim Leslee pushed her, adding a few more years to Leslee's sentence. But Coco isn't sure what happened. She must have slipped, in which case the faulty latch on the back gate could be a problem for the Richardsons should Coco decide to sue.

What we don't know in the days following these events—and what we won't, in fact, find out for many months—is that Coco won't sue the Richardsons. Instead, she writes a screenplay titled *The Personal Concierge,* set at a gracious and iconic house on Nantucket that is purchased by a couple who set out to infiltrate and dominate Nantucket's summer social scene. There are familiar details in the screenplay: The personal concierge has a handsome boat-captain boyfriend and a best friend who takes selfies of the two of them and sends them to her ex-girlfriend. The couple the concierge works for throw extravagant parties that involve wigs, nudity, and partner-swapping. The wife cheats at pickleball; the husband pits two local real estate agents against each other in a land-development deal.

Coco sends her screenplay to three producers in Hollywood

whose contact information she acquired from creeping into Bull's email account (Coco has been saving Bull Richardson's password for the right moment). A bidding war ensues. Warner Bros. buys the screenplay for an undisclosed seven-figure sum.

Bull Richardson sells *Hedonism* back to Northrop and Johnson for a fraction of what he paid for it (the accident devalued the boat severely). There will be no insurance payout on the house, but Bull puts the empty land on the market for seventeen million—he wants to recoup his money somehow, though both Eddie and Addison agree he'll be lucky to get a third of that, and it will likely take years for some abject climate denier to come along.

Bull stays with Leslee despite her two-and-a-half-year sentence at MCI-Plymouth (he, at least, meant every word of his vow renewal). Leslee makes friends in prison, of course, and shamelessly flirts with the corrections officers. Six months before her release date, she arranges for a viewing of *The Personal Concierge,* which earned great acclaim on the big screen before finally coming to Netflix.

"This movie," Leslee tells her cellblock mates, "is about me."

Leslee generally approves of how "Layla" in the film is depicted; they cast a beautiful, award-winning actress. Leslee *loves* the scene near the end where Layla takes the boxes of cash and escapes from Pocomo Harbor on her speedboat, *Decadence* (why didn't Leslee think of doing this in real life?), before being caught by the Coast Guard.

The only moment in the movie that Leslee ponders later is Coco slipping and falling off the boat.

Leslee (who, as Coco once acknowledged, is a human being with a point of view) remembers the events happening this way: As news of the fire breaks among guests of the sail, Leslee decides to sneak a couple of drags off a cigarette to steady her nerves (her house is going up in flames; she will have to do the best acting of her life in a moment). She finds Coco at the back of the boat all alone, taking a picture of the sunset. The idea comes to Leslee swiftly: If she pushes Coco off the boat, it will look like Coco is trying to run because *she* set the fire.

However, before Leslee can decide if she's actually going to go through with pushing Coco, she hears a splash and watches Coco's pink-and-white-clad form hit the water. Leslee is stupefied; she very nearly calls for help, but there's a disorienting moment when Leslee wonders if she *did* push Coco or if Coco somehow knew Leslee's intentions and fell in as she tried to avoid being pushed. Yet another part of Leslee wonders if Coco might have…jumped. This is obviously absurd; why would Coco ever jump off the boat?

But then, look how things turned out: Leslee and Bull are ruined and Coco has a blockbuster movie—and Leslee just heard that Warner Bros. has green-lit *Rosebush* as well. Talk about a clever revenge.

If Leslee didn't hate Coco so much, she might admire her.

Nantucketers are known for bouncing back from even the most troubling events and by Labor Day weekend, nearly all the uproar caused by the Richardsons has receded into the background. Life, after all, goes on. Eddie Pancik and Addison Wheeler apply for a substantial construction loan from Nantucket Bank to develop Jeanne Jackson's property out in Tom Nevers. Kacy Kapenash decides to stay on Nantucket for the foreseeable future. She accepts a position at Nantucket Cottage Hospital in labor and delivery, a job that will become especially meaningful in the spring because her brother, Eric, and his girlfriend, Avalon, are expecting a baby in April. Kacy has started dating Stacy Ambrose; if things work out, Kacy might consider moving to Baltimore and taking a job at Johns Hopkins.

Busy Ambrose tells anyone who will listen that Leslee Richardson never made the seventy-five-thousand-dollar donation to her husband's scholarship fund that she said she did. Busy sounds surprised by this. *She sent me a picture of the check!*

A space at the Homestead opens up for Glynnie Oakley. She's placed on the same floor as all her best friends. It's just like being back in the college dorm, she tells Lamont.

This frees up Lamont to leave the island, at least for the off-season. He and Coco are thinking of Los Angeles. Coco is starting work on a screenplay that might be based on certain real-life events, and Lamont has an interview for the director of sailing position at the Los Angeles Yacht Club.

As Blond Sharon drives home from pickleball, her phone rings with an unfamiliar number, area code 954. *Telemarketer,* she thinks, but she answers anyway. It's none other than Lucky Zambrano.

"I submitted your short story to an online literary magazine called *Modern Romance,*" he says. "It's grown wildly popular with the Tik-Tok crowd and has nearly half a million subscribers."

"I've heard of it," Sharon says. "*Mo-Ro!*" She can't believe Lucky took the initiative with her piece. Nancy and Willow will be so jealous when they find out. "When will we hear back?"

"I just did," Lucky says. "They want to publish it, and they're paying fifteen hundred dollars."

Fifteen hundred dollars! Sharon nearly drives off the road.

When she gets home, she shares the news with her kids: "*Mo-Ro*—TikTok-approved—is going to publish my story and I'm getting paid."

Robert is playing Minecraft and doesn't look up.

The twins are briefly energized by the mention of TikTok and come over to give Sharon desultory hugs. She knows she shouldn't expect much more than this. They're kids; they see her only as their mother.

She calls her sister, Heather, who, although once again in the middle of a desk lunch, whoops with abandon and says, "I'm so proud of you! Am I in it?"

No, Sharon thinks, *but I need to talk to a certain someone who is.*

She drives down to the Steamship just as the noon boat starts loading. She hears her name and sees Busy Ambrose sticking her head out the window of her Subaru. She beckons Sharon over. "Your boyfriend is so *influential.* I was number one hundred and seventy-seven on the standby list, but Romeo pulled some strings and *got me on*!"

Sharon waves goodbye to Busy—"Have a nice fall, see you at Christmas Stroll!"—and waits until Romeo has loaded all the vehicles (packed to the tippy-tops with tennis rackets, boogie boards, buckets of candy from Force Five, golden retrievers, and sunburned children in need of haircuts) onto the ferry.

When he's finished, Sharon lowers her sunglasses and says, "You let Busy on the boat after all?"

"I wanted to get rid of her," he says with a wink. He gathers Sharon in a bear hug. "To what do I owe this honor?"

Sharon beams. "My short story is getting published in *Modern Romance,*" she says. "They're paying me fifteen hundred dollars."

Romeo picks Sharon up and swings her around. "I'm taking you out to dinner tonight."

"And then maybe karaoke?" she says.

Romeo kisses her nose. "Of course. I'll come get you at seven."

As Sharon pulls out of the Steamship parking lot, she notices the bench where she first spied Coco and Kacy getting off the ferry. She's so glad she abandoned Coco and Kacy as her characters, because who can keep track of all that drama?

Sharon is going to stick to love stories.

42. Your One Wild and Precious Life

The weekend after Labor Day, the entire island turns out at the Oystercatcher for Chief Ed Kapenash's retirement bash. The Chief's family is there—his wife, Andrea; Eric and the newly pregnant Avalon; his daughter, Kacy, and her date, Stacy Ambrose; and Chloe and Finn, back from their summers abroad.

"What'd we miss?" Chloe asks.

"Trust me," Eric says, "you don't want to know."

Carson Quinboro is behind the bar slinging glasses of frozen rosé and Mount Gay and tonics; she fetches the Chief a can of ice-cold Whale's Tale. There's a huge raw bar with local oysters and cherrystones; servers pass sliders, fried chicken sandwiches, fish tacos. The band, Cranberry Alarm Clock, plays as the sun begins its descent.

Ed isn't used to this much attention. For the past thirty-five years, whenever he walked into a party, the chatter and laughter stopped. What Ed would like to tell everyone is that he never judged the citizens of this island; he merely tried to keep them safe. He likes a stiff drink and a good dirty joke as much as the next person. He's far from perfect.

Ed looks around and realizes he's surrounded by stories. Fast Eddie and Grace are in attendance, which reminds the Chief of when he had to call the FBI because he suspected Eddie was running a prostitution ring out in Sconset (he was right). When the Chief gets a second beer from Carson Quinboro, he thinks about how the poor girl lost her mother, Vivian Howe, in a hit-and-run accident on Kingsley Road. The tragic stories are the ones that come to mind first—when Penny Alistair drove her Jeep off the end of Hummock Pond Road; when Meredith Delinn was hiding out in Tom Nevers and someone left a dead seal on her front porch; when Chloe and Finn's parents, Greg and Tess MacAvoy, drowned in a sailing accident—but Ed chooses to focus on resilience. Look, for example, at Coco and Lamont. They've seemingly recovered from their strange and eventful summer working for the Richardsons. Right now, they're sitting in Adirondack chairs next to Kacy, who is holding hands with Busy Ambrose's daughter, Stacy.

Ed feels a hand on his back and turns to see Zara Washington on the arm of Joe DeSantis, the owner of the Nickel sandwich shop downtown. The last unofficial piece of advice the Chief gave Zara was where to get the best lunch, and he apparently did a nifty bit of matchmaking in the process (Dabney Kimball Beech would be proud).

"This is a nice party, Ed," Zara says. "Everyone on this island really loves you. I'm not sure I'll ever be able to fill your shoes."

"You're going to be a huge success, Chief Washington," Ed says. "This is an island of good people—everyone in the community shows up for one another."

"Amen to that," Joe says.

"Just be sure not to miss Joe's grilled shrimp po'boy special on Wednesdays." The Chief clicks his beer can against Zara's wineglass. "Now, if you'll excuse me, I'm going to dance with my wife."

The Chief finds Andrea with Phoebe and Delilah. Andrea is trying to pick a grandmother name. Phoebe says, "We're basically the same age and Reed hasn't even started high school. I'll be a hundred before I'm a grandmother."

The Chief says, "I'm taking Granny for a spin on the dance floor."

The band plays "Stand by Me," and Ed holds Andrea close.

"You did it, Chief," she says. When she looks up at him, her eyes are shining. "Thirty-five years of service, none of it easy."

"The worthwhile things never are," the Chief says. He gazes around the dance floor to see Eric and Avalon, Kacy and Stacy, Coco and Lamont, Blond Sharon and Romeo, Delilah and Jeffrey, Addison and Phoebe. Addison raises his cocktail to Ed over Phoebe's head, and Ed thinks, *Is it okay if I get in my feelings now?* Even grouchy old Pamela from the Wauwinet gatehouse has shown up to wish Ed well.

When the song is over, the Oystercatcher staff roll out an ice cream cake from the Juice Bar. The top of the cake says *Thank you, Chief Kapenash.* Andrea whispers, "People wanted to make toasts but I told them you'd hate that."

"You know me too well," Ed says.

"That I do," she says. "So don't go crazy on the cake."

"Actually," the Chief says, "I think I'm going to walk down to the water. I need a breather." He kisses Andrea's forehead. "I love you."

"I love you," Andrea says. "And for the record, I can't wait to be sick of you."

The Chief wanders down the boardwalk that leads from the Oystercatcher to the shore of Jetties Beach. There are a few beachgoers, people who understand that the best part of the summer are these golden September days. Ed waves and smiles, though his face feels numb and his chest is tight. He breathes in through his nose, focusing on the sun as it sinks into the water, shooting orange and pink feathers across the sky. Down the shore to the left, the Chief watches a young man taking down blue, green, and canary-yellow umbrellas at the Beach Club. He watches the steamship glide out of the harbor. Its stacked white decks remind him of a wedding cake.

Suddenly...he's in the garden of the Chanticleer cutting into his own wedding cake. It has a basket weave and is garnished with sugared cranberries. He feeds a piece to Andrea, nicely, neatly, but she has a rebellious streak and smashes her piece into the Chief's face, to the boisterous delight of her Italian uncles.

"*Ed!*" Andrea cries. "Someone call 911! Is Stu Vick still here?"

The Chief strolls the docks of the Boat Basin. Eric has brought him out to show off his new fishing boat, *Beautiful Day*. The Chief sits in the fighting chair and thinks how smart his son is to have started this charter business. Every day, he gets to work on the water.

The Chief is cruising down the Milestone Road, ten thirty on a Saturday night in November. He cuts left into the moors, and as he nears Gibbs Pond, he sees the Jeeps lined up, then he hears the music, and finally he gets close enough to see the blaze of a bonfire and the silhouettes of teenagers. He sighs. How many high-school parties has he broken up over the years? Hundreds. He turns on his lights and blasts the siren for just a second, and the kids scatter. The Chief steps out of the car, announces that the fire must be extinguished and nobody who has been drinking should drive. Hobby Alistair, captain of the football team, stays to put out the fire, then lopes over to shake the Chief's hand.

Sorry, Chief, he says.

Ed says, *Nice win against Barnstable today, son.*

It's late June and the Chief is out in Sconset. All of the tiny cottages are blanketed in pink and red roses. Every year it's a fairy tale come to life, a village enchanted, all the more magical because it's fleeting. Ed nearly stops to take a picture, but how silly is that, a grown man photographing a place he's lived most of his adult life as though he's a tourist.

"Daddy!" Kacy says. "Dad, we're all right here. Just stay with us, please, please stay."

The Chief is supervising a house move out on Madaket Road when he gets a call from Jennifer Speed, the dispatcher. *You're needed at the hospital pronto, Chief.*

Can it wait? the Chief asks. *I'm in the middle of something here.*

Andrea is in labor, Jennifer says. *Contractions are two minutes apart.*

Ed hops into his car, throws on his lights and siren. They're going to have a baby.

When he gets to the hospital, the person in the delivery room isn't Andrea. It's...Avalon. She gives birth to a boy, his grandson, the next Edward Kapenash. They're calling him Teddy.

"Dad," Eric says. "We love you."

They love him. He's been lucky to live with so much love, day in and day out.

But there's another reason he's been lucky, one that is every bit as powerful as the people in his life—and that is this island.

The pearlescent gray of the south shore in the fog.

The flock of sheep that graze in the hidden meadows of Quaise.

Wading into the chilly water of Polpis Harbor with his rake on the first day of family scalloping season.

Main Street at five in the morning after a blizzard, the cobblestones blanketed in snow, the whole town immaculate, white, silent.

The first glimpse of spring during Daffodil Festival: mild sunshine on his face as he drives a 1962 Oldsmobile Starfire in the classic-car parade, the taste of a deviled egg, everyone wearing their yellow and green, buoyant with the knowledge that another season is beginning, summer is on its way.

It seems like nothing short of a miracle: He found a home on this island, thirty miles out to sea.

Nantucket.

Acknowledgments

It's a daunting task to thank everyone who contributes to my work in a regular year, never mind this year, when I have come to the end of an era. *Swan Song* marks the last of my Nantucket-based summer novels (for now — there may very well be another one or two somewhere down the road!).

I want to start by thanking you, my readers. It is no secret that Elin Hilderbrand readers are the most devoted in all of publishing. You have trusted me with your summer reading hours, and I am grateful. I want to give a shout-out to a few longtime readers who have become friends: Jessica Jackson, Lizz and Elaine Backler, the entire Bello family, Derek White, Tara Fox, Mary Parker, Eileen Bratton, Deena Dick, Kim Ritzke and the late Jennifer Wells, Lisa Hitt, and the reader named Katherine who handed me a letter at the Oxford Exchange in Tampa, a letter so meaningful that I read it whenever I do a speaking engagement. A writer does her work alone, but because of all of you, I have never felt alone, and my work has always had purpose — to entertain, certainly, but also to give you an all-expenses-paid mental vacation to one of the most magical places in the world.

Next I'd like to thank my editor, the amazing Judy Clain, for her sharp eye, her keen insight and intelligence, her attention to detail, and her enthusiasm. She edited this novel so brilliantly that all I can say is I don't know how she does it. I also must thank the great Reagan Arthur, who edited twenty of my novels (from *Barefoot* through *28 Summers*). It is not an exaggeration to say that without Judy and Reagan, there would be no Elin.

Thank you to my incredible publisher, Little, Brown. Back in

January of 2007, Michael Pietsch stood up at a media luncheon and told everyone that Little, Brown was going to "bring Elin Hilderbrand to the world." At the time I thought, *Now, there's some hyperbole.* But that is what happened. I owe my career to Michael, who led by dynamic example, and to the following people at L,B, both the past and present: Terry Adams, Craig Young, Bruce Nichols, Karen Torres, Ashley Marudas, Danielle Finnegan, Brandon Kelly, Asya Muchnick, Jayne Yaffe Kemp, Karen Landry, Bryan Christian, Lauren Hesse, Sabrina Callahan, my darling Mario Pulice, Annie Martin, Tracy Roe, and my beloved publicist, Katharine Myers.

Michael Carlisle and David Forrer at Inkwell Management are not just agents; they are my superheroes, my protectors, my counselors, and my friends. For all these many years, they have been everything great agents should be: supportive, kind, wise, and, at times, tough. In Hollywood, huge and sincere thanks to Jason Richman and Addison Duffy at UTA. May my future (and yours) include more Elin adaptations to the screen.

I have wanted to be a writer since I was seven years old and everyone at Arrowhead Elementary School knew it. I want to thank my teachers, many of whom have attended at least one (and in some cases more) of my signings: Linda Izett, Lisa Yanak, Fran Rapp, Terry Underkoffler, and, of course, John Hersh. Special shout-out to Lydia Buckwalter, who, along with Jessica Polashenski, gave me the "Top Author" award at the end of second grade. Maybe they saw some kind of rare talent in me at a young age or maybe they just sensed my enthusiasm for making up stories, but in any case, they believed in me and are responsible for setting me on my path. This is the incredible power of being a teacher.

Thank you to Nantucket's recently retired harbormaster, Sheila Lucey, who explained in detail what happens on Nantucket when someone falls off a boat. I speak for all of Nantucket when I say: Thank you for your service, Sheila. There will never be another harbormaster like you.

Thank you to Carla Castillo for her help with all things NICU-related. To all my nurses out there, thank you for making a difference every single day.

Thank you to Jeff Allen, who served for years and years with the Nantucket Fire Department, for all the background on fires. Any inaccuracies or inconsistencies are mine alone or are included in service of the narrative.

Thank you to Patrick McGee for suggesting pickleball. I do not play myself—as you might be able to tell—but maybe with retirement, I'll learn!

Thank you to Heather Brinson Clymer for describing what it's like to live with type 1 diabetes and for explaining how the Dexcom app works. Sending you so much love.

Thank you to my vote for a future College Sailor of the Year, Emily Doble. Emily answered all my sailing inquiries with great patience. Georgetown is lucky to have you!

Shout-out to Madison from Alt Nation and Lithium for compiling a list of Coco's favorite bands and songs. I figured if anyone would know what Coco would listen to, it was Madison. I'm so lucky to count her as one of my readers.

A special shout-out to my ride-or-dies on each summer book tour: Susan at Browseabout Books in Rehoboth, Zandria and Jackie at Bethany Beach Books, and Marla and Tony Sofia at the Parker House.

Jenn Sherman: Thank you for being with me first thing nearly every single day. #peloton

TGF: There isn't space in these pages to express my gratitude for the ways you have brightened my life. You always have my heart—and you work a signing line like nobody else.

And now for Nantucket.

To the *Nantucket Current:* What would we do without you?

To Nantucket Food, Fuel, and Rental Assistance: Thank you for all you do to serve those among us who need a little help. (If anyone feels moved to give back to Nantucket after a visit, this organization is a great way to do it. Visit assistnantucket.org.)

To Nantucket Book Partners, including Mitchell's Book Corner and Nantucket Bookworks: Thank you for being the best hometown independent bookstore a writer could ask for. My undying love to owner Wendy Hudson as well as Suzanne Bennett, Cristina Machiavelli, Annye Camara, and Dick Burns. In a category by himself, of course, is my work husband, Tim Ehrenberg. Tim, who is the creator of the Bookstagram platform @timtalksbooks as well as my cohost on the podcast *Books, Beach & Beyond,* is the secret to my success. This is a person who sits with me in the basement at Mitchell's for hours while I sign and personalize; he's the genius behind all the marketing and merchandising ideas; he makes all the magic happen, including getting five thousand copies out the door and into the hands of people across the country. He is also one of my closest friends.

I have never been blessed to have family on Nantucket, so over the past thirty years, I created my own family. In good times and terrible times, they have stood by me. Thank you to Rebecca Bartlett; Wendy Rouillard; Wendy Hudson; Debbie Briggs; Chuck and Margie Marino; Elizabeth and Beau Almodobar; Matthew and Evelyn MacEachern; Anne and Whitney Gifford; Jeannie Esti; Melissa Long; Frank and Sue Decoste; Linda Holliday; the fabulous Jane Deery; Julie Lancia; Deb Gfeller; Helaina Jones; Heidi Holdgate; Roy and Shelly Weedon; Jana and Nicky Duarte; the Powers sisters, Sarah, Lulu, Julie, and Sue; Richard Congdon; Norm and Jen Frazee; David Rattner and Andrew Law; West Riggs; Jay Riggs; Manda Riggs; Sally Horchow; the real Corwin Moore; Holly and Marty McGowan; Kit Noble and Emme Duncan; Connie Anne and Jere Harris; James Scheurell; David Handy and Donald Dallaire; Elizabeth Harris; and Mark and Gwenn Snider.

Acknowledgments

Thank you to my family—my mother, Sally Hilderbrand, and the rest of the gang: Eric and (my incredibly talented interior designer) Lisa Hilderbrand, Randy and Steph Osteen, Todd Thorpe, and Doug and Jen Hilderbrand. Plus all my many (!!!) nieces and nephews. Now that I'm retired, I will have more time to focus on my auntie duties. (Watch out, Patrick!)

My sister, Heather Thorpe, is the person who reminds me I'm not alone in the world. She supports, she runs interference, she handles, she encourages, she brightens, and when I am standing on the knife-edge of my sanity, she is my phone call. She is my end-all, be-all. Everyone should have a Heather.

I dedicated this novel to my ex-husband, Chip Cunningham. Chip has believed in me as a writer since the days when I used to send stories to *The New Yorker* in a manila envelope—and he comforted me when the inevitable rejections arrived. He spent two grueling winters out in Iowa City while I was in graduate school; one winter he worked at the Oral-B factory inspecting toothbrushes for "wild nylon" so we would have extra money. His support is invaluable and we have successfully headed the Cunningham family with all its various challenges for twenty-five years. I am eternally grateful for his humor, his sunny outlook, his fearless leadership, and his friendship. In the summer of 1993, I went to Nantucket on my own, but it was because of Chip that I returned and it is for this that I owe him the biggest thank-you. It seems nothing short of a miracle: I found a home, thirty miles out to sea.

This brings me to the reason I do anything and everything: my children, Maxx, Dawson, Shelby, and Alex. The four of you are my favorite people to spend time with, so I must have done something right. I love you all beyond the beyond. Thank you for being patient. Now that I'm retiring, I'm free to hang out! Let's go to the Box!